STATE OF PANIC

LORI GORDON

This book is a work of fiction. The characters, incidents, and dialogue are drawn from the author's imagination and are not to be construed as real. Any resemblance to any actual events or persons, living or dead, is entirely coincidental.

FIRST SOFTCOVER EDITION

ISBN-13: 978-1-61706-078-6

Cover art by Gary McCluskey
Cover design by Jessy Marie Roberts
Published by Pill Hill Press
First Printing: August 2011

Visit us online at www.pillhillpress.com

Dedication

For my fabulous group of writer friends for their Amazing friendship, support, and for encouragement. I couldn't have done this without you.
Orlando Stephenson, Wayne C. Rogers, Ellen Shaw, Deb Dormitzer and William Stroupe.
You guys are the best.
To Victoria Wegner for cheering me on and making me laugh.
a special Thank you to Bill for the many hours of help, and for always believing. I couldn't ask for a better friend.
With Love to My parents,
John and Lorraine Gordon
Thank You...
...For everything
and for being the best people I know.

STATE OF PANIC

LORI GORDON

Pill Hill Press

Chapter One

Sierra writhed beneath him. Her nails dug into his arms, urging him to go faster. His body was slick. A bead of sweat dropped onto her cheek. Her back arched, she was so close.

"Quiet."

At first she thought he was kidding. He froze above her, body rigid with tension. She groaned, thrusting her hips against his, trying to pull him closer.

He was off her in an instant.

She opened her eyes, blinking in confusion. Her hand groped in the dark for the sheet. The air conditioning was a blast of ice against her overheated skin. "What's the matter?"

"I said, quiet. Don't you understand what quiet means?" He sat perched on the edge of the bed. His head was cocked, like he was listening for something.

An angry flush stained her cheeks. She loved him. *She was about to marry him, for Christ's sake,* but there were times he tried her patience. It had been a long day and she was exhausted. She was tempted to roll over and go to sleep, but she was getting tired of his strange outbursts. It would serve him right if she got dressed and went home.

"Are you going to tell me what's wrong or not?"

He ignored her. *The hell with him.* Sierra reached down and grabbed her clothes off the floor. His hand clamped down around her wrist before she could reach them. "Go to the kitchen. *Now*."

"What for?"

"Fix us a snack. I need something to eat."

That wasn't like him. In all the years she'd known him, he never once ordered her to do something. She studied his face. He looked tense, haggard; his face drawn, lines of worry creasing his brow. A chill ran up her spine. *Something wasn't right.*

"Please," he begged. "You know what I like. Fix us something to eat."

She was too tired to argue, but she was damned sure going to let him know she wasn't happy. She wasn't his damn servant. Her voice was cold and tight. "Fine."

His hand loosened on her wrist. He leaned over and kissed her forehead, "Thank you, Sweetheart. Wait for me in the kitchen, okay. Please?"

"Why?"

He ran his hand through his hair, "Will you stop with the questions already?" He snapped. "I'll be there in a bit."

Sierra pursed her lips and yanked on her bathrobe. He could be a real sonofabitch at times. When she reached the bedroom door, she stopped to glare at him.

"Please, don't be like that," he pleaded. "I love you."

Tension snaked through her. Something was definitely wrong. *But what?* One minute he'd be fine, the next he was on edge, cranky. Her stomach growled. She hadn't realized how hungry she was until she reached the refrigerator door. Hunger could put anyone in a foul mood, herself included. She exhaled in an effort to calm down. They'd missed dinner. Maybe the evening—and the mood—could be salvaged if they ate.

It was a hot night and she opted to fix a cool snack. She grabbed a plate from the cabinet and loaded it with goodies from the fridge. Melon, prosciutto, swiss, and cheddar. A bit of salami to add some bite. At the last minute, she reached for the bottle of pinot grigio chilling in the fridge. Maybe the wine would help settle him down.

She rummaged through a drawer to find the corkscrew. He never put it back in the right place. Things would have to change after they were married. She reached for the wine glasses, and they clinked together as she removed them from the cabinet.

Click. Boom.

Something exploded.

Sierra jumped. The edge of kitchen counter dug into the small of her back as she slammed against it. The wine glasses slipped from her fingertips, tumbling down to the carpet. An ungodly shriek split the air, sending tremors of terror through her. She raced towards the hallway, heart slamming inside her chest. A thought stopped her cold. *Neil's odd behavior, the way he sent her to the kitchen, telling her to wait there for him. He'd known something was wrong, and had been trying to protect her.*

She forced herself to slow her pace. Running straight into danger wouldn't help anyone. It might even get her killed. Instinct kicked in. She flattened her back against the wall and crept towards the doorway, then offered up a silent prayer and peered around the corner.

The stench of burning flesh assailed her nostrils, hitting her hard. Bile splashed the back of her throat. She gagged, struggling to make sense of the horror in front of her. Disbelief chugged through her mind. Neil's body, engulfed in flames. She could hear the hiss of fire licking the flesh from his bones.

He fell to the floor, screaming in agony. Her hands flew to her face. It was already too late; there was nothing she could do to help him. No way he could survive. He rolled, an angry ball of fire, hurtling towards the front door.

Someone set him on fire. She looked up. A stranger stood framed in the doorway, face impassive, watching her fiancé burn. He had cold, dead eyes. Their black depths seared into her mind, and she knew she'd remember them forever.

Sierra stumbled back in shock, breaking out in a cold, clammy sweat. *I have to get out of here.* Her stomach cramped. She clutched her belly, fighting the urge to vomit. Her mind splintered in a thousand directions. *If he sees me, he'll kill me too.* Panic washed over her, rooting her in place. If she ran, she could wind up a suspect. If she stayed, she could end up dead.

Get. Out. Now.

She peaked around the corner one last time. A sob welled up in her throat, almost choking her. Neil, or what was left of him, was melting into the floorboards. *The very last thing she had done was glare at him. Oh God! Would she ever be able to forgive herself?*

No time for that now. She had to pull herself together.

The stranger's eyes remained fixed on Neil. This might be her only chance. She hugged the wall, moving towards the back of the house, darting into the bedroom to grab her purse. Neil's laptop sat beside it. All her contact information was stored in his computer. Under the circumstances, she didn't want to leave it behind. She shoved the laptop inside her bag, praying she wouldn't get caught.

A quick glance down the hall told her it was safe. She hugged the purse against her body and dashed into the kitchen. Her hands were shaking so hard the doorknob rattled when she eased open the back door. One step closer to safety. She slid through the crack into the stuffy night air. Fear pumped inside her; she started to hyperventilate the moment she shut the door behind her. Fighting back tears, she stumbled, falling headlong into the grass. She knew she was going to be sick and scrambled behind a bush, terrified the killer might hear her retching. Her body heaved; the contents of her stomach splattering the ground. She couldn't stop shaking.

Her mind clicked away at warp speed. Her first instinct was to flee, to run to her car and tear through the night. What if the killer chose that exact moment to leave? She'd be setting herself up as bait. She should call 911, but she knew enough to realize she was an automatic suspect. Her face would be plastered all over the news, alerting the killer to her identity. She couldn't run, not dressed in a bathrobe. She'd stick out like a sore thumb on the deserted streets. Best to sit tight. With any luck, the killer had no idea anyone else had been in the house.

A chill prickled the back of her neck. *He would know. Her clothes lay scattered in the bedroom; two wine glasses were on the kitchen floor. He was going to come looking for her any minute now. Oh God, she had to get away.*

Her eyes darted around the yard, desperation reared up inside her. There had to be a place to hide. *The garage. She had a set of Neil's keys.* Her legs went weak with relief. She dug inside her purse, crying when her fingers closed over them. She stayed in the shadows until she reached the garage, and then made a quick run for it.

She could see the house through the small garage window. Lights blazed inside. The killer was on the hunt, turning on light in every room. *He's looking for me*. Her palms were sweaty. The key slipped twice when she tried to fit it in the ignition.

The minute the garage door opened, she gunned the engine. Her heart skipped a beat. She was safe. For now.

With the immediate danger behind her, a combination of shock and grief exploded inside her. *Who would want to kill Neil? And why?*

It made no sense. He was an average guy. There was nothing in his past that would make him a target. *At least nothing she knew of.*

The image of him rolling on the floor, unable to escape the flames torching his body, sent a fresh wave of pain ripping through her. The scent of burning flesh lingered in her nostrils. She would never forget the smell. It would be with her forever. The horror of what she witnessed churned inside her. She was shaking so hard, she had to pull over. There was no way she could drive in her current state.

She found a side street, far enough away from Neil's house that she felt safe, and gave into the sobs racking her body. Her nerves tingled, and her head pounded with questions.

Neil had been afraid. Even making love, he was attuned to danger. He'd been listening for it, damn it. It took a moment before the implication set in. He knew he was at risk, and he hadn't told her. Worse yet, he'd exposed her to danger. He had gambled with her life by having her with him. *What kind of man would do such a thing to the woman he loved enough to marry?*

Sierra slumped back against the seat. Her life had blown apart in an instant, but at least she was still alive. She needed time to process everything. When she got home, she'd pour herself a stiff drink and try to put the pieces together.

Home. *Dear God,* she thought, *I can't go home. The police will want to question me. Whenever there's a murder investigation, they look at the loved ones first.* She'd fled the scene, which meant she already had one strike against her. She had to give herself a fighting chance and calling the police wasn't an option. There was no way in hell she'd give the killer a roadmap to find her.

She felt better for half a second and then her stomach sank. Neil's killer knew someone else had been in the house. Her clothes were a dead giveaway. Once he found them, It wouldn't be too hard for him to connect the dots.

They'd been finalizing their wedding plans. Taking the computer had been useless. Her name was everywhere. So was her address. He'd been doing a sweep of the house when she drove away. If she went home, she was a dead woman.

A car turned onto the street where she'd parked. Headlights glared in her review mirror. Sierra shrank down into her seat, terrified the killer was on her trail. She held her breath until the car passed.

She plunged into a state of panic, finding it impossible to separate logic from raging paranoia. Nothing had ever prepared her for this type of life or death situation. There had to be somewhere she could hide, someone she could call for help.

Grace was the logical choice. *Which*, she realized, *meant she had to stay as far away from her best friend as possible.* Sierra knew in her gut that Neil's death hadn't been random. The monster who'd killed him wouldn't leave loose ends. There was a fifty-fifty chance the killer was lying in wait for her at her house. When she didn't come home, he would look through her contacts. She couldn't risk putting her friends in danger.

There was only one person she could call, one person who could help her.

Chapter Two

Considering the way things ended between them, would he even take her call? There was a good chance he wouldn't. It had been years since they last spoke.

He still kept in touch with Grace; her friend had inherited him after the break-up. Following in his father's footsteps, he'd joined the FBI straight out of college. He was a rising star in the bureau, quickly climbing the ranks. According to Grace he lived in Washington now, was something of a big deal. There was even talk of him running for political office in the not too distant future.

Their relationship had been messy, the break up complicated. He'd never forgiven her for choosing Neil over him. Now Neil was dead and he was the only one she could turn to. It was an ugly twist of fate.

Closing her eyes, she took a deep breath, blowing out a long stream of air. Her heart was doing crazy little palpitations in her chest, her palms slick with sweat. She wiped them on her robe and grabbed her cell phone before she lost her nerve. It was insane to be this nervous. They were all adults and she was in trouble. He wouldn't turn his back on her once he heard her story.

No one could be *that* unforgiving.

Just make the call and get it over with. Deciding she'd have a better chance of reaching him if she blocked her number, she swallowed her pride and dialed.

A woman answered. *Shit.* She hadn't expected that.

"I'm looking for Donovan St. James."

"Van isn't here right now. May I ask who's calling?"

Van? The implied intimacy rattled her. The cool, cultured voice set her teeth on edge. This was not a woman to whom she could blurt out her problems to.

"Hello? Are you there?" the woman asked, haughty and impatient.

Sierra scrambled for something to say that wouldn't make her sound like a complete idiot, "I have information on one of his cases. Do you know how I can reach him?"

"He's out of town until tomorrow. If you'd care to leave your number, I'll be sure to give him a message when he checks in."

A rock formed in Sierra's stomach. Waiting for a call back wasn't an option. She hung up and tossed the phone in her purse.

There was no choice. She had to run.

***

She'd been driving for hours. It would be dawn soon and she needed a plan. It was hell not knowing how much of a head start she had on the killer. The police might already be swarming over Neil's property. They would find her things, notice his missing car, put out an APB.

Or not.

She thought about the last thing she'd witnessed. Neil *melting* into the floor. The flames from his body should have ignited a blaze. *But they hadn't.* The house wasn't on fire when she escaped. Then again, she hadn't hung around long to watch. A fire took time to smolder. The house could have turned into an inferno *after* she drove away. It was possible evidence of her presence went up in flames. If the killer was smart, he'd torch the place to cover up the murder. *Wouldn't he?*

Then again, given the coldness in the stranger's eyes, he might have simply walked away from the crime scene. Maybe Neil's death was meant to send a message. *But to whom?* She ran her hand through her hair. There were too many questions. Trying to guess at the answers would make her crazy. If she had any chance of remaining sane, she had to focus on what she did know.

It was Friday night. Neil didn't have any weekend plans, so no one would report him missing. Neil's remains could conceivably lie undiscovered until Monday when he didn't show up for work.

Unless the house caught fire and they'd already discovered what was left of his body.

"Damn it." She banged the steering wheel with the palm of her hand, reminding herself that speculation was pointless. Going back and forth over every possible scenario wasn't going to do her any good. It was impossible to know whether she had hours or days to vanish.

The sick feeling in the pit of her stomach leapt into her throat, leaving her with a sour taste in her mouth. Not too many hours ago, she'd been in bed with her fiancée, pissed off at his inattentiveness. Now she was thinking of him in terms of his remains.

Sierra pulled over and threw up again on the side of the road.

Cars whizzed past her, people going about their business, like it was an ordinary night. There was nothing ordinary about it. Her life was falling apart, her mind frayed. She slammed shut the car door, collapsing in her seat. If she didn't get a grip soon on her situation soon, Neil wouldn't be the only casualty tonight. Her life was on the line too.

Back to square one. She frowned, fingers tapping the steering wheel. She needed a plan…getting rid of Neil's car and finding a rental would be a good place to start. She had credit cards and cash. Hysterical laughter bubbled up inside her. How the hell was she going to rent a car clad only in a bathrobe?

Holy shit. A new set of worries blindsided her making her head spin. Rent a car? Why not go ahead and paint a bull's-eye on her back? Even if she paid in cash, she'd have to provide the rental company with identification. Tracking her would be easy. Heart thundering, she checked Neil's GPS. It was off. Thank God she hadn't turned it on without thinking. Her cell phone was a dead giveaway to her location too, wasn't it? She shoved her hand inside her purse, searching for it. The phone slipped between her trembling fingers three times before she managed to fish it out it. The last call she made was to Donavan, which could work to her advantage. If she were guilty, would she seriously be calling an FBI agent?

Sierra glanced down at her phone. She couldn't bring herself to toss it out the window. Her life was on it. She pressed the off key praying that was good enough.

Her mind raced as she retraced her steps. She'd taken the skyway out of Chicago. Toll booths were equipped with cameras; there was a record of her crossing the state line into Indiana. If she used an ATM or a credit card anywhere along the way, she was screwed.

How the hell did people vanish?

A horrid gasp echoed in her ears. At first, she didn't realize it came from her. For a terrifying moment, she couldn't breathe. She could feel her chest tightening. In a corner of her mind, she realized she was hyperventilating again. Clutching the wheel for support, she warded off the anxiety attack.

The dark road stretched out before her. She'd been driving blind through the night, desperate to put as many miles as she could between her and the killer. She couldn't think straight and it was getting harder and harder to focus. No surprise since she was operating on fumes and adrenaline. She needed food and sleep, but rest wasn't an option—not until she was certain the imminent danger was behind her.

The gas gauge veered towards empty. She couldn't stop for gas in a bathrobe and bare feet. Even out here in the middle of nowhere, her appearance would raise eyebrows. It would also make her easy to remember.

What the hell am I going to do? She had to get off the highway. Even in the pre-dawn hours, rest stops and main exists would be crowded with tourists and truckers. Too much of a risk. Elwood, Indiana was two miles ahead. She would take her chances there.

It was a ghost town. All the gas stations had shut down tight for the night. She banged her head against the steering wheel, tears trailing down her face. *Something* had to be open. She was about to give up when a distinct shape caught her eye. At the back of a gas station was a dark green charity bin, where people dropped off used clothes. It was overflowing.

"Thank you, God," she whispered, pulling up alongside it. There was no time to be fussy. Anything would be better than a bathrobe. Luck was on her side. She found a couple pair of worn out jeans that looked close to her size, a few t-shirts, two plaid shirts, and an oversized denim blouse. She changed in the car. The pants had to be rolled up at the waist and the shirts were a few sizes too big for her small frame; she wanted to hug the person who had dropped them off. Now she could blend in.

The clothes gave her confidence. She got back on the highway and had just enough gas to make it to the next rest stop. While the gas was pumping, she headed into the mini mart. A tiny bell announced her arrival.

A tired looking man glanced up at her from behind the counter, a newspaper spread out in front of him. His eyes followed her long enough to make her want to bolt. She snuck a look at him when she passed by, telling herself to calm down. There was no way Neil's murder would be in the paper yet, and it wouldn't have made national news. *This was Indiana, close enough for his death to be newsworthy,* she reminded herself.

She wasn't sure what to do. *Murders might be a dime a dozen in Chicago, but most were a result of gunshots, stabbing or the occasional strangulation. Neil's death would certainly make the local news.*

The bell jangled. She almost jumped out of her skin, afraid the police had found her. What if the clerk pushed a panic button hidden beneath the counter? Her eyes darted towards the door. It was a young couple, giggling, and holding hands. She winced, fighting back tears. *She and Neil had been the same way once, goofy with love.* Things had grown tense between them in recent months. It seemed they were always at each other's throats. She'd hoped it was a phase, and that they'd get back to normal. Now they'd never have the chance.

She realized she was staring when the girl looked in her direction and blushed. Sierra quickly turned away, noticing the clerk was watching them with the same dull-eyed stare he'd focused on her. She trembled with relief. The attendant viewed all his customers with suspicion; he hadn't singled her out.

Still, she'd need a better disguise. The clothes were good, just not good enough. Keeping one eye on the security mirror mounted high overhead, she roamed the aisles, picking up a couple of baseball caps and two pairs of sunglasses. Her eyes lingered on a package of scrunchies. She'd never been a pony-tail girl, but what the hell. It would add to her disguise.

The young couple stepped up to the counter to pay. Condoms and Pepsi. The girl fidgeted with embarrassment, her boyfriend draped his arm over her shoulder and told her to relax. It was a wakeup call for Sierra. The teenage girl was trying too hard to be inconspicuous; her nervous energy drew attention to her. She might as well have stood under a spotlight.

Sierra murmured a silent thank you to the girl. No doubt Sierra's fears were making her stand out. No wonder the clerk had been eyeballing all of them. He'd picked up on their weird vibes.

Sierra took her purchases up to the counter.

"Disgusting," he said, his lip curling up in a sneer that revealed yellowed, rotten teeth.

Her cheeks flamed. *Was he referring to her?*

"Damn kids now-a-days. All they do is get hopped up on caffeine and fornicate. What's this world comin' to?"

She searched her mind for an appropriate response. The man had a good twenty to thirty years on her. His generation hadn't been any better behaved; they'd just been less brazen. *Remember,* she warned herself, *blend in, don't say anything to stir up trouble.* "There's no discipline anymore. Parents let their kids run wild," she replied, matching his tone.

"Damn straight. If my sister had been caught buying rubbers, our Pa would have tanned her hide but good."

"Yup, I hear ya. If I missed my curfew by a minute, there was hell to pay." This time she wasn't lying.

"The world's going to hell in a hand basket," he growled with a shake of his head. "It's a damn shame these kids ain't got no values."

"Ain't that the truth."

He nodded and smiled, exposing his broken teeth, "Haven't seen you around before. Are you new to town?"

"Just passing through."

"Too bad. We could use more of you around these parts."

She thanked him and hurried from the store. *Please God, let this get easier.* She pulled her hair back into a high ponytail and plunked the baseball cap on her head. Funny how a small change could make such a big difference. She'd chosen sunglasses big enough to swallow her face. Add the rolled up jeans and huge flannel shirt and all, in all, it wasn't bad, for a makeshift disguise. She'd pass the first glance test.

Sierra tossed the empty bag onto the passenger seat and started the car. She still needed a different vehicle. It felt like there was sign slapped on the hood of the car, screaming, *here I am, come get me.* At least in a city, she could get lost. Out here on the Indiana Highway, there wasn't much action. It was all fields and farms on either side of the road, and the exits came at long intervals. Outside of the semi's, she was pretty much alone, making her a moving target.

She clicked on the radio and surfed for an all-news station. The tension in her body was tight enough to bounce coins off. Her heart jumped every time they announced local news on the eight's. The tears came out of nowhere. Her future was gone, her present, uncertain. She needed time to grieve; instead, she was stuck in a no man's land of emotion.

Emotion was the devils handiwork. She half-laughed, half-sobbed. *Where had that come from? Talk about a bastardized phrase.* She was slap happy from lack of sleep. It made a strange kind of sense though. Emotions had a way of clouding perspective, making it easier to over-react instead of thinking things through.

Oh, Jesus, was that what she'd been doing? Reacting? Survival mode had kicked it, her fight or flight instincts engaged. It was burn and die or run. She ran. But where was she running to?

The sound of brakes squealing snapped her back. The semi's surrounding her screeched to a halt. It was like being in a metal cave. She couldn't see what was going on. Her eyes slid to the clock. 6:00 AM. Too early for rush hour but traffic was at a standstill. Her stomach chose an inopportune moment to growl, reminding her how long it'd been since she'd last eaten. It was suicide to keep up at this pace. Time to make a list and formulate a plan.

She needed food.

A car.

Money.

Disposable cell.

Sleep.

Somewhere to stay.

She needed a town large enough to accommodate those needs, big enough for her not to stand out. Banks didn't open till nine. She'd have to bide her time until then. Indianapolis was her best bet.

A horn blared, demanding her attention. The trucker next to her was making lewd gestures, and wiggling his eyebrows at her. She shivered in disgust. He probably had a wife and four kids at home, and she sure as hell wasn't looking particularly good in her charity clothes. What was he thinking? Pig. She pitied his poor wife, slaving away at home, while her husband looked to get lucky on the road. *How many men kept secrets from the women they claimed to love?*

Like Neil. Why had he become standoffish and irritable? He'd been hiding a secret, a secret big enough to get him killed. He'd been willing to risk their relationship to guard it. They'd always told each other everything, what made this different?

He'd shut her out, leaving her angry and frustrated. If she wanted to be brutally honest with herself, she'd been sharing a stranger's bed for months. He'd kept her close physically, while he pushed her away emotionally. Had she been so desperate that she'd ignored important signs and hadn't known when to walk away? She twisted the engagement ring on her finger. A pledge to stand by each other, for better or worse. It didn't get much worse than this.

There was a break in the traffic. She edged forward. Her heart jumped into her belly. She caught the reflection of flashing strobe lights against the trucks up ahead. *The State Police. Jesus, God,* she prayed, *please don't let them be looking for me.* Sierra looked around in desperation for an escape route. There was no way to slip into the right lane. The tuckers were lined up nice and tight. She mumbled The Hail Mary under her breath and pulled the cap lower to hide her face.

Sierra died by inches. She craned her neck, wishing she could see what was going on. The sea of brake lights ahead of her blurred into a giant red, hot mess. She gripped the steering wheel hard, thinking of Neil swallowed by angry red fire, pictured him writhing on the floor, desperate to douse the flames. The chilling look on the dead-eyed killers face. Her eyes burned, she couldn't cry, not now. She had to stay strong—her life depended on it.

There was a box of tissues on the back seat. They were useless, she couldn't reach them. Keeping her eyes on the road, she fumbled with the glove compartment, praying Neil stashed some napkins inside.

The truck in front of her moved forward. Her hand rummaged inside the glove box, closing around anything she could grab. She spotted flares up ahead. The knot in her stomach loosened. The two rights lanes were shut down; everyone was being forced into the left lane. *It was an accident. No one was looking for her. Thank God. She'd dodged another bullet. Her nerves couldn't take much more.* She dumped the contents of the glove compartment onto her lap, glancing down for napkins, papers, anything she could use. A picture stared up at her. She couldn't look at it, she couldn't risk seeing Neil's face or a reminder of happier times. It would be too damn painful. She sifted through the stack by touch. At the bottom were a few crumpled paper towels. She reached for them, and dabbed at her eyes, wishing for a bottle of water to wash the taste of tears from her mouth.

A cop stood several feet ahead, using a glow light to direct the flow of traffic down to one lane. She averted her eyes; she didn't want to look at the accident sight. Didn't want to think of another tragedy. Not today. She picked up the pile resting on her lap. Curiosity would make her go through it eventually; for now, she'd dump it on the passenger seat.

She flipped on her turn signal and turned the wheel to the left. While she waited for her turn to merge into the left lane, she glanced at the stack. A face in the picture jumped out at her. *Grace McGinley.* Her best friend. *Grace.* With Neil. They had their arms around each other. Grace's head was nestled against Neil's chest and there was an implied intimacy in the pose; enough to make her wonder if something had been going on between them.

A sharp rap on the car window made her jump. A state trooper, barely old enough to shave stared inside the car. *Shit. What else could go wrong?*

The picture slid to the floor. *God Damn it. She couldn't ignore the photo or the possible implications. If Grace and Neil were having an affair, the police could view that as a motive for murder.* Ironically, that had been her one saving grace in this whole mess. There was no reason for the police to believe she wanted her fiancée dead. Until now. This changed everything.

The trooper motioned for her to roll down the window. *Great. Fine.* This was it. There was an APB on the car and they'd run the plates. She was screwed. Less than twenty-four hours ago, she'd awoken to a perfectly normal life. Since then, she'd witnessed the man she loved murdered in cold blood, the killer almost certainly knew her identity, and her best friend and her fiancée might have been hitting the sheets. She was running for her life, and a baby-faced cop was about to arrest her.

She searched the car for the right button. The window glided down. Her throat tightened again. The trooper bent at the waist, staring inside the car.

"Mornin', Ma'am. Don't know if you're aware of this, but your left rear wheel is pretty low. Drive too fast on that thing and you'll be risking a blowout. We already have one bad accident to deal with tonight. Don't need us another. "

Nervous laughter bubbled up inside her. *A low tire? He was stopping her for a low tire?* She sucked in her cheeks, giddy with relief. It wouldn't do for her to laugh in his face. She schooled her features into a smile. "Thank you, officer. I'll get the tire taken care of right away."

He studied her face a moment too long. Sweat broke out beneath the baseball cap. *Good Lord, I can't risk any trouble.* She took off her sunglasses and batted her lashes, "I'm very grateful, Officer. It's been a bad night. My grandma took ill, and I'm on my way to the hospital."

He patted her door, "I know you gotta take care of your grandma, but take care of you too. Don't you go driving back into Illinois with that tire."

"I won't. Thank you again. You're most kind." She treated him to a flirtatious smile. He blushed.

"You be safe, now," the cop said, his voice an octave higher than it had been earlier. If she wasn't mistaken, he was blushing

"Thank you. Don't you work too hard." Despite her turmoil, she was flattered by his response. It rook the edge off her nerves and she was able to breathe easy for the first time since she'd seen Neil burn to death.

He grinned like a schoolboy. "I'll try not to. Hope your Grams is all right."

She nodded. "Say a prayer."

"Will do."

She could use a prayer. She'd take as many as she could get. He stopped the slow flow of traffic and motioned her through. Her hands shook on the wheel. This was the strangest day ever. *What else could go wrong?*

Chapter Three

A sharp pain on the left side of her neck woke her. After she'd maneuvered her way through the rest of the traffic jam, her nerves screamed for sleep. Knowing she had a long road ahead to safety, she listened to her inner voice and pulled off at a rest stop. She didn't think she'd be able to sleep, but she drifted off as soon as she turned off the car.

Sierra rubbed the stiffness in her neck, shifting into a sitting position. The sun was blazing overhead, it was going to be another scorcher. Her whole body ached from a combination of stress and the cramped position she'd slept in. Her bladder throbbed. It was going to be a hell of a day.

She grabbed her purse and headed to the restroom. While she washed her hands, she glanced at herself in the mirror. She barely recognized herself. The sunglasses covered half of her face, but she couldn't wear them at night. She'd have to pick up a pair of lightly tinted glasses for later. She removed her sunglasses, splashed cold water on her face and blinked at her reflection. She looked horrible. Her make-up streaked across her face. Deep bags and dark shadows made her red-rimmed eyes look sunken in. Her cheekbones were hollowed out, and she was pale as a ghost. Using her hands, she scrubbed off the remaining make-up. She tilted her head to the side; without all the gook on her face, she looked younger. Considering her outfit, all she needed was a backpack and she might be able to pass herself off as a college student if no one looked at her too closely.

Time was wasting. She dried her hands and headed back out to the car. Her stomach reminded her she needed food. Counting calories wasn't a priority anymore. Her eyes watered. She didn't have to worry about fitting into her wedding dress now that her fiancée was dead. *Would he have gone through with the ceremony while sleeping with Grace?* She bit her lower lip… maybe she was jumping to conclusions. There could be a reasonable explanation for the picture—one that didn't involve a tawdry affair behind her back.

A McDonalds loomed ahead. The pull on the steering wheel when she made sharp turn into the drive though reminded her the back tire was low—a small problem in a sea of big ones. She ordered two sausage McMuffins with egg, a hash brown, two large coffees, and parked under a tree to enjoy her meal.

The first bite was pure greasy bliss, reminding her how much she loved junk food. She dumped a packet of salt over the hash browns, and closed her eyes, chewing slow enough to savor each decadent bit. Good food, hot coffee, a beautiful summer day, for a minute she was able to fool herself into believing life was normal. Amazing what sleep and fast food could do for the soul.

The sullen clerk had only included one tiny napkin in her bag. The kid was probably on the fast track to management, looking out for bottom line. She tossed the useless napkin onto the floor and wiped her hands on her jeans.

Sierra knew she couldn't stall any longer. She drained the last of the first large coffee, picked up the stack of pictures, and felt a fresh stab of betrayal slice her heart. The picture was recent. Neil wore the shirt she'd bought him last month for his birthday, and Grace's hair was styled in the new bob cut she'd debated over getting. For a moment, Sierra couldn't breathe. Betrayal cut through her heart. The picture was proof they'd been doing *something* behind her back. Something they wanted to keep from her. She gnawed on the side of her cheek, searching for a reason they might be together, and came up empty. *How dare they do this to her? Was this the reason for Neil's recent short temper and odd behavior? Was he hiding an affair?*

No. That didn't quite jell. It had to be something else. She flipped through the other pictures; there were more of Neil and Grace, wearing different clothes, taken at different times. Some of the photos were group shots, which only confused her more. She scrutinized each one, looking for any small clue, which might provide an answer.

The group shots were too blurry. Sierra couldn't make out the faces of the other people. She skipped back to the pictures of Neil and Grace, focusing on them. They had their arms around each other in a couple of the shots, but in each one, they were staring into the camera, robbing her of the chance to see how they looked at each other. Their eyes might have revealed if they were friends or lovers.

Who was she kidding? She was grasping at straws. Neil and Grace were friends, but she'd never known them to get together without her. If their meetings were innocent, why keep it a secret? A caldron of emotions boiled inside her; she was pissed off, heartbroken, terrified, and alone. She didn't suffer well in silence. There had to be a way to confront Grace; otherwise, suspicion would fester inside her, clouding her judgment. Her mind needed to be sharp, not muddled with thoughts of how they'd made a fool of her. Grace had some serious explaining to do.

Sierra slammed down the pictures beside her and started the car. She couldn't bear to look at them again, not now. Turning her head, she backed out of the parking space. When she glanced to the right, something caught her eye. Something was written on the backs of the pictures. She swung into traffic and grabbed the stack again.

A single word.

Foxtrot.

What the hell did that mean? Dance lessons? She quickly discarded the idea. Neil was an excellent dancer; he wouldn't have wasted time or money on lessons. The word had to refer to something else. *But what?* She picked up the stack again, and skimmed through the others. One of the group photos had something written on it as well. *The First Wave.* Great. Now she had two clues, neither of which made any sense. The perfect chaser for her morning coffee.

She rammed the pictures into her purse and threw them on the backseat. Out of sight, out of mind. She didn't have time for distractions—not if she wanted to stay alive.

When she hit Indianapolis, she glared at the GPS. Great technology at her fingertips and she couldn't use it because it could pinpoint her location. For the first time in her life, she felt Big Brother peering over her shoulder. *It might be a free country*, she thought, *but we're turning into a society so eager to protect ourselves that we're handing over our privacy and our freedom.*

Frustration ticked inside her. She wanted to get in and out of the city in a hurry, a difficult task with the odds stacked against her. She knew what she needed; where to find it was another matter altogether. She drove around until she spotted several satellite branches of her bank within reasonable proximity from each other. Back home in Chicago, there were banks on every other corner.

For the first time she was glad she'd never gotten around to investing the bulk of the insurance payout she'd received after her parent's death. The settlement may have left her a wealthy woman, but dealing with the money was a painful reminder of the accident. Everyone she knew kept telling her she was crazy to let so much cash sit in a savings account, turns out she wasn't so crazy after all.

Her hand froze when she reached for her purse. Her plan was simple enough. Empty her accounts by visiting several banks, withdrawing enough at each to not raise eyebrows, or be stuck waiting while they requested more money from the safe. She hoped to do it fast enough for the withdrawals not to have posted to her accounts by the time she hit the next bank. All it would take was one overly curious self-important, bank manager to question why someone from out of town was taking out large wads of cash and she'd be toast.

She remembered how freaked out she had been by the gas station attendant and the cop. Bank tellers back home had a way of making her feel like a criminal every time she withdrew more than a few hundred dollars. Up until now, she'd been lucky. Luck had a way of holding so long before it turned. She needed a cover story.

Sierra leaned back against the seat. She unconsciously twisted her engagement ring around her finger. "Think," she whispered, trying to come up with a plausible reason for needing large amounts of cash. Her lips curved in a slow smile. She scrounged around on the floor for the discarded napkin. When her hands closed around it, she felt like she'd won the lottery. It took her a minute to locate the ashtray. Using the lighter, she set the napkin on fire and let it burn in the tray.

The flames, small as they were, jarred her. A chill ran up her spine at the memory of the heinous way Neil had died and why she was on the run. She folded her arms against the steering wheel, and buried her face in them as a gut wrenching sob tore through her. A part of her agonized over whether he had cheated on her; another part of her hated herself for being angry with a dead man. *The emotion was wrong on so many levels.* In the end, it didn't matter what Neil had done, no one should suffer such a horrendous death.

She wiped away her tears and glanced down at the ashtray. The napkin burned itself out. She dipped her fingers inside and smudged the ashes across her face beneath the sunglasses. For good measure, she added a second slash of soot across her chest. Steeling herself, she went inside.

Keeping her head down to avoid surveillance cameras, she filled out a withdrawal slip and made her way to the window. She wordlessly slipped her ID and piece of paper through the window.

The teller studied the withdrawal slip for a good long time. "You want to take all this money out?"

Sierra fought her anger. What gave tellers the right to question people? It was her God Damn money. She repressed her anger and let the tears flow. "My poor sister. Her house burned to the ground last night. Her husband lost his job a while back. He worked for GM. They don't have no insurance. I wish she would have told me they'd fallen on hard times. They've got three kids. I would have paid the insurance for them. Now I just got to help. Do you have a sister?"

The teller's face turned cherry red. "I do. My baby sister makes a habit of doin' all the wrong things, for the right reasons, God help her."

Sierra leaned over the counter, nodding. "So you know what I'm going through."

The teller reached out and patted her hand, "I sure do."

"I could have given them a couple thousand or so each year for insurance. She was too proud and headstrong to ask."

It worked like a charm. The teller scurried over to the pregnant manager. They couldn't have been nicer. Sierra brushed her hand over her tears. "You know what? Maybe I should take out a little bit more. Just in case."

She walked out of the first bank twenty two thousand dollars richer, breaking into a wide smile when she reached the car. *What an adrenaline rush.* She hadn't done anything wrong, yet it felt like she had gotten away with something. Confidence bolstered, she drove to the next bank. When all was said and done, the nice people in Indianapolis were a hell of a lot more compassionate than Chicago folk. Six banks later, she drained everything except her 401k and CD's. She thanked the Lord for her inheritance money. Next stop, discount stores.

There was a Wal-Mart right around the corner. She picked up a couple pillows, blanket, backpack, small suitcase, disposal cell, undies, clothes and snacks. Then she hit the ATM's and maxed out her available cash advances.

The next town up was Terra Haute. She found an internet café, and checked the Chicago papers on-line, biting her fingernails while she read. Every muscle in her body tightened. She had one ear cocked, expecting to hear sirens racing in her direction any moment. Wiping out her bank accounts left a major trail. It was like painting a big red X on her back, screaming come get me. She scrolled through each article, terrified of finding her name or her photo splashed across the page. She sagged with relief when she finished. There was nothing about Neil. No one had found him, no one reported him missing. Thank God. She felt a pang of remorse at her relief. This wasn't how things were supposed to be. Under any other circumstances, she would be beside herself with grief. Instead, she was running from a killer. The whole situation reeked of insanity.

Her gaze scanned the café. Satisfied that no one was paying attention to her, she did a Google search for The First Wave. *A dead end,* she thought, quickly typing in Foxtrot. No double meaning for the scribbled word jumped out at her. She knew the pictures were going to gnaw at her until she had answers. Her neck was in knots. She rolled her head, and heard her muscles crick. This line of thought wasn't doing her any good. Self-preservation first, everything else had to wait.

Sierra logged off the computer and bought a coffee, sitting back down at another table, there was no need to leave a trail in a single computer's history. If anyone was following her, she planned to make it as difficult as possible to find her. She went on Craig's list, and scribbled a list of phone numbers. There were quite a few used cars for sale; buying one was going to be tricky.

She headed back to the car and started dialing, hitting pay dirt on the fifth call. A seventeen-year-old kid who rebuilt cars was trying to earn cash for college. She begged him to meet her outside a local diner. When he hesitated, she realized she'd made a mistake by sounding too desperate. Afraid that he was about to hang up, she turned on the waterworks to help convince him. It took some doing but he finally agreed to meet her in forty minutes

Sierra shoved a few things in the backpack and ripped the plaid shirt she was wearing. Gritting her teeth, she opened her car door, and slammed it into her chin. *Damn, that hurt.* If she was going to play a role, she was going to own it. Method acting. Who could have predicted her high school drama classes were going to pay off after all? She banged the door into her forehead too, and with a grunt of satisfaction felt a bump start to rise.

She stuffed six thousand dollars into her jeans pocket and buried the car keys in another. Then she went to sit on a curb, rubbing her already reddened eyes to make them look worse. A quick look around told her no one appeared to be paying attention to her and her cell phone burned a hole in her hand. Before she could talk herself out of it, she hit star sixty-seven and dialed Grace's number. It went to voice mail.

Odd. Grace should have been home. Sierra screened her calls. Grace always picked up, no matter what she was in the middle of doing. The unanswered call fed her paranoia. She imagined Grace pacing in a motel room waiting for Neil to arrive and warned herself she was jumping to conclusions. The truth was it was far easier to feel betrayed and angry, than to give into grief.

Two cars pulled up alongside her. The 2002 black Honda Accord gleamed from a recent polishing. She could care less about the dings and dents riddling the back door. The kid burned rubber squealing into the parking lot. The motor hummed, that was only the sales pitch she needed.

A pimply faced teen tumbled out of the Honda. His buddy, a bit cooler in a souped-up Camero, followed. Sierra felt old looking at them.

The kid thrust his chin at her, "You the lady lookin' to buy?"

"Yeah." Sierra used her sleeve to wipe her tears and hurried over to them.

"Whoa." The kid eyed her battered face, backing away. "What happened to you?"

She cast a furtive glance around her. "Hey, listen, I want the car okay? I came here to get a soda after class. And what do I see? My fiancée with the local rich bitch. I confront him. He pulls me outside, threatens me, smacks me in the face and takes off with my car. His Daddy is some big shot with the Chicago police. He dumped me, right on the spot. Said if I caused a scene or messed things up with his new girlfriend, he'd make all kinds of trouble for me. He would too, he's that mean. I don't even want to go home and get my stuff. I just want a car so I can go back to my family in Illinois. I don't want trouble."

The kid looked at his buddy. "Neither do I."

She batted her lashes, "Please, help me. You're asking five grand for the car. I'll give you six, if you can promise if anyone ever comes asking, you've never seen me. No matter what."

The buddy nudged pimple face, "An extra thou, man. Ain't nothin' to sneeze at."

The kid shifted from foot to foot. "You know what you gotta do, right? With the plates and title and all?"

"Yeah, of course."

"You wanna have it checked out or take it for a ride?"

"No. I just want to get far away from the asshole before he comes after me again."

"You wanna buy it? Just like that?"

"Yeah, just like that. If we have a deal. You've never seen me. I'm scared he might kill me…or worse. You don't know his temper."

"And you'll pay an extra grand?"

She shoved her hand into her pocket, and pulled out a wad of cash. "It's right here."

"Well." He looked at his friend again.

"Well?"

He eyed the bills in her hand. "All right then, you got yourself a deal."

"Even if the cops starts talkin' trash about me?"

"Hey, I ain't never seen ya."

Sierra shoved the money into his hand before he could change his mind. "Thank you. You saved my life." The teen had no idea how true that was.

"Shit, for a thousand bucks, it's the least I can do." He handed her the keys and the title. "Get that taken care of okay? Like, right away?"

"You bet. Thank you."

"Anytime. She's all yours." He started to walk away, and then turned back. "You know, maybe I should go with you for the title exchange."

Shit, this was a complication she didn't need.

"My fiancée is probably gonna be lookin' for me. He's a big guy who thinks with his fists. I promise, I'll take care of it right away. I don't want him giving you any trouble."

The kid hesitated before he nodded. "All right. Just don't mess me up, okay?"

"Okay." Poor guy, she *was* going to mess him up. She should have given him more than an extra thousand for his troubles.

He scuffed the tip of his gym shoes on the pavement, deep in thought. He was probably remembering all the good advice his parents gave him about what *not* to do when selling a car. Her heart stood still. She needed the Honda.

The buddy poked him. "A grand, man. Let's book."

"Yeah." He raised trusting brown eyes to hers. *She would remember those eyes.* "Good luck."

Sierra forced a smile and a waved. She waited until they were out of sight before tucking the title into her back pocket, and transferring her belongings to the new car. *Now what to do with Neil's car?*

There were woods within walking distance. She gnawed on the side of her cheek, thinking. Sierra drove in as deep as she could and pulled over. There was a tool kit in the trunk. She located the VIN number, and hacked away at it with a screwdriver. If anyone were looking for her, they'd have figured out by now that she'd taken Neil's car. The longer they thought that the better. Squatting down, she removed the license plates. She sat back on her heels, tracing the numbers with her finger. Whenever Neil picked her up, she'd watch for the familiar plate number. Another thing she'd never do again. She sighed, shuddering with emotion. This wasn't the time to break down, not if she wanted to outwit the killer.

Sierra steeled herself to take last look through the car; she didn't want to leave any of his personal items behind. One day, she might look back and regret it. She emptied out the glove compartment, it contained mostly junk, nothing worth keeping. Out of the corner of her eye, she noticed something sliver glinting under the driver's side seat. She stretched forward to reach it, surprised when she found a netbook, one of those small mobile laptops that allowed instant access to the internet. Neil never mentioned owing one. It was becoming apparent there was a lot she didn't know about her fiancée.

For good measure, she left the driver's side window open, and the keys in the ignition. If Indiana were anything like Chicago, someone would steal the car or chop it up for parts. Abandoning Neil's car to be picked clean by scavengers felt like a second death.

Sierra wrapped her arms around her body. "Good-bye, Neil."

With a final nod, she turned ready to face the unknown.

Chapter Four

Sierra rolled down the windows, and relished her first taste of freedom since the whole debacle began. She unfastened her ponytail and let the wind whip through her hair. Somewhere along the line, she'd made an unconscious decision to figure out what happened to Neil and what his connection to Grace, Foxtrot and The First Wave was. Curiosity was her downfall; she'd dig for answers, twisting questions until she got the truth.

Let's just hope my curiosity doesn't get me killed this time, she thought, staring out at the fields on either side of her. Every mile looked the same. She wished the scenery wasn't so monotonous.

It took her over four hours to reach Lexington, Kentucky. Sierra kept the radio loud to drown the voices of doubt in her head. *Best not to think right now,* she warned herself. Riding the roller coaster of emotions plummeting inside her would make her crazy.

She hadn't eaten since early that morning, and was starving; stress had a way of making her crave food. She pulled into a local market and stocked up on a blocks of cheese, crackers and Pepsi, using her credit card. Sooner or later, someone besides the killer would be looking for her. The deliberate clues leading from Illinois to Kentucky would help to establish a false trail. Once she got far enough away, if her plan worked, she'd be untraceable.

Her mouth salivated for a bite of cheddar. She ripped into the package and bit off a large chunk. She washed it down with Pepsi and picked up the disposable cell.

Grace still didn't answer. A bad feeling slithered over Sierra's spine. Her friend was a creature of habit; if Grace wasn't answering her phone, it meant something happened to force her to change her routine. She wouldn't have found Neil's body. Not yet anyway. Not with Sierra supposedly still there.

So where the hell was she?

Sierra gulped down more Pepsi and rubbed her eyes. She was running on fumes. Between the traffic jam, waiting for the banks to open, and the pit stops she'd made, fourteen hours had passed. Fourteen life-altering hours.

***

She couldn't rest yet. Sierra managed to keep her eyes open and hunger sated until she reached Nashville. The cheese wasn't cutting it anymore. She fueled up, and found a hole- in- the- wall restaurant where she dug into a full slab of the best damn ribs she'd ever eaten.

The joint was jumping. Groups of people laughed over steaming plates of food. Bad jokes rang out from good old boys seated at the bar, and the juke box blared country music.

Sierra rested her chin on her hand and took it all in. She envied them. They looked so normal. Everyday people, with everyday problems, letting off a little steam at the end of the day. What she wouldn't give to be like them, to be a part of the revelry, instead of on the outside looking in.

"That's a mighty wistful expression for such a pretty lady."

The voice startled her. She glanced up and stared into the blackest eyes she'd ever seen. Two frosty mugs of beer sweated in his hands. "Mind if I join you? The beer is yours whether I can sit or not."

"I have a long drive ahead," she answered with a tired smile, "I probably shouldn't be drinking unless you're ready to provide me with shelter for the night."

He grinned. "That could be arranged," he drawled with a mischievous wink.

Her cheeks flamed red. "No, I didn't mean…"

"Relax, I know what you meant." He chuckled, setting one beer on the table in front of her. "I'm not in the habit of taking advantage of strangers. I can offer you a single bed and safety for a night. If you need it, that is."

Sierra frowned, studying him. He wasn't her type, but he wasn't half bad looking. Long black hair slicked back and caught in a ponytail. An interesting face, chiseled good looks, weathered by life. His body was long and lean. He wore soft, faded denim jeans and a loose plaid shirt over a pristine white tee. There was something familiar about him, but she couldn't put her finger on what it was. When he cleared his throat, she realized she was staring.

"Do I pass inspection?" He lifted his beer, and gestured to the empty seat across from her. "May I?"

She looked around the crowded restaurant. He didn't reek of cop, and she didn't think anyone had followed her. A vein throbbed in her forehead. The last thing she should be doing was taking up with a stranger, but couldn't shake the feeling she'd seen him somewhere before. Curiosity got the best of her again. "Yes, you may."

He raised his beer and motioned for her to do the same. Bemused, she complied.

"To fortuitous meetings," he toasted, clinking his glass against hers.

A chill gripped her. She drained a fourth of the beer in a single swallow, "Why would you say that?"

He leaned back in the booth, and stretched out his legs. "Most meetings are fortuitous, wouldn't you say?"

Sierra took another swig of beer. The cold drink soothed her dry throat. "No, I don't necessarily agree." She cringed at the crack in her voice. Inviting him to sit with her had been a bad idea.

He was nonplussed by her tone. "Ah, come on, think about it. Don't most people, the people you really connect with, come into your life for a reason? They show up right when you need them most, even if you don't realize it at the time."

She grew uncomfortable with the direction their conversation was taking. Sierra shifted in her seat, prepared to bolt.

He laughed. A deep, pleasant belly laugh that cut through her fear. "I didn't mean to freak you out. I guess I delved too deep to start."

"Yeah, you think? You're a bit intense."

He leaned across the table and winked. "Livin' life with intensity. That's me. Never do anything half assed. You only get one chance."

She laughed, surprising herself. "What, are you Batman or something?"

"Or something." He extended a hand. "Name's Skinbone Harris."

She choked on her beer, covering her face as it shot through her nose.

"Yeah, I get that reaction a lot." He shrugged.

She peered at him over her hand, trying to stifle her laughter. "That's your name? Seriously?"

"Seriously. White Daddy and a Hopi Momma. Both with a warped sense of humor."

She mopped her face with a napkin. "That explains a lot."

He crossed his long legs. "It does, doesn't it? And see, you're not wistful anymore. You're laughing, and…sputtering. See? I did come into your life for a reason."

Sierra raised her eyebrows and finished off her beer. She shouldn't be drinking, but it felt good to unwind. "Well then, Skinbone, serve your purpose and buy me another beer."

He signaled to the waitress for two more. "You want to talk about what's troubling you?"

"Nope."

"I guess I shouldn't be asking what a nice girl like you is doing in a dive like this."

"No. You shouldn't. And who says I'm a nice girl?"

He raised his brows, "Careful now or I might get it into my head that you're flirting with me."

"That's not at all what I was implying," she shot back. *What the hell is wrong with me,* she thought, *why do I keep saying things that stink of flirtation?*

Skinbone lifted his hands in mock defeat. "My mistake."

An awkward silence fell between them. The waitress arrived and set their drinks down on the table. Sierra cupped her hands around her glass, and met his gaze, unable to restrain her curiosity any longer, "Why do you look so familiar?"

Her question caught him off guard. He lowered his beer, studying her face carefully. "I have no idea. Fortuitousness?"

"I'm being serious."

"Okay, Serious, I don't have a clue why I look familiar, but the fact you think so intrigues me."

It was on the tip of her tongue to ask him if he'd ever been to Chicago when she realized that would be a grave mistake. She needed to stay anonymous.

"Maybe if we got to know each other a little better, you'd figure out why I seem familiar. Could be I remind you of someone. Speaking of which, are you ever going to tell me your name?"

She hesitated, divulging too much information wasn't a good idea. She settled on telling him her childhood nickname instead, "Seri."

"Okay, Seri. Here's a clue about me. I'm an enigma."

Her eyes narrowed, but she couldn't suppress her grin. "Oh, that's real helpful."

"There's more. I'm a Noetic Scientist, a Native American Spiritualist, and…"

"And?"

"An assassin."

"Assassin?" she croaked. *Oh my God,* she thought, *it was his eyes that made him look familiar. Black eyes, just like Neil's killer.* It couldn't be the same man, *could it?* She swallowed hard, trying to recall the killer's face. All she could remember were his cold, dead eyes. *Had someone put a hit out on Neil…and had they found her now too?*

Sierra gripped the edge of her seat, forcing herself to remain calm. *Was he taunting her?* Her fingernails dug into the wooden booth, a splinter piercing the tender skin beneath them. The pain jolted her back to reality. This had to be a bizarre coincidence. There was no way the killer could have found her… let alone been lying in wait at this out of the way bar. She forced herself to meet her companions gaze.

Skinbone took a sip of beer, gauging her reaction over the rim of his glass. His eyes twinkled.

She wasn't sure how to read him; didn't know if she should be angry or scared. "You expect me to believe you?" her voice was haughty, daring him to continue.

"What I expect doesn't matter. It's what you believe." His face was solemn, but his eyes crinkled with amusement.

The hell with him. His answer tipped the scales towards fear. She slapped money on the table and stood up, banging her shin against the wooden booth.

He gripped her wrist. "Hey, slow down. Sit. Drink your beer. You are not in any danger. Not from me, anyway."

The blood drained from her face at his touch. She looked down at his hand, feeling a jolt of arousal down to her toes. Her eyes widened, and the breath caught in her throat. *Jesus. Did he have electricity running through his veins instead of blood?* Her knees wobbled, she grabbed the edge of the table to steady herself. There was no way in hell she was going to let him see how he affected her. She bit her cheek and slipped back into the booth.

"Whoa, come on, now. You look like you've seen a ghost." He flashed a pearly white smile, oblivious to her inner turmoil. "Chill. If I was an assassin, do you really think I'd announce it to a total stranger I just met in a bar?"

"No. Of course not." She took a jittery breath and composed herself. Okay, so he was joking—he had no way of knowing what a sick joke it was under the circumstances. Still, there was something unnerving about him. She couldn't shake the feeling she'd seen him somewhere before. The coincidences were starting to add up. His ink black eyes continued to disturb her. She couldn't ignore the fact that they were the same color as the killers. Up until last night, she'd never seen eyes that shade before.

He reached for her hand; his eyes were gentle, as if he was trying to reassure her. "Listen, Seri, I don't know you from Adam, but something made me approach you tonight. We were meant to meet at this dive of a restaurant. There is a reason for it. You may think I'm crazy, but I believe in predestination. We met for a reason that is, as yet, is unclear to both of us. I apologize if I scared you. I didn't mean to, I was just having fun with you. You're white as a sheet. The bags under your eyes tell me how exhausted you are, and you're half-bagged from the beer. I may come on a little strong, but I mean well. Seri. Look at me."

She looked.

"Let me help you."

She shook her head, feeling skittish. Skinbone, if that was even his name, was hitting too close to home.

"I mean you no harm. I was drawn to you because I sensed you needed help. That may sound strange to you, it may even alarm you, but you need to understand I am a very spiritual person. Our lives are destined to be intertwined. You need to trust me."

His face had an urgent quality. He was throwing off a weird vibe, and she was on the verge of being sucked in. The man had a compelling presence. If she wasn't careful, in another few seconds she'd be spilling her guts to him. That would be a huge mistake. She gathered her things."I really need to be going."

"You're not from around here, are you?"

Did Skinbone know who she was, and what she had seen? He could be toying with her, trapping her like a mouse in a maze.

"Why does it matter?" she answered, scanning the restaurant. Would anyone come to her rescue if he tried to drag her out of here?

"It doesn't matter, Seri. Listen, I apologize again if I made you jumpy. It wasn't my intent. I'm sorry. I go too far sometimes. Pushing the envelope, you know? I wanted to get your mind off whatever's troubling you."

Instead, he'd added to it. If she was going to survive until the killer was caught, she couldn't get spooked every time someone brought up an uncomfortable topic. She might as well wave a huge white surrender flag.

She took a deep, calming, breath. *I can do this. I've done it already, at the gas station, the banks, with the cop and the kid who'd sold her the car.* "No, I'm sorry. You're right. I'm on edge tonight. I'm also seriously out of practice at bar banter. Does it show?"

He flagged down the waitress and ordered another round before answering. "What shows is you're raw and you're hurting. You're also blowing my moment. So much for being Batman, and rescuing a damsel in distress."

The laugh formed in her belly. She wasn't proud of it, but she guffawed, right then and there. "If this is your idea of rescuing, you have a lot to learn." Tears of laughter ran down her cheeks. The tension was broken. She could feel the effects of the alcohol kicking in.

He leaned back in the booth and crossed his arms, shooting her a quizzical look. His expression only made her laugh harder. The waitress deposited their drinks on the table with a confused smile, and quickly backed away eliciting a fresh round of laughter from her.

Skinbone leaned across the table. "Are you trying to get us thrown out of here? I mean, if you're that desperate to go back to my place..."

Sierra waved at him with both hands. "Stop," she gasped, trying to catch her breath. She really shouldn't be drinking. Hell, she shouldn't be laughing either. The stress and the beers were catching up to her and laughing was the only way to relive her bottled up tension. As inappropriate as it was, once she started, she couldn't seem to stop.

"You know, if you laugh yourself to death, you can't blame me. This is not the reaction I'm used to getting from women."

Her sides ached. She snorted. *Way to go, Sierra,* she thought, *that shows what a classy chick you are.*

Skinbone looked around the restaurant in mock embarrassment, "Would you like to be alone? I feel like I've suddenly been dropped kicked into *"When Harry Met Sally."*

The entire situation was too much. Sierra dipped her head to her hands, utterly spent. She pounded the table. "Stop. Please."

"I would, but this is all you. I believe you were the one who dubbed me Batman. Trust me; I'm really not this funny. You're messin' with my MoJo."

Sierra grabbed her beer, despite the fact she was already tipsy. Raising her head, she gave him a wary look, and pointed a finger at him. "Don't you dare make me laugh again."

He raised both hands in surrender, "Far be it from me to amuse you into convulsions."

She struggled to keep a straight face. "God, I hate you."

"Yeah. I can see why. I made you forget your despair."

"Well, thanks for the reminder." Her fingers curled around the glass. "Here's to reality."

Skinbone touched her glass with his and took a drink. He reached for her hand. She stopped laughing. "Reality is what you make it."

She pondered his words, looking at him with bleary eyes, "That's bullshit. Reality is what's thrust upon you."

His gaze turned serious. "Come on now, do you honestly think this was a happenchance encounter?"

"I'd prefer to think so, yes."

"Amateur. Give me your cell phone."

Her eyes narrowed in suspicion. "Why?"

He reached out his hand. "Phone first. Then I'll tell you why."

She was drunk enough to oblige. Sierra dug around in her purse, searching for her disposable cell.

"I'm programming your number in my phone. And I'm giving you mine. Fate will bring us together again."

"I highly doubt it."

He arched a brow, "You wait and see. No. Uh-Uh. Don't you give me that look. Just when you need me most, when you feel like your world is falling apart, I'll call you. Mark my words. And the same goes in reverse. If, or when I'm in trouble, I expect a call from you."

"All because of a chance encounter?"

"There are no chance encounters. Do you know what Noetic Science is?"

"Nope, don't have a clue."

"Thought not. I'm going to text the phrase to you. Look it up at your convenience. I think you'll find it fascinating. Of course, you'll have to temper what you learn with my Native American Spiritualism and my proclivity at being an assassin, and all."

She glared at him, "That's not even remotely funny."

"Not meant to be. Let me ask you something."

"Oh, God. Do you have to? Why do I get the feeling I'm not going to like it?"

"Just roll with this, okay?"

"Okay. But you're buying the next round." The alcohol was loosening her up.

He raised a brow, but signaled to the waitress to bring them another round. "We've gotten to know each other a little bit, and I stress, little bit."

"Agreed."

"For the purpose of this conversation, if I was an assassin, would you hate me or hate what I do?"

Sierra leaned back, running her hands through her hair with a groan. "Why are you stuck on this topic?"

He grinned, "Because it's interesting. And it pushes your buttons."

The humor faded from her face. She wanted to move away from this subject.

"Well, would you hate me or what I do?" he prodded, leaning over the table.

"Honestly? Both." There, she'd said it.

"Ouch." He covered his heart with his hand. "Here I thought I was a charming guy."

"There's nothing charming about death," she snapped.

"Point taken. And I never said there was. But what if I only killed bad people?"

"Bad people?" She blinked, turning his words over in her mind.

His brow creased and he hurried to explain. "People who pose a threat to national security, to life as we know it, the world at large. Bad guys."

Sierra shivered despite the heat. *What was he saying?* She regretted drinking so much. The bar noises seemed amplified the crowd eating and drinking, ominous. She fidgeted in her seat, sweat beading up on her forehead. The conversation had taken a disturbing direction.

"Hey." Skinbone touched her arm gently. "Are you okay?

Why did his fingers feel like lightening against her skin? The too bright lights burned her eyes. Her stomach lurched at the compassion etched across his face, like he genuinely cared. *Play along,* she decided, *give him the answer he wants and get the hell out of here.*

"I guess that would make you one of the good guys."

"I rest my case." He smiled in triumph and raised his arms, resting his head against them. "You ever gonna tell me what's chipping away at you?"

She collected her things and slid out of the booth. "You know, I think I'll save that revelation for another time. I need to get going."

"You okay to drive? My offer of a bed is still open." He stood up with her and gripped her hand.

Sierra studied his face for a good long while. She wanted to remember it. "I'm fine."

"Make your own reality, Seri. Don't make surface judgments. Sometimes there's a fine line where good and bad blur and nothing is what it seems. We will meet again. We're in each other's orbit now. The world is a hell of lot stranger than you think, kiddo. How you perceive it is up to you."

Rattled, she snatched her hand from his grip. She had one foot out the door, when she realized he was messing with her head. Skinbone was one part charm, two parts con, and who the hell knew what else. She turned back, ready to give him a piece of her mind.

He'd vanished into thin air.

CHAPTER FIVE

Five minutes later, Sierra couldn't stop shaking. *He must have gone out a back door.* She drove with one eye glued to the review mirror in case she was being followed. Talk about strange encounters. She had no idea if he'd been warning her or sending her a message. What if he'd slipped out and was lurking out here somewhere, lying in wait? She never should have talked to him; their conversation did nothing to sooth her nerves.

Skinbone Harris was trouble. She could rationalize things sixth ways to Wednesday, but one thing was certain: Sierra Montgomery always trusted her gut, and it was telling her he had a connection to everything that was happening to her right now.

How close had she come to death tonight? She resisted the urge to press her foot harder against the gas pedal. The beers had gone to her head; she couldn't risk getting into an accident.

She drove past a motel without thinking. *Damn it, stick to the plan.* She had no idea what she'd gotten caught up in; she couldn't afford any more foolish mistakes, she needed to stay under the radar. No cars were behind her; she backed up and pulled into the parking lot.

The motel was a dump. Thank God, she had no intention of staying. She checked in under her own name and used Neil's license plate number. She scattered her empty Pepsi cans and cheese wrappers on the nightstand and dresser to make it looked like she'd stayed overnight. When she pulled the covers down on the bed, a roach scurried over her foot, and she jumped in alarm. The idea of touching the bed disgusted her, but she grit her teeth and smashed her hand into the pillow to create an indent so that the bed looked slept in. Satisfied with her handiwork, she slammed the door behind her. *Good Lord, how could anyone sleep in these hovels?* She shuddered at the thought.

The clock was ticking; there was only a small window of opportunity for her to execute her plan. It didn't take long to find the train station where she bought a one-way ticket to New Orleans; once purchased, she jammed the ticket in her purse, and walked out, a cup of strong black coffee in hand.

She had an hour to kill before she boarded the train. Fortified by the coffee, she drove to an abandoned lot she'd noticed earlier and tossed Neil's license plates into the pile of junk that lie rotting near the side of the road. If anyone were still searching for his car, the trail would end here, just like she intended.

A few minutes later, she was back in the train station's parking lot, with time to spare. Sierra picked the disposable phone. Grace still wasn't answering. She racked her brain, trying to remember if Grace had mentioned any weekend plans. Between organizing the wedding and Grace's excitement over a new project at work, their conversations had been hit and miss. It hadn't seemed like a big deal at the time. Now she regretted not keeping in better touch. Their last conversation had been on Tuesday.

It was Saturday night. If she was lucky, she had one day left to dig up answers. She took a sip of coffee. The shot of caffeine cleared the fuzz from her eyes. There was one more phone call she could make.

Chapter Six

"St. James."

Sierra closed her eyes. It was odd to hear his voice after all these years. Memories came flooding back. She swallowed hard, trying to push them away.

"St. James," he repeated. She caught the hint of irritation in his tone. He'd always been impatient.

"Donovan, its Sierra."

There was a long silence. She dug her nails into the palms of her hands. This wasn't the reception she'd been hoping for. "Are you there?"

"Yes, I'm here."

No, hello, or how have you been. He wasn't going to make this easy on her. It seemed time and distance hadn't quelled his anger.

"Hi." God, she sounded like a fool. His chilly reception threw her off guard.

"What do you want, Sierra?"

Her heart sunk at his clipped tone. "I… I need to talk to you," she started, her voice breaking.

"Really? Neil's gone, so you decide to come running back to me. What? Did you think we'd pick up right where we left off?

She didn't hear a word after *Neil's gone.* How did he know? She'd been tracking the news; there'd been no report of his death.

"What do you mean 'Neil is gone'?" Fear crackled in her voice.

Another long pause. A full minute passed before he answered. "Isn't that why you're calling?"

"Why did you say 'Neil's gone'?" She repeated. Her hands had turned icy cold. If news of her fiancée's death had trickled up to the FBI, she was in deep trouble. Eluding the CPD by crossing state lines was one thing—evading the FBI would be a hell of a lot harder. Calling Donovan had been a huge mistake.

"Sierra, I'm in no mood to play games. Either he left you or you dumped him. Why else would you be calling?"

She almost wept with relief. He didn't know. She still had a chance. "No, we didn't break up."

"Oh." The word hung in the air. Donovan cleared his throat. "My mistake, then. Things are good?"

"Yeah, they're good." Dear God, what was she saying? For a crazy, mindless second, she'd automatically lapsed into telling him things fine between her and Neil. She started over. "No. No, things aren't good. Neil is dead." A train rumbled by, blowing its horn. "I'm in trouble. I need your help."

There was silence on the other end. She had spoken the words so fast, she wondered if Donovan understood her, or if he heard her at all over the blare of the train. "Donovan? Are you there? Did you hear me?"

"Sierra, where are you? What's all the noise in the background?"

"Never mind the noise! Did you hear me? Damn it, Donovan, this is important."

"No, I have no idea what you're mumbling about. Frankly, I don't understand why you're calling me."

She glanced around. No one else was in the parking lot but she didn't want to shout.

Another train was approaching from the opposite direction. She yelled into the phone, "I said, Neil is dead. Did you hear me this time?"

She only caught the end of his sentence.

"... you said."

"You heard what I said?"

"… what you want."

Damn it. His voice cut out again. "Donovan, we have a bad connection. Let me call you back."

"...say, don't bother."

"Please? It's a matter of life and death." No answer. She glanced at the phone. No bars. *What else could go wrong?* She headed back to the train station, praying the cell would work inside.

It didn't. The phone was dead. She'd forgotten to charge the battery while in the car. She considered running back out when they announced her train was boarding. She dragged the luggage behind her, feeling every ounce of the stress she'd been under since the previous night. She stopped to rest, watching the other passengers rush past her. It was embarrassing not to be able to keep up.

Gritting her teeth, she pushed forward. By the time she made it to the front of the train, she was soaked with sweat, and out of breath. There was only one seat left. She'd bought a business class ticket, hoping to sit alone. No such luck. She stored the suitcase in the overhead compartment and fell into the seat with a resounding thump. Her seatmate didn't even blink. *Thank God.* With any luck, he wouldn't be much of a conversationalist either. It would be a short trip, at any rate.

She planned to get off the train at the first stop. Until then, she intended to rest. Every inch of her ached with exhaustion. She closed her eyes, feeling some of the tension drain from her body. She was safe, for now. No harm could come to her here. Lulled by the soothing motion of the train, she drifted off into a dreamless sleep.

***

The singing woke her. No, not singing—humming. Sierra opened her eyes, disorientated. She was always groggy when she woke up. For a split second, she thought she was at home in her own bed. Then it all came rushing back to her. She was on a train. Neil was dead. And she was running for her life.

The nap hadn't helped at all; if anything, she felt worse. She rolled her neck and shoulders trying to work out the kinks, and was rewarded with a snap, crackle, popping sound for her efforts. On top of everything else, she had a raging headache. The pain crested when the humming grew louder. *Where the hell was it coming from?*

The tune was familiar…from a Broadway show, though she couldn't quite place it. Sierra rubbed her eyes. Irritated, she sat up straight in her seat and glared at the man next to her. He didn't seem to notice her annoyance.

Sierra grabbed her purse, leaping out of her seat. She needed coffee, lots of it. Caffeine often dulled her headaches. She bought a large regular and took a sip, burning her tongue in the process. It hurt like hell, but it helped clear her head.

She finished her coffee, throwing several dark glances at the man beside her. He was tall and sinewy, with an intriguing, craggy face. She guessed him to be in his early sixties. His long brown hair was graying and pulled back into a ponytail exposing a gold hoop earring in his left ear, the slight stubble of five o'clock shadow peppered his chin. There was a large gold ring on his middle finger and several ropes of leather and gold bracelets adorning his wrists. The man liked his jewelry.

At least she was finally able to put a name to the tune he was humming. *If I Were a Rich Man, from Fiddler on The Roof.*

She glanced at her watch. Half an hour until they stopped. At some point, she needed to take a few risks if she was going to save herself. Neil's netbook seemed like a good place to start. She had no idea if it functioned like a regular laptop, or had a GPS built inside it like a cell phone, but if the police didn't know he owned one, they wouldn't be tracking it.

She shook the numbness from her hands; she'd been clenching her fists hard enough to lose feeling in them. A few people started to gather their belongings from the overhead bins. She wrestled with her luggage, cramming it in front of her legs, and pulled out the computer, balancing it on her lap as she powered it up.

Damn it. Password protected. She knew his e-mail password and tried it. Nothing. Twisting her engagement ring, she stared at the screen. Neil was a creature of habit. He'd use a password easy to remember. Her fingers flew over the keyboard, trying different combinations, groaning in frustration when none of them worked.

Grace. Ignoring the pang in her stomach, she typed in the name. Invalid password. Sierra breathed a sigh of relief. It would have killed her if he'd used Grace's name. She thought of the pictures she'd found earlier. One blow today was enough. *The pictures*, she thought excitedly, *the words scribbled on the back... one of them is the password.*

Foxtrot. As soon as she hit enter, the computer started to boot. The conductor's booming voice reminded the passengers that they would be arriving in Greenwood, Mississippi in ten minutes. She didn't have a lot of time to access the laptop's files. Sierra clicked on a random folder, drumming her fingers while she waited for it to open. A warning popped box up. It too was password protected.

Jesus. Sierra ran her hands through her hair in frustration. *Again? Really?*

Shaking her head, she went with her best guess, typing in The First Wave.

Bingo.

The file opened. Classified splashed across the front page in big bold letters, right beneath a U.S. Government seal. Air rushed from her lungs. She didn't know what she'd expected to find, but it wasn't this. She bit her lips, nervous energy exploding inside her. *What was Neil doing with classified information?* A quick glance around the cabin assured her no one was paying her any attention. She located the arrow key. Her hand shook while she strolled down.

TriCon Lab appeared on the page. Her nerves relaxed. The file was work related. *Whew.* She leaned back in seat, waiting for her pulse to stop racing.

In an instant, all hell broke loose.

The man beside her sprang to life, slamming her netbook shut and shoving her head between her knees.

"What the hell—?" Before she could finish her sentence, her attacker pushed her out of her seat, towards the ground. She kicked hard, grabbing her possessions, and holding onto them for dear life. He deflected the kick, covering her with his body.

How did they find her? Sierra scratched and elbowed, stunned at the bold attack in such a public place.

A man seated nearby jumped up and headed towards them. Sierra opened her mouth to scream for help. Her attacker pressed her face into the ground, his bracelets scraping her cheek.

"Go," he hissed in her ear, "stay down. Crawl towards the door."

She twisted in his arms. "Are you out of your..."

Bullets slammed into the train, metal hitting metal with horrifying deliberateness. Sierra cringed, deafened by the noise. Without thinking, she looked up in time to hear a distinctive pop and see the window next to their seats shatter. She froze, blood turning to ice, when a bullet burrowed into the headrest she'd been leaning against moments earlier.

If the man hadn't shoved her down, she'd be dead. She crumbled, covering her head with her hands. Whimpering, she flattened herself against the floor to protect herself from the spray of bullets. "I can't take anymore, I can't, I can't, I can't."

Her seatmate ignored her piteous sobs, and yanked her up by the hair. "Get to the exit, now. *Hurry.*"

She shook her head, fingers searching for something to hold on to before her dragged her away. "No. I need my things."

Screams tore through the cabin, people were diving for cover. The passenger coming to her aid staggered backwards as a bullet slammed into his right arm. His eyes glazed over in shock. He raised a hand to staunch the flow of blood, collapsing into a seat. A brave couple rushed to help the injured man.

Her protector took advantage of the confusion and tossed Sierra the backpack and purse. He grabbed hold of her suitcase.

Pandemonium continued. Another volley of bullets sailed overhead. There was no time to think. Staying low, Sierra scurried to the back of the cabin. The train was screeching to halt.

Sierra made it to the end of the cabin. "The doors are locked."

"For security reasons. They don't want whoever is shooting to get on board."

"Now what?"

He pushed himself in front of her. She glanced over her shoulder, praying no one was coming after them. When she turned back towards her protector, the connecting doors were open wide enough to squeeze through. The exit doors remained locked down tight.

"What do we do?"

"Hush." He faced the outside door, turning his gaze on it. Within moments, it slid open.

Her mouth dropped open; she stared at her companion, "How the hell did you do that?"

"That's not important right now." He took hold of her arm, pulling her forward, "You need to jump."

"Jump?" She looked down. The train had slowed, but it was still moving.

"Jump or I'll push," he growled.

She decided not to argue. They tumbled down to the pavement, her bags rolling to a stop beside them. Her knee stung where her worn out jeans ripped.

There were sirens in the distance. The gunshots stopped. The man stood up, slinging her bags over his shoulder, "Stay down."

They'd exited on the opposite side as the shooters. He prowled the length of the train from the outside, until he neared where they had been sitting. He crouched low, peering underneath the train, then ran back towards her, motioning for her to get up. Without stopping, he grabbed her hand and the handle of her suitcase, "Let's go."

He almost wrenched her arm out of its socket. She wasn't about to complain. He'd saved her life. Their feet pounded the sidewalk. When she was able to catch her breath she yelled, "Where are we going?"

"Quiet."

The word sliced through her. She saw herself in bed with Neil, felt his body tense beneath her fingers as he rolled off her. He'd barked at her to be quiet. Sadness mingled with anger coursed through her and her feet slowed to a stop. She was about to tell him where he could shove his 'quiet' when he took hold of her upper arm and yanked her along with him.

If she didn't run, she had no doubt he would drag her. She ran. They made it to a parking lot. He tried every car door they passed until one of them opened. "Get in."

"You're stealing a car?"

"You have a better idea?"

She looked at the car, then at the four men running in their direction and back again. The shooters. She scrambled into the car without a word. He hotwired it in an instant, holding a finger up to his lips. Then he gunned the engine.

The tires squealed. She flew back in her seat inhaling the distinctive scent of burning rubber.

Sierra closed her eyes and prayed.

Chapter Seven

The car jerked to a stop. Sierra opened one eye, scared to death. She had no idea why this stranger was helping her, or how he knew what to do. Deep down, she was terrified she'd somehow alerted the killer to her location by logging onto the netbook.

But that was crazy, wasn't it? She hadn't logged onto the internet. The gunmen were already lying in wait in Greenwood. So if they weren't after her…

Oh God, what else had she gotten mixed up in?

The driver's door slammed closed. They'd pulled up alongside a river. Her companion ran around to her side of the car, pulling her door open. "Get out."

She eyed him with suspicion, "Who are you?" She asked, half-afraid of the answer.

He ignored her, "Get out," he repeated in a growl. There was a sense of urgency in his tone.

Sierra shrank back in her seat. His piercing blue eyes glittered with anger, but she was determined to hold her ground. "Not until you tell me who you are."

"Suit yourself." He opened the back door and unloaded her stuff. Without so much as a word, he picked her things up and jogged towards the dock.

"Wait. You can't take those," she yelled at his back. He kept going. She got out of the car, hurrying after him, "Stop."

Without a word, he deposited her things into a speedboat, and jumped inside. Sierra teetered on the edge of the water. She wasn't going to allow him to take off with her stuff, but she couldn't force herself to jump. The river was dark, and murky—and she couldn't swim.

He looked up at her, "You coming?"

She extended one foot, pulling it right back. She couldn't make it into the boat.

"Oh, for crying out loud." The man extended his hands. "Grab on, I won't let you fall. Don't take all day," he jerked his head towards the shore. "We have company."

Sierra didn't have to turn around. She heard tires screeching behind them. Reaching for his hands, she let him help her into the boat. Before she settled into a seat, he was speeding away. Her head flew backwards, she screamed and grabbed onto the sides of the boat for support. Waves crashed around them, water slapped her in the face, blinding her. She grit her teeth as the nose of the boat flew upwards, skimming the river. They were going so fast, the wind tore the breath out of her lungs, making conversation impossible.

He raced forward, cutting through the darkness. Her hands tightened on the guardrail, terrified they would tip over at any second. Without warning, he made a sharp turn. She fell sideways, mumbling an incoherent prayer.

The boat stopped. Sierra sat back up, brushing the hair off her face; the baseball cap had flown away the minute he took off. She felt the touch of his hand against her shoulder, and glanced up. He pointed towards the shore, an intent look on his face.

The gunmen ran towards the edge of the river, firing off shots in their direction. Sierra cringed, ready to dodge for cover. *Why had he stopped the boat? They should be running* away *from the shooters.*

She watched as the gunmen reached the edge of the riverbank. They had to have seen the river; there was no way they could have missed it. They had to *know* all that was ahead of them was water, but when they reached the drop-off where the land ended and the water began, they kept on running towards the boat, continuing to shoot. From her vantage point, it looked like they couldn't stop themselves. One by one, their legs carried them over the river's edge, plunging them into the murky waters.

They didn't surface. Her companion clapped his hands together once, threw back his head and yelled, "Ha!"

Sierra shivered, watching him out the corner of her eye. This was no accident. He knew this was going to happen. It was why he stopped the boat, and why he pointed the gunmen out to her.

"Do you know what they call the Yazoo River in Choctaw? River of Death."

His words didn't register, she didn't care what the river was called in Choctaw.

She was in a boat with a killer.

A killer who saved her life.

There was no doubt in her mind that he was responsible for the gunmen's death, though she couldn't figure out how he had done it. She felt lightheaded, her breath was coming in short little gasps. Her bottom lip trembled, but she fought for control. There was no way in hell she was going to give into her fear.

She couldn't imagine what was coming next.

The air went still around them; the only sound came from waves licking the side of the boat. She scanned the area. They were alone on the water. She couldn't swim, she couldn't escape. The gentle sway of the boat was deceptive. Her life was anything but calm.

"Who are you?" she asked again, determined to learn more about her companion, "What the hell happened to those men?"

He squeezed her shoulder and winked. "We'll talk later. Follow my lead."

The boat started up again. He removed something from the glove compartment. Music blared, startling her. Another Broadway soundtrack. *Zorba the Greek*. He waved his arm, humming along, motioning for her to do the same. The man was crazy. Pure and simple.

Sierra inched back in her seat, teeth chattering. *Could she trust him?* Wild theories tormented her. What if Neil's killer knew where she was all along? What if the gunmen were from the FBI or the police, and her savior was actually her captor? *But then why not let her die?*

It was too much of a coincidence for her to write off the shooting as random. Sierra slumped down in the seat, too raw to think. She rubbed her arms to keep them from trembling. If only she'd called the police after she'd run from Neil's house. All she wanted to do was stay alive, and not be falsely accused. In retrospect, jail would have been a hell of a lot safer.

The boat sped out into the night. She had the oddest sensation of being swallowed by darkness. Her life was swirling into an abyss of terror and death. And a crazy man humming *Zorba the Greek* was at the helm.

Chapter Eight

Sierra saw lights in the distance and perked up. If he wanted her dead, he would have already killed her, he'd certainly had enough opportunity. She felt the first glimmer of safety since she'd boarded the boat. They were heading towards shore.

"Where are we?" she yelled over the music.

His head snapped towards her. He looked surprised, like he'd forgotten she was there. Instead of answering, he held up two fingers. He pressed them to his mouth, and pointed towards civilization, signaling they would talk there.

She nodded. Good enough. All she wanted was answers, and then she'd be on her way. She'd lost a few hours, but had enough time to carry on with her original plan.

He slowed the boat to a glide. Sierra did a mental happy dance, breaking into a smile when she saw solid ground. Her eyes drifted towards her companion, emboldened at the prospect of a sidewalk under her feet. He had a quiet strength and charisma she hadn't noticed before. She studied his face, trying to figure him out. His looks were deceiving: half-hippie, with his long hair and jewelry, and half warrior, with a penchant for show tunes. Together, they made an odd-looking pair. For some reason the image made her burst into hysterical laughter.

They were docking. He swung a rope towards a poll, and shot her a look. "Are you all right?"

His question triggered another laughing fit. "No."

He secured the boat and wrapped an arm around her. "It's okay, you're in shock. I've seen this kind of reaction before. Let it out, you'll feel better for it."

The comforting gesture did her in. She stiffened at first; uncomfortable at his touch until she reminded herself that he'd saved her life twice that evening. He couldn't be all bad. Life and death situations made strange bedfellows. She leaned against his shoulder, her laughter turning to sobs.

He patted her back. "Shhh, everything's gonna be all right. You've held up remarkably well under the circumstances. I'm sure you're not shot at every day."

If he only knew. Sierra pulled away, wiping her face with the bottom of her shirt, answering with a watery chuckle. "It was a first."

"You have chops, I'll give you that. You're a brave little thing."

"Do you know what happened back there?"

He stood up. The boat rocked from the abrupt movement. This time she wasn't afraid of falling overboard. His head tilted, like he was listening for something. From what she could see, there wasn't much around them.

"We may not be safe to talk here. Let's get to somewhere where there's a lot of white noise."

"White noise?"

He held up a hand. "You'll see."

***

They ended up at the train station in Memphis. For once, fate had worked in her favor. She'd left the Honda parked in the lot right outside. She was right back where she'd started hours ago. By the time they got there, questions were burning a hole in her head. She collapsed on the first available bench, shrugging off her purse and backpack. He set the suitcase beside her and looked around.

"I'm going to see if I can find us some coffee."

"Sounds good." Sierra waited until he walked away and unzipped the backpack. The netbook was there, safe and sound. She had to know if it still worked. The first file she'd clicked on may have been work related, but there had to be a reason Neil had hidden the computer. If she could unravel whatever secrets he was hiding, she might be able to solve the mystery of his death. She might also find out whether or not he and Grace had been having an affair.

Her finger hesitated over the power button. Maybe it would be better to wait until she had a clearer head to investigate, without the threat of her companion looking on.

She didn't hear him come up behind her. "Don't touch that."

His voice boomed in her ear, loud enough to make her jump. The computer bounced in the air; she lurched forward to grab it before it crashed to the floor.

Her heart pounded. "Why did you do that? You scared me half to death."

He walked around the bench holding two cups. He offered one to her. "Here. Put down the computer and take this. It's scalding my hands."

Sierra was too tired to argue. She set the computer down between them and reached for the cup.

"Thanks." The aroma hit her immediately. Lifting it to her nose, she inhaled. The cup of coffee was the best thing she'd ever smelled, good enough for her to close her eyes and smile.

"It's only coffee, you know, not even a shot of whiskey in there, though we could sure use it."

She sniffed again, sighing with pleasure, "You have no idea how much I love coffee."

"Apparently not."

They sat in silence, sipping their coffees. She felt odd, sitting in the train station with him, drinking coffee like they were old friends. A few people milled about, minding their own business. Sierra drained half the cup, and turned to look at him.

"Luke," he said.

"Excuse me?"

"You're wondering who I am. I'm Luke."

"I'm wondering a lot more than that. What happened back there on the train?"

"Aren't you going to tell me who you are?"

"Sierra."

"Interesting name."

She shrugged. "Are you stalling? I'm grateful to you for saving my life, thank you for that. But I'd like to know what almost got us killed."

He turned, looking her in the eye, "I don't know."

Not the answer she was hoping for. The blood rushed from her face. If the men hadn't been shooting at Luke, then… "I don't believe you," she challenged. "You reacted too quickly, knew exactly what to do. You had a boat waiting, for Christ's Sake. You *knew* you were in danger; otherwise, you wouldn't have had an escape route mapped out. " She folded her arms, meeting his gaze head on. " I have a right to know."

He tilted his head; the gold earring he wore caught the light. "I'm not entirely certain the shots were meant for me."

"Oh for…" She crushed the empty coffee cup in her hands, losing her patience. "What do you mean?"

"You're running from something, Miss Sierra. The outfit, the bruises on your face, they way you clutch your bags like your life depended on them. You're in trouble." He held up a hand to stop her cry of protest. "Now, I do have enemies, yes, I'll grant you that, and I'm trained to outwit them; I'll give you that too. I'll even admit, at first, I did think they were gunning for me. But they shouldn't have been able to find me. I wasn't trackable."

"Not *trackable*?" She brushed a strand of hair behind her ear, and tapped her foot in irritation. "Please, if you're aren't going to tell me the truth, say so. I'm truly grateful you saved me. I'm even more grateful you didn't kill me. But as you so succinctly stated, I have my own problems. And in case you've forgotten, I was on my way to New Orleans before all this happened.

I need to know if I'm in danger."

"Wait. Hear me out." Despite the lines of fatigue that showed on his face, he maintained an air of authority. "No, I didn't forget you were on your way somewhere. In fact, in case I'm the reason we got shot at, I plan on buying you a new ticket for your trouble. But you need to be straight with me too, because if you are in danger, I can't help you if you're keeping secrets from me."

"Go on."

"First off what's on this computer of yours?"

She drew back, suspicious. His piercing blue eyes rocked her to her core. "Nothing important. Work stuff. Why?"

He laid his hand on the computer resting between them. "This isn't yours, is it?"

Her body tensed. *What if the gunmen had been a ruse? A way to make her trust Luke so he could get his hands on Neil's computer?*

"Technically, it was my boyfriends. I bought it for him as a gift. Things ended when I found out he was cheating on me with my best friend. It got ugly, I grabbed what I could from the house, and I was on my way out of town until things cooled down. You happy now?"

"Happy, no. Satisfied, yes." He patted her hand, his bracelets brushed against her skin. "I'm sorry about what you've gone through. I'll tell you why I saved your life. You saved mine, I was returning the favor."

"I don't understand?" He'd piqued her interest.

"Before you told me your story, I was thinking it was an awful coincidence we got shot at minutes after you turned on the computer. I know how crazy that sounds, but in my line of work, you never know who you can trust. It was clear to me you were in trouble. I thought the men might have been after you."

His words petrified her. The scenario he described fit. *Dear Lord, maybe she wasn't paranoid after all. They could have been shooting at her. Luke's quick thinking might be the only reason she survived.* It was dumb luck she'd sat next to someone skilled enough to have gotten off the train alive.

"Sierra? Are you okay?"

"Sorry. Guess I'm a still a bit shaken up. Please, go on with what you were saying." She noticed a young family walking past them. A little boy, not more than five, or six turned around to stare at them.

Luke noticed too. The station was filling up. He lowered his voice, "Where was I? Oh yes, I had my eyes closed, tuning everything out but my music. When you turned on the computer, and kept bungling the password, the light from the screen annoyed me. I opened my eyes to glare at it. The way you had it angled on your lap, the screen worked like a review mirror. I saw the men running towards the train, saw them aim their weapons."

"Which is why you shoved me down."

"Yes. They were aiming at us and I didn't want your blood on my hands."

Neil's computer had saved their lives. It was a sobering thought, how one random act was the difference between life and death. If she hadn't taken the netbook out of her backpack right when she had…she couldn't bear to think about it.

"Thank you for keeping me safe." A million questions buzzed in her mind, but she settled on the important ones. "You don't seem all that shaken up. Do you know why those men were shooting at you? Are you in some kind of trouble?" Sierra thought of how the shooters plunged into the river and how Luke had stopped the boat, instructing her to watch as if he had known what was going to happen. She remembered how the doors of the train had opened, allowing them to escape even though they'd been locked when she'd them. "*Who* are you?"

"That, my friend, is something you are better off not knowing. It's nothing you want to get any more tangled up in than you already have."

"I'm already tangled up in this. You did something, didn't you? To make those men drown? I need to know what I'm involved in."

Luke stared straight ahead, rubbing his palm over his chin. He turned to her with a smile, but his eyes were somber. "You're safe now, that's all that matters. We were running for our lives, it's reasonable to assume you were in a heightened state of anxiety, you may not be remembering things quite the way they occurred."

She opened her mouth to protest. He shook his head, changing the subject.

"I will say this, it was extremely fortuitous you sat next to me on the train. Otherwise, I might be a dead man. I never would have seen them coming. Thank you."

His words struck a nerve. Her throat went dry. "What did you just say?"

"I said it was extremely fortuitous you sat next to me on the train. Otherwise, I might be a dead man."

She didn't hear anything after fortuitous. The word chilled her. She knew she was over reacting, but Skinbone Harris had also called their meeting fortuitous. Both men were intense and compelling, unique and mysterious, each in their own way. She narrowed her eyes. What were the odds two men would chose the same words to describe their meeting on such an extraordinary night?

It felt like an omen, and not a good one.

"You look beat," Luke said. "Why don't we go get those train tickets? We should have gotten them first thing when we arrived. Now there's a line."

Sierra had no intention of getting on another train. The ill-fated trip to New Orleans was a smoke screen, the final step in the false trail she created. She'd planned on getting off when they stopped at Greenwood, double backing to her car in Memphis.

She glanced at the line. "Why don't you go ahead? I need to use the bathroom. I'll meet you in line."

"Do you want me to watch your things?"

"No, thank you. Considering all that's happened tonight, I feel better keeping them with me. No offense, it's not that I don't trust you, I just…"

"I understand. In case bullets start flying, you want to make a quick getaway."

She blanched at the imagery. "I'm joking," he laughed. "Go. I'll see you in a bit."

"Okay." She smiled, hoping she'd kept the regret out of her voice. Sierra watched him walk away, and gathered up her things. Anxious to slip away, she forgot about the netbook left lying on the vacated bench.

The bathrooms were near the exit. Luke wasn't paying attention to her; a blue haired woman decked out in gold jewelry was making a move on him. Sierra smiled. That should keep him busy for a while.

She ducked out the back door, and tossed her things in the car. She'd had enough fortuitous encounters with ponytailed men for one night. The mystery of Luke played on her mind, but she had her own problems to solve. If anything, coming close to death tonight strengthened her resolve. She was going to get her life back. No matter what the cost.

Chapter Nine

Sierra made it back to Chicago before daybreak. She picked up a McDonalds Big Breakfast and a Tribune, pouring through the news while she ate. No word about Neil, although the shooting on the train to New Orleans warranted a blurb.

She crumpled the paper in her hands, saddened that someone could lie dead for days with no one the wiser. No one deserved to be forgotten in death.

Still, the fact his body remained undiscovered worked to her advantage. Sierra needed to learn the meaning behind Foxtrot and The First Wave. Odds were the shooters had been after Luke, but the experience left her hesitant to turn on the laptop she'd taken from Neil's house until she knew it was safe. Besides, there was an easier way to find out the meaning behind the pictures.

The two people she loved most in the world had kept secrets from her. Now one of them was dead.

She needed to talk to Grace.

Popping the last forkful of pancakes and sausage in her mouth, she hit the road. Grace McGinley owned a modest brownstone in Old Town. Sierra wasn't worried about anyone noticing her here; people came and went at all hours and the neighborhood had a lot of foot traffic. No one would give her a second glance.

The moment she pulled into the small parking spot behind Grace's yard, the acrid smell hit her. Smoke and fire. *Oh, God. Please no.* She flung open the car door, panic thumping in her chest. She fumbled with the seatbelt, tearing at in frustration.

Grace always answered her phone and she hadn't answered.

Please God, let her be okay.

The seatbelt gave way. Sierra raced through the back yard, not even noticing when the neighbor's door opened. Corrine Lawson stood there, poised to take her shitzu, Tara, for a walk. Sierra froze in place when the dog yelped, certain Grace's neighbor would see through her through the flimsy disguise. The two women stared at each other. Corrine broke the silence.

"Are you the insurance adjuster? What a shame about poor Grace. God bless her soul. Such a good neighbor. And so young."

The implication ripped through her. Grace was dead. *Dead.* She shook her head in denial. *No, this couldn't be happening. There had to be a mistake.*

Reeling with shock, Sierra dug her fingernails into the palms of her hands. It took every ounce of strength to keep it together. Corrine was staring at her, anxious to gossip. It sickened her how the neighbor could be so blasé. She felt like grabbing her and shaking her. Instead, Sierra nodded, struggling to find her voice. "Yes, ma'am. Sorry for your loss."

"The flames were terrifying. I was up all Thursday night, afraid the fire would start up again. My poor baby here was shaking from all the commotion. I didn't even go to work on Friday."

"Did you say Thursday night?" The hairs on the back of her arms stood up on end. *Grace had died before Neil.*

"Oh, yes. I'll never forget it. Don't you know the date of the accident?" Corrine shot her a suspicious glance.

Sierra tipped the brim of her cap lower to evade Corrine's scrutiny. "My paperwork says Saturday. It must be a clerical error."

"Oh my," the woman's hand fluttered to her chest. "I hope there weren't any other mistakes. The way the house exploded, I thought a bomb had been dropped on us. The nice, young fire chief said the fire was so hot, there was only a little bit of bone fragments left. Can you imagine?"

Imagines of Neil's death sprang to mind. Yes, she could imagine.

"You'll make sure that house is safe now, won't you?"

Sierra didn't trust herself to speak. She nodded and took a step towards the back door.

Corrine smiled absently and went on her way. *Cold -hearted witch.* Sierra waited until she was out of sight. A gut wrenching sob erupted from her. For Grace. For Neil. For herself.

Unless she found a way to disappear, she'd be next. She should have gone to the cops when she had a chance. They might have been able to protect her. She was on her own, and needed to stay underground for a good long time. *How was she going to pull it off?* Her mind spun into overdrive. Corrine hadn't bothered to lock her door when she took the dog for a walk. They were similar in height and weight, though the neighbor had a few years on her.

She needed a new identity. This might be her only chance at getting one.

There was no time to think it through. She had fifteen minutes tops. Sierra ran back through the gate and hurried through Corrine's yard. She yanked open the back door. The woman's purse was on the kitchen counter, in clear view. *How careless could she be?*

Up until now, Sierra hadn't done anything illegal. Her Social Security card was tucked into the side pocket of her wallet. Sierra lifted the card with shaking fingers. Corrine's driver's license was prominently displayed in a plastic window. It was at least six years old. Sierra studied the photo carefully. It was unflattering, but it would work. She replaced the wallet exactly how she'd found it.

Taking a deep breath, Sierra went in search of a desk, and found one in the dining room. A stack of bills lay in a haphazard pile. She grabbed the electric bill. *Was that enough? No, she would have to forge Corrine's signature.* She found a stack of canceled checks in the top drawer. *Perfect.*

By Sierra's calculations, she had a couple of minutes to spare. She found a small office at the back of the house. A Bible rested on the top shelf of a bookcase. She grabbed it and rifled through the pages. A birth certificate fell out. There was an all in one copier next to the bookcase. She kept the original, pressing the copy between the pages.

Sierra exited the house, and headed back to Grace's yard, adrenalin pumping through her. The entire front of Grace's house was gone. The back was partially intact. The police and fire department had probably gone through the house to determine if it was arson, Sierra wished she could get her hands on the report.

No matter how thorough their investigation, they didn't know what they were looking for. Murder by explosion had to be pretty rare. Covering her mouth and nose with her hand, Sierra jerked the door open and steeled herself to enter.

The smell of burnt flesh assaulted her. She retched in the kitchen sink and splashed cold water on her face. When she'd run from Neil's house, she'd been fleeing a killer; there wasn't a lot of time to dwell on his death. She had to focus all her energy on putting as much distance between her and the monster who'd taken his life as possible.

This was different. She grabbed a kitchen towel to hold over her face, and made her way to Grace's bedroom in the back of the house, overlooking the garden.

"Ah, shit." Sierra sank down on the bed, thinking of how much Grace had loved her garden. Would Grace and Neil even get a proper burial?

Skinbone Harris's words sprang to mind. *"Just when you need me most, when you feel like your world is falling apart, I'll call you. Mark my words."*

Another empty promise. Good old Skinbone was full of shit; she kicked herself for almost buying into it. It bothered her she cared enough to be pissed off. She wasn't even certain if she could trust the man.

She stood, brushing soot from her pants. She didn't know where to begin. It was almost impossible to comprehend how much had happened in little more than forty-eight hours. Of all the scenario's she'd imagined, the one thing she hadn't considered was that Grace's life was in danger. She rubbed her arms against a sudden chill, reminding herself Grace was killed first, before Neil.

Sierra went back into the kitchen, crouched down and peered under the sink. Grace hated gardening gloves. She used latex hospital gloves because they were more pliable.

Sierra found the box of gloves behind the bleach, and slipped a pair on. Before the fire, her fingerprints would have been all over the house. She had no idea if the hoses would have washed them away and decided it was best not to take any chances.

She returned to Grace's bedroom and went to work. If she were going to find any answers, they would be among Grace's personal belongings. Opening a closet, she dumped old clothes out of banker's boxes, and began throwing in all of Grace's mementos.

When she got to Grace's desk, she hesitated. Her friend's laptop sat in plain view. If Grace was hiding something, there was a good chance it would be on her computer. Sierra added it to the pile. A glossy brochure had been neatly tucked underneath the laptop. She frowned, stashing it in her pocket to look through later, wondering why it had been hidden.

What next? Her fingers tapped on Grace's jewelry box. She lifted the lid, hesitating for a second, remembering that the box had a false bottom. Grace had been enchanted with it and had shown it to Sierra on several occasions. Sierra slid it open and stared down at the wad of cash concealed inside. Her hand hovered over the money. Grace had no family; there was no one else to claim her things. She put aside her misgivings and stuffed the money in her pocket.

Standing in the center of the room, childhood memories came flooding back. She thought of how they'd giggled over boys, how their diaries were their most treasured possessions. They hid the keys to their journals in bottles of vitamins, thinking they'd come up with the perfect hiding place. Spotting a cluster of pill bottles on the nightstand, Sierra emptied them. Sure enough, a key spilled out. She grasped it in the palm of her hand, knowing Grace left it there for her to find in case anything happened.

Oh Grace, she thought, *what are you hiding?*

Tucking the key in her pocket, she kept searching. Dresser drawers held the usual. There weren't many other hiding places she could think of. The fact that she had no idea what she was looking for made the job even harder. Piles of old record albums stacked on the bottom shelf of a bookcase caught her eye. Unless Grace had saved warped LP's, the jackets appeared thick and lumpy. Sierra kneeled down and pulled one from the stack. Inside the sleeve were several sheets of paper.

Curious, she sat back on her haunches, and examined the papers, frowning when she realized the contents contained a computer-generated code. She'd have to figure out a way to decipher them. She shoved her hand inside to make sure she had all the sheets and came out with a bundle of hundred dollar bills. Flipping through the stack, she counted five thousand dollars. She stared at it a good long while, mouth dropping open in shock.

Coded files, stacks of money, not a good sign.

Sierra tore through the rest of the albums, dumping the contents on the floor. There were at least a hundred documents and two hundred thousand dollars. She jammed the money and the papers inside a box and slammed the lid over it. *Whatever Grace was involved in, she'd gotten in over her head, and she'd somehow managed to pull Neil down along with her.*

She searched the rest of the room with increasing urgency. It was looking less and less likely that Grace and Neil had been having an affair, and more like they were mixed up in something dangerous and illegal.

Grace was savvy enough to hide the money and the key. Neil had hidden his netbook for a reason. It made sense Grace would have one too. It would be somewhere no one would think to look, somewhere safe. *Where else had they hidden things as kids?*

Pillow cases. Grace had three pillows stacked up on each side of the bed. Sierra threw the top two off and checked the bottom ones. Sure enough, zipped into a pillow sham was a netbook. She'd bet anything they used it to correspond instead of their regular computers.

Sierra saved the desk for last, rifling through the drawers. Mostly office supplies and a handful of stuffed envelopes. As there wasn't time to look through them all, she tossed them into a box and pulled on the last drawer. It was locked. Whatever was in the drawer was important. Sierra jimmied it open with a bobby pin. A stack of unmarked file folders lay at the bottom. Her hands trembled when she lifted them out. The evidence was mounting.

Taking a final look around the room, Sierra noticed the giant old sea shell she had given Grace years ago resting on a shelf above the bed. Grace always swore she hated it, yet she'd kept it out, displayed with her other treasures. Biting back a twinge of nostalgia, Sierra carefully tucked it in a box. She needed at least one untarnished memory to remember her old friend by.

Chapter Ten

He stared out the window, tucking a strand of black hair back behind his ear. Not a single cloud marred the sky. A good omen. He could use one of those. He hated second-guessing himself. The jobs had been clean and he shouldn't have this residual worry. Everything would have gone off without a hitch, except for the damn woman.

She was trouble. Once the shit hit the fan, it was going to be bloody complicated to spend time and resources tracking her down. His lips curled in disgust. He hadn't expected Neil Thornton to have company. He'd watched the man for weeks. Like Grace McGinley, he was a creature of habit. He spent Friday nights alone in front of the TV with a drink in hand. It should have been the prefect night for him to die.

The entire plan had been perfect, meticulously thought out and executed.

The explosion had been brilliant. The house imploded in a spectacular blaze of fire shooting sparks high into the sky. He would have liked to have stayed and watched, but the neighbor came running outside and began searching the street for anyone who didn't belong. Patrol cars must have been in the area when the neighbor called nine one one. Moments after the blaze began, a squad car came tearing down street, followed by a second unit, robbing him of the opportunity to enjoy his handiwork

With Thornton, he needed a different M.O. Two explosions within a mile of each other would have resulted in the Chicago PD sniffing around. He killed the man on the spot, intending to take his time searching the house, when he realized the Thornton hadn't been alone—he wasted precious time by going after her.

He flicked a fuzz off his shirt in annoyance. He was stuck on a plane to establish an alibi. Not that he expected to need one, but he couldn't risk blowing his cover. Killing McGinley and Thornton had been a personal mission. Their deaths were not part of the assignment.

He expected to be jubilant on the flight, planning a night of celebration. Instead, the kill left a bad taste in his mouth making him wonder if he had more to worry about. All because of the damn woman.

What if she was in on it? Could Thornton and McGinley have brought her into the fold? Shared their secrets? It didn't matter if she wasn't working with them. What mattered was how much she *knew,* and what she might do about it.

He couldn't take chances. He'd waited a lifetime for retribution. The woman had to be dealt with. Eventually, she'd get tired of hiding. If she'd seen him, she was keeping it to herself. The twit was probably scared out of her mind. She should be. He didn't plan to leave any loose ends.

Sierra Montgomery had to die. It was just a matter of when and where. She couldn't have gotten far, considering she'd left her clothes strewn all over Thornton's bedroom.

A rustle beside him disturbed his train of thought. His seatmate fussed with her things, anxious for the plane to land. She'd made the mistake of trying to converse with him early on. She dug under her seat, banging his shin with her laptop. Her high-pitched laughter threatened to shatter his eardrums.

The stupid cow. Did she think a giggle and fluttering her eyelashes at him would make up for her clumsiness? He began his ritual of clenching and unclenching his fists while he counted to five.

The wheels bumped the ground. The woman crossed her legs, knowing full well her skirt would hike up. She looked at him, tilted her head, and gave him an appraising look. Two little dimples popped in her cheeks as she smiled at him. "Would you like to grab a drink?" she purred.

Women these days had no subtlety. Her meaning was crystal clear. *Stupid girl,* he thought, *didn't your mamma ever warn you about talking to strangers?* The little tramp had no idea who she was messing with.

Chapter Eleven

Sierra carried out the bankers boxes and stashed them in the trunk. Back inside the car, she examined the brochure. It was for an old Victorian house in Shadow Lake, Michigan, a realtor's card neatly stapled to it. Grace never mentioned looking at real estate, let alone a lake house.

She frowned. The property was out of character for Grace. Sierra loved the water. Grace abhorred it. When they were in college, it became a bone of contention between them when deciding on vacations. Grace would never stay on a lake. Not voluntarily.

Unless...the possibility still existed that Grace and Neil were having an affair. Was it possible Grace was thinking of buying the property as a love nest? Doubtful. It would have been too obvious if they kept leaving town at the same time. The charade wouldn't have worked long enough for the investment to pay off.

Tired and frustrated she rubbed her forehead, wondering if the property could be a clue. Maybe Shadow Lake was a rendezvous point, having to do with Foxtrot.

Sierra shoved the brochure in her purse and started the car. Her mind and body ached. She pulled into a Seven-Eleven and attempted to tidy up in the bathroom. Leaning against the sink, she studied her reflection and groaned. A zombie stared back at her. Grabbing a paper towel, she let cold water run over it, and pressed it against her face. It did nothing to relieve the bags under her eyes. She grubbed in her purse for her make-up bag and fished it out, and attempted to make herself presentable. She examined herself in the mirror. *Too much Sierra, not enough Corinne.*

Closing the lid on the toilet, she sat down, shaking with anger. She didn't want to be a fugitive, or be on the run from a killer. She'd done nothing to deserve any of this, except love the wrong people. Her hands fisted in her hair. *Damn them. How could they have put her in this position?*

She couldn't even mourn them properly; she was too pissed off at the both of them.

Someone tried the doorknob. *Time to get a grip.* She needed more make-up. There was an old compact wedged in a zipper compartment. Powder caked up in lines, it would make her look older. She piled it on. She and Neil had attended a work banquet in his honor a few weeks ago; she'd bought a red lipstick and new eyeliner. Lining her eyes heavily, she slashed on the lipstick. Much better. She twisted her dark blonde hair into a bun and pinned up her bangs. Another smudge of blush to finish things off. Not great, but not half bad either.

She opened the restroom door. A woman with three little boys glared at her. *Sorry, lady,* she thought, *I've got bigger problems than cranky kids.* On the way out, she ordered two large coffee's to help keep her awake, and headed to the DMV.

***

Nailing Corrine's signature was a snap. The woman never outgrew the rounded letters they taught in second grade. Marching up to the desk at the DMV was a hell of a lot harder. She wiped her sweaty palms on her jeans and mimicked the clerk's disinterest.

"I lost my license and I need to get a replacement."

The woman looked up long enough to frown. Perspiration dribbled down her chest, despite the large fan pointing in her direction. The woman's scrutiny was unnerving. Sierra reminded herself that so far, she'd done nothing wrong. She had no reason to sweat under the woman's scrutiny.

The woman's hand shot out. "ID."

Sierra passed the stolen documents over, cringing when she noticed they were damp where she'd clutched them. The woman plopped them down in front of her, still frowning. She slapped her hand on the ID's and scanned the room.

Sierra tapped her foot in an attempt to calm her nerves. This was taking too long. The woman had passed the people ahead in line ahead of her right through. *What was the problem?*

The clerks gaze settled on someone. "Leroy," she called out, gesturing across the room. A large black man dressed in a security guard uniform finished off a conversation and headed towards the desk.

Sierra's line of vision narrowed to a tiny pinpoint. She watched the guard lumber towards her, thinking, *Oh God, why had she stolen the stupid ID's?* Her stomach churned; she swallowed hard. Leroy stared at her, picking up his pace.

It was over. She hadn't done anything wrong, not yet anyway, and he was going to cart her off to jail.

Leroy hurried towards her. Sierra gripped the counter, her bones turned to jelly; the room started to swim. Ice cold fear shot through her veins.

"Leroy," the clerk banged her hand on the counter. "Can you move the fan closer in this direction? It's hot enough to melt glue in here. I can't work like this no more."

Leroy held up a hand. "One minute Shawana. This lady here looks like she's about to pass out. You okay, miss?"

Sierra blinked at the fog covering her eyes, dizzy with relief. She touched her chin to her chest, holding onto the counter. When the worst of it passed, she wiped the cold sweat from her forehead and met Leroy's eyes, giving him weak smile. "I'm okay. The heat's getting to me. The air conditioner in my car gave out, and it's not much better in here."

"Ain't that the truth? You know on my break, I saw the temperature on the bank across the ways was one hundred and six. Can you imagine? You need to get yourself something salty and stay hydrated, young lady. This heat wave is dangerous," the security guard said

"*I'm* going to get dangerous in a few minutes if you don't move that fan," the clerk retorted.

Leroy winked at Sierra. "These ladies love to boss me around. Like I don't get enough of that at home."

"You men wouldn't know what to do if your women didn't give you the what for."

Sierra forced a smile. "I think you'd better listen to her."

"Pay attention to the young lady, she knows what she's taking about." The clerk flashed her grin, and passed back the ID's. "Take a seat, and watch for your number. Try and stay cool."

Sierra thanked the DMV worker and took the papers in a daze. She collapsed into a chair. She'd been inches from passing out from pure fear. If she survived getting a fake license, the first thing she was going to do was check into a hotel and sleep for a week. She longed for her own bed. *Would she ever get to sleep in it again?*

Her number flashed overhead. Whether or not she'd have chance at a new life boiled down to this moment. She swung her purse over her shoulder and approached the counter, forcing one foot in front of the other. The tiled floor stretched out before her. She might as well have been walking towards a firing squad.

An older gentleman peered at her over his glasses. She handed him her papers and offered up a silent prayer. The list of crimes she'd been racking up since Neil's death flashed through her mind. She counted them off in order: driving an unregistered vehicle without insurance, stealing Corrine's ID's, lifting money and documents from Grace's house. What she was about to do next was full-blown identity theft. She could go to jail. Or, she could do nothing and wind up a sitting duck for a killer.

She straightened her shoulders and looked the clerk straight in the eye while he asked a laundry list of questions. Luckily, Corrine had no blemishes on her record and she answered each of them correctly.

"You're all set. Pay at the next window and follow the yellow line."

Courage bolstered, she started to walk away. She stopped and turned back, giving him what she hoped was an appealing smile. "You know, the picture on my license is at least six years old. Can I get a new one?"

He waved her back to the counter. She paid the additional fee and followed the yellow line blurring in front of her. Sierra couldn't shake the feeling she was following the yellow brick road.

It took less than five minutes to get her picture snapped and a brand new driver's license handed to her. She clutched it like a lifeline. The last traceable evidence of Sierra Montgomery would officially die in New Orleans. She managed to buy herself time to sort things out.

Sierra felt inside her pocket for the key she'd found hidden in the bottle of vitamins. Her fingers curled around it. The key would unlock the answers Sierra needed to stay alive. In a city this big, trying to figure out where the key fit would be like looking for a needle in a monster size haystack.

She didn't have a hell of a lot to go on.

Chapter Twelve

Luke dropped his bag on the floor and flipped on the lights, whistling the theme song from *Brigadoon*, one of his favorite Broadway classics. He needed a drink since sleep wasn't an option. His batteries needed recharging, but he knew himself well. Rest would elude him until he set his mind at ease.

He poured himself a vodka rocks and opened the terrace doors. The Sedona, Arizona night should have brought him comfort; he couldn't remember a time when it didn't. Until tonight. The incident on the train worried him. It could have been Karma biting him back for taking a holiday in the middle of a sensitive project. *Wishful thinking*. He could try to whitewash it any way he liked; the truth was something more sinister was at work.

The assault had come out of nowhere. No one should have been able to track him and there was no way in hell gunmen should have been lying in wait in Greenwood. He rolled his neck, trying to ease the tension. *Call it like it is, old man, no one should have* known *he was someone worth killing. Far as the world knew, he was retired, kicking up dust in this old Arizona town.*

Downing the vodka in a single swallow, he chuckled. He'd been a hell raiser back in the day, for sure. Never fit into any one damn mold. His colleagues may have laughed at him in private, but they sure as hell respected him on the job. He'd been damn good at it.

Luke hadn't been what the starched-shirt type higher-ups expected. Instead of playing by the rules, he shook things up. The problem with shaking things up was that sometimes bad things fell out. The way Luke saw it, two wrongs didn't make a right. So he bided his time until he could retire and work on his own dime.

So far, retirement had been good to him. Until the train, when bullets started flying. He looked up at the stars, feeling the crick in his neck. Damn thing traveled down his back. It was hell getting older, especially since his mind felt no different than when he was young. He was smarter, maybe, certainly wiser. But shit, when he looked in the mirror, he kept expecting to see a man in his prime.

He thought of the woman, Sierra. She was an impressive little thing, a real trooper. She reacted with lightning speed, and had known when to keep quiet in a crisis. She should have been firing off questions the moment he threw her to the floor. Shock didn't set in until after she knew she was safe.

He rolled that around in his mind, wanting to pinpoint what troubled him. Looking back, a few things didn't make sense. It was almost like she'd been waiting for trouble. When the gunmen opened fire, she accepted the danger. She might have been running from a boyfriend, but it was doubtful a cheating ex would hire four hit men to come after her.

Ah, who was he to judge. He'd seen worse. The heartbreak in her eyes was real, so was her determination to access her ex's files on the netbook she'd left behind.

The least he could do was return it to her. She'd almost gotten killed, for the simple mistake of sitting next to him. He might not know her last name, but the netbook was registered to her boyfriend. He didn't believe in coincidence or chance. There was no such thing as random encounters. Everything happened for a reason. It was up to him to figure it out.

If the bullets had been meant for Sierra, he'd know soon enough.

***

Skinbone Harris wanted to go to Mexico; he settled for Texas instead. These days, it didn't matter where he hung his hat. He was in constant contact with the team. Trouble was brewing and they were going to have to speed up their efforts.

They were a motley group. Probably went together as well as bees and gators, but hell, they got the job done. He tossed his keys in on the table and relieved himself of the semi-automatic tucked in the small of his back. After removing the clip, he poured himself a whiskey. Before he could raise the glass to his lips, Garber and Sadie galloped through the house, almost knocking him down. Garber, a three-year-old black lab, leapt at him, resting two paws on Skinbone's shoulders. Sadie, a six-year-old tortie cat, bucked against his ankles before settling back on her haunches and giving him a reproving glare. Sadie never forgave him easily when he was gone too long.

"Guys, I'm sorry. I have to work. Don't give me those faces. Maria's been feeding the two of you pretty well, based on your bellies."

A pair of tails thumped on the ground. They looked at him expectantly. "Oh, all right." He set down his glass and headed to the kitchen. He couldn't help himself; he had a habit of taking in strays, spoiling them rotten. They were beside themselves when he opened a cabinet door, gobbling up their treats before he could set them down on the floor.

A thick steak waited for him in the fridge. God bless, Maria. There was nothing like a thick steak, done just right on the grill, making him happy he had returned to Texas. He could have stayed at one his other homes. Lord knew he had enough of them. But a man could think in Texas and he had a lot of thinking to do.

Skinbone slapped the steak on a plate and headed out to the patio to fire up the grill. Garber and Sadie bounded outside, eager to play. The entire property was surrounded by a seven-foot brick wall. In his line of work, you couldn't be too careful.

While the steak grilled, he changed into a t-shirt and retrieved his drink. There wasn't anything on Earth like a Texas sunset and he was looking forward to watching it later tonight. He stretched out on a chaise lounge and crossed his long legs, willing himself to relax. The dog and cat dashed between the Black-Eyed Susans and Mexican Sage, enjoying their freedom. *Freedom, what a concept.*

Skinbone tossed back the whiskey and poured another, flipping the steak. He'd bought this place with the intention of enjoying his freedom. He'd had a good run, made a load of cash, and wanted to get out at the top of his game. He almost made it too. Until he got the call, sucking him back in. Once he heard the man out, he couldn't turn him down. Problem was the job wreaked hell on his social life. Not too many women were willing to cozy up with a cold-blooded killer.

He smiled, thinking of the woman he'd met in Memphis. Seri. She was a pretty little thing, and feisty enough when she let her guard down. She only laughed when she forgot herself, and that wasn't damn near often enough. A shame too, because her whole face lit up, turning her into a real beauty. There was trouble lurking behind her sweet blue eyes, bad trouble. He knew, because his gut told him he helped put it there.

It had been a crazy assed thing to tell her his line of work. The words just came tumbling out, like he was in a confessional. He'd felt a connection the moment he laid eyes on her. It came on unexpected, like a sucker punch to the gut. Proved what a dumb sonofabitch he was.

Aw, hell. What was done was done. He'd have to do a better job of sweet-talking her the next time—and they would meet again. Skinbone knew there was no such thing as chance encounters. Within seconds of meeting her, he knew she was going to play a role in his life. She would have known too, if she wasn't wrapped up in her troubles.

The steak sizzled on the grill, reminding him of the here and now. Skinbone picked up the tongs to flip the steak when he heard a sound behind him. He dropped the tongs and turned, a double-edged blade ready in his hand. Tawny, the three month old kitten he'd adopted, came out of hiding. She rubbed her small body against the patio door, eager for some attention. Skinbone sheathed his knife and chuckled. This job was making him too damn jumpy. Either that or he was getting too old.

He bent down and held his hand out for Tawny to sniff. She took a tiny step forward, and darted into the yard to play with her siblings. Damn, he had about as much luck with pets these days as he had with women.

He warmed tortillas, slathered them with mayonnaise, piled on strips of steak, and dug in. Nothin' could beat home cooking, that was a certainty. He took his meal with his small family. Garber gobbled up a couple slices of steak, while Sadie and Tawny nibbled the tiny pieces he'd cut up for them.

The phone rang while he was finishing off the last of his whiskey. He listened quietly, his face settling into a hard line. Their operation had been severely compromised. There was only one way that could have happened.

Bad news had no place on such a beautiful night.

In the morning, he would hop on a plane to Chicago.

Someone had to die.

Chapter Thirteen

The euphoria of snagging a new identity wore off in a hurry. Sierra's brain felt ragged by the time she got to the hotel. Realizing the world preferred plastic over cash, she stopped at a currency exchange and purchased a preloaded credit card.

She bypassed the cheap motels and checked into a decent hotel near O'Hare airport. Kicking off her Wal-Mart sandals, she stashed Grace's boxes in the closet and turned the AC to high.

The urge to fall on the bed and collapse was tempting, but her stomach growled in protest. Nothing was going to drag her out again. She picked up the room service menu, ready to order a club sandwich, when the steaks caught her eye. Deciding to splurge, she ordered filet mignon, fries, a dinner salad, and a bottle of wine.

With time to spare, she headed to the bathroom to take a shower. She stood under the pulsating shower head, letting the water beat down on her exhausted muscles. Halfway in between washing several days of grime from her body, and running out of hot water, the soap slipped through her fingertips. She'd been running on auto-pilot for almost seventy-two hours. She sank to the bottom of the tub, oblivious to the water raining down on her.

"Damn it," she beat the tub with her fists; anger churning inside her. *What right did the black-eyed bastard have to detonate her life?* Sierra rubbed her burning eyes, drawing strength from the hatred pumping inside her. The sonofabitch was going to pay. Once she put together the puzzle pieces of what her friend's involvement with Foxtrot and The First Wave was, she'd have a better idea of what she was actually dealing with.

Her cell phone rang for the third time while she was in the shower. She'd tucked it away in her purse. Since it was a disposal cell, she'd never bothered to set up voice mail. No one had her number, so what did it matter?

No one except for Skinbone Harris, and she wasn't expecting to hear from him.

Sierra toweled off in time to collect her dinner.

The bell boy wheeled the cart in and set her dinner on the table, "Would you like this billed to your room, Miss Lawson?"

Sierra opened her mouth to correct him and snapped it shut again. For a second, she'd forgotten she registered under Corrine's name. Her new identity was going to take some getting used to.

"Yes, that's fine, thank you." She tipped him hastily, double locking the door behind him. Her near slip-up left her shaken. After all she'd gone through to get a new identity, she'd come close to blowing it. There was no room for sloppy mistakes.

Pushing everything else from her mind, she sat down to her supper. She polished off the steak and sopped up the fries in the steak juice, enjoying every last bite. Stomach appeased, she turned down the blankets and slipped into bed. The cool sheets were heaven against her body. Even the hard pillows were a welcome relief from the car's headrest.

A crack of lightning flashed outside the hotel room window. She pulled the blankets up around her face, listening to the rain beat against the windows.

A summer storm suited her mood. Sierra welcomed the darkness, wishing she could lose herself in it. She closed her eyes and fell into a deep, dreamless sleep.

***

Skinbone Harris walked towards his small pond, sitting down alongside it. The sun hung low in the west, coloring the cloudless sky a magnificent golden pink. He stared down at its refection in the pond, concentrating on the orange center of the sun.

In the white man's rush to embrace technology, they ignored the powers the universe so freely offered. Skinbone never turned his back on a gift; he embraced what others rejected.

It was one of the reason's he was so good at his job.

He tuned out everything except for the sun's reflection. The night was still, there wasn't even a hint of a breeze. He opened his arms, drawing the energy of the sun towards him. He imagined a circle at center of the sun's image. Next, he drew a mental line around the circle, separating it. He could see the blue waters of the pond easing through the lines, like blood seeping through a clean cut. With his mind, he lifted the center of the sun from the pond. When it began to rise, he willed it to turn at a ninety degree angle. A ray of sunlight blazed towards him. The picture was so strong; he saw specs of dust flicker in the light. He pulled the energy into his body, feeling the power of the sun flow inside him. Golden light flowed through his veins; heat soared through him, giving him strength.

Skinbone closed his eyes, seeing the ray absorbed by his body. When it was over, the excursion of the mental exercise left him dripping with sweat. He wiped his brow with the back of his hand, needing to test himself.

He dampened his finger and held it up to the air. It dried without a breath of wind. Turning his attention back towards the pond, he focused on the quiet waters. He chose a spot towards the waters center. Using only his mind, a small ripple disrupted the center of the pond. He willed it to grow bigger. Soon the entire body of water was disrupted by a series of ripples.

A butterfly flew past him. His head turned towards it. He willed it to fly back to him. The butterfly hung in the air and changed direction. When it rested on his shoulder, he used his energy to direct it towards the tree across the pond.

Willing a living creature was harder than causing a pond to ripple. It entailed changing their will or going against instinct. The butterfly hovered next to him for at least a minute. He could feel its confusion. A flower bed lay to the right. He had disrupted its path. It wanted to fly towards the flowers. He used his mind to guide it to the tree instead.

Once he accomplished his goal, he released the butterfly; it immediately raced to the flower bed.

Skinbone smiled. Dusk was settling. He was ready.

The operation couldn't be compromised. It had to move forward.

The threat had to be eliminated.

He'd given his word.

***

A bolt of lightning startled her awake. For a split second, Sierra thought she was home until a clap of thunder rattled the thin walls of the hotel room. She sat up in bed, brushing the hair from her eyes. She glanced towards the windows. It was so dark, she couldn't tell if it was day or night. It didn't matter. She was still exhausted.

A dull headache throbbed behind her eyes. She missed her house, and her familiar belongings. Being isolated from the world was a strain; there was no one to talk to about all the crazy theories bouncing around in her head. No way to make sense of what was happening.

The resolve she felt after escaping with Luke had taken a severe hit. Grace's death changed everything. She was up against something far bigger than she'd imagined.

Pushing aside the covers, she padded towards the tiny coffee pot the hotel provided. She foraged around on the tray, frowning. *One stinking little package of coffee?* With the rates they charged, they could have at least provided two.

Sierra filled the small pot and opened the closet door while it brewed. She had to start somewhere. The items she'd taken from Grace's house were her only leads. If she could put enough pieces together, maybe she'd be able to go to the police. *And get my life back,* she thought.

She dumped the contents of one box on the bed, groaning at the pile.

There was so much to go through, it could take days. Did she have that kind of time?

Sierra shook her head, rubbing at a spot between her eyebrows. She poured herself a steaming cup of coffee, hoping it would help ease her headache. Lightening sliced through the sky. She jumped, sloshing hot coffee on her hand.

"Damn it." She wiped her hand on her t-shirt, casting a dark look at the window. The storm continued to rage. Rain was one thing. Thunder and lightning always got under her skin, making her skittish and jittery. She shuddered, feeling a renewed sense of urgency.

She took a sip of coffee before placing the mug on the nightstand. The brochure she'd placed there the night before beckoned to her. Sitting down on the bed, she examined it.

What did Grace see in the place? The exterior was foreboding at best, run down at worst. The inside was another story. It was fabulous; the type of place Sierra would imagine a celebrity or CEO living in. No surprise there, beachfront property didn't come cheap. The home boasted six bedrooms and baths, among other amenities.

Why would Grace need all that room? To say nothing of the fact while they'd all done okay for themselves, none of them had the kind of money to afford a place like that. There was a wide divide between well off and wealthy, and this place was way out of their league.

At least it should have been. She thought of all the cash she'd taken from Grace's house. There'd been the two hundred thousand hidden in the old record albums. Fifty grand in the jewelry box, another fifty thousand in Grace's emergency hiding place.

Where had the money come from?

Sierra spent the next hour and a half separating the contents of the first box into two piles: treasured but useless memorabilia and items that warranted further exploration. So far, her two best leads were the brochure and the netbooks. She was afraid to access Grace's computer from the hotel. She knew just enough to worry about the IP address being traced, thanks to an episode of *Law and Order*, but not enough to know how all the techie stuff worked. Besides, she couldn't chance a repeat of the train episode. Her cell phone, on the other hand, couldn't be tracked back to her.

If she'd gotten a warmer reception from Donavan St. James, she could have tossed this whole mess into his lap and let him sort out what had gotten Grace and Neil killed. His chilly response proved what her mother always told her: don't count on anyone but yourself.

Grace wouldn't be buying the beach house on Shadow Lake. With any luck, there weren't other potential buyers waiting in the wings. Sierra wanted to take a look at the property.

Skinbone Harris had been right about one thing. It was time to trust her instincts. Logic wasn't giving her a hell of a lot to go on.

Sierra dug her cell phone out of her purse, intending to call the realtor. The blood drained from her face. *Three missed calls*. They could only be from one person. Skinbone Harris. A wave of uneasiness crept over her, remembering his words. *"Just when you need me most, when you feel like your world is falling apart, I'll call you."*

That should have been reassuring. It meant there was at least one person out there who cared about her. It wasn't. She closed her eyes, picturing Skinbone's self-assured smile, and probing black eyes; eyes that looked through her carefully constructed façade and straight into her soul. Their meeting at the hole in the wall Memphis rib joint had been surreal. The last thing she wanted to deal with was his gibberish about fortuitous encounters. She had enough on her plate. And she sure as hell wasn't about to trust him, not with his crazy talk about assassins.

"How did my life get so complicated?"

Skinbone managed to intrude on her sanctuary, leaving her feeling edgy. The sun broke through the clouds, promising another steamy day on the horizon. She wasn't crazy about the idea of hitting the city streets, but she needed a decent cup of coffee and a place to access Grace's computer. If she stayed in this part of town, there was less chance of being recognized. Twisting her hair back into the dreaded ponytail, she slapped on the baseball cap and sunglasses.

No point in taking chances.

***

Skinbone arrived in Chicago ten minutes ahead of schedule, courtesy of the private jet that had been provided for him. It was a hell of a lot better than flying commercial. With all the traveling he'd been doing the last few days, he was starting to feel like a ping pong ball.

He slicked back his jet-black hair. There was a damn good reason for this trip. He had to cover his ass. When he got the call saying the project had been delayed, he had to show his outrage, demanding they stick to the original time-table.

He couldn't let on that he knew Neil Thornton and Grace McGinley were dead.

With the operation in jeopardy, they needed someone on the inside. An insurance policy to make sure they weren't being double-crossed.

Needing a distraction, Skinbone powered up his cell to check his messages. Seri hadn't returned his calls. He couldn't shake the feeling that she was in trouble. Resisting the urge to call her again, he shoved his phone in his pocket. Things would play out between them the way they were meant to. Life had a funny way of working things out on its own.

Besides, he had a job to do. This was no time to get tangled up with a woman, especially one with a shadow of trouble following her around like a dark cloud.

CHAPTER FOURTEEN

There were no internet café's in the immediate vicinity. The day was not starting out well. Annoyed, Sierra pulled into a Starbucks, and ordered a large black coffee and two pastries. The place was jammed. She took the only table available, next to a kid engrossed by his laptop.

Sierra couldn't shake the feeling she was running out of time. Unless she could be productive, she shouldn't be wasting it here—not when she had a huge pile of Grace's things to go through waiting for her at the hotel. Her fingers itched to access Grace's computer. She pulled it out of her bag, wondering if she should risk it. Starbucks had wifi, so she'd be using another network. *Was that enough to protect her?*

Sierra glanced at the table across from her. The kid's fingers flew over the keyboard with lightning speed. She was on the verge of asking for his help when he cried out.

"No, no, no. This can't be. It just can't be." He slammed his laptop shut, burying his face in his hands. Telling herself not to get involved, she forced herself to turn away.

She looked around the coffee shop, hoping to see someone else who looked approachable. There were several groups of men congregated together, talking about last night's Cub's game. A few couples enjoying a relaxing Sunday morning. That left a smattering of older men, well past retirement age, who probably knew less about computers than she did.

She picked up her coffee cup and snuck another look at the kid. He'd reopened his computer, typing furiously. He leaned in close, absorbed in something on the screen, lips moving as he read. When he was finished, he slapped his forehead with his hand, and sank down in his seat, a stricken look on his face.

"The peril is even greater than I imagined. Am I the only one seeing this?" The kid glanced up to see her looking at him. Their eyes met for a split second.

"Deepest apologies," he muttered, his face turning a deep red. " I didn't mean to disturb."

"No apology necessary. Are you okay?" Sierra asked.

"I'm most defiantly not okay, but that's no excuse for intruding upon your solitude." His black rimmed glasses slipped down his nose. He pushed them back up and loosened the tie he wore over a crumbled white shirt.

"You're not bothering me. In fact, it's the other way around. I was about to interrupt you, but you've obviously gotten bad news, so…"

He looked around, seemingly to reassure himself she was referring to him. "Really? You wanted to talk to me?"

"I did, yes."

He perked up for a moment, then his eyes narrowed in suspicion. "You don't work for Kepler do you? Because as I've already stated, The Shark will not be returning, no matter what he offers."

"Huh?"

"The Shark will not be bribed or enticed to return to the job or the heartless daughter. Even The Shark has his pride, battered though it is."

Sierra stared at him. "Who is The Shark, and what in God's name are you talking about?"

He raised soft, doe brown eyes to hers, and sent her a lopsided smile. "Then you've not been sent by Kepler or the demanding, self-centered, two-timing Angelica?"

"I honestly don't have a clue what you're talking about, sharks or no sharks." She pushed back her chair. This was a bad idea. The guy was way out in left field. Best to walk away now.

He jumped up to his feat. "No, wait, please. Don't leave on my account. I would be most grateful for the distraction of assisting you." He took a deep breath and plunged on. "Let me start over. I am The Shark. Kepler is the father of my former fiancée, the traitorous Angelica."

"You're name is actually Shark?" Sierra blinked in surprise.

"No." He wiped his right hand on his jeans and extended it, "My given name is Walter Marx, but I'm known in the cyber world as The Shark."

Sierra was bemused. The kid was a character, and a cyber-shark was exactly what she needed. She decided not to rush to judgment. "Nice to meet you, Shark."

"Likewise. I apologize for my earlier faux pas in thinking Kepler sent you. I seem to have overestimated myself once again."

Her right eye started to twitch, the kid…Shark…had the whole exuberance thing backwards. He seemed to have boundless energy for being down on himself. He reminded her of a puppy who'd been kicked one too many times.

"May I ask why you initially wished to speak to me?"

What did she have to lose? "I need to know, if I access the internet from here, would anyone be able to trace the IP address?"

"Will you be accessing sensitive information?"

"I might be, yes."

"Then I would advise against it. The IP address itself would be the same as everyone here using their laptops. The IP would only be traceable to this location. However, the connection host can intercept any data being sent over the connection."

She thought of the government seal she'd seen on Neil's file. It was possible she would find the same type of files on Grace's computer. She couldn't risk it.

"My new friend appears distressed. If you tell me what you wish to achieve, perhaps I can help?" He shot her a hopeful smile.

"It's complicated. Besides not wanting to get you involved, what I need is probably beyond your capabilities."

"I assure you, nothing is beyond my capabilities in the cyber world. The Kepler's found me more than capable."

The name clicked, piquing her interest. "These Kepler's you keep talking about, any connection to Kepler International?"

"I suppose everyone has heard of the company," The Shark sighed. "I was the head of their IT department."

Sierra choked. Kepler International was a multi-billion dollar tech corporation. "Forgive me for saying this, but aren't you a bit young to hold that kind of position?"

"I'm older than I look. I'm twenty-six, and if I do say so myself, a cyber-genius." His face fell, "An unemployed, unloved, homeless cyber-genius."

He looked so crestfallen, she couldn't stop herself. "If you worked at Kepler, you had to make decent money. How can you be homeless?"

"I cohabitated with Angelica. Since I've walked out on her, I've nowhere to hang my hat, so to speak."

"You must have enough money to rent a place."

"Oh, I have more than enough money. But what's the point? I've been betrayed by the woman I love, the world is in peril, there's no meaning or purpose to my life."

"That's awfully drastic. You can get another job."

"I signed a non-compete, and I am certain I would get a less than stellar reference from my former employer. If you allow me to help you, at least I'll feel useful."

She weighed her options. The guy was in worse shape than she was, but she was desperate. "You're really a computer shark?"

"I am."

"I have three computers I need to get information from. One is a laptop two are netbooks. I have to do it in a way that can't be traced—by anyone. The last time I turned on one of them, bullets came flying out of nowhere. Do you still want to help?"

His eyes widened. "Seriously? Actual bullets?"

"It's a long story, but, yes, actual bullets."

"I will most definitely assist you." His eyes came to life at the prospect of a challenge, "The Shark is at your service."

***

The bigger the corporation, the more shrouded in bullshit it was. Give a man offices in a glass enclosed skyscraper, and he thought he had the right to play God.

Skinbone Harris brushed past the receptionist, ignoring her frantic instructions to sign in and be awarded a badge before he was granted entry. Hell, let her call security. He didn't give a damn.

A long-legged brunette in the inner sanctum stood ready to block his way. The receptionist must have forewarned her. At least this one recognized him. "I'm sorry, sir, he's in a meeting."

"Not anymore, he's not." Skinbone pushed his way through the glass door, enjoying the startled look on Kepler's face. It was clear Jared Kepler hadn't expected to face him this soon.

"I need a status report." Skinbone eyed the younger man with Kepler, "You may want to tell your flunky here to leave so we can talk business."

Kepler's protégée bristled at the insult, glancing at his boss. With a nod from Kepler, he moved forward, extending his hand. "Ethan Wilde. And you are?"

"Your boss knows who I am." Skinbone didn't wait for an invitation. He pulled out a chair, "Who the hell are you?"

Kepler rearranged his features into his trademark slick smile. "Gentleman, no need for a pissing contest. We're all on the same side."

Skinbone jerked his chin towards Ethan, "He can be trusted?"

"Absolutely. He's well aware of our project. And what a vital player you are." Kepler leaned his elbows on his desk. "What can we do for you?"

This was a twist Skinbone hadn't anticipated. Kepler usually played things close to the vest. He preferred dealing with the man in private. The fewer eyes on him the better. He took a minute to weigh his options. There wasn't much of a choice. "My people are getting anxious. By our timetable, the project should be near completion. Instead, I get a call from your office advising me of a delay."

Kepler inclined his head toward Wilde. Skinbone noticed the subtle shift in both men's eyes. No surprise, Kepler was going to make the kid the fall guy.

"I am going to ask my question again, this time in hope of getting an answer. Will we have Foxtrot next week, or not?" Skinbone demanded

Ethan played it well. It was clear the kid was being groomed. He perched himself on the edge of Kepler's desk, schooling his features to reflect conflict, keeping his voice smooth. "We've hit a slight snag. Mr. Kepler has put me in charge of this project. I was out of town over the weekend on business and returned to discover an issue concerning the scientists. I can assure you, the problem is being addressed as we speak." He lowered his voice to a conspiratorial tone. "Between the three of us? We all know the value of swift delivery to the Venezuelan government. We are working day and night to rectify the situation and at this point, do not anticipate further delays."

Something about Wilde rubbed him wrong. He disliked the kid's calculated, condescending attitude, and clipped British tone but there was more to it. Ethan Wilde was too smug. Kepler was slipping if he didn't see the kid was chomping at the bit to run the show.

Skinbone decided to knock him down a peg. Ignoring Wilde he locked eyes with Kepler. "My government needs assurances. With the kind of money we're paying you, we need a guarantee the project won't be compromised. The balance of the funds will not be transferred until our tests are completed."

Wilde's face turned a mottled shade of red. He jammed his hands into his trouser pockets. "That was not part of the original agreement. The funds are transferred up front at the time of the exchange."

Skinbone's eyes never wavered from Kepler's. "I don't think so. You see, we've done a little digging into your background. Does The First Wave sound familiar, gentleman? It may not ring any bells with young Ethan here. After all, that goes back what twenty, thirty years?"

Kepler's voice tightened. "I was not running the company back then. Do not confuse me with my father."

Skinbone crossed his legs. "A little hard not to, don't you think? Like father, like son? You take government contracts from the U.S. and then sell the formula to the highest bidder? So, tell me, what happened with The First Wave? How did it get into the hands of the Chinese and the Mexicans? Or are we pretending the timing of the first Indigo Children is nothing more than a bizarre coincidence?"

"We had nothing to do with that." Anger simmered in Kepler's eyes. Skinbone touched a sore spot.

"Then how about this? You certainly had a hand in what you provided the Americans back then. How many lives exactly, did your company destroy?" Skinbone countered.

"Again, a tragic mistake. Not intentional." Kepler leaned back in his chair, loosening the collar of his shirt.

"Tell it to the children, and the parents. Oh, that's right. You had a nice little cover up going. No one knew the children were being experimented on. So no one could ever point the finger at you." Skinbone sneered, refusing to let the subject drop.

Kepler fought to keep the anger out of his voice. "I don't know where you are getting your information, but you are way off base. I resent the implication. Had the project been a success, we would have been lauded as national heroes. Instead, it failed. It was too ambitious an undertaking for that day and age."

"Nice speech. You know what concerns me though? When the project went bad, you blamed the scientists. They took the fall. It was *their* failure, not Kepler's. And now I'm hearing this project has been delayed, due to an issue with the scientists. Do you see where I'm going with this?" Skinbone's tone was cold and deliberate.

"I repeat, The First Wave was a tragic mistake. We did nothing wrong. Intentionally or otherwise."

"At least not in any way the United States could prove. You came out with clean hands on that one. I am going to make sure our deal stays clean." Skinbone directed a steely gaze towards both men.

Ethan Wilde adjusted his tie, "We don't appreciate threats. The terms are not negotiable."

"Your underling speaks for you now?"

Kepler cleared his throat, raising a hand to silence Ethan. Beads of sweat dotted his brow. "*Are* you trying to renegotiate?"

Skinbone leaned forward. "We've paid quite a bit upfront. My job is to make sure we get what we paid for. Once the formula is in our hands, all research is destroyed. The scientists are being well compensated by us for their work *and* their discretion. Their employment with Kepler and any of its subsidiaries must be terminated, effective immediately after the exchange."

Another look passed between Kepler and Wilde. Skinbone stood up. "Take it or leave it, gentleman."

Kepler's eyes narrowed. "That was part of our agreement all along. We have no problems abiding by our original terms."

"Then you understand we are simply protecting what is ours. I require a guarantee Foxtrot is not compromised. To that end, an associate of mine from the States will be joining your scientists throughout this final phase to assure everything goes according to plan."

Before they could respond, he walked to the door and opened it. "Gentlemen, I'd like you to introduce you to my associate."

Donovan St. James stepped into the room.

Chapter Fifteen

Sierra hesitated before swiping the key card. The Shark bounced back and forth on his heels behind her, whistling tunelessly. Twenty-six or not, he had a child-like innocence. He was already nursing a bruised heart courtesy of the two-timing Angelica. Did she want to add to his problems? "I don't know if I feel right about this."

He blinked. "About what? Bringing me to your hotel room? I doubt you have any nefarious plans for me. If what we need to discuss is of a confidential nature, your hotel room is the most advantageous location, wouldn't you agree?"

She stifled a smile. He certainly had a unique way of putting things.

The Shark raised his eyebrows and gestured towards the key card she held. "Shall we get to work?"

Sierra leaned against the door. She didn't want him to get hurt. "Listen, maybe you could show me what to do with the computers and let me take it from there. I wasn't kidding earlier when I said this was dangerous."

"Understood. But I assure you, I am up to the task. To be honest, I'm intrigued. It's not every day The Shark meets an actual damsel in distress."

"That's the thing. I'm worried you think this is some kind of adventure. It isn't. It's life and death."

"My apologies. I did not mean to make light of your situation. I realize said damsel is in grave danger."

She studied his face a good long time. Sighing, she inserted the key card and opened the door a crack before turning towards him. "Then we make a deal. Once I tell you the whole story, if there is any part of it you aren't comfortable with, we part ways. All I ask is what I tell you remains between us. I need to know I can trust you, Shark."

"I am honored you trust me enough to tell me your story. A deal, then, on both counts." Expression solemn, The Shark extended his hand. She accepted it, and they shook. It felt ridiculous, like they were making a pact. Given all that was going on, she surprised herself by holding back a chuckle. Intentionally or not, The Shark had a way of lightening her mood.

She pushed open the door, gesturing for him to enter first. He came to a dead stop, staring open-mouthed at the bed. "Holy Mother of Moley. What is all that stuff?" Frowning, he sniffed the air, "Do I smell…fire?"

"Close. You smell smoke. All this stuff was rescued from my best friend's house."

He whirled to look at her, stricken. "Oh. Your friend? Is she okay?"

Sierra gripped the back of a chair, tears burning her eyes. It was one thing to know Grace was dead, she couldn't bring herself to say the words out loud. She shook her head, "No, she isn't."

He cocked his head, and placed his things on the desk. They stared at each other, bonding in the silence of grief. Shrugging, he walked over to her, awkwardly patting her shoulder. She smiled through her tears. "Couple of sad sacks, aren't we?"

He nodded. She knew he was thinking of his loss too. She felt his shoulders shake and patted his back, before gingerly pulling away. Pressing her palms over her eyes, she wiped the tears away, smudging her mascara. He used the bottom of his shirt.

"Sorry," they said in unison, breaking the somber mood.

Sierra found an empty spot near the edge of the bed and motioned him to the chair. "It's still so hard to get used to, you know? I know they're gone, but so much has happened in the last few days, I really haven't had time to grieve."

"They?"

"My fiancée."

He mouthed a silent O, covering his heart with his hand. "I am so very sorry for your losses."

She looked down at her ring finger, thinking of all the secrets they'd kept from her, wondering how to explain everything without sounding like a lunatic.

The Shark broke the silence. Whether it was out of respect or caution, she wasn't sure, but he was careful to speak in hushed tones. "Forgive me for asking, but at a time of such devastating loss, it seems odd you are fixated on computers. Unless…am I correct in assuming they met with foul play?"

His words jarred her to the bone. Foul play didn't begin to describe the danger she was in. Or the jeopardy she'd be placing Shark in if he agreed to help. She was insane to drag him into this, even crazier to expect him to believe her. She couldn't risk his life, or hers.

The walls felt like they were closing in on her—up until a few days ago, she never would have invited a stranger into a hotel room—let alone reveal sensitive information to someone she barely knew. Her fingers curled around the blankets edge. Her throat closed up on her, leaving her gasping for breath.

The Shark jumped up, dumping the odds and ends they picked up at the grocery store onto the desk. He shoved the bag in her face. "Breath. In and out. You're hyperventilating, this will help."

Sierra gripped the bag like a lifeline, feeling like a fool. She was making a scene. When her breathing returned to normal, she dropped her hands to her sides. "Thank you. Really. For everything. The more I think about this, it's a bad idea. Nothing good can come out of it."

His head dropped. Minutes ago, he'd come to her aid, now his shoulders sagged. She'd hurt his feelings, which was the last thing she wanted to do.

He raised soulful eyes to hers, "I do see you are struggling with the predicament you are in. I can assure you, I also see you are in great pain and under severe duress. You may think whatever you have to tell me will sound crazy, but the world is full of crazy. It just so happened to pull you into the middle of it. My heart has already gone out to you, and while I know there would never be any romantic connotations between us, you are indeed a damsel in distress, and it would be my privilege to be your knight in shining armor, so to speak. You need someone to help you, and I need someone to help. Tell me your story, and let me be the judge of whether I want to get involved or not. Please?"

Taking a deep shuddering breath, she realized in order get the help she needed, she was going to have trust someone. Sierra told him everything, beginning to end, leaving nothing out. He listened with rapt attention, nodding here and there. When she told him about Skinbone, and Luke, his eyes glazed over.

"What's wrong?" Her panic was on the verge of coming back.

He pondered her question, "I'm not entirely certain. I felt something strange, like an odd tickle up my spine. *Fortuitous*. It's a great word, and not one you hear every day." Straightening up in his chair, he shot her a sheepish smile. "Based on all you've told me, I would even go so far as to say that I believe our chance encounter was fortuitous."

She groaned, "I wish you hadn't said that. The word is freaking me out."

He held up a hand, leaning towards her in excitement. "No. There's something to it. Fortuitous, The First Wave, Foxtrot, these things have meaning."

Sierra shivered. She stood up, paced. "So you think they are connected?"

He turned up his hands, shrugging. "I believe the possibility exists."

"You don't think I'm crazy?"

"No, I truly don't. What does surprise me is your hesitancy to contact your FBI agent friend again. Perhaps he was cool to you because of your break-up, but surely he would know you didn't kill anyone."

"I was in terrified when it first happened, when I saw Neil die. The only thing I could think of was running. I tried calling Donovan. When I couldn't reach him, I did what I had to do. Now it feels like it's too late."

Nerves had a way of working against her. Hunger yawned like a looming pit inside her stomach. Her eyes wandered to the desk. They'd bought snacks, but none of them appealed to her. In lieu of decent food, she bit her bottom lip. "Okay, you don't think I'm crazy and you know the risks. You can leave if you want to. No hard feelings."

"Leave?" He looked thunderstruck. "While being sympathetic to your most dire plight, I find myself embroiled in the odd set of circumstances you've become entangled in. Simply put, wild horses couldn't drag me away."

Relief flooded through her. Without realizing it, she'd been holding her breath. She wasn't in this alone anymore. Tucking a stray strand of hair behind her ear, she smiled, nodding at him. "Thank you."

"You are most welcome. I am honored to help. Where do we start?"

"With pizza."

***

The Shark shared her affinity for food. After much debate, they settled on a large thin crust, mushroom, onion and pepperoni, and a medium stuffed spinach pizza with extra cheese. There was a small fridge in the hotel room. What they didn't eat now, they could save for breakfast.

While they waited for the pizza delivery, Shark went to work, setting up the computers and attaching the cables and gizmo's they'd picked up at Best Buy. Sierra attacked the pile of Grace's things. They were easier to go through with another person in the room; maybe because she wasn't getting lost in the memories each time she handled something.

So far, the key Grace had hidden with the files and brochure were the most promising items. Then there were the treasures she wanted to keep to remember her friend by. Sierra's fingers stroked the seashell Grace kept all these years. Not wanting it damaged, she wrapped it carefully in the bags from their shopping trip and tucked it among her clothes in her suitcase.

Picking up the Shadow Lake brochure, she pulled a chair over to sit beside Shark. "I wanted to show you this. Can you talk or do you have to stay focused?"

"The data is transferring. By all means, talk away."

She handed him the flyer. "I found this tucked underneath Grace's computer. She had a thing for odd hiding places, and I know she didn't want anyone to see this. At first, I thought maybe she was considering it as a trysting place for her and Neil. I ruled that out because I don't actually know they were having an affair. I think they were involved, but not in the way I was originally thinking."

"I tend to agree."

"What if this is a clue? It could have something to do with Foxtrot or The First Wave."

His lips moved while he read. She reached over and grabbed the stack of folders. "Then there are these. They are all in some sort of code."

He put down the flyer and flipped through the folders. "These are hard copies of encrypted files. I suspect we will find more of the same on the computer. I might be able to break the encryption, but it will take time."

"I have a thought. I'd like to see if the house in Shadow Lake is still available."

"You mean purchase it?"

She nodded. "Or rent it, whatever Grace was going to do. I should have enough money, I think."

"Bad idea. You may need the money to live on, and financing is out of the question with a stolen identity. We could create a way to divert a background check, or even divert funds from your friend's bank accounts…"

That made her nervous. "You mean hacking?"

He grimaced. "Hacking is such a malicious word. I prefer to think I possess a highly specialized talent for infiltrating and manipulating certain systems when the situation warrants it."

"No. No, absolutely not. I don't want you involved in anything criminal."

He raised both his hands. "Dear damsel, you didn't let me finish. I was about to suggest you allow me to purchase or rent the house in my name. That way, there will be no tie to you whatsoever. And while I applaud your cleverness in assuming a new identity, if indeed this house is important, a large purchase in Corrine Lawson's name could raise too many red flags. My name will be meaningless to anyone tracking you or investigating your friend's death."

She had to admit his idea was brilliant. "I can't let you actually *buy* the house."

"I don't see why not. I do need a new residence and I no longer have any ties to the city."

"Do you know how much a house like that would cost?"

"I have more money than I know what to do with and a house is an investment."

A vein throbbed in her forehead. It was a generous offer. Too generous. "Look, you barely know me. It's one thing for me to buy the house. It's my life and my freedom on the line. My fiancée, and my best friend who were killed. I appreciate your offer to put the house in your name, but the financial risk should be mine."

"My apologies. I did not wish to upset. I propose a compromise. Initially, we split the cost. If I choose to remain there after we have cleared your name and solved the puzzle, I buy you out. If not, we sell. Agreed?"

"Counter proposal. We make the call. If the house is still on the market, we make the appointment with the realtor in your name. We sort out the rest of the details later."

"Fair enough. Shall I make the call?"

She nodded, too nervous to listen. While he dialed, she grabbed a handful of change from her purse and headed down to hall to get a couple of sodas.

His face was solemn when she returned. "The plot has thickened. It appears you were correct in your assumption that the house factors into recent events."

Her heart skipped a beat. "Can we see it?"

"First off, the house is not for sale. It never was."

"Then how does it factor in?"

"It's a month to month rental. Grace has been renting it for the past month and a half. According to the realtor, her stay was open ended. She has stayed there with a man on occasion. I don't know if it was your Neil or not, sorry."

"It's a dead end." She couldn't keep the disappointment out of her voice.

"Not necessarily. It may not be what it seems. There's more"

"Do I want to hear this?"

"Based on what the realtor told me, I improvised a bit on the call. I explained Grace was unable to fill her rental agreement, and that I wanted to sublet. The realtor was amiable; however, there are two problems."

"Which are?"

"Hurdle number one; the property isn't available until August first, due to the request of the owner. The realtor advised me that Grace was aware of this when she rented and agreed not to be on the premises for a two-week period. The owner is having minor renovations done. Hurdle number two, she wanted to know if the others would be joining us."

"Others? What others?"

The Shark tried to look hopeful. "Perhaps there are unknown allies who can aid us on our mission in uncovering the truth."

"Or unknown people that want to kill us. We could be walking straight into the enemy's hands."

***

The toughest part of any job was to know when to walk away. Skinbone left Kepler and Wilde in Donovan St. James capable hands. The man's presence would shake them up a hell of a lot more than any threats he could make.

St. James would report back once the shit hit the fan. With a watchdog shadowing their every move, they couldn't keep the cover-up going for long. If they had Foxtrot in their possession, they'd turn it over quick enough.

Skinbone couldn't see Kepler walking away from the cool five million the "government" he claimed to represent offered, unless they were planning a double cross. Donovan's presence would ensure that didn't happen.

The problem with men like Kepler and his protégé was they thought they were untouchable. Skinbone had seen that kind of arrogance before. Some men never learned that cockiness and crime were a deadly combination—not until seconds before he put a bullet between their eyes.

Kepler was smart enough not to wind up dead. Not if he could help it. He'd play ball when he realized the odds weren't in his favor. He was the kind of man who'd do anything to save his own sorry skin.

Skinbone itched to get to work. There was another reason he'd come to Chicago, one that couldn't wait. The meeting had served a dual purpose. He'd effectively tied Kepler's hands by giving him a babysitter; he wouldn't be able to make a move without St. James breathing down his neck. As an added bonus, it was an effective way to keep the fed busy. The last thing Skinbone wanted was St. James trailing him, he needed to attend to his business undeterred.

The trip also served as a smokescreen, giving him a damn good reason to be in Chicago.

***

The pizza was a welcome reprieve. They dug in like scavengers, making a mess.

"We should have bought paper plates," Sierra mumbled between bites.

"We should have bought napkins." The Shark scooped up another slice, using his hand to mop up sauce from his chin.

She tossed her half eaten slice back in the box and stood up, rubbing her arms. The latest wrinkle in her plans bothered her. They couldn't go to Shadow Lake blind. If they didn't know what they were up against, it could be suicide.

Sierra walked towards the window, staring out at the sky. There was a hint of daylight left. Out towards the west, it was clouding up again. The rain would probably hit sometime after midnight. She hated storms. Chicago was notorious for violent thunderstorms following a heat wave. Considering how hot it had been the last few days, they were probably in for a doozy.

She turned away from the window and looked at all of Grace's things scattered around. They had so much work ahead of them. It was hard to figure out which problem they should tackle first.

Skinbone Harris's words came to mind. *Reality is what you make it.* Damn, why did she keep thinking about him? When she closed her eyes, she could visualize every angle and shadow of his face; feel the way her skin tingled when he touched her. *She couldn't get him out of her mind.*

Irritation rubbed at her like an itch she couldn't scratch. She needed to temper her memories with what she knew to be true. Every line he'd fed her was bull; he'd claimed he would know if she needed him. She wasn't ready to talk to him, but that wasn't the point. He'd made a promise and, if she'd ever needed help, in her life it was now.

Sierra gnawed on a fingernail—she shouldn't even be thinking about him. It was too dangerous. No matter how hard she tried to recall the image, the killers face eluded her. All she could visualize were those damn black eyes—and their similarity to Skinbone's.

Her cell phone rang, scaring her. She jumped, banging her shin against an end table. Gooseflesh prickled her skin.

Shark leapt out of his chair. "Don't answer it."

"I won't." She crossed her arms fighting a sudden chill.

"It could be your FBI agent friend."

She shook her head, spooked by the coincidence. "No, it isn't. I never gave him the number."

"I don't know if you are aware of this. A disposable cell is untraceable, however, law enforcement, and probably other organizations as well, can pinpoint the general location of a disposable phone. You still need to exercise caution when using one."

"I wasn't planning on answering, but thanks, I didn't know."

"You are most welcome. However, if you have no intention of answering, you're reaction to the ringing phone is most distressing. You're trembling. And, forgive me for saying so, but you're white as a hotel sheet. The phone itself cannot hurt you."

"I think I made it ring," she whispered.

He tipped his head, a perplexed look on his face. "How could you *make* it ring?"

"I was thinking about the man I met, Skinbone Harris. I was standing here thinking how everything he'd said was bullshit; otherwise, he'd be calling."

"And the phone rang."

"And the phone rang. I think I *willed* him to call."

"Surely that's happened to you before. It's one of those utterly bizarre, cosmic coincidences. You hear of it happening all the time. People think of someone they haven't talked to in years and suddenly they call or run into each other. It happens to everyone."

He made a good point. "I guess you're right. My imagination is starting to play tricks on me."

"With good reason, I should say. I don't mean to be a harbinger of doom, but the situation you find yourself in is most unusual. I admire your courage and wherewithal. I would have been a basket case from the get go, and would most likely be on a slab somewhere right now courtesy of the madman. You truly should be patting yourself on the back. You've outwitted a killer thus far on your own. There is no reason to believe we will not triumph in the end."

Sierra wished she had his optimism. Right now, she was plain overwhelmed. Shark, on the other hand, bristled with energy. If she ever wanted her life back, she was going to have to shake off her mood and force herself to keep going.

"Okay." She slapped her hands on her thighs, "Let's get back to work. How far have you gotten with the computers?"

"I've transferred all of the information from the laptop. I can begin to work on one of the netbooks or we can take a look at the files I've retrieved."

Worry nagged at her. "I think you should finish transferring everything first. If we start looking at files now, we could get caught up in it."

"Excellent thinking. I suspect Dear Damsel will feel better once all the files are in a central location. I shall get started on Grace's netbook post haste. It may take a while to retrieve the password."

"Try Foxtrot or The First Wave. Those were the passwords Neil used."

"Will do."

While The Shark occupied himself, Sierra decided get Neil's netbook ready for him to work on next. Her heart stopped. *It wasn't in her backpack.* She dumped out the contents, hoping she'd missed it. She hadn't. It was gone. Thinking backwards, she remembered Luke asking about it. She'd taken it out at the train station, placing it on the bench between them.

"Oh, God, please no." Hands shaking, she tore through all her things, praying she'd put the netbook somewhere else. The room looked like a disaster area by the time she was done.

She sank down to the floor, cradling her knees against her chest. *She didn't have it.* In her haste to leave the train station, she'd left it behind.

How could she have been so careless? Neil's computer was a vital piece of the puzzle. The information he'd stored on it was critical to figuring out why he'd been killed. She was certain of it.

Sierra tried to calm down telling herself that what they had might be enough, provided Grace had been working with Neil when a thought struck her. *Someone else now had access to Neil's netbook.* If Luke noticed it lying on the bench and picked it up, things might be okay. He was involved in something sketchy himself he hadn't wanted to talk about. Neil's secrets might be safe with him.

If anyone else took it, she was in deep trouble. Bullets started flying minutes after she'd turned it on. They could have been meant for Luke, or they could have been aiming for her. Her panic mounted. How many people would turn it in to lost and found? There was a better chance someone walked off with it. Good Lord, her mistake might have put someone's life at risk. And if that person wound up in the path of a bullet, the netbook would become evidence. Her fingerprints were plastered all over it, tying her to Neil and his death.

Leaving the netbook behind had been a dangerous mistake. One that could get her killed.

***

Slipping away hadn't been easy, but he didn't have a choice. He'd made a critical mistake. Loose ends had a way of unraveling when least expected. He never should have let the woman slip away. There was no excuse. How could he have been so sloppy? He brushed back an unruly strand of long black hair and surveyed the scene.

The plan had been simple enough. Kill Thornton and McGinley and take off with Foxtrot before anyone was the wiser. Nothing should have gone wrong.

Sonofabitch. He slammed his fist into the closest wall. *He had to clean up his mess before any fingers starting pointing to him.*

Neil Thornton's remains were nothing more than a stain on the floor. Wouldn't take much to clean it up. No body, no murder. If the CPD wasn't breathing down his neck, it would buy him some time. Let the cops spin their wheels looking for a missing person. They'd forget to keep looking soon enough. Bigger and badder crimes would take precedence. The Thornton case would end up in the cold case file before winter.

The next step was to remove all traces of Sierra Montgomery. She hadn't come back. If she had, she would have taken her things and cleared away any evidence of her presence that night. Everyone knew the cops looked at the significant other first. He was surprised she was willing to risk the cops fingering her as the prime suspect. Then again, she wasn't very smart.

He helped himself to a shot of Neil's whiskey. Makers Mark. The man had good taste. He settled down on an easy chair to think, crossing his long legs in front of him.

The woman might not be smart, but so far, she'd managed to be damn lucky.

The situation had to be cleaned up fast, before it became any more complex. It was critical he recover the netbook. In the wrong hands, the fallout could be catastrophic.

How the hell had she gotten it? It hadn't been in the house the night he'd eliminated Thornton—that much he was certain of. She must have been working with McGinley and Thornton all along. He crushed the shot glass in his hand. Having no prior knowledge of her involvement was a major slip-up.

He'd clean up Thornton's remains; make sure there wasn't a trace left. Sierra Montgomery would be all his. He smiled. No one could run forever. When enough time passed with no report of Thornton's death, one of two things would happen: she'd get nervous and start making mistakes, or she would think it was safe to come home. Either way, he'd win.

Chapter Sixteen

Skinbone Harris stood inside the shell of the burnt out building, rubbing his face with his hands. It was his third stop of the day, and this one was bad. Someone had picked through Grace McGinley's things like a vulture picked flesh off the bone. Except for a few things that stood out, like the missing computer, a casual observer wouldn't know the place had been tossed.

This was trouble.

His foot creaked on the warped floorboards. He ventured down the hallway until he came to the spot where nothing but jagged beams remained and the sky served as ceiling. The explosion should have leveled the place; he was surprised to see a part of the back half of the house still standing. How the hell had it survived the blast?

The need to know itched inside him, like a mosquito gone mad. He jammed his hands inside his pockets and went back inside. Knowing it was useless, he searched anyway, hoping to find a crumb or two of Grace's work.

Nothing. Not one damn thing. Well, hell.

He stood in silence, picking up on a strange vibe, a wrong scent. He could feel it down into his bones, and bones never lied. If someone had come back looking for information, the place would have been ransacked. Instead, it had been searched with painstaking care, everything put back in order, respectful of the house that once was and the woman who had made it her home.

It didn't fit.

Skinbone's lips settled into a hard line. A new player had tossed his hat in the ring and this threat was a wildcard. His eyes glittered; fury cooking up inside him. Someone must have leaked information into the wrongs hands. Right about now, the problem was hemorrhaging, and it was up to him to fix it.

The house had something to tell him, he just had to open himself up to it. Shaking off the anger, he squatted down on his hunches, clearing his mind. A violent death occurred here. Closing his eyes, he breathed in and out, long slow breaths, concentrating on the room.

Walls did talk; Skinbone knew it was just a matter of knowing how to speak to them. This room was Grace McGinley's haven. It was where she worked, and where she'd kept her secrets. He picked up a nightgown tossed on a chair. She must have worn it the night before she died. He wrapped it around one hand and pressed his other palm against the wall, establishing a connection.

The vision threw him backwards. He felt the explosion, saw her blown to pieces, flesh and bone smattering across the living room and bursting into flames. All that lingered was her death. No answers, no secrets, only the violence remained.

He squinted. There had to be something. *Damn it, what was he missing?*

Outside, a door slammed, breaking his concentration. A dog yapped in the distance. High heels clicked against wooden stairs. Skinbone sucked in his breath, easing into the shadows, hoping whoever it was kept on walking. The back gate clanged shut.

Her voice cut through the air. "Hello? Hello? Is someone there?"

Brushing soot off his hands, he yanked his shirt over his jeans to cover his weapon. Wanting to discourage conversation, he stuck his head out the back door.

"Sorry, ma'am, I have to ask you to vacat the property. It's not safe for you to be here. The structure isn't sound."

She folded her arms, a petulant look on her face. "And who are you?"

"I'm the guy telling you shouldn't be traipsing around back here unless you want to get hurt."

She pursed her lips, "I'd like to know your business here—I also need to see some ID."

Skinbone worked his jaw, hiding his irritation behind a smile. He rammed his hand in his pocket. He'd come prepared with various identities in case he ran into someone legitimately inspecting the house. "Dept of Alcohol Tobacco Firearms and Explosives. This scene is under investigation, so once again, I have to ask you to leave."

Her eyes widened. She staggered backwards, gripping the fence for support. He felt a twinge of relief. In a minute, she'd be running home, and on the phone, gossiping with neighbors.

Skinbone turned to hide his chuckle, glad to be rid of her. The door was closing behind him when she called out.

"Oh Dear Lord, I knew it. I haven't gotten a wink of sleep since this whole thing began. My life's been turned upside down. I knew too many people kept coming and going, and so I told the fire Marshall when I called him a little while ago."

Skinbone closed his eyes and counted to ten trying to gather up his patience before he faced her.

"I mean, how could I sleep? Some of her things are still in there. I have to keep an eye out for looters. I'm terrified they might rob me next. Or homeless people might start squatting inside, attracting all kinds of druggies and thieves to the neighborhood."

He opened his mouth to talk. His mistake. She'd only paused for a breath.

"And now you're telling me her house was *bombed*? That's what you people do, right? Investigate bombings?" She clutched her chest. "Here I was, thinking she died so young, and I should overlook all the trouble she's caused me. Now I find out she brought this on herself. Houses don't get bombed for no reason. I should have kept a better eye on things. If I'd have known she was up to no good, all this commotion could have been avoided."

Skinbone swore under his breath. He should have used a different ID. Now he had to calm the woman's hysteria. He took the stairs two at a time, jogging over to her. "Miss…I'm sorry, what's your name?"

She sniffed daintily, dabbing at her eyes with the back of her hand. "Lawson, Corrine Lawson."

He saw her sizing him up, checking his left hand for a ring. Damn, she was a cold-hearted broad. He'd use it to his advantage. "Miss Lawson," he rested his hand on the fence, touching her shoulder with his arm, "I hate to see a pretty woman like you distressed. I assure you, there's nothing to worry about. There was no bomb. They send us out to do routine checks after every major fire. I give you my word; the most exciting part of this inspection was meeting you."

She batted her eyelashes at him. "Really?"

"Scouts honor."

Her body inched closer to his. "Well, thank you. I feel much better. You are so much nicer than those other people who were here. Most of them are so abrupt. I even saw one of them carrying a box out to her car. I didn't think I needed to keep an eye on her. I was on my way to take my Tara for her walk, and the woman said she was an insurance adjuster. It worries me she might have been stealing; she might have even taken more than one box. She drove away before I could catch up to her

Skinbone zeroed in on someone carrying out a box. *This was information he needed.* Gripping Corrine's shoulder hard, he spun her around to look at him. "When was she here?"

Corrine gasped, glaring at his hand, "Ouch. That hurt. What's the matter with you?"

He loosened his grip. "Sorry, I wasn't thinking."

She rubbed her shoulder, thrusting her lower lip out in a pout. It wasn't attractive on her. She peered up at him from beneath her lashes, looking like he'd run over her dog. Knowing he had to suck it up and get back into her good graces, he swallowed his impatience.

He leaned in close, letting his words brush against her ear. "I really am sorry. I hope you'll let me make this up to you sometime."

Worked like a charm. Shoulder forgotten, she smiled. "I'd like that very much."

"So would I. Right now though, you could really help me out. If that woman committed a crime, I need to know about it. What can you tell me about her?"

Corrine preened. She was in her element, puffed up with self-importance. Skinbone fought the urge to shake her. "Let's see. She was here in the morning. Late morning, I think. I remember thinking it was strange she was working on a Sunday, but what do I know about such things? Insurance adjusters work all kinds of hours. The other thing that struck me as odd was she had the night of the fire wrong. She thought it happened on Saturday night when it was on Thursday. That seemed to rattle her, although she blamed it on a clerical error."

So the woman had a day's jump on him. "What else?"

"Well, we didn't talk much. My Tara was anxious for her walk… she's been high strung ever since the fire." Corrine stopped in mid-sentence, remembering. "Oh dear, I thought of something. This is all my fault. When I saw her coming up the walkway, I stopped her. I asked her if she was the insurance adjuster. I gave her an excuse to be here."

"You did the best you could, Corrine. Did you get a name? Can you describe her?"

"She was a little thing. I remember thinking it was a strange job for her to have."

"How little?"

"Maybe about my size?" She gave him a sidelong glance, running her hands down her body, "But not as…filled out….as I am."

Filled out? That was one way to put it. Another would be plump. He bit back the words. "Hair color?"

"Oh, that I don't know. She had on a baseball cap and huge sunglasses. Wasn't dressed very professionally, either. Ratty jeans, with a plaid shirt worn loose over a t-shirt." Corrine shuddered. "I didn't approve at first until I decided she really couldn't wear nice clothes working in all that mess."

Skinbone froze. She was describing the woman he'd met the other night. He tuned Corrine out. It had to be a coincidence. How would a woman he'd met in a Memphis rib dive know Grace McGinley? Besides, she'd been sitting there, minding her own business. *He* was the one who approached *her*. No way was she tangled up in this mess.

The woman rambled on, voicing her disproval about women working masculine jobs. Skinbone wasn't listening. His eyes narrowed, the tips of his fingers started to twitch. *Had she played him?* That didn't set right, no matter how he shook things out. He couldn't wrap his mind around the idea of Seri being involved. Corrine had to be mistaken; no way was she talking about the same woman. The one he'd met was a sweet little gal, fighting hard to hide the trouble in her eyes.

Corrine was still talking. He dragged his mind back to the present. Maybe delving into Grace McGinley's personal life would serve up some answers. "Did she have many visitors? Did you notice any suspicious comings and goings in the weeks before the fire?"

She folded her arms, lips pursing in a prim line. "There *was* something, though I hate to speak ill of the dead."

He flexed his fingers, trying to hide his annoyance. Dimwitted woman. If she'd seen something suspicious, shouldn't she have mentioned it before now? "It's not speaking ill if it will help us with the investigation."

"Well, if you think it might help." She smiled up at him. "Would you like to come inside for a glass lemonade first? It's awful hot out here."

"Wish I could, but that could get me in trouble." He winked at her. "Another time, when I'm not working."

She giggled. The sound was like razors piercing his skin. "What did you see, Corrine?" he prodded.

"I don't mean to gossip, you understand."

"Of course."

"And I don't know any details."

He was losing patience. In another minute, he'd be hard pressed not to strangle her. "Understood."

Corrine sidled up to him, leaning in close to whisper. "A man was sneaking around here at all hours of the night. Very suspicious, like he was making sure no one saw him coming or going. I think she was having an affair with a married man."

His ears pricked, *this could be useful.* "What did the boyfriend look like?"

"Nice looking man, about six foot tall, sandy brown hair, blue eyes. Good build, like he worked out."

Neil Thornton.

That sure as hell raised the stakes. Was the woman he met in Memphis the same woman who claimed to be the insurance adjuster?

He had to find her.

Question was, would he have to kill her?

***

Luke's eyes were bloodshot. For the first time in his life, he felt older than his years. Neil Thornton and Grace McGinley were dead. Their blood was on his hands.

"Ah, Sweet Jesus." He pushed his chair away from the computer and poured himself a shot of vodka. He didn't give a damn if it was morning. He'd never made it to bed last night.

The guilt was eating him alive. It had been his idea to stir things up. He raised the glass to his lips. "You should have let things rest, damn fool old man."

He'd tracked down Foxtrot to settle an old score, had wanted the bastards who started the project to pay. Now he was just as bad as they were, taking lives and almost losing his own in the process.

How had they known?

He'd stayed up all night looking for flaws in the plan. Not a single thing jumped out at him. They'd covered their bases. The whole operation should have gone down smoother than an eighty year old bottle of scotch on a cold winter's day.

So what the hell went wrong?

Bad as all that was, something bigger caused the burn in his gut. He'd waited a long time to exact revenge. The sonofabitches had cost him his only son. To rub salt in the wound, years ago, when the initial project—The First Wave—was under investigation, the government couldn't dig up enough evidence to make a conviction.

Luke vowed to do two things before he died: find his son and destroy the men who robbed him of his family.

He stared at the glass in his hand, and slammed it down on the desk. "Time to meet the morning, old man. Sitting on your ass feeling sorry for yourself, ain't gonna fix a thing."

Stretching to relieve the kink in his back, he walked over to the blinds and opened the slats. He grimaced, temporarily blinded by the blazing sunlight pouring in. He needed coffee. A piece or two of toast probably wouldn't hurt either. Might do some good at sopping up all the vodka he'd consumed and help clear his head.

While he waited for the coffee to brew, he went back to his computer. He had private eyes all over the world looking for his son. The older he got, the more important it was that he find him. What happened to the boy wasn't entirely his fault, but he shouldered much of the blame.

The world was a different place back in the late sixties and early seventies. *Anything* seemed possible. Man landed on the moon, genetic testing and modification opened up new avenues in science, and the first test tube baby was born.

And somebody, somewhere, decided it would be a good idea to test random children for psychic abilities. Camps sprung up in various parts of the country. Gifted children selected by invitation only. The First Wave.

Only the project had gone terribly awry. The children weren't tested; they were put through rigorous mental training and injected with hallucinogens to make their minds more susceptible to psychic preconditioning. Doped up and brainwashed. Tortured in the hopes that one day the U.S would have elite squads of soldiers and government agencies able to predict attacks and protect the country from any threat.

After they left the camps, the children were carefully monitored for ten years without the knowledge or consent of their families. Not even the children were aware of what they endured. Memories were wiped clean and replaced with false experiences through drugs and extensive hypnosis. By the early eighties, it was the clear the project was doomed to fail—not even the trigger word implanted in their minds awakened their hidden abilities. The memory suppression had been too severe.

During the final years of the project, when it was clinging to its last dying gasps, they decided to become more selective in their search. Science was evolving. Though there was no testing available to substantiate their theory, it was their hope that psychic abilities could be passed on genetically. To that end, they began to seek out children whose parents had known psychic abilities.

Luke was one of those parents.

He never suspected what type of camp he'd sent his son to—not until his son returned and exhibited odd behavior. It took Luke almost a decade to dig up the truth. By then it was already too late.

He'd come home one night after a week away. He'd been working a tough case, the brutal kidnapping, and murder of a young girl. Made him grateful for what he had, no matter what their problems. When he unlocked the door, nobody greeted him. He'd called out their names, his voice was the only one that echoed back.

There was a note taped the refrigerator door. His wife had taken his son and fled the country. He'd made the mistake of telling her his suspicions about the camp a few weeks before he was called out of town.

She'd taken their son to protect him. Luke knew it didn't work that way.

That was in nineteen eighty-four. His son had been six years old at the time.

He never saw either one of them again.

***

High atop his stainless steel throne, Jared Kepler held court among a chosen few. It was a term coined by his daughter to describe his luxurious penthouse apartment a few floors below the top of the John Hancock building. Her other term, far less flattering, was reserved for private company.

Angelica smoothed the front of her Ralph Lauren linen dress and crossed her legs, tossing her comment over her shoulder. "Honestly, Father, I don't see what you are making such a fuss about."

Jared Kepler stood looking out the floor to ceiling window facing Lake

Michigan, holding an untouched martini. "That's the problem with you, Angelica, you've never understood people."

She raised a hand to her raven colored tresses, neatly done up in chignon and cast a wicked look in the direction of Ethan Wilde and Donovan St. James before turning her attention back to her father. "I understand *people.* I just don't happen to like many of them."

Jared turned to look at his daughter, a sour expression on his face. "You are so like your grandfather. But then, I suppose that's how he built an empire."

She shrugged an elegant shoulder. "This is an old argument, Father, one you should learn from. Grandfather Kepler employed scores of immigrants who otherwise who would have begged for their bread. They had nothing more to offer than strong backs, which Grandfather used. That was how big business was built back in those days."

Ethan Wilde sensed an argument brewing. He smoothly stepped in, handing Angelica a fresh glass of merlot. She accepted it and took a delicate sip, leaving a red stain from her lipstick at the edges. She gave Ethan a sideways glance, her mouth turning up in a seductive smile.

Jared Kepler was getting angry. "We are not talking about the unwashed masses here. Two brilliant scientists, two of the brightest minds in the country are gone. One missing and one dead."

Angelica's dark eyes slid between Ethan and Donovan St. James. "Gentleman, would you excuse us? I need a private moment with my father."

She waited until the men took their leave. Once the door closed firmly behind them, she turned on her father, "You are embarrassing yourself. Gail McKinney isn't worth it."

"*Grace McGinley,*" he corrected between gritted teeth. "And yes, she *was* worth it."

"There are other scientists with brilliant minds who would jump at the chance to step into this project."

Jared smashed his martini glass into the window. "Damn it, Angelica, without them *there is no project.* All the research, the prototypes, the *final components are gone.*"

She raised a well-shaped brow, "How could you allow this to happen?"

"I didn't *allow* it to happen. The project should have been secure. Knowledge of it was on a need to know basis only. There was no way I could have foreseen this happening. For God's sake, I took every step necessary to ensure its safety."

She pursued her lips, examining her perfectly manicured fingernails, "What are we doing to address the problem?"

"We've had no choice but to contact the government and the proper authorities."

Angelica placed her glass on an end table and stood, walking over to him. She placed a hand on his shoulder. "This does not bode well for you. How did you allow the project to exist without proper back-up?"

He snarled at his daughter. "We could have retrieved the information if your *indiscretion* hadn't cost me Walter Marx."

"I could not abide that man," she shivered in distaste. "I only accepted his ridiculous marriage proposal at your instance. It never would have lasted."

"It could have, if you were discrete about your affairs," Kepler countered.

Her face reddened. "That's a distasteful comment. I demand an apology."

He ran a hand threw his hair, "Fine, I apologize. This entire situation has me on edge."

"Clearly."

He whirled, grabbing her arms. "What do want me to say? This is a disaster. You may find this hard to believe, but I have blood in my veins instead of ice. I get to be upset, damn it. Any normal human being would be."

She patted his back. "Of course. Go ahead and nurse your wounds if it makes you feel better."

Jared moved to the bar to mix another drink. "We need to come up with a plan. There has to be a way to salvage this."

Angelica stared out at the magnificent skyline surrounding the water's edge. Her lips curled in a calculating smile. "Have your drink, Father, and get some rest. In fact, why don't you retire to your room? I'll call Ethan and Donavan St. James back in. Let me brainstorm with the two gentleman. We can run our ideas past you in the morning."

He looked at her and nodded, "Fine. Go speak with them and see what you can come up with. Let's all meet in my office at 9:00AM. We need to jump on this."

Her eyes glittered. Raising her wineglass to her lips, she turned her powerful gaze on the city outside the window. "Don't worry, Father, I'll jump right on it."

***

He paced the room like a caged animal, jaw set in an angry snarl. At least he didn't have to keep up the façade while alone . Dissatisfaction over the recent turn of events raged through him—he never could abide failure.

He shrugged off his suit jacket, throwing it across the room. His muscles strained against the starched fabric of his shirt. Rolling up the sleeves, he strode to the bar to fix himself another drink, catching sight of his reflection in the mirror. The image mocked him, worsening his mood.

Damn fools. Everything he'd worked for was in jeopardy. How the hell had this happened?

He downed his drink in a single swallow, flinging the empty glass at the mirror. A line of cracks immediately appeared, distorting his reflection. He ran his hand across his jaw, deciding the distortion was appropriate. He wore many faces and had become quite the chameleon in recent years. A necessary evil if he was going to achieve his goal.

He'd set the wheels in motion well over a year ago, when he engineered his first meeting with Angelica Kepler. He assumed he'd have his work cut out for him, convincing her to align herself with him and embrace his plan. He couldn't have been more wrong. In Angelica, he'd met a kindred spirit, one who shared his vision.

From that point on, they shared a clandestine relationship. The secrecy resulted in a heightened sexual tension between them; the forbidden aspect was titillating for both of them. He drew an added perverse pleasure from their union. Angelica had no idea he'd manipulated their affair, no reason to suspect he was pulling all the strings.

He was the Puppet Master.

Impatience ground away inside him. *Where the hell was she?* They needed to talk, in private, to rehash the day's events and reformulate their plans. He gnashed his teeth and checked his watch for the third time in as many minutes. He didn't like to be kept waiting.

He glanced around the chrome and leather living room, looking for something to break. His hand tightened around a heavy black vase. Just then, he heard a key turn in the lock. Still holding the vase, he turned to face her.

She smiled, clicking her tongue when she saw was he was about to do. Her hands moved over the shoulders of her dress. She advanced towards him, sliding the garment down her arms. Her breasts glowed in the soft evening light, calming some of his rage. He set down the vase, enjoying the way she pressed up against him.

He caught her chin in his hand, forcing her onto her toes. Her smiled deepened, his nostrils filled with her scent. She dampened her lips, straining against him, eager for his kiss. His left hand tightened on her shoulder, hard enough to make her cry out and then he pushed her away.

"What the hell went wrong with Foxtrot?" he growled. "We've worked too hard for this to come crashing down on us now."

Her eyes narrowed. She glared at him, placing her hands on her hips, and shrugging an elegant shoulder. "Then I suggest we get busy."

"Don't toy with me," he warned. "I'm not in the mood."

"But I am…" She dropped her dress to the floor and turned towards the bedroom. She cast a fleeting glance over her shoulder. It was her way of inviting him to follow.

He smiled at the sight of her retreating back. He had her right where he wanted her. After all, he was the Puppet Master, and for now, he would play her game.

Chapter Seventeen

Skinbone needed to clear his head. Things weighed on his mind and he did his best thinking near the water. Chicago wasn't the same city it was years back. He'd liked it fine before Navy Pier had turned into a tourist trap. There used to be a small beach nearby on Grand Avenue which no one much went to, especially past sunset. A man could sit there listening to the waves lap up on the shore and watch the dusk settle. He could lose himself there, back turned to the city, and forget about things for a while.

It wasn't like that anymore.

Skinbone had a boat docked in Belmont harbor, but he didn't want to fuss with it. Instead, he parked in an overpriced lot near the lake, jostled his way past a sea of humanity, and walked along the beach till his legs grew tired.

He wasn't any closer to figuring things out.

After ditching Corrine, he'd gone back inside Grace McGinley's house. This time, he looked for clues as to whether her relationship with Thornton had been intimate, or anything that might link Seri to Foxtrot. He came up empty handed, walking out of the rubble a far more troubled man then when he'd first arrived.

In the glint of the dying sun, he spotted shards of glass embedded in the sand. Keeping his eyes fixed on the water, he couldn't help thinking about the Foxtrot's predecessor, The First Wave. Another reminder of how things could go terribly wrong.

On which side did Seri weigh in?

He picked up a rock and tossed it towards the lake, watching it skip over the water and sighed. He couldn't ignore the fact Seri had been running from something.

Truth was, he'd taken a real liking to her. She'd been on his mind, digging herself deep under his skin. He'd been hoping to turn their meeting into something more somewhere down the line. *He wanted her to be innocent.* He needed to do his job.

There were ways to find answers. He wasn't ready to go down that road. Not yet. He'd try giving her another call or two, see if he could charm his way into making her open up. He was nearing the parking lot when his phone rang. Checking the caller ID, he shoved the phone back in his pocket. He'd call back when he was ready.

There was another reason he didn't want to take the call. His sixth sense told him it was news he didn't want to hear. He let it go to voicemail, and shut off his phone

***

Skinbone stopped off at Gibson's before heading back to his hotel. The steak and whiskey hadn't improved his mood. He let himself into the hotel room, not bothering with the lights. He dumped his key card, gun and phone on the nightstand and stretched out on the bed fully dressed.

He wanted to give her a chance to explain herself.

Skinbone thought of the way Seri reacted when he'd touched her. There was no denying the chemistry between them. He'd felt the jolt clear down to his toes. No woman ever had that kind of effect on him.

He pushed aside his romantic feelings. He had no business starting up something. His work was dangerous. He couldn't pursue her until he knew if he'd come out the other side dead or alive.

Proof might be staring him in the eyeballs that she was mixed up in this mess, but the facts weren't shaking out right for him. What had she been doing in Memphis, looking like her world had just been blown apart? And if she was involved, why double back to Chicago and put herself right back in the thick of things?

Ah, hell. He couldn't let himself get swayed by soft eyes and a sweet smile. A woman could be a dangerous weapon—especially one that knew how to play a man. He wouldn't be the first to be fooled by a pretty face and enticing form.

The idea of being played spurred him to action. Swinging his legs over the side of the bed, he checked his voice mail. St. James wouldn't return to the hotel for another hour or so. That should give him enough time to squeeze in a workout. He was hoping it might help clear out the sludge in his brain.

He changed into gym shorts and a T-shirt before raiding the bathroom for a towel. He thought he'd passed a hot tub downstairs too. After a day like today, that might be a good place to unwind.

The night suddenly sparkled with promise. All he needed was a workout, a good steam in the sauna, time in the hot tub, and a stiff drink. Hell by morning, he'd be his old self again.

Draping the towel around his neck, he crammed the trunks into his pocket and headed towards the elevator.

***

Angelica arched her back and examined her fingernails. She had a bit of his skin underneath them. It pleased her to know he would bear her mark for the next day or two. Sighing languidly, she narrowed her eyes as she watched him pull on his pants. "Are you sure you have to go?"

"You know I have work to do. Besides, I have to keep up the charade. We also can't risk your father finding me here. It would *not* work to our advantage if he knew I was the one who screwed up your relationship with Shark. That wouldn't suit our plans, now would it?"

She shuddered delicately, pulling the sheet up around her breasts. "My father was a fool to think I would marry that outcast. He was an embarrassment."

He stopped short of zipping up his trousers, and arched a brow. "Did you use me?"

"Whatever do you mean, Sweetheart?"

His voice held a hint of coldness. "Do I need to spell it out for you? Did you use me to get rid of your fiancée? Was it part of your plan for him to catch us in bed?"

She reached out and opened her nightstand drawer, pulling out a cigarette case. She took her time lighting one, exhaling a stream of smoke towards the ceiling. "You make it sound so tawdry. Walter had a key. He and came and went as he pleased. He could have stayed with me if he wanted to, although I suppose it would be cold comfort to share my fortune and not my bed."

"The man's stuff is still here, Angelica. You could have told me he lived with you. He could have ruined our plans."

She sat up in bed, glaring at him through the darkness. "What is wrong with you? I thought we both want the same thing."

"We do." he grabbed his shirt off a chair.

"Then what is your problem? We share a common goal. You share my bed and you stand to gain a great deal more. Do you really think it's wise to cross me?"

"I'm not crossing you, darling. I have no interest in being played for a fool."

"Stay useful to me and you won't."

"Marx was useful." He countered, running a hand through his carefully styled hair.

"He was useful to my father, not to me." She stubbed out her cigarette. "I need a real man."

He stared into her eyes for just short of a second before yanking the sheet down and grabbing hold of her breast. "You mean like this?" He squeezed her hard, twisting a nipple between his fingers. Her eyes rolled backwards. She fell back against the pillows, gasping in ecstasy. He straddled her, taking hold of her with both hands. "A man who will treat you like the slut you are?"

Her arms wound around his neck. "Show me what a bad man you are."

He ripped away the remaining sheet clinging to her body. "This is no game, Angelica. I give you what you want, you give me what I want." His hands moved roughly over her body. "Do you understand me?"

"Yes. Yes, fine. Please."

"Please what?" He grabbed her wrists and pulled her arms above her head. He gave her a rough kiss. "Are we a team? Are we in this together?"

She couldn't bear the pressure cooking inside her. "Yes, we're a team."

He ran his hand down the small of her back. There was a dangerous light in his eyes. "Don't even consider crossing me."

"No, never."

"You know what I'll do to you if you try."

A slight trickle of fear ran down her body. She quickly dismissed it, succumbing to her darker urges. "*This* is what I need. You're what I need. As long as we have this…"

He grabbed her by the hair, tilting back her head. "Don't ever forget that."

"Never," she whimpered.

Satisfied, he lowered his body onto hers.

Chapter Eighteen

Sierra hated to admit it but Shark was right. As ridiculous as it seemed, a massage was exactly what she needed. She had scoffed at the idea when Shark first suggested it, but had been convinced when he said he could work on the computers faster without her pacing the room, looking over his shoulder. Her muscles had been balled into tension knots for days.

The masseuse tsked in dismay at how tight she was and talked her into their deluxe package. Lulled by the hands kneading her pain away, she agreed. It would be a relief to move without hearing every part of her body creak in protest. In the space of a few days, she'd forgotten what it felt like to feel normal.

Every time his fingers moved to a fresh spot on her body, Sierra bit her lip to keep from whimpering aloud. She sucked up the pain, thinking maybe once she felt better; her situation wouldn't feel so dire.

"You need to relax, Mon Cherie," the masseuse admonished, "I feel you tensing up again."

"Sorry," she murmured. She wondered if Neil and Grace had kept her out of the loop to protect her. They would want her to be okay. A single tear slid down her cheek. It was the least she could do for them. Closing her eyes, she forced herself to relax.

The hour sped by much too quickly. She wasn't certain, but she might have dozed off.

"I leave you now so you can get changed. Bathing suit for the hot tub, *oui*?"

Sierra didn't want to move. She was as limp as a newborn kitten. Wrapping a towel around herself, she sat up, blinking the sleep from her eyes. "No, no hot tub. I don't have a bathing suit with me."

"We have in the gift shop." He glanced at a clock. "It is still open. You should go. Hurry, they will be closing soon."

Sierra smiled politely. One indulgence today was enough. It was impossible for her to wrap her mind around a second. Not when Shark was upstairs toiling over the computers, and she was desperate for answers. Reaching for her clothes, she started getting dressed. Her smile deepened when she thought of what a Godsend Shark was. His quirky witticisms already hit home several times, saving her from going off the deep end or plowing headfirst into making a mistake. Meeting him in the coffee shop truly had been fortuitous.

She passed by the hot tub without a second glance. Noticing the gift shop up ahead, she wandered in that direction. Standing outside, she peered in through the window, debating whether to pop in. It might be nice to pick up something for Shark—nothing big, just a book or a magazine, or maybe even a box of candy. She wanted to do something nice for him. Even though he strong-armed her into getting the massage, it turned out to be a good idea after all.

She frowned, realizing she didn't have a clue what he liked. *Okay, maybe a book wouldn't be a good idea,* she decided, *but everybody liked chocolate, didn't they? Or fudge. Gift shops were notorious for selling fudge.*

Sierra lingered outside the shop, pondering whether to get fudge with or without nuts, when the hair on the back of arms stood up. A nervous tingle slithered down her spine. She tensed, aware of the unmistakable sensation of being watched.

Pretending to check her pocket for money, she counted to ten. When nothing happened, she told herself she was being ridiculous. The trail she'd left ended in Greenwood, Mississippi. No one would be looking for her here. *Stop being paranoid. Nothing to worry about.*

If people are watching me, it's because I'm loitering, she decided, ignoring the goose bumps rising up on her arms. Resisting an almost overpowering urge to run towards the elevators, she took a step towards the shop entrance.

It happened fast. A pair of arms slammed against the store window on either side of her, boxing her in. Her stomach did a series of somersaults.

They found me.

A sense of finality settled over her, even as she realized, she had no idea who *they* were.

She stood still, terrified to move. She had no idea if the person behind her was waiting to kill her or arrest her. Her eyes flew to the right, followed by a quick glance to the left. The arms surrounding her rested right above her shoulders. If she ducked down fast enough, catching whoever was behind her off guard, she had a chance of making a decent run for it.

It was worth a shot.

Taking a deep breath, she ducked. She wasn't quick enough. The arms tightened around her shoulders. Warm breath tickled the back of her neck.

"You're a hard lady to get a hold of and, apparently, almost as hard to hold on *to.*"

Good Lord. She knew that voice. Her legs went weak. She recognized his touch from the thousand little electric shocks racing up and down her body. Taking a deep breath, she struggled to pull herself together. Sierra didn't want him to know how much he'd frightened her.

Blowing out a long stream of air, she forced herself to relax. No easy feat, considering the way her heart was hammering away inside her chest. This time, it wasn't due to fear; it was her reaction to him. Placing a hand on his arm, she turned to face him, a bright smile plastered on her face.

"Skinbone Harris." She was surprised she managed to squeak out his name in a relatively calm manner.

"The one and only," he grinned and dipped down in a shallow bow.

For a crazy instant, seeing him again felt like finding a familiar face in a den of insanity. His black eyes at close range appeared to have silver flecks. She forgot herself for a moment, wondering if the unusual coloring was the reason they twinkled. Then she remembered how careful she had to be.

His smiled broadened. "Have I rendered you speechless?"

"No, more like scared me shitless. Why did you sneak up on me like that?"

"It was either that or risk you running away from me again. Most women usually run *towards* me. You're approach to flirtation is rather unique."

"You're the one who vanished into thin air." She regretted the words the minute they left her mouth.

He raised an eyebrow. "You came back to look for me?"

She felt a flush creep up her cheeks. "I didn't say that."

"You didn't have to." His voice lowered to a seductive drawl. "It's enough that I know you did. Although I would like to know why."

"I don't remember."

His eyes bore down on her. "I don't believe you."

"Okay. I went back to give you a piece of my mind. There, are you satisfied?"

"Been a while since I've been satisfied, but thanks for asking."

"Oh, that's…you're…" She glared at him, trying to think of an appropriate comeback.

"That's twice now I've left you speechless, but who's counting?"

He had a way of getting under her skin. No witty reply sprang to her lips, leaving an awkward silence hanging between them. Now that the initial shock of seeing him was wearing off, suspicion crawled back. Her eyes narrowed. "What are you doing here?"

His smile faded. Warning bells went off, flooding her with adrenaline. She remembered he didn't know she was from Chicago. She had to play it cool; act like this was a wild coincidence. Better yet, let him think she was happy to see him.

"I told you I'd show up when you needed me, *Seri.*" His expression turned serious.

His playful demeanor changed, giving her a distinct chill. *Was it her imagination or did he emphasize the nickname she'd given him a little too much?* "What makes you think I need you?"

He reached out, brushing a lock of hair away from her face, skimming her cheek with his hand. He leaned closer. "I can feel it. Why do you think I've been calling you?"

An older couple walked by, staring at them. The woman glared her disapproval, making Sierra uncomfortable. It was clear she thought they were sharing a very public, intimate moment. She swallowed, struggling to deflect the intensity between them. In an attempt to lighten things up, she smiled and joked, "Mmm…yes. That mysterious connection you mentioned last time we met."

He didn't take the bait. Instead, his eyes searched her face, looking for confirmation. "I *know* you felt it too."

She could feel the heat radiating from his body. *He was standing too damn close.* She shrugged a shoulder, looking up at him innocently. "I'm not sure. Is it anything like that jittery feeling you get when a known *assassin* sneaks up behind you?"

He looked startled for a moment, then threw his head back and laughed. "There you go, messin' with my mojo again. You're not a very good sidekick for Batman. In fact, you're brutal for my ego."

Her lips twitched. She didn't want to laugh. The truth was his being here scared the living hell out of her. The giggle erupted from her in spite of her fear.

Skinbone grinned along with her. She glanced down, noticing for the first time he was dressed in shorts and a T-shirt. When she looked back up at him, she caught a flicker in his eyes. *She'd swear he was looking at her with a modicum of apprehension. Why? What changed since the last time they met?*

He covered quickly, giving her new reason to worry. Now she *knew* she wasn't imagining it. "Ah, that's better. I like seeing you laugh. I also like the new hairdo. Suits you much better than a baseball cap and a ponytail."

"You have a new look too. I don't know why, but I wouldn't have pegged you for a shorts and a T-Shirt kind of guy."

"Ah, well, that's where you're wrong. These aren't shorts. These are swim trunks."

"Oh. Well. That makes all the difference," She fixed her eyes on his trunks, biting back a smile. "You wear those in public often then?"

"How did I miss the fact that you're a smartass last time?"

"Guess you weren't looking hard enough." *What was wrong with her? Flirtatious words spilled out of her mouth whenever she was around him.*

"I was looking plenty hard. I recall enjoying the view while I tried to figure you out."

She wasn't going to take the bait. Sierra shook her head, pressing her lips together in a frown. "Not all that much to figure out, I'm afraid. I'm a simple girl with all the predictable problems."

There it was again. A glint of mistrust buried deep in his eyes. *Shit.* Something had definitely changed since Memphis. He'd made her skittish last time with some of the crazy things he said, but he'd been totally at ease. Tonight, they were circling each other like boxers, dancing to the tune of inane dialogue, waiting for the first punch to be thrown. The last thing she needed was more trouble. She needed to find a way to escape. The glass elevators were exposed, providing guests with a view of the entire hotel; the rooms surrounded a courtyard. All you had to do was look directly up in order to see people entering or leaving their rooms. Her stomach plummeted. *There had to be away for her to beat a hasty retreat. It was only a matter of finding it.*

"Which is why I think we should go to Vegas. Unless you prefer Monte Carlo."

Damn, she hadn't been listening. "What did you say?"

He cleared his throat. "I was saying, I suspect there isn't a damn thing simple or predictable about you. Not that you were paying attention. For a minute there, it looked like you were a million miles away."

"You caught me." *Was that disappointment she saw flit across his face? Don't read too much into his every expression,* she warned herself. *Stay on your toes. Play the game*. She looked up at him, letting her teeth tug on her lower lip. "I was thinking what a strange coincidence it is that we've met twice now, far away from home. *My* home at least. I don't know where you're from?"

Skinbone released his hold on her shoulder, staring at her. "Means something, don't you think?"

"I don't know. I'm not in a position to start anything with you, which I think you're angling for."

"And why's that?"

"Like I said, I'm a simple girl with predictable problems." She held up her left hand. "See this ring?"

It was clear he hadn't noticed it before. His face tightened.

"This ring should mean something, right? It's a promise. To love me and to marry me."

His body shifted away from hers. "You're telling me you're spoken for?"

The tears came easy and she hated herself for it, but she had a hell of a lot of pent up emotion inside her. "The ring is a joke, yet I can't make myself take it off. Turns out my *fiancée* is a two-timing bastard. I left a man who loved me more than life itself to be with him. Only to find out, *months before our wedding,* that he's cheating on me. And I'm still wearing the damn ring."

Her body shook with tears. Real ones. She raised watery eyes to his. "So yes, okay. You're an attractive man and I feel the chemistry between us. But it means nothing to me because my heart's been broken and I'm still raw. *That's* why I've been avoiding your phone calls. The last thing I need right now is another man in my life. I'm throwing myself into my work and traveling all over the country to run away from the hurt."

He believed her. His expression changed, flashing from pained to sympathetic. She didn't feel guilty, because it wasn't a lie. Her heart was broken. For all she knew, Neil had cheated on her, though it was looking less and less likely. Either way, he was gone.

Skinbone's eyes bore down on her. He was wrestling with something. She wished she could read his mind. She had every reason to be wary of him, but why was he wary of *her?*

He gathered her into his arms, patting her back, taking her by surprise. "We got us a confusing situation here. It seems to me we need to get to know each other better some."

"I think it's best if I just go."

"The only place you are going is into this gift shop here. We're gonna buy you a bathing suit and you're going to join me in the hot tub."

***

Skinbone Harris got one thing right; they did have themselves a confusing situation on their hands. The man had a disturbing effect on her. A few minutes alone with him and she felt like a ping-pong ball, bouncing back and forth in an emotional game of one up-men-ship. There was no doubt in her mind he was hiding something, the same way she was.

Secrets had a way of getting people killed.

Besides, she'd come too far to get tangled up in something that would lead nowhere. She couldn't take the chance he was working for the enemy. It was in her best interest to put as much distance between them as possible. No matter how convincing his words, his eyes betrayed him. He'd come looking for her, she felt it in every fiber of her being.

Like he'd said in Memphis, there was no such thing as coincidences.

She was starting to believe him.

"We should go in." He gestured towards the shop. "Looks like they're getting ready to close."

Skinbone held out a hand to her. She reached out to take it, nervous energy dancing inside her. Before they reached the entrance, she swayed. Sierra grabbed onto his t-shirt to steady herself. Her fingers slipped off the soft cotton, her cheek brushing against his chest.

He slipped his arm around her. Concern flashed across his face. "You okay?"

"Yeah. I think so. I got a little dizzy"

"Why are you holding your stomach?"

She glanced down at her hand. "I don't know."

He studied her face a good long while. "Don't take this wrong, but you don't look so good."

"No, really, I'm fine."

"Don't lie to me. You aren't very good at it."

If he only knew, she thought. Taking a shaky breath, she rested her head against his shoulder, breathing in his clean scent. "Okay. I'm lightheaded and I'm queasy. It's a hundred degrees outside and my life is pretty much a mess right now. I haven't been taking care of myself. I'm probably dehydrated."

"I'm taking you back to your room."

"No." She fought to keep the panic out of her voice. *That wasn't part of her plan.*

"Good God, woman, I'm not going to take advantage of you when you're sick, if that's what you're worried about. Trust me; I don't need to stoop that low."

She waved a hand, "I'm okay."

"No, you are not okay. I'm putting you to bed."

His words brought on a fresh onslaught of images she forced herself to ignore. "I have a better idea," she said.

"I doubt it, but go ahead. Say your piece."

"Let's find a bathroom so I can splash cold water on my face. Then we can go to the bar and have a drink."

"The last thing you need is a drink."

"If I'm dehydrated, I absolutely need to drink. Coke, lemonade, iced tea, whatever they have."

Skinbone eased back a bit and studied her face. He had one arm looped around her shoulder; his other hand buried in his pocket. The sharp angles of his face gave him an aura of mystery and his black eyes were impossible to read. She had the eerie sensation he was looking right through her, trying to decide if she had something up her sleeve. Luke sprang to mind. She remembered the way he'd listened to music on the train so no one would be able to track him. It seemed silly at the time, now she wasn't so sure. Skinbone Harris had the look of someone itching to read her mind. Sierra cleared her thoughts of everything except the fear of fainting and a sense of betrayal. She let those run rampant, slumping beneath his arm. Standing straight was too much effort. The heat was getting to her, in more ways than one.

She had no idea if she diverted his suspicion or if she was giving into raving paranoia, but the shift in his expression was immediate, lightening the mood. He grinned at her and winked. "I think I like your plan. I suspect if I took you upstairs, you wouldn't let me in your room."

"You suspect correctly. I'm fading fast though. Can we please find a bathroom? I don't want to faint on you. You might get a complex."

"I'm used to women fainting at my feet," he teased.

Sierra cringed at his joke and punched him in the arm, "You're lucky I'm too weak to do any real damage."

"Are you kidding? I'm crushed."

"Crushed?"

"That you don't believe me."

"Sure you are." She patted his arm. "If it's not too much to ask, can we focus on me for a while? Before I keel over? We can get back to your ego later and how it needs to be taken down a peg."

He chuckled. "I think I can manage to guide you safely to the restroom. After which, I'm assuming, you will spend the next hour or so extolling my many virtues, and expressing your eternal gratitude."

It felt good to have Skinbone back in good spirits without any hint of suspicion lurking in his eyes. "I'm sure I'll just be beside myself," she laughed.

"Figured you might be." They reached the ladies room. "Take as much time as you need. I'll be right out here, waiting for those compliments to start rolling off your tongue."

Her smile faded as soon as she pushed the bathroom door open, relieved he'd bought her act. Running into him plunged her into a state of panic. *The odds of Skinbone Harris turning up in the same hotel was too much of a coincidence. What the hell was he doing here?*

It didn't take a rocket scientist to answer that question, she admitted to herself. He was hunting someone. The glint of distrust in his eyes was terrifying. *What if he was hunting her?*

No matter how impossible it seemed her instincts screamed he was mixed up in the same mess she was. Grabbing her cell phone out of her pocket, she hurried to the last stall and dialed her room, praying Shark would answer. The call went straight to voice mail.

Sierra left a detailed voice mail, telling him what she needed him to do. Knowing she didn't have much time, she headed to the sink, splashed cold water on her face and neck. Taking a chance, she decided to call back a second time. Shark picked up on the third ring, panting and out of breath.

"Damsel, I've been frantic. I was out looking for you."

"I can't talk," she whispered. "Please listen to the voicemail I left you. Gotta go." For good measure, she dampened her face again, staring at herself in the mirror. Swallowing her anxiety, she forced herself to smile and tried to think of something pleasant before going back out to meet him.

It would be suicide to let him see the fear in her eyes.

***

Calling Shark gave her confidence the boost she needed. Now that she'd put her plan in motion, she was looking forward to having a drink with Skinbone. An idea occurred to her while she was in the bathroom—there was a certain amount of risk involved, but at least she would know if she had reason to worry.

Skinbone leaned against the wall opposite the ladies room, waiting for her. He'd taken advantage of her absence to make a call of his own. Her heart plummeted. Was there another woman waiting in the wings or was he calling for back-up?

He snapped shut the phone and shoved it in his pocket. "You look a whole lot better. Let's go find a table."

She arched a brow, unable to keep the jealousy her voice. "Cancelling a date or making one?"

His eyes twinkled, "I wasn't aware we'd reached the point of full disclosure in our relationship."

"We don't have a relationship."

"Then it shouldn't bother you whether I was making a date or not, now should it?"

"It doesn't." She shrugged. "I was only asking because I don't want to hold you up if you have something better to do."

"So you were just being considerate."

"Now you're catching on."

"And your cool tone, that has nothing to do with the fact you think I was talking to another woman?"

He was exasperating. He was also right. She had no business delving into his personal life. "Were you not listening to me earlier? I just had one man cheat on me. I'm not about to get involved with another."

Skinbone surprised her. "You're right. I'm sorry. It's hard to look at you and imagine any man would be fool enough to leave you. If you want the truth, I was talking to a colleague and I was wrong to yank your chain the way I did. It made me feel good to think you had a soft spot for me. I admit I was pressing the subject to get a rise out of you."

His admission was a hell of a lot more than she'd expected. "I admit I didn't like the idea of you planning a date while waiting for me. It brought back memories. Made me wonder how many times my fiancée called his girlfriend when I was in the bathroom or getting popcorn at a movie."

"Not all men are like your ex-boyfriend."

She couldn't keep the emotion out of her voice. "Maybe not. I think what worries me most was I didn't know he was keeping secrets from me. How could I not have known?"

"Don't put this on yourself. You should be able to trust the people you love. He was the one who violated that trust, not you. A man gives you a ring; you should be able to count on him."

She nodded, tilting her head up to look at him. "Keep this up, Skinbone, and I might develop a soft spot for you."

"Now *that* would be a dangerous thing to do."

His eyes threw off heat. Sierra had the strangest urge to lean over and smooth out the lines etched across his face. She guessed he was in his early forties, a hard living man who'd spent a lot of time in the sun, taking any risk life threw at him. She was on the verge of asking why it would be dangerous when they were interrupted. The waitress chose that moment to come by and take their order. Whiskey neat for him, an iced tea for her.

"Sure is crowded," he noted, changing the subject. "We got the last free table."

"Hotel bars are usually crowed. I'm guessing most of these people are here on business. What else is there to do?"

"A lonely life."

He'd opened a door, one she had every intention of walking through. "You speaking from experience?" she asked.

He leaned back in his chair, crossing his arms. She noticed he scanned the crowd and the lobby every few seconds, "Yeah. Hard to build something when you're not home enough to maintain it. Guess that's partially why I'm a lone wolf."

"Have you always been alone?"

"Never met a woman who could hold my interest."

His eyes spoke volumes. She had the distinct feeling of being swallowed up by their pitch black depths. Shaking off the implication, she cleared her throat. "You bore that easily?"

The drinks arrived. He took a sip, and shrugged. "The women I meet? They're after one of two things. An adrenaline rush or my bank account."

She warned herself to stay detached. Unfortunately, curiosity won out. "That's sad. Don't you meet any normal women?"

He downed more than half of his drink, cocking an eyebrow. "Is there such a thing?"

"Of course there is. I'm normal."

He choked on the whiskey. "You are the least normal woman I've ever met."

"Are you kidding me?" She waved down the waitress. "Number one, I've had enough adrenaline rushes recently to last me a lifetime. Number two, I inherited more than enough money to last me a couple lifetimes."

"Somehow that doesn't make you normal. Granted, you are not in the same league with the women I've dated. You, lady, are in a class of your own."

The waitress approached. Sierra ordered another drink for Skinbone and a dry vodka martini for herself.

"Whoa, there. Should you be drinking?"

"I'm feeling much better."

"Bring another iced tea too, please," Skinbone instructed the waitress. Once she left, he gave her a pointed look. "If you're dehydrated, alcohol is a bad idea."

"I need it. You're making me nervous."

"Me? What did I do?"

Sierra glanced down at her ring, reminding herself she was saying too much. She needed to steer the conversation to a lighter topic. "If the first time we met was fortuitous, what does that make this?"

"Now there's a damn good question. I'd have to call it fate."

A slow burn worked its way up her body. "If you don't believe in coincidences, how can you believe in fate?"

"Two entirely different things."

The waitress delivered their drinks. Sierra took a long swallow of her martini. "How so?"

"Fate is something that pulls you in a direction, whether you want to go there or not. It just is, something that was meant to be."

She speared an olive and popped it into her mouth. "Why are you in Chicago?"

"Business. You're avoiding what I said."

"Because I can't imagine why fate would bring us together at such an inopportune time."

"See, now, that's because you're putting your own spin on fate."

"What do you mean?"

"At the risk of getting slapped, I'm guessing you're thinking of fate in a romantic context."

She wanted to die of embarrassment. *Where the hell was Shark?* Her cheeks flushed. She'd walked right into that one. "Okay, so I'm a romantic at heart. When I think of fate, yes, that's exactly what I think."

He reached out and gathered her hands in his. "I never said you were wrong. Fate has all kinds of possibilities."

She eased her hands out of his grasp and took another drink. *No topic was safe with this man.* "Don't you believe in choices?"

"Sure I do." His eyes creased at the corners. "We don't always make the right ones. I think fate sometimes jumps in to lend us a hand, steering us in the right direction when we veer too far off our intended path."

"You really are always this deep, aren't you?"

He threw back his head and laughed. "I do remember you saying something of the sort the first time we met."

Sierra brought her glass up to her lips, watching him. She liked the way he laughed. He didn't hold back. There was a passion to everything he did. He was a deep thinker with a dangerous edge, a man who made his own rules. She'd never met anyone quite like him before. He fascinated her and scared the hell out of her.

She smiled along with him, wishing she could feel at ease. It would be nice to enjoy his company; under the circumstances, she couldn't relax. The gritty truth was she didn't know if he was more likely to romance her or kill her. Her eyes drifted to the elevator. Shark got off and was wheeling a cart through the lobby. Her stomach tightened. She'd know soon enough.

It was time to turn on the charm. Sierra ripped her eyes away from the lobby and treated Skinbone to what she hoped was a seductive smile. "Why do you think fate brought us together tonight?"

"Damned if I know, but I'd like to take my time and find out. There's a reason for it, I'd stake my life on it."

"You intrigue me," she said boldly, letting her gaze linger on his.

"Careful now." He picked up her martini glass and set it down in front of him. "You're sending out some mixed signals. Never play with fire unless you're willing to get burned."

His words sickened her. She didn't have to fake the nausea or the stomach cramps. Grabbing her midsection, she leapt up from the chair. "I think I'm going to be sick."

He jumped up, blocking her way. "I'll come with you."

She shook her head, trying to get past him. He moved along with her, like they were dancing, "Stay, please, so we don't lose the table."

He looked around. The crowd at the bar was three deep. "Okay."

Sierra stepped forward, he took one step back. She eased to the right, he did too. "Jesus, Skinbone, I need to get to the bathroom, not dance the Foxtrot."

There it was. His eyes zeroed in on her. He grabbed her arm hard enough to leave a bruise. "What did you say?"

Fear rushed her. *Oh God, she'd prayed paranoia had gotten the best of her and she was imagining Skinbone's involvement. She didn't want him to be the enemy, but there was no mistaking the hard line of his face and the steely look in his eyes. His hand was a vise on her arm, digging into her bare skin. How was she going to get away?*

Shark came through. She didn't know how he managed to pull it off, but thank God he did. A man carrying four drinks collided with Skinbone, dumping the contents down his front. In the ensuing commotion, she whispered, "I'm gonna be sick," and dashed towards the bathrooms.

Out of the corner of her eye, she caught a glimpse of someone walking into the hotel. Blinking in disbelief, she didn't stop for a second look. Her feet pumped on autopilot, sprinting past the bathroom and out the emergency exit.

A car idled outside the door. She grabbed the handle and hopped in.

He sped away before she could slam the car door closed.

CHAPTER NINETEEN

Sierra fell into the car seat, gasping like she'd run a marathon. Her nerves were going haywire. She rubbed her arms, trying to recover from the shock.

The Shark peeled rubber out of the hotel lot. "Where to?"

Was anyplace safe? She shook her head. "I have no idea." Her heart was still racing. Covering her chest with shaking hands, she tried to calm herself. Again.

Skinbone knew.

Fate, fortuitousness, chance encounters, all the seductive lies that came out of his mouth were bullshit. Her instincts were spot on. He was connected to Foxtrot.

Skinbone Harris was the enemy.

She'd almost been stupid enough to believe the attraction between them was real. Not that she wanted to pursue it, but that hardly mattered. The horrible truth was he was here to kill her. What kind of arrogant, cold blooded bastards were they dealing with?

Her stomach curdled. He'd touched her, laughed with her. She would have bet her life there was an honest connection between them. Exactly what he wanted her to think and feel.

Damn him. Damn everything.

"Pull over," she yelled.

The Shark looked confused, "Pull over? Are you sure?"

"Yes. Hurry." She swung open the car door, needing fresh air. Death didn't agree with her, neither did being treated like a fool. She thought of the other shock she'd received that evening. While she was running towards the exit, a familiar face entered the hotel lobby.

Donovan St. James.

She wanted to sink to the ground and wake up from this nightmare. Her circumstances were so far flung they were unimaginable. The universe had to be playing a wicked, cruel joke on her.

She needed to take a good hard look at her situation and take another stab at piecing things together. There had to be something she was missing. An assassin and the FBI were both after her. What was her crime? The only thing she was guilty of was spending a quiet Friday night with her fiancée. Her head was swimming. Sierra grabbed the car door for support and eased her way back inside. Things were starting to click in her brain. Shark came around to her side of the car to check on her. She held up a finger, tapping her forehead.

A quiet Friday night.

She never saw Neil on Friday.

He hadn't been himself for weeks. She'd been afraid he was getting cold feet. Desperate for answers and wanting to fix whatever was broken, she'd made an impromptu decision to stop by his house and seduce him. He hadn't been thrilled, but since he wasn't willing to tell her what was wrong, she put him in a position where he couldn't refuse her.

The night he was murdered, Neil was supposed to be alone. She wasn't supposed to be there.

Neil and Grace were keeping secrets from her, secrets big enough to get them killed. She was connected to both of them.

It wasn't personal. The killer wasn't afraid she could identify him—he was afraid of what she knew.

He was after her for information.

Skinbone Harris wasn't in Chicago looking for her. He was here to recover whatever project Grace and Neil had been working on. She'd beat him to the punch. She frowned, finding a flaw with her logic. If Skinbone was working with the killer, why would he have shown up in Chicago *after* her? Shouldn't he have gotten here first?

And why hadn't the killer taken what he needed to begin with?

Because, Grace's house should have been destroyed, and any "secrets" she had should have been destroyed along with it. He couldn't get what he needed from Neil because she'd grabbed his laptop, and the netbook had been hidden in Neil's car.

Whatever information she had was incriminating enough to kill for.

That didn't explain why Donovan was here. If he'd come looking for her, or learned about Grace and Neil's deaths, he would have stayed downtown. Why commute back and forth from O'Hare wasting precious time in Chicago's never ending rush hour?

Shark's voice pulled her back to reality. "We are wasting precious time if we need to escape. Perhaps if you fill me in on whatever has you so upset, I can be of some assistance."

She looked at Shark through blurry eyes. The entire night took on a surreal quality. Thunder rumbled directly overhead. He was standing under a street light which turned his skin a ghastly shade of pale. His worried brown eyes appeared far too huge for his face. The unregistered car's doors stood open on the deserted street, motor humming.

Her only hope out of this mess depended on an illegal vehicle and a kid named Shark.

God help her.

***

She knew about Foxtrot. Damn her. She taunted him with her knowledge right before she ran. Did she have a death wish?

The punk who'd dumped the drink on him stumbled forward, grabbing onto his shoulders, "Hey, man, I'm sorry."

Skinbone peeled the kid's hands away, shoving him aside. The guy fell headfirst into a near-by table. Chaos ensued. A couple of beefy sales types leapt up from their chairs, intent in taking him on. He fixed his eyes on them, stopping them dead in their tracks, and hopped the railing sectioning the bar off from the lobby.

She'd set him up. Her performance was worthy of an academy award. He might have had his misgivings about her, but he'd never, for one moment, doubted she was sick. The minute he rounded the corner towards the bathrooms, he understood. He'd caught her off guard showing up at the hotel. She was looking for a way out and she'd found one. The emergency exit was a stone's throw away from the ladies room.

He didn't bother to check the bathroom; he knew she wouldn't be there. He hit the exit door with both hands and flew out into the night. Rain pelted him from every angle. There was no sign of her. He ran towards the front of the hotel before the door had a chance to slam behind him.

Two valets dressed in rain gear huddled together near the doorway. Skinbone jogged towards them. "Did a woman just leave here?"

They shook their heads.

"Did you see anybody drive off? Anybody ask for their car in the last ten minutes?"

The older of the two, a pimply faced kid of about twenty, stepped forward. "No one's left in the last half hour. We've only had people coming in."

"How about the garage? Did you see anyone leave from there?"

The two kids exchanged a look. "We had our backs to the garage. We were watching for cars coming in, trying to stay out of the rain."

Skinbone worked his jaw, staring down the road. Nobody was out walking in the downpour. "How about anyone running? Did you notice anyone on foot?"

"Sorry. Haven't seen that either."

The area was well lit. Skinbone dashed around the outside of the hotel, on the lookout for hiding places. He came up empty. She'd vanished into thin air. Considering she had, at best, a three minute head start, her disappearance was nothing short of miraculous—unless, she darted out and ran back in through the front. "One more question. Did a woman on foot enter the hotel?"

"You mean, like, without dropping her car off?"

"Yeah."

"Not real sure. We just pay attention to cars, you know?"

Skinbone grit his teeth. She could be long gone or upstairs in the comfort her room, congratulating herself on pulling a fast one. His right eye twitched; that only happened when someone got the best of him.

She was a hell of a lot sharper than he'd given her credit for. First she'd turned up in Memphis, and now she was here, smack dab in the thick of things. The question was, was she a killer? Had she murdered McGinley and Thornton and come back to clean up her mess? Was it possible she had manipulated her way into both of their lives to gain access to Foxtrot?

Anger boiled in his veins. Not one damned thing was going according to plan. He stormed through the hotel entrance, kicking himself in the ass for taking the job. In all his years, he'd never seen such a nightmare of a mess.

The job should have been simple. Kepler had a reputation for selling government secrets to the highest bidder. Word of the project leaked out, a pretty clear indication they were open to offers. Whoever got their hands on Foxtrot could disable an entire government without anyone being the wiser.

Skinbone's mission was clear-cut. Outbid any interested parties and bring down Kepler. Now someone was one-step ahead of them, causing a major ripple in the plan.

He slammed his fist into the wall. Disappointment settled over him, making him feel older than his years. Ten minutes ago, he would have sworn the only thing Seri was guilty of was having bad judgment in men. There was a spark between them; a connection he'd decided had possibilities of running deep.

He'd finally met his match all right—a woman who could outsmart him. It was too bad they were playing a dangerous game.

The way things stood, he was might have to kill a woman he was already more than half in love with.

How the hell was a man supposed to live with that?

***

Sitting idle didn't set well with Luke. He wanted to be in the field instead of laying low. It pissed him off that his hands were tied, but setting foot in Chicago could blow the whole mission apart. His face was too recognizable.

Hell, *retirement* was going to be the death of him, cover or not. He itched to be at the epicenter of the action. He was a ground zero kind of guy and sitting on the sidelines irked him. It wasn't his forte. He might be a bit older and a bit greyer, but hell, his mind was sharper than most men's half his age. The incident on the train proved his reflexes were as good as ever. If anything, longevity had given him greater skills.

It had also given him a what-the-hell attitude. *Really, what did he have to lose? What mattered most to him was already gone.*

That, he knew, was the root of his frustration. He had the means, the connections, and the money to hire the best to search for his son. Another day, another empty inbox. His wife had done a damn good job of hiding. Luke had no idea if either one of them was dead or alive.

He'd probably go his grave not knowing.

No excuse to be reckless. There was a fine line between taking risks and putting someone else in danger. When he'd learned about Foxtrot, he'd assembled his own team. Luke figured he didn't need much help. Two men, one of them was like a son to him. Hell, except for the age difference, the man could have been his son, they looked enough alike. He smiled, thinking what an unlikely pair they were, but hell, they shared a bond.

Luke always recognized other men who had *"the gift."*

He thought about how naïve they all were back in the day. They were crazy times, back before the end of the cold war, when China was making a lot of noise. The FBI set up a special task force with Luke at the helm.

New recruits underwent extensive testing. If it was determined any of them possessed so much as a hint of psychic ability, they were assigned to the force.

It didn't amount to a hill of beans. Only a rare few actually possessed any real abilities. What most people, including the government, didn't fully understand was there were varying degrees of psychic ability. And qualifying factors. A man might be capable of telekinesis, but that didn't mean he had the gift of precognition. True psychic power was rare, and it sure as hell wasn't one size fit all. In the end, the majority of agents moved on soon after being recruited. They didn't want any part of a Psychic Squad, fearing it would hurt their long term careers.

Inadequate as it was, the task force existed to this day and not much had changed since its inception. The force normally contained only one or two *"good men."*

Luke always chose the good ones. He kept hoping one of them would have the power to help him find his son. Knowing he was treading dangerous waters, he pushed his chair away from his desk and decided to get some fresh air.

The evening was hot and still, the sun on the tail end of another spectacular orange and purple display. How many sunsets had he missed, locked away in his office looking for clues that didn't exist? There were long spells where he could get through the day without obsessing about his boy. Then something would trigger a fresh need to find him and he'd get sucked in. Almost getting riddled with bullets on the train to New Orleans was one of those triggers;

death had a way of making you want to cling to life—made you want your life to count, to do some good.

Luke loved the spiritual quality of Arizona. He laughed aloud at his whimsical thoughts and went inside to pour himself a drink. The sun went down a lot smoother with an ice cold vodka in hand. He filled a glass and headed back outside. There was no denying he could sit in his backyard and feel the power of nature all around him, but he would be a hypocrite to call himself a saint. He'd led a rowdy life full of adventure, women and excellent liquor. He indulged, imbibed, and lived like he had ten lives, and didn't intend to apologize for it.

He stayed outside, long after the sun went down and the temperature cooled. He thought about driving into town and frequenting his favorite establishment, deciding against it in case one of his men reported in. Without much else to occupy his time, he decided to work on Sierra's netbook. It beat sitting around watching the wind blow.

If he was lucky, maybe he'd be able to find her and tell her what secrets her boyfriend was keeping from her.

***

The sky opened up overhead. A steady downpour of rain bounced off the car in a rhythmic pattern. The wipers squeaked against the windshield, trying to keep up with the downpour. Sierra kicked off her shoes and folded her legs on the car seat. All she wanted to do was curl up in a warm bed and wait out the storm. It was the only way she could think of to escape the terror that seemed to be lurking at every turn.

Her thoughts echoed the jagged streaks of lightening across the darkened sky. Rare moments of illumination, interspersed with zig zag lines which didn't quite fit. She knew Shark was waiting for answers. He deserved that much.

"Thank you for helping me, and for not asking questions. I know I didn't have time to explain anything when I left you the voice mail. You saved my life."

Shark turned to her, confused. "You're most welcome, but I am completely in the dark. I knew something was wrong when you didn't return from your massage, but I can't even begin to fathom what happened. Your cryptic and somewhat desperate message, to pack everything up and meet you behind the hotel, was most alarming. Especially in light of…"

She waited for him to continue, with a growing sense of concern. He was white knuckling the steering wheel, eyes glued to the road. He looked shaken up, bordering on grim. She assumed it was because of the threat of danger and navigating the storm. Now she wasn't so sure, "In light of *what*, Shark?"

"Forgive me, Damsel, it seems we have much to talk about. It would help me to concentrate if I knew what happened to you first. Maybe then we can determine our destination. Once I am not driving aimlessly, I promise to tell you what's going on with me."

Sierra closed her eyes, knowing she didn't have the energy to handle another problem. She already knew she wasn't going to like what Shark had to tell her. More to stall than anything else, she began to tell him about Skinbone.

"I can't imagine what was going through your mind when you saw him. You knew it couldn't be a coincidence."

"In those first few seconds, I didn't know what to think. When I saw the suspicion in his eyes, I knew I needed to figure out how to get away from him. I couldn't just walk away, he would have followed me. Once he knew my room number, it wouldn't be too hard to find out I'm using a fake name."

"Good thinking. You keep a clear head in times of crisis."

"I'm starting to think it's not enough. There's obviously a hell of a lot more going on than Neil and Grace's murders. I'm convinced those bullets on the train were meant for me and that Luke was an innocent bystander. Oh my God…"

"What's wrong?"

"If Luke picked up the netbook, he could be in danger. I don't know his last name or where he's from. There's no way for me to warn him."

"There might be something we can do. Let me think about it for a while."

"How?"

"As I said, let me try and come up with something. I sense you have a certain fondness for this Luke character. If there is a way to warn him, I'll figure it out."

"Thank you. He helped me. Scared the death out of me first, but he got me out of danger. I would hate to be responsible for putting him in harm's way."

"Peril does indeed seem to follow you."

Sierra's fingers curled around the door handle. She stared out into night, watching the rain come down in sheets. She couldn't ignore the fact that something was bothering Shark. He'd been a good friend; he deserved the same consideration from her.

"What happened with you?"

"Please, before we embark on this discussion, can we figure out where we are going? Staying alive has to be our first priority. The rest we can deal with later."

"You're right." They had good chance of getting away. Whoever was after her didn't know about the car, and hadn't figured out she was traveling under the name Corrine Lawson. No one knew about Shark. If they were going to make a run for it, they had to do it now.

Flying out of O'Hare was too risky. They knew she'd taken a train before, so it made sense for them to check the airports and railroad stations once they realized she was gone. Staying on the road seemed like the best option.

Her first instinct was to tell Shark to head towards Indiana. Only a fool would retrace her steps twice so It was the perfect route to take. She quickly discarded the idea. If they were smart enough to find her in Chicago, they'd find her in Indiana, too.

The next logical place was New York. Anyone could get lost there. The problem was the long drive on a lot of open road. They could easily be overtaken.

Which left North or West. They could head towards Milwaukee, and from there, Canada. Under normal circumstances, that was exactly what she would do. Which meant they had to do the complete opposite.

"Let's head west."

"West? Really? Won't we be too exposed?"

"That's what I'm counting on. It's the least logical choice. They can't look for us everywhere at once. I'm hoping this will give us a good head start." Her mouth went dry. A new fear crept up on her. If Donovan and the FBI were involved, she was a fugitive. She had a lot more to worry about than Skinbone Harris.

Shark hit the brakes and made a sharp u-turn. "West it is. I've always wanted to see the Grand Canyon."

The road stretched out before them. He glanced at her out of the corner of his eye, looking uncomfortable.

"What is it?" Sierra asked.

"I have dire news."

"What do you mean, you have dire news? How could you possibly have dire news?"

"It's about your friend. Grace McGinley."

"What about her?"

"She was having an affair, but not with Neil. Grace was involved with Jared Kepler."

***

Sierra didn't think she heard right. She could have sworn Shark said Grace was having an affair with Jared Kepler. "What?"

"Grace was intimately involved…"

"No, I heard what you said. I don't understand why you would say something like that?"

He shrugged, keeping his eyes fastened on the road. "I have firsthand knowledge of the affair."

She shook her head, frowning. She couldn't imagine how he'd come up with such a ridiculous scenario. A knot formed between her brows. "That makes no sense at all. You have to be mistaken. Grace didn't even know Jared Kepler."

"My apologies, Damsel, I know you may not want to believe it, but I witnessed it with my own eyes. I didn't make the connection until you called and asked me to pack up all your things. I came across the pictures of Grace and Neil, and that's when knew I'd seen her before. It was in Kepler's penthouse, enjoying a romantic evening. The memory is crystal clear. Angelica caused a bit of a scene." A shadow crossed his face when he mentioned Angelica. "She didn't think Grace was good enough for her Father."

Sierra absorbed the information. How many other secrets had she not been privy to? If what Shark said was true, it added yet another wrinkle to an already complex situation. "You have to be mistaken. How would Grace meet a man like Kepler?"

Ignoring her question, Shark said, "It gets worse."

Worse? How could things possibly get worse? They were pretty damn bad already.

Shark reached over and awkwardly patted her leg. She supposed he was trying to comfort her before dropping another bombshell.

"Did you know Grace worked for Jared Kepler?"

Sierra shifted in her seat to look at him, dumbstruck, "No, she didn't. I don't know where you're getting all this from, but none of it can possibly be true."

He held up a hand, "I understand you're confused. The general public may not be aware of this, but TriCon Labs is owned by Kepler International."

"Grace didn't work for TriCon, but Neil did. Neil worked for TriCon. Grace worked for GenStar."

An animated look crossed Shark's face. He slammed his palm against the steering wheel. "Yes. This is all starting to make sense. GenStar is another of Kepler's subsidiaries."

She rubbed her temples. Shark was almost jumping out of his socks in excitement. "I must be missing something. Why is this dire news? I don't understand how this is relevant to…anything."

"You're early deduction that Grace and Neil were working together was indeed correct. The fact that they were working for Kepler sheds a great deal of light on the whole situation."

"How?"

"How much do you know about Kepler International? Or corporate espionage?"

A vein in her neck started to throb. Did this explain the four gunmen lying in wait for the train? Was Shark trying to say Kepler's minions had been shooting at her? "Please, if you have something to tell me, blurt it out. You don't need to lead into it."

"I don't mean to mislead. I have no facts as of yet, only theories. When your call came in, I had pulled up the first file on Grace's netbook and recognized the name TriCon. I myself have painfully little knowledge of corporate espionage. I would, however, have to assume a company as large as Kepler would be at great risk. Considering the types of things Kepler and its subsidiaries work on, it's not at all surprising people would kill to possess a small portion of the technology Kepler is creating."

Her exhaustion vanished. "You have an in with Kepler. We call him, make arrangements to return the computers…" her voice trailed off, remembering the large sums of money found in Grace's home. *Damn it.* "And possibly be accused of being a party to espionage."

"To say nothing of the fact that you could be giving the killer an engraved invitation to your whereabouts."

They lapsed into silence. Sierra digested this latest information. Some of it she'd already suspected. Shark's news tied a few missing pieces together. If Grace was working for Kepler, and sleeping with him, where had the money she found stashed in the record albums come from? Had he been paying her off? Or was there a far more ominous meaning?

She stared out the window at the pouring rain. The air conditioning was on and the windows were starting to steam up. She wiped a spot clean with the palm of her hand, wishing the night could provide more answers. Did *Skinbone* work for Kepler? Was it within the realm of possibility that a corporation would hire an assassin to recover stolen information?

It was a sobering thought.

Chapter Twenty

Luke leaned back in his leather chair, cracking his knuckles before settling into work on the netbook Sierra left behind. A steaming cup of strong black coffee rested beside his dinner on the edge of the desk. A warmed corned beef on rye, slathered with yellow mustard, and melted cheese. He took a bite, wiping his hands on his jeans.

Time to get started.

Cracking the password wasn't a great chore—it was a matter of time and being patient. The program would run through millions of possible variations; it had never failed him. While he waited, his mind wandered. He was drifting, and that made him edgy.

If and when he managed to take down Kepler, he had some decisions to make. Continue searching for his son or move on with his life. He could toss his hat back in the ring and work with the FBI as a consultant on a regular basis. He'd also been entertaining the thought of opening up his own agency, with a few strong people on his team. It would keep life interesting, maybe allow him to sleep at night instead of obsessing over his lost family.

He didn't want to die holding onto a vendetta and not much else. After this operation was done, he would have resolution, one way or another. He'd have to move on.

Luke scarfed down the rest of the sandwich, scalding the back of his throat with coffee. He looked out the window and counted the stars dotting the sky, trying to remember the last time he was truly content. Sure there'd been good times, and happy occasions scattered here and there throughout the years, but had he ever been satisfied? Had he spent his life chasing misguided dreams?

He wasn't going to find those answers tonight. The computer program alerted him to a match. The password was cracked. His fingers flew over the keyboard, looking for information on Sierra's boyfriend.

The computer was registered to Neil Thornton. Luke rubbed his eyes, unable to believe what he was seeing. He rolled the chair closer to the desk, hunching his shoulders, and began to pull up files.

TriCon

The government seal.

The Foxtrot Files.

Jesus Christ, the information he'd been searching for had been right at his fingertips all along. He reached into his drawer for a flash drive, saving everything to it. Once the transfer was complete, he stashed the flash drive in his pocket. He'd put it in the safe later. Right now, he wanted to devote himself to deciphering the contents of the netbook.

The files were encrypted; he'd have to find a way to decode them. It would be time consuming, and there was a chance all of the information wasn't here. McGinley might have information that was pertinent to Foxtrot on her computer, but decoding these files would be a damn good start.

He'd get started as soon as he searched for information that would reveal Sierra's full identity. He'd bet his last dollar she was the one they'd been looking for, the one who had stolen the information. He banged the desk with his fist. Not only had he saved her life, he'd let her slip right through his fingers.

How the hell had he been so stupid? The shooters hadn't been after him, they'd been after Sierra.

Luke realized the implication a half second too late. Yanking open his drawer, he pulled out a semi-automatic as the first volley of bullets shattered the window.

Taking cover, he rolled to the floor, holding up his weapon. The bullets continued to fly through broken glass. The sound didn't drown out the noise of other men bashing in his door. Luke positioned himself to fire at the doorway when the men came crashing through it.

He was seriously outnumbered. They stormed through the house, firing in a full out onslaught. Any move Luke made would send him headlong into a wall of bullets.

He calculated his odds, knowing he was a goner. He would never find his son, never see another sunrise. *The hell if he'd go easy.* For what it was worth, he fired a single shot into the computer. No reason to give them what they'd come for. If he was lucky, he destroyed the hard drive. If nothing else, he'd shut down the computer. They'd have to do their own due diligence to recover the password.

His move pissed them off. They rushed the room like soldiers on the front lines. Luke took out three of them out before taking a bullet in the chest. Pain ripped through him, knocking him flat on his back, his gun flying out of reach. He lay there, gushing blood, unable to take action, the barrel of a gun pointed directly at his head. The bastards grabbed the computer, grunting in jubilation at their success.

Pain blasted through his chest with each breath. He refused to give them the satisfaction of hearing him grunt or whimper. Screw them. His last thought wasn't going to be wasted on wondering when the man holding the gun on him was going to pull the trigger. Closing his eyes, he thought of his family, of happier times when they were young and the house was full of laughter. It'd been a good life, right up until the day he lost them. There were times that weren't half bad since they'd been gone.

He could feel himself getting weaker. He knew they'd never let him raise his hand to try and staunch the blood pouring out of him. Luke wondered if he would have known his son by sight now that he was a grown man in his thirties, or if there was a chance he could have passed him by on the street, never knowing how close they'd come to meeting.

His mind was getting cloudy. He wasn't sure if he was hearing right, but it sounded like the men were leaving. In an instant of clarity, he understood Sierra's role. Before he could think it through, he coughed up a mouthful of blood.

The gunman didn't bother putting another bullet in him.

They left him lying on the floor, waiting to die.

***

Skinbone Harris swiped at the water dripping down his brow, swearing under his breath. The hotel lobby felt like the inside of a refrigerator after his futile chase through the heat and rain. He had about fifteen seconds to make a choice and the hell of it was he didn't know what damned thing to do. He'd never faced down so much doubt in his life.

The heart wants what it wants. He remembered hearing that quote a time or two and never understood it, he'd figured it was a load of bull. Besides, there wasn't a whole lot of room in his life to worry about his heart given his line of work. Until now.

If only she hadn't slipped away. They needed a sit down, a face to face conversation laying out all their cards on the table. Too much of what she'd said rang true. He believed she was running from a broken heart. No matter how good a liar she might be, she couldn't fake the shadows lurking in her eyes.

On the other hand, if she was innocent, she wouldn't have known about Foxtrot and be so damn good at running. If he had any real chance at catching her, he should be in his vehicle right now, pursuing her like he would any other mark. What kind of man did it make him to be standing in a hotel lobby, dripping wet, pissed as hell, thinking with his heart? Not one he recognized.

He needed a damned drink. Hell, he needed to be home in Texas, before he'd ever laid eyes on her. St. James spotted him, and hurried in his direction.

"Shit, man, why did you go tearing out of here like a bat out of hell? Where did you go?"

"If you saw me go tearing out of here, where the hell was my back-up?" Skinbone snarled. St. James didn't have so much as a drop of rain on him.

"By the time I got outside, you'd vanished into thin air."

Skinbone didn't buy the excuse, but he let it pass. "Buy me a drink and catch me up on what went down today."

St. James slapped him on the back. "It was an interesting day. I have plenty to tell you. Let's go get that drink, but first are you going to tell me why you flew out of here or not?"

"Mistaken identity." Skinbone listened to his own words with surprise, reckoning he'd made his decision. "Thought I'd recognized someone. Turned out I was wrong."

They found a table, and ordered their drinks. Skinbone turned his chair sideways, stretching out his legs. He kept one eye on St. James, watching him flirt with the waitress. The man had a stellar reputation in the field, but to Skinbone's way of thinking, he kept his college boy image a bit too spit polished. With his blonde haired, blue eyed, movie star good looks and slick edges, Skinbone would bet his last quarter St. James had political aspirations in his crosshairs.

"So, Hollywood, what happened at Kepler?"

Donovan smiled. Skinbone couldn't help thinking his teeth were a shade too white. "You know I hate it when you call me that, Chief."

Skinbone laughed, drawing the other patron's eyes towards them. He imaged what a mismatched pair they made. Mr. Slick, in his designer suit, flashing his pearly whites, and him with his damp t-shirt clinging to his muscles, American Indian features, and jet black ponytail dripping on the floor. "Good one, Hollywood. Now start talking before I scalp you and make a fortune off your stylish locks."

Donovan chucked and waited for the waitress to set down their drinks. Raising his glass, he said, "I've missed working with you, man. You never take my shit. There's too much tip-toeing around in Washington. People shake your hand and stab you in the back at the same time."

"Takes a special breed," Skinbone drawled.

"You've got that right." Donovan missed the sarcasm and took a swallow of whiskey, exhaling after it went down. "I can tell you're chomping at the bit to hear about Kepler. I hate to say this, but I think he's clean."

"What the hell do you mean, clean? He thinks I'm working for the Venezuelan government and he's got no problem selling me information he's got a damned United States government contract for. That's not *clean* in my book."

Donovan rested his elbows on the table and leaned towards Skinbone. "No, that's not what I'm saying. Kepler didn't order the hit on Neil Thornton and Grace McGinley. He didn't know they were dead. The way it looks, there's a chance, however slim, that Thornton's alive. The intel we received on his murder may have been wrong."

Skinbone raised his glass to his lips, studying St. James. "That would be a load off your mind, considering you had them recruited for the job."

"Yeah." Donovan ran a hand through his carefully styled hair. "That part sucks the worst, man. I'm pretty broken up. The three of us go way back."

Skinbone had something to say on the matter but he let it slide for now. "What makes you think Thornton could be alive?"

"After you left, I demanded to be taken to the lab. It took some arm twisting and a hell of a lot of threat's, but I got Kepler to admit he had his scientists working independently. He told that British asshole, Wilde, to get them on the phone and arrange a meet at the TriCon lab. I know what you're going to say. The explosion at McGinley's house did make the news, but it turns out her identity was never released. Chicago PD was trying to track down her next of kin. Wilde was gone a hell of a long time. When he admitted he couldn't reach them, Kepler blew a gasket. Guess he was worried about you withdrawing your offer. He had Wilde take me to their homes. It didn't take much to confirm Grace was dead. One call to the CPD and we had our answer."

"How did Wilde react?"

"He was harder to read. Looked shocked enough, but you know the British, with their stiff upper lip and all."

"You keep saying British. I thought Wilde was from India."

"Wilde's mother spent time in India when he was a boy. She eventually married a Brit, whose business was headquartered in India. After that, Wilde spent time in boarding schools. The trail ends for a bit, until a few years ago, when Wilde moved to London and resided there while working for Kepler UK."

"Okay. Enough of the history lesson. Wilde is incidental. What happened next?"

"We went to Thornton's house. No sign of him, but the place was ransacked. I got a forensic team out there. If Thornton was killed, it wasn't in his house. No evidence of foul play."

Skinbone's eyes narrowed. "So he could be out there. He could be our wildcard."

"Could be. When we got back to Kepler and broke the news, the man took it hard. Real shook up. Yeah, he could see your millions blowing up in smoke, but I knew there was more to it. After a long day of back and forth, we went back to his house. He called his daughter to be with him. It was pretty damn clear Kepler had been personally involved with Grace McGinley. The daughter was none too pleased about it either."

"You think the daughter had something to do with it?"

Donovan looked around to make sure no one was within earshot, "Angelica? No, she's too self-absorbed. One of those socialite celebs. Ethan

Wilde strikes me as a hanger on; he seems pretty tight with the family."

Skinbone finished his drink in a single swallow, absorbing what he'd learned. The next step, one he would take without St. James's interference, would be to see if he could find a link between the Kepler's, Wilde and Seri.

He set down his glass and looked Donovan in the eye. "You think Wilde has a motive?"

St. James shrugged, "Not sure, at this point, I'd only be able to make a guess. Greed? Or maybe he wants to discredit Jared Kepler in a bid to take over the top spot, though I doubt the daughter would allow it. Who the hell knows? England and India may be our allies, but they have enemies. Maybe they want Foxtrot. Or maybe Wilde wants to make his fortune by selling it to the highest bidder. Lot of countries would pay through the ass for Foxtrot. Whoever takes possession could own the whole goddamn world."

Skinbone couldn't argue the point. Foxtrot equaled power. Whoever owned it could start a new world order. A superpower, unlike any before, could arise out of nowhere. In a bid to win the weapons race and push the technological envelope, the world was going to annihilate itself. Skinbone figured it was damn arrogant stupidity to create what could destroy you, unless you spent an equal amount of time developing a failsafe.

"What about Thornton?" Skinbone asked.

"What do you mean?"

That wasn't the response Skinbone expected. "If Thornton is alive, could be he killed McGinley and has his own agenda."

St. James swirled the ice in his glass, pondering the idea. He stared down at his drink a good long while before answering, "Or Wilde could have kidnapped Thornton and is keeping him somewhere."

Tit for tat, Skinbone thought, giving Donovan credit where it was due. He hadn't considered that scenario. Based on what he knew, he was pretty damn certain Thornton had been Seri's fiancée. The pieces fit.

He glanced at St. James. His partner was busy signaling the waitress for another round. The bar crowd was starting to thin, although there were plenty of holdouts. Conversation hummed around them.

Hollywood turned on the charm when the harried waitress approached. Skinbone frowned, realizing what was bothering him. Kepler had been on their radar for a good long time. St. James had worked the system to make sure Thornton and McGinley were selected to develop Foxtrot. There was history between the three of them. Wouldn't it stand to reason that St. James was aware of Thornton's fiancée's identity? Shouldn't he have mentioned at least getting in touch with her to see if she was knew Thornton's whereabouts?

The waitress giggled at something Hollywood said. Skinbone tilted back in his chair, lifting the legs off the floor. He refrained from slapping his forehead when he figured it out. *That's* where the tip had come from, alerting them that something was wrong in the first place. *Seri* must have called St. James to report her fiancée's disappearance or death, setting everything in motion.

Skinbone's eyes narrowed. Seemed they *both* were protecting her. A wall of silence. What were St. James' motives?

Drinks ordered, Donovan turned his attention back to Skinbone. "Listen, Chief, I haven't been entirely straight with you."

Skinbone felt an unexpected shiver run down his spine. He bolted upright in his chair knowing instantly something was very wrong. He shook his head, holding up a finger to signal Donovan to hold his thought.

Sierra Montgomery.

The name came out of nowhere, pounding in his head, taking root in his brain. A chill overtook him. *Sierra Montgomery.*

Seri.

The noise in the bar took on a dull roar. He saw Donovan looking at him strangely, could see his lips moving. The name came from somewhere else. He jammed his hand in his pocket, searching for his phone. He'd turned it on silent when he'd planned on having a workout. Flipping it open, he saw he had one message. He punched in his password with a shaky hand, afraid of what he would hear.

A weak, thready voice. Two words. Sierra Montgomery. The clatter of the phone on the other end as it fell. He leaped up out of his seat, color draining from his face. Donovan stood up, staring at him with concern.

There wasn't any time to waste. Ignoring St. James worried expression, he gripped the phone like a lifeline. "I gotta run. Hold down the fort. I'll call when I can."

He was already keying in the number to prepare the private jet. Sprinting from the bar, he placed another call. Skinbone didn't take the time to bother with his car. He stole a cab coming to collect a twenty-something couple, pushing them out of the way like his life depended on it.

In a way, it did.

***

Ethan Wilde splashed cold water on his face, staring at his reflection. The killing had to end. The mission was hemorrhaging, and racking up bodies wasn't going to stop the disaster from widening.

He could kill with the best of them, never batting an eye. Death was inevitable. It didn't faze him when there was meaning and purpose behind it.

He smoothed back his hair and studied his features. He'd lived his life preparing for the opportunity to be Jared Kepler's right hand man. Considering his background, it hadn't been easy. Then again, he had higher than average intelligence and a plethora of talents, most of which remained untapped. With any luck, they would remain that way.

Until the time was right to reveal his plan.

He was playing a dangerous game. He'd come to the States for two reasons and he was positioned exactly where he wanted to be. Kepler was going down and he was the heir apparent to the throne. Provided, of course, that he kept Angelica happy.

No easy feat, considering she was an insatiable bitch who thought nothing of taking on other lovers. *Did she think he'd meekly accept being cuckolded?* He knew he wasn't the only one to share her bed—But he would be the one who ultimately held the fate of Foxtrot in his hands.

Angelica Kepler gave herself entirely too much credit.

In the end, she would beg him, *beg him,* for mercy. Despite her phenomenal beauty and staggering net worth, she wasn't a very good judge of character. She should exercise greater caution when choosing her men.

He dampened his toothbrush, squeezing a precise amount of toothpaste onto the brush. He wouldn't rest until he'd accomplished what he'd set out to do.

There was a soft knock on the door. He frowned. The doorman hadn't buzzed, advising him of a visitor. *Who the hell could it be?* He finishing rinsing and wiped his hands on a towel. Moving stealthily to the door, he stood back, pressing himself against the wall. Ethan didn't want to be an easy target if bullets started flying. "Who is it?" he yelled.

A sultry voice answered from on the other side, "It's me, Sweetheart."

"Damn," he swore under his breath, swinging open the door. She stood there with one arm raised to rest against the doorway, the other posed seductively on her hip. Her red lips were curved in a sexy pout. Despite the heat, she wore a raincoat. His eyebrows raised until he saw droplets of rain dotting the fabric.

He should have known better than to give her the benefit of doubt. "What are you doing here, Angelica? I told you I had things to do."

She smiled, unbuttoning the coat right there in the hallway, revealing a sheer, frothy white negligee beneath it. "It's after midnight," she purred. "If you had things to do, you should be done with them by now." She took a step closer, wrapping her arms around his neck, pressing her body against his, "Besides, I missed you, darling."

"Shouldn't you be playing the dutiful daughter, consoling your father?"

She shrugged; the coat slipped off her shoulder, revealing more skin, "He's a big boy. He can take care of himself. You, on the other hand, need to be taking care of *me*." Angelica slammed the door shut with the heel of her black patent leather pump, drawing his lips down to hers. She nipped his bottom lip with her teeth, "I've worked up quite an appetite. Take me to bed."

He looked down at her. Her elegant exterior was a striking contrast to the animal passion beating inside her. Ethan imagined the fit she would pitch if he tossed her back out into the hall unsatisfied. The thought amused him. Her voracious hunger blinded her. That suited his purpose. For now. He slid his hands down her back, cupping her backside, smothering a laugh when she started to grind against him.

There were worse ways to topple an empire.

Ethan wrapped his hand around her raven hair, pulling her towards his bedroom. An unexpected chill stopped him cold. "Do you feel that?"

Her face twisted into an unflattering scowl, "The only thing I feel is that I don't have your full attention."

Ethan heard the petulance in her voice. She was getting ready to stir the pot. Angelica liked angry sex. He wasn't in the mood to indulge that particular whim tonight. He brought his mouth down on hers hard, crushing her lips beneath his. She wrapped herself around him, groaning with pleasure.

He went through the motions, giving her just enough to satisfy her, but his mind was disconnected. He was thinking about the chill he'd felt. Something, somewhere, had gone terribly awry.

The question was what?

***

Sierra bolted upright in her seat. She twisted her head, trying to peer out the back window. Between the steam and the rain, she couldn't see a damn thing. She shivered violently, rubbing her arms to ward off a chill. "Did you turn up the air conditioning?"

"You feel it too?"

She looked at him strangely. "You mean the cold?"

"I fear it is more than sudden coldness. I have the most unsettling sensation. A foretelling of bad news, perhaps, or impending doom." Shark's voice was a pitch higher than usual.

Sierra nodded, not trusting herself to speak. Biting her lower lip, she fought to not to give in to a fresh set of worries. It wasn't easy, given her unexpected encounter with Skinbone Harris and the bizarre news Shark delivered this evening. The storm didn't help either. Even under the best of circumstances, electrical storms made her jumpy. The last thing she needed was the eerie feeling that an unknown, monumental *bad thing* occurred.

Clearing her throat, she said, "We need a better plan."

"I agree."

"Good." Taking note of how quick Shark jumped at the idea, she kept nodding. *Planning is good,* she thought, *less time to dwell on the craziness.*

"So do you have one?" he asked.

"No. Not yet." She tucked her legs beneath her and pulled the wet hair off her face, gathering it into a makeshift bun. Understanding the enemy was the best way to stay one step ahead of them. "Let me ask you something."

"I am here to assist Dear Damsel in any way I can. Ask away."

"Earlier you wondered how much I knew about Kepler International. I feel like I'm missing something. Aren't they basically a technology company?"

Shark's face turned wistful for a moment. She guessed he was thinking about Angelica and the future they'd planned. Sierra had a sudden urge to tear out the woman's hair for breaking poor Shark's heart. He was one of the sweetest, most giving men she'd ever met. Come to think of it, if Angelica was shallow enough to cheat on her fiancée what possessed her to get involved with Shark to begin with? There had to be a reason. Sierra sure as hell bet it wasn't love.

No matter what direction her thoughts took these days, she was finding ominous undertones. Lord knew, she had more pressing matters to worry about than the two-timing Angelica. If they managed to get out of this mess alive, she wondered if she'd ever trust again, or if her faith in people was destroyed forever.

"Tell me about Kepler International."

Shark sighed. "They have a hand in everything, including government contracts. The list is staggering, when you think about it. They are a major military supplier, defense contracts, weapons, also cutting edge medical research, pharmaceuticals, genetic research, technology, science, electronics, to name a few. Kepler has very long arms, reaching into almost every corner of the world. If there is a profit to be made, Kepler will make it. They are leaders in developing new products, concepts, ideas. I'd say they are the closest thing to Royalty we have in this country."

Each word felt like a knife twisting inside her. They were in way over their heads. "That has to be why I didn't know what Neil and Grace were working on. I'm sure they signed confidentially agreements, non–disclosers, and God knows what else. They worked in different fields though. I can't figure out how or why the two of them ended up working together. It's too much of a coincidence to be random."

"Kepler only recruits the best people. People don't apply to Kepler as a general rule; they have an entire department dedicated to seeking out the best and the brightest. I would most certainly think your friends were approached by Kepler, and not the other way around."

"Why would Kepler have recruited them specifically? They were highly regarded, but certainly not the top in their respective fields. Even if they were, what are the odds they'd both be recruited for the same project? There has to be more to it," Sierra continued.

"There is much about the entire situation we don't understand. With any luck, the computers will provide us with much needed information. It's a shame I had to abandon my work when I did. Still we may have discovered a few tidbits to work with."

"Don't take this the wrong way, because it was a wonderful idea, but I can't help thinking if I hadn't gone down for a massage we could have been safely tucked in for the night."

Shark's shoulders sagged, "Regretfully, I've been thinking the same thing. There is no reason to blame yourself, Dear Damsel. The fault lay entirely at my door."

She patted his shoulder. "It was a great idea at the time."

He made a half-hearted attempt at a smile and shrugged. "It *was* well meant."

Sierra could almost hear Skinbone Harris's voice chiding her that everything happened for a reason. She could beat herself up with if only's. If only she hadn't gone downstairs for the massage. If only she hadn't chosen that particular Memphis rib joint. If only she hadn't insisted on seeing Neil Friday night.

She rested her cheek against the window, feeling uneasy. She knew she was missing something vital—some clue that would tie everything together, and tell her what their next move should be.

A bolt of lightning sliced through the sky, striking a near-by tree on the side of the road. Sierra's fear of storms got the best of her. She screamed and grabbed onto Shark's arm. Startled, he lost control of the steering wheel. He slammed on the breaks, fighting a losing battle with the wet pavement. The sickening squeal of tires rent the night air. Panicked, he overcorrected. The car spun out of control on the dark, deserted road.

Chapter Twenty-One

Skinbone Harris was sweating bullets. He gripped his phone like a lifeline; all the while praying to whatever God was willing to listen to his sorry-assed soul. Times like this reminded him he had more of a heart than he cared to admit.

Grinding his teeth in impatience, he ran his hands through his hair, undoing the short ponytail he wore. *It's a good sign the phone isn't ringing,* he assured himself. He needed to believe that in order to hang on to hope.

It had been a damn horrible night and it wasn't over yet. He felt like his guts had been filleted and broiled over hot coals. *This is it,* he swore to himself and the God he hoped took pity on his blackened soul. *No more.* He knew better than to try and barter a deal, but he did it anyway, promising if things turned out okay, he would change his ways.

He was still a young man, just shy of forty. Too young to retire, even though he had enough money put away to last several lifetimes. He'd find a good use for his talents. Maybe open up some kind of agency. And he'd damned sure make a point of including the old man, maybe even let him think it was his idea.

If the old man survived.

And if he would call off the hit on Sierra Montgomery. That had to be part of the deal.

Who the hell was he kidding? Making plans he had no right to make. He'd gotten mixed up in this mess because of the old man's life-long vendetta. Hate something or someone that long, and it was sure to rot your soul. Yet there was nothing rotten about the old man. Go figure.

The plane began its decent, Skinbone's face steeled into an expression of pure granite. He didn't love much, and he sure as hell didn't love often. He couldn't lose the only two people he associated with love in a single night. He'd be damned before he let that happen. Hollywood could take over. He had no doubt Donovan would find a way to parlay a successful end to the mission to further his political aspirations

The minute the plane bumped down on the runway, Skinbone headed towards the exit. He grunted his thanks to the pilot for making record time, despite the storm sitting over the Midwest, and dashed down the stairs to the waiting limo.

He boned up on courage, not sure what he would face when he reached his destination. If the news was bad, he would single-handedly ring Kepler's neck. He slammed his fist into the door, realizing he'd broken his deal with God. He folded his hands, begging forgiveness. He never begged. Lord, he was a mess. If he could only rewind the clock, and be back in Texas with Garber, Sadie and Tawny, grilling steak and sitting by the pond, thinking about the sweet little gal he'd met in Memphis.

He'd gotten over what Kepler did to him a lifetime ago. He hadn't let it poison his life. If only the old man had done the same and been able to let go.

The driver got them to the hospital in no time. Skinbone spent a good long time staring at the imposing structure. He didn't want to go in, but he couldn't rest easy until he did.

The sterile hallways caused a knot to form in his gut. The only two times he'd set foot in a hospital was when he'd lost both his parents. It was little wonder he associated hospitals with death.

He headed straight to the emergency room. *You've stared death in the face more than a few times,* he reminded himself, *you can do this.* The nurse on duty was his type, a tall, buxom brunette, with the face of an angel. He couldn't help comparing her to a certain blue-eyed blonde, who was five foot two at best. His taste in women had taken a decided turn in the last few days.

His feet propelled him to the nurses' station before he was ready. The nurse instinctively backed away. No wonder. A wild eyed, long haired Indian with blood in his eyes, was descending on her. He gripped the desk, feeling every bit as dangerous as he looked. He barked out the name. His voice was as raw as he felt.

"He just got out of surgery. He's in intensive care. Room 301."

Skinbone whispered a thank you. His body sagged in temporary relief. *Intensive Care.* That meant the old man was in bad shape. Pushing himself away from the nurses' station, he found the elevators, frantically pushing the up button. Precious seconds ticked away while he waited.

Two things were on his mind: the man who had been like a father to him the last twenty years, and the woman he was growing to love. They were intertwined, at opposite ends of the spectrum, but they both had a place in his heart.

He rode up in silence, bracing himself for the worst. He hovered at the doorway of room 301, sucking in air at the image that confronted him. The man was hooked up to a plethora of machines. His body had shriveled since the last time he saw him, he looked at least twenty years older. He was pasty white, but he was alive, and he was breathing. Skinbone offered up silent thanks and walked quietly into the room.

Luke opened one eye. He raised a frail hand to push the oxygen mask off his face. "I suppose I have you to thank for calling the ambulance."

"Damn straight. Although you could have mentioned you were shot in your message."

"Too much work. How the hell did you manage to round up an ambulance so fast all the way here in Arizona."

"I think on my feet." He smiled down at Luke, "After all, I learned from the best."

Luke grunted. "Somebody had to take you under their wing. You were a damn wild one, would have gotten your ass killed if it weren't for me."

Skinbone would always be grateful. He'd been headed for trouble after his parents died. If the old man hadn't given him a home and taken him in, Lord knows how he might have ended up. Couldn't have been easy for Luke to saddle himself with a trouble making thirteen year old, but he was damn glad the man did.

Skinbone pulled up a chair and reached for Luke's hand, trying to keep the tremor out of his voice. "What the hell were you thinking, getting shot while I'm clear across the country on a mission?"

Luke made a feeble attempt at smiling, "You know me. I like to shake things up."

"You trying to keep me on my toes?"

Skinbone fought to keep a stiff upper lip when Luke raised a hand to his chest to stifle the cough resulting from his attempt at laughter. "Somebody's gotta keep an eye on you."

"I'm a big boy now. I can take care of myself."

"That's a load of bull. You need to find yourself a good woman to keep you in line."

"Not much chance of that happening. Besides, who else is gonna look after you in your old age?"

"I got a ways to go before I'm a doddering old fool. Plenty of time for you to have yourself a life with someone who loves you by your side."

"You really think that matters to me right now? Let's get you back on your feet before you start harassing me about my love life. You got that?"

"Fair enough, but don't think I'm going to drop the topic permanently," Luke croaked. "Sierra Montgomery. Did you even bother to look for her?"

"First things first. I got a little distracted with saving your life."

Luke became agitated, gripping Skinbone's hand while struggling to sit up in the hospital bed. Wanting to calm him, he told a bold-faced lie. "Hollywood is handling it."

"No," Luke gasped, "You have to find her."

"Save your strength. You need to rest."

"You don't understand. She's…"

Luke's eyes rolled back in his head. Skinbone recoiled when the alarms on Luke's monitors went crazy, bleating out a deathly cry. A platoon of medical personal rushed in, screaming code blue. They had to peel Skinbone's hand away, escorting him from the room.

He stood outside in worried silence. He didn't even notice the tears streaming down his face.

***

Sierra's head slammed against the window. Blood dripped into her eye and down her cheek. Grimacing in pain, she raised her hand, wiping the blood away.

Shark.

His head rested against the steering wheel, shoulders heaving. *Thank God,* she thought, *he's alive.* She sat up straight, fighting a wave of dizziness. Her shoulder ached where it rammed against the door. She pushed herself towards the driver's side, and reached out for his shoulders.

"Shark? Are you okay?"

He nodded, making no attempt to sit up. His hands were wrapped around the steering wheel in a death grip, alarming her. The accident shook her out of her fog, snapping her back to alertness. Shark wasn't moving. She looked around at their surroundings. They were lucky that the car hadn't hit anything. They could have crashed into the concrete embankment or ended up in a ditch. That was the good news. The bad news was they were sitting ducks in the middle of a dark road and visibility was poor. The car had turned around, facing the wrong direction. Any minute an unsuspecting car or truck could barrel into them, killing them instantly.

She shook Shark gently, "We can't stay here like this. If you can't drive, scoot over. I'll move the car."

He raised himself slowly, still in shock.

"Let me drive," she repeated It was up to her to get them out of danger, especially since the spinout was her fault.

He shook his head. "I made a grievous error. I never should have slammed on the brakes. We could have flipped over, or worse. I am so sorry. I could have caused severe harm."

"Don't worry about it. I'm the one who screamed and made you lose control of the car. If anyone's to blame, it's me. But let's get out of the middle of the road before we do get hurt."

"Damsel is far too generous." He released the brake, pausing to look at her. "Oh my gosh, you're injured. Your face, you're bleeding."

She touched a spot on her forehead. "No, it's okay. Seriously. It's a small cut and a bump. Honestly, it looks a lot worse than it is." Her words sounded braver than she felt. Her head was spinning and she was slightly nauseous, but she wasn't about to tell Shark. Knowing him, he'd probably insist she see a doctor and there was no way she was about to do that. "We should pull over to the side of the road. I'll grab a t-shirt out of my bags to hold on my forehead. The pressure will help staunch the bleeding."

He eased the car forward, making a u-turn, and stopped as requested. Sierra breathed a sigh of relief. They were out of danger. He hopped out of the car before she could object, handing her one of his own freshly laundered white t-shirts.

She thanked him, holding it over the gash with a firm hand. "Listen, I think I do have a plan. We can't drive all night without a break. It's insane to think we can keep up a good driving pace. Not in the condition we're in. Where are we, anyway?"

"If memory serves, I believe the last signs we passed place us near Davenport."

"Iowa?"

"The land of corn. Not to be confused with Idaho, which of course, is famous for its potatoes."

Her lips twitched. Smothering a laugh, she tried to ignore her howling stomach. The mention of food reminded her she was starving. Food was fuel and they both needed to keep up their strength. "Okay, so here's our plan. We find a diner. Iowa *has* to have an all night diner somewhere along this road. All those truckers hauling corn need to eat."

"A diner?" Shark made a face.

"Yes, don't look so dubious. Diners are great. Trust me, you're in for a treat."

He didn't look convinced. "If you say so."

"Then we find a place to sleep. Davenport has to have some decent hotels. We won't go to a motel. That's too obvious. People on the run always check into cheap motels."

"And you know this how? Have you known many people on the run?"

She made a face at him, turning up the palms of her hand, "Okay, so maybe I know that from TV and movies, but what I've learned kept me out of danger so far. Don't laugh; I picked up a lot of useful tips from *Law and Order*."

"This is your big plan? Eat at a diner and survive off tips from *Law and Order*. I think you hit your head harder than you're admitting."

"No, of course that's not my plan. Well, except for the diner part."

"I find myself, oddly enough, not comforted."

"Oh, diners have the best comfort food. I could go for some mac and cheese, with a side of mashed potatoes and gravy. Or a nice, big greasy burger, tons of fries, and gobs of ketchup. You know what I really have a taste for? Al's beef. Have you ever had Al's beef?"

He shook his head.

"You don't know what you're missing. Anyway, once I accidently laid my sandwich down on some ketchup, oh it was so good. I always dip it in ketchup now. Carson's ribs, those would be good too. Love Carson's ribs. You have had those, right?"

"No."

"Oh my God. Don't you eat? When we get back home, I am taking you out. How could you never have had those things?"

"How do you stay so skinny?"

"Luck, I guess. I'm sure one day it'll catch up to me and I'll wake up big as a whale."

"I'm confused. We have an accident and your first thought is to find a place to eat. Clearly you're a nervous eater."

"Which is why we need to find a diner before I starve to death. Keep your eyes peeled."

"If I must."

"You must. Getting back to the plan… after we rest, I think we should ditch the car and hop a cab to the airport. We take the first available flight to Arizona."

"Arizona? Seems an odd choice."

"It's the perfect choice. People from Chicago flock to Arizona for spring training. So it stands to reason that's the last place we'd go, making it the perfect place to hide."

"Spring training? It's the middle of summer…"

"The Cubs? Spring training? You are from Chicago, aren't you? I'm not even a baseball fan, but everybody knows about spring training. The point is, Chicagoans have an affinity for Arizona, no matter what the season. We won't go to Mesa though. We'll go somewhere interesting like Sedona."

"Damsel seems to be bursting with unexpected energy since our spinout calamity."

"It's adrenaline. Trust me, I'm exhausted. We need to put a lot of distance between us and Skinbone Harris. Kepler too. Driving will take too long. Even if they are checking the airports, they won't be looking for Corrine Lawson." She remembered seeing Donovan St. James at the hotel. *How had she forgotten?*

Up until now, she'd been running from a cold hearted, calculating killer, and random gunmen. She hadn't been running from the FBI. She hadn't kept up with the news. For all she knew, her face was plastered all over by now as a wanted fugitive. Her spirits plummeted.

"On second thought, flying might not be such a great idea after all."

"Why not?"

She explained her reasons. The Shark listened quietly. "We should tune into the news once we find a hotel. But we can still fly to Arizona."

"It's too risky."

"Not if we use the private jet."

She laughed. "Oh sure, a private jet. How do you propose we manage that?"

"Simple. I'll call the pilot and tell him meet us at the airport tomorrow morning."

"Why didn't I think of that? Let's just call the pilot. I'm thinking you're the one who hit his head too hard."

"No, I'm being serious."

Dumbstruck, she gaped at him. "You mean to tell me you actually have a private jet?"

"Not me, personally. It's the family jet—more specifically, my fathers. He, however, is out of the country and he has often told me it's at my disposal any time I wish to use it."

She had a hard time controlling her astonishment. "Here I am feeling bad for you because you're homeless and you have a *jet?* Don't get me wrong, I still feel bad for you because of the whole Angelica fiasco. If I ever met the woman, which is extremely unlikely, I would claw her eyes out for doing what she did to you. But how on earth can you be homeless when you're family has a plane?"

A smile played at the corners of his mouth, "I told you I had money. It's true, I don't have a home. My pride would not allow me to return to my parent's house, so technically I am indeed, homeless."

"That's quite a technicality." She couldn't help laughing, "You, Mr. Shark, are one of a kind."

"I shall take that as a compliment. Look to your right. I think I see a diner looming up ahead."

"Prepare to have your taste buds dazzled."

He slid into a parking spot and reached for the door handle, doubt etched across his face. Watching him, she was overcome with emotion. She grabbed his hand, stopping him from opening the door.

"Is something wrong?" he asked.

"No. I just wanted to say thank you. Not too many people would get involved in my mess. You're a good man, Wally Marx. I need you to promise me something, though. If my situation gets too dangerous, I want you to run. I appreciate your help, more than you know, but I don't want you getting hurt."

He smiled his lopsided smile. "I have every faith in the world in you, Damsel. Most women in your shoes would have buckled under the tremendous strain you've been under. You are a survivor. No harm will come to you."

"Thanks for the vote of confidence, but no one is indestructible. It's hard to fight back when you have no idea what you're up against, or who the enemy is."

***

Ethan Wilde stood under the shower; hot water poured down on his body, loosening tight muscles and washing away Angelica's cloying scent. He felt the sting where her nails left deep grooves down his back. The lady enjoyed drawing blood. He'd had a hard time getting rid of her; she'd sensed his distraction and had gone in for the kill.

Angelica was a necessary evil. Kepler was powerless to get rid of him as long as his daughter was sharing his bed. He was positioned right where he wanted to be—Not that it was doing him a hell of a lot of good.

His mouth curled into a sneer. Until he had his hands on Foxtrot, his time at Kepler International was an exercise in futility. Jared was weak; he didn't have the balls to stick to his principles. He allowed himself to be manipulated into selling the weapons to the highest bidder. The man was a fool. He was too busy protecting the family name and fortune to realize how the weapons would be used against him.

The asshole hadn't thought it through, didn't know the full extent of his mistake. He'd put his own damn country at risk. He hadn't learned a thing from his father's screw-ups. Greed obviously flowed freely through the Kepler's bloodline.

Had the man been stupid enough to think that by sleeping with one of the scientists the project was safe?

Ethan had no patience for fools. He was also numb to normal human emotion, courtesy of Kepler International. His childhood had been stolen from him, so it was only fitting that he used Kepler's daughter to further his own agenda. An eye for an eye, wasn't that what the Bible said?

He yanked a towel off the bar and turned off the water. His earlier sense of unease lingered, putting him in a foul mood. Nothing was going according to plan. All because a woman named Sierra Montgomery had been in the wrong place at the wrong time.

He had to find her, and eliminate her.

Nothing was going to stop him.

***

Skinbone Harris hovered outside the room, desperate to know what was happening to Luke. Precious minutes ticked by without word. The waiting was unbearable. He paced the hallways, willing the door to open. The stench of fear assaulted his nostrils, his hands coiled into fists. There would be hell to pay of Luke didn't make it. He'd strangle the doctor on staff with his bare hands.

Then there was Sierra. Luke all but confirmed she was responsible for his shooting. Why else would he have said her name right before the monitors went off? He bared his teeth, scaring the nurse wheeling a dinner cart. He wanted to kick himself in the ass for letting Sierra slip away. His romantic feelings for her made him sick to his stomach.

It wasn't like him to be compromised by a pretty face and enticing figure. He'd never had any trouble finding beautiful women to pass the time with. He never should have let her crawl under his skin. Even now, knowing what he did about her, he still wanted her. What the hell was wrong with him?

He should have told Hollywood about her back in Chicago. Instead, he'd given her a head start. She could be anywhere in the country by now. He vowed to find her no matter where she went and if it turned out she'd ordered the hit on Luke, she'd pay for it.

The door to the hospital room finally swung open. Skinbone jogged to the doorway, momentarily blocked by hospital personal wheeling out the crash cart. He tried to push his way through, his heart pounding a mile a minute, praying Luke was okay.

He almost made it through the door when a doctor blocked his path, closing the door behind him. Skinbone's stomach twisted. "How is he?"

The Doctor paused, ignoring Skinbone's question. "And you are?"

"Skinbone Harris. Can I see him?"

"Only immediate family can visit patients in Intensive Care."

"I *am* his immediate family." Skinbone advanced on the doctor, fury in his eyes. "Tell me how he is."

"Again, Mr. Harris, I can only discuss his condition with an immediate family member."

"I've already told you, I am family."

The doctor hesitated, giving him a skeptical look. Skinbone felt his blood boil, knowing the doctor was judging him. He could see the wheels turning in the man's mind, thinking this wild eyed Indian couldn't be related to the frail white man lying just beyond the door in a hospital bed.

"You have two seconds to update me on his condition. That man in there is my father, and not you, or anybody else, is going to keep me from him." Skinbone tried to tone down his fury.

The doctor held his ground, "I do not appreciate being threatened, Mr. Harris."

Skinbone's eyes glittered dangerously. He caught the doctor's gaze and held it, his penetrating stare unwavering. "Do you have any idea who that man in there is? Luke Preston is an important man in this town and anyone who matters will tell you he took me in as a boy when I had nowhere else to go. He raised me as if I were his flesh and blood. Our skin may not be the same color, but he is my father in every way that counts."

For a moment, neither man budged. Skinbone held the doctor's gaze, using all his energy to bend the man's will. The doctor relented. "Okay. No need to cause a scene. I'm just protecting my patient. Mr. Preston is in critical condition. The bullet did a lot of damage. It missed his heart by fractions. He's lost a lot of blood; if he'd gotten here five minutes later, we wouldn't even be having this conversation. We managed to remove the bullet and repair the damage during surgery, but Mr. Preston was in a weakened condition. The strain apparently was too much. He went into cardiac arrest. We got his heart started again, but he hasn't regained consciousness. The next twenty-four hours are critical. We are doing everything we can."

A lump formed in Skinbone's throat. "So, he may not make it? Is that what you're telling me?"

"I'm sorry, yes."

Skinbone nodded once, feeling the breath knocked out of him. *Luke had to make it. He was too strong, too vital.* "I'm going in to see him, and I am not leaving his side."

The doctor moved aside. Skinbone rushed through the door, stopping cold when he saw Luke. He looked ten times worse than he had before. Skinbone sucked in a lungful of air, covering his face to hide the tears spilling from his eyes. He took a moment to compose himself and then pulled up a chair to Luke's bedside.

He took Luke's hand in his, shocked at how cold and fragile it felt. "You're going to be okay," he whispered, making a promise he had no right to make. "You just have to fight and then you have to fight some more. You can't let Kepler beat you, you hear me? You have to snap out of this so we can take him down. Don't you dare even think about leaving me to do this alone. You fight. I'm going to be here, fighting right along with you. Don't give up on me. I need you."

Skinbone's shoulders started to shake. He laid his head against Luke's hand. White hot tears ran down his face.

***

Donovan St. James was restless. He checked into a hotel in downtown Chicago. With Skinbone gone, there was no need to stay out in the suburbs. He'd missed the glitter of the skyscrapers reflecting in Lake Michigan. He'd always loved this city.

He thought of the woman waiting for him back in D.C. He was going to have to end things with her—she didn't figure into his plans anymore. There was only one woman he burned for, one with whom he could share his life; strong enough, bold enough, and beautiful enough to be his bride.

He'd have an easier time controlling Kepler and Wilde without Skinbone Harris breathing down his neck. It irked him that Luke put Harris in charge. The man lacked his finesse, and put Kepler and Wilde on edge. It didn't help their cause. Then again, that's why he was in Washington, and Harris was nothing more than a hit man for hire.

Donovan shook his head, thinking about Sierra. She never should have gotten tangled up in this mess. Sierra had no idea what a dangerous game she was playing. He didn't know how much longer he could protect her. Too many people were hunting her. This was all her own damn fault for choosing Neil Thornton over him. She'd put herself in the line of fire.

His biggest worry was what she was going to do with the information. Hell, she probably had the prototypes in her possession too. She had enough power at her fingertips to destroy the United States government, or *any* government for that matter. The only saving grace was she didn't know what she had. There was no way in hell Sierra would be able to decipher the encrypted files.

But what if it fell into the wrong hands?

Or worse, what if either Thornton or McGinley had confided in her, and she played a far more significant role in this whole debacle?

He couldn't think about that now. He needed to plan his next move. So far, he'd managed to keep their connection under wraps but he wouldn't be able to hide it forever—unless he managed to get to her first, things would go badly for him when their past came to light.

He still loved her, but that wouldn't be enough to save her.

Foxtrot was too big, the ramifications too explosive.

Odds were Sierra Montgomery was going to die.

It was just a matter of when and where.

Chapter Twenty-Two

Sierra tossed aside the blankets, and tip toed out of bed so she wouldn't disturb Shark. She smiled, remembering the way he dug into his baked mac and cheese, fresh corn on the cob and mashed potatoes, professing an instant fondness for diner food. They'd gorged themselves, ordering apple pie ala mode afterwards for desert.

The heavy meal added to Sierra's exhaustion. It was still dark out when they checked into the hotel. Shark insisted on sharing a room with her, declaring there was safety in numbers. She was too tired to argue. They checked in under his name, securing a room with two double beds. True to his word, he called his pilot, no doubt waking him from a sound sleep. The jet would be fueled and waiting to go. Shark even arranged for someone to ditch the car, so it wouldn't be abandoned at the airport.

Everything was set. *So why was she on edge?* Shark would have all the time he needed to break the encryption. She'd be able to go through Grace's things and look for answers without fear of being caught.

Stress twisted her shoulders into knots. She had a bad feeling about all of this. For the millionth time, she questioned her decision to run. Even if Shark did manage to break the code, then what? How would that make them any safer? In the end they'd be turning the information over, either to Kepler or the FBI. In the meantime, they could wind up dead.

She raked her fingers through her hair. Maybe the best thing to do was call Donovan again. He knew damn well she wasn't capable of murder or corporate espionage. Now that she was certain Neil and Grace hadn't been having an affair, she had no motive. Donovan could broker a deal, granting her immunity and protection. Shark would be safe and she could start over somewhere new.

It was the smart thing to do.

Knowing if she thought about it any longer, she'd change her mind, she dug inside her purse for the disposal cell. It was time to put an end to the insanity. She was terrified that the next time she crossed paths with Skinbone Harris he would kill her. It sickened her that she'd developed real feelings for him. *What kind of woman did it make her if she was falling for an assassin? What kind of person was she, feeling such a deep connection to* anyone *so soon after Neil's death?*

Not wanting to face the awful truth about herself, she flipped open her phone and stared at the keypad. She hesitated, wondering if she was reacting out of emotion; swallowing hard, she started to dial. *This was best for everyone,* she assured herself, feeling a lump the size of watermelon form inside her chest.

The phone was wrenched from her fingers. She heard it snap shut before she could register what was happening. She looked up to see Shark standing over her, a worried look on his face.

"What are you doing?" His grip tightened on the phone

She felt a red stain creep up her cheeks. "I was calling Donovan St. James."

"Oh my God." His hand flew to his forehead "*Why* would you do that?"

"Because it's crazy not to. We have no idea what we're dealing with," her voice cracked, "What if…what if Skinbone…" She couldn't finish her sentence.

Shark sat down next to her, keeping a firm hold on her phone. "You have feelings for him, don't you? That's where all this is coming from."

She couldn't look him in the eye, "Of course not, that would be ridiculous."

"Would it?" His voice was gentle, "We can't help who we fall in love with, Damsel. Against all odds, Grace loved Jared Kepler. Look at me. I fell head over heels for Angelica. Who wouldn't? She was the most gorgeous woman I'd ever laid eyes on and she seemed to return my affections. Truth be told, she was the one who pursued me. I never would have dared to approach such a perfect creature. She was my world and I loved her more than life itself. I would have forgiven her anything had she not cheated on me. In retrospect, I can see now, Angelica was perhaps not a very nice person. Still, I was blinded by my feelings for her. Love works in mysterious ways. It's beyond our control, sometimes even beyond our comprehension."

She raised her eyes to his. "But she's not a killer."

"True," Shark reached out and patted her hand. He stared straight ahead. Sierra got the impression he was summoning up courage. "Forgive me for saying this, but is it possible you've turned Skinbone Harris into the enemy as a way of denying your feelings for him?"

She felt like he'd slapped her. Her shock must have shown. Shark raised his hands, stumbling over his words. "I meant that in the nicest way possible. Think about it…what proof do you have he's a bad guy? You enjoyed spending time with him, and yes, I know he told you he was an assassin, but no person in their right mind would blurt that out if it was true. And you said he grabbed your shoulders when you mentioned Foxtrot, but wouldn't you have had the exact same reaction if he'd said that to you?"

Sierra looked at Shark like he'd sprouted horns. "I don't believe this. You're *defending* him?"

"No, I am not defending him. You are missing my point."

"Yes, you're right. I am missing your point." She folded her arms. Shark hit a nerve, but she wasn't about to admit it.

"All I am saying, Damsel, is I fear you are letting emotion cloud your judgment."

"Because I'm a woman?" she snapped.

"No, because you are human."

They sat in silence. Misery churned inside her. "It doesn't matter. None of this matters. I can't risk running into him again. I need to concentrate on what's important: clearing my name, finding Neil's killer, and figuring out Grace's role in all of this."

"I fear that is where you are wrong."

Sierra threw her hands up in exasperation. "Jesus, you are like a dog with a bone about all of this." She got up and went to stand near the window. The first streaks of dawn were breaking through the night sky. "How can I be wrong?"

Shark took his time, mulling over his next words. She could see his reflection in the window. He fidgeted on the bed and she knew he was uncomfortable.

"Damsel? I have known you for a short amount of time, but I already consider you a treasured friend. It is not my intent to cause you pain or duress. However, as your friend, there are some things that appear crystal clear to me that perhaps you might not see because you are too close to the situation."

She squeezed her eyes shut, touched by his words. He was only trying to help, she had been wrong to snap at him. Turning away from the window, she met his eyes. He reminded her of a puppy who'd had been kicked one too many times. She felt like a wretch.

"I'm sorry, Shark," she said, sitting down beside him. "I consider you a treasured friend too. I just…I feel like my world is spinning out of control. From the moment this whole thing started, I've been second guessing myself. I never expected any of this to spiral into such a huge mess. I don't mean this the way it's going to sound, because I know what I'm about to say will sound bad, but…"

"It's okay, go ahead. I promise not to judge."

She blew out a stream of air, trying to think of how to phrase what she wanted to say. "I was furious with Neil. He'd pissed me off and I was in the kitchen, trying to cool down."

Her face twisted in anguish. Putting herself back in that place, reliving her feelings was harder than she imagined. It put her in a bad light, made her less than noble. Covering her mouth with her hand, she looked up at the ceiling in a vain attempt to keep her tears at bay. She was dimly aware of Shark stroking her back, telling her it was okay.

She shook her head, biting the inside of her lips. "It's not okay. Nothing will ever be okay again."

"Tell me about Neil."

Her voice cracked. "I don't know what I was thinking. I don't know what's wrong with me."

"You've been through a horrible ordeal."

"No," she sniffed, wiping her nose with the back of her hand. "That's not what I meant. The night he died, I was furious with Neil. He'd been cold and distant and I went there with the intention of making a last ditch effort to save our relationship. I wasn't supposed to see him that night—we rarely saw each other on Fridays, but I insisted. I thought, if we could just have one good night, maybe everything would be okay."

"There's nothing wrong with that. He'd been shutting you out because of Foxtrot. You had no way of knowing."

She glanced at him out of the corner of her eye, shaking her head. "But I *did* know. Things hadn't been good for us for a very long time. It was almost like a switch had been flipped somewhere along the line."

Sierra wrapped her arms around herself and began rocking back and forth. "Grace pushed us together. She thought Neil would be perfect for me. I was seeing Donovan back then. We were pretty serious, even talking marriage." She laughed, but it was a bitter sound. "At the beginning, Neil pulled out all the stops. He was sweet, romantic; he was the perfect guy." She looked down at her hand; the diamond she wore seemed to mock her. "He was too good to be true, you know? I was dazzled. How many people get that? I thought I was the luckiest girl in the world."

"It sounds as if you were."

"I was, for a while. It was all so perfect. *Too* perfect. I don't even know how to explain it. It was like he could read my mind. Corny as it sounds, he made every single one of my dreams come true. The first year of our relationship was the happiest of my life. When Neil proposed, I was on cloud nine. We both agreed to a long engagement. To be honest, it was my idea, but a few months after our engagement Neil started to change. I told myself that was normal, the first bloom always wears off. This was long before Foxtrot. At least I think it was. I won't bore you with a play by play. Suffice to say, I was thinking of ending things with him."

"And then you had the misfortune of witnessing his murder."

"I still loved him, or, at least, I loved the memories of what we had in the beginning. Stupid or not, he had reason after reason why there'd been such a shift in our relationship. I let him convince me the problems were temporary, that we'd get back to how we used to be. When I watched him die…" She went silent, waging an internal war with her emotions. "I'd clung to hope for so long, I fought hard to fix whatever was broken between us, because I knew how good it could be. Do you have any idea how guilty I felt? How petty, for starting fight after fight? For being angry at him in those last few seconds before he died? It's eating me up inside when I have time to stop and think. On the one hand, I couldn't let myself see the truth. I couldn't admit to myself he'd stopped trying. But then I blame myself, for not realizing the trouble he was in, and for making his life miserable by trying to turn our relationship into something it wasn't anymore."

"I think, perhaps, Damsel is being too hard on herself."

"That's kind of you to say, Shark, but I have to live with this guilt. In a way, it was easier when I thought he was having an affair with Grace. At least then I wouldn't have to shoulder all the blame. How horrible does that make me?"

"If I may be so bold, my impression, after listening to your story, is that in your heart, you knew things were over. You knew you deserved better than what you were getting from him. But you are a woman who honors her word and you gave him chance after chance."

"I did. I really did."

"And now here you are, wracked with further guilt, because in the midst of all the turbulent emotions you are feeling, you met a man you truly connected with and you feel that's wrong. If I was a shrink, and I am the first to admit I am the furthest thing from it, I would hazard a guess you don't think you deserve to be happy. You don't trust yourself not to fall for the wrong man again, so you have found every reason in the world not to trust your feelings for Skinbone Harris. It's far easier and far less painful to push him away right from the start. Unfortunately, he's given you the ammunition to do it."

"Even if Skinbone hadn't given me ammunition, I haven't even mourned Neil. How could I possibly have feelings for another man? That's just so... coldhearted."

"I think you have. Perhaps not his death, but you've already mourned the death of the love you shared. You need time to put this all into perspective. You've taken the first step tonight. And as you've said, you have far more pressing matters to deal with. Give it time. If, you are in fact, meant to be with Skinbone Harris, you have his number. Until then, you need resolution. Let the dust settle, as it were. If he is involved with Foxtrot, you'll know soon enough."

***

"We should be out celebrating. Too bad every decent bar is closed at this hour."

He jerked awake, instinctively going for the gun beside his bed. In a flash, he pointed at her head.

Her laughter pierced the room. "Relax, Darling, it's only me."

"What the hell are you doing did here?" he swore, lowering the gun. It would have served her right if he'd blown her head off.

"Does it matter?" Angelica purred. "Neil Thornton's netbook has been recovered. It should be in our hands by tomorrow. The tracking device worked. You are a genius." She draped her arms around his neck and lowered her mouth to his, kissing him full on the lips. "I'm sorry I doubted you when the first attempt on the train failed."

He was in no mood for her shenanigans. He pushed her away, his brow knotting into a frown. "Jesus Christ. Couldn't this wait until morning?"

"Don't be testy," she pouted. "We have precious little time to formulate our plans."

He threw the sheet back and pulled on a pair of shorts. "Don't you think you're jumping the gun? Thornton's computer may not contain everything we need."

"Sleep must have addled your brain. This is a major victory for us. If Neil Thornton's netbook contains the formula and the prototype, we can move forward." She sidled up to him, running a finger down his chest. "Isn't that what we both want?"

He bit back his impatience. Angelica was cunning, but she lacked the prowess to pull off the plan on her own. She would be nothing and nowhere if he hadn't come into her life. The woman had no concept of the obstacles they faced. "Where exactly was the netbook found?"

Angelica sat down in a huff, crossing her legs. "Can't you enjoy our victory for once before going off on one of your tangents?"

"*Where* was the netbook *found* Angelica?" he repeated through clenched teeth.

"Oh for God's Sake." She glared at him, rustling around in her purse for a cigarette. He wanted to throttle her as she took her time lighting one and blew out a long stream of smoke.

"Answer me," he demanded, knowing full well the type of game she was playing. She wanted to punish him for ignoring her advances by making him wait for an answer.

"One of your teams recovered it in Arizona, at the home of Luke Preston."

He was trained at schooling his emotions. Keeping his face impassive, he strode to the wet bar and poured himself a drink. Angelica came up behind him, wrapping her arms around his waist, pressing her body against his. He fought the urge to peel her off him. There was work to be done but Angelica was in the mood to play. If he denied her, she would cause a scene and time would be wasted.

"Pour me one too, would you darling?"

He splashed some vodka into a glass and passed it to her, ignoring her seductive gaze. Angelica revealed a turn of events he hadn't anticipated. There was only one way Luke Preston could have gotten possession of Thornton's netbook.

Sierra Montgomery.

Up until now, he'd written her off as an inconvenience, someone who'd been in the wrong place at the wrong time. He was beginning to think he'd underestimated her and that she'd somehow managed to align herself with the enemy. She'd disappeared without a trace and had been smart enough to send them on a wild goose chase, leaving a deliberate false trail for them to follow. Then she vanished off the radar, after she'd placed Thornton's netbook in Luke Preston's hands. Her fiancée had been murdered. Not too many women would be able to keep their wits about them after something like that. Not the way Sierra Montgomery had. The single slip up she made was turning on the netbook and even then, she'd escaped four gunmen with enough firepower to take down a small army.

He was going to have to cast a wider net, use whatever means necessary to smoke her out.

Aligning herself with Luke Preston had been a fatal mistake. He flexed his well-muscled arm. Sierra had to die.

Chapter Twenty-Three

Sierra fumed, she was having a difficult time containing her anger.

How dare they? The bastards thought they could play with her emotions? They'd made a huge mistake, underestimating her ability to separate fiction from fact.

Unable to sleep, she'd asked Shark if she could use his laptop. Since no one knew of their connection, she reasoned it was safe to access the internet from his computer. Before they delved any deeper, she wanted to check the news to see if the Chicago Police department had any leads in the brutal slayings of her friends.

She hadn't expected to see her own face staring back at her alongside a current photo of Neil. Sierra read the accompanying article in shock, not quite able to grasp what she was reading.

"Shark, are you awake?" She spoke in a whisper, in case he had fallen asleep.

"Yes. The pillows here are far too lumpy to provide a restful night's slumber. I have not been able to get a wink of sleep."

"Can you come take a look at this?" She pushed back her chair, biting a fingernail.

He sat up in bed, rubbing his eyes, before fumbling on the nightstand to find his glasses. "Has something happened?"

"Something's happened, all right. The Chicago papers are printing a bunch of lies."

"What do you mean?" He located his glasses and shuffled over to the computer, sitting down in the chair she'd vacated.

"Take a look."

Shark glanced at the monitor. Sierra hovered behind him, impatient for him to start reading. "That's a lovely picture of you."

"Thank you." It was a reflex response. She laid her hand on the back of his chair. "Read the article."

He pushed his glasses up higher on his nose, and nodded reading aloud.

"Chicago Police still have no leads in the disappearance of scientist Neil Thornton. Thornton, age thirty-three, was reported missing Monday morning, days after the death of Grace McGinley, another Chicago area scientist.

"Thornton's fiancée, Sierra Montgomery, also remains missing. Initial reports indicated the couple were victims of an apparent robbery attempt. In a statement released earlier today by Chicago area police, robbery has now been ruled out as a motive in their disappearance.

"It remains unclear whether the couple was abducted or are the victims of foul play. Police are urging anyone with information about their whereabouts to contact their local authorities."

Shark quietly re-read the passage a second time, looking at Sierra in dismay. "How can this be? According to this article, Neil is alive."

She folded her arms, pacing the floor. "He's not alive and he sure as hell isn't missing."

"Is there any chance he could have survived?"

"You didn't see him, Shark. No one could have survived what happened to him. No one. That," she pointed to the computer screen, "is a bold-faced lie. Don't you see what they are doing?"

"Uh…" his eyes moved between her and the computer. "No."

"They're setting me up."

"You've lost me."

She grabbed a chair and pulled it towards Shark. "The killer. He must have gone back to Neil's house and removed all traces of his remains." She shuddered, flashing back to the horrific memory. "They, whoever *they* are, want me to believe Neil is alive."

"Why?"

"They probably assume if I see this, I'll come forward. They want to plant a seed of doubt in my mind, hoping I'll start wondering if he is alive."

"And if you come out of hiding, they can recover Foxtrot."

"Exactly. But they're smart enough to cover their bases. Not only do they suggest Neil is alive, they allude I might have been kidnapped. Plenty of people out there want to be heroes, Shark. They're counting on that, hoping if someone spots me, they'll call the authorities."

"Unwittingly leading the killer or killers right to you."

"A scenario I never counted on."

"It's insidious. Using a potential Good Samaritan to do their dirty work, leading you like a lamb to slaughter."

"Please, Shark, I don't need any help visualizing."

"Oh, yes, of course. My apologies. I got a bit carried away."

She rocked back on her heels. "They've also put you at risk."

"Me?" he blinked. "How?"

"If anyone spots me with you, they could assume you're a kidnapper."

Shark's mouth dropped open, "Surely no one would suspect me?"

"Why wouldn't they suspect you? Because you don't think you look or act like a kidnapper? How many people originally suspected Ted Bundy of murder? Looks can be deceiving."

He tilted his chair back, covering his face with his hands. Sierra turned away, unable to look at him.

She heard the front legs of the chair hit the floor. Shark let out a tuneless whistle. "These people are pure evil. They want to isolate you from anyone willing to help you and have enlisted millions of people to try and 'save' you. It's ingenious, really. One has to applaud their efforts."

"I don't think I'll be applauding any time soon."

"I detect a note of bitterness in your voice, Dear Damsel. None of this should come as a surprise. You've known all along your adversaries are dangerous people, willing to stop at nothing to further their as yet unknown agenda."

"Am I supposed to be comforted by that?"

"Indeed you are. You are missing a succinct point."

"Which is?"

"You have them scared. You've successfully eluded them. They have no idea how much you know or what you plan to do with the information. Employing the general population to assist them in their efforts to find you smacks of desperation. This press release clearly shows you maintain the upper hand."

On impulse, she leaned over and hugged him, planting a kiss on the top of his head. "Thank you. You always know the right thing to say." Shark's face turned an immediate shade of red.

"Does this mean you're not giving up?" he asked.

"Damn right it does. Let's get to Arizona and nail those bastards."

***

They landed in Sedona earlier than expected, much to Sierra's relief. She arched her back and tried to work out the kinks in her neck. She'd dozed off a time or two during the flight, only to be awakened by vivid nightmares and a stiff neck. So much for rest.

Shark used the time to work on breaking the encryption. "Any luck?" she asked.

"Won't be much longer." His fingers flew over the keyboard. His lips moved while he read, although he didn't utter a sound. Satisfied, he snapped the laptop shut and smiled at her, a glazed look in his eyes. "Have we landed?"

"We have. You really get into this computer stuff, don't you?" she asked, amused by his enthusiasm.

"It's my life."

"I can see that." She unfastened her seatbelt, stifling a yawn. "Thank you for doing all of this, Shark."

"No thanks necessary. It is my pleasure to help." He peered out the window, "Ah. I see our car is waiting."

She turned to look "Is that a rental?"

"Nope, it is ours. And on that note, wait here. I will be right back." He left her sitting while he ran down the stairs and hurried to the car. He withdrew a shopping bag from the backseat and was back within minutes. Shark handed her the bag. "Look inside."

Not sure what to expect, she took a cautious peek. "What is all this?"

"Your disguise. Since your picture is in the news, and since you've already been seen in your baseball cap and pony tail, I took the liberty of providing you with a new look."

She reached into the bag and pulled out a short red wig, a straw hat and designer sunglasses, squealing in delight. "This is perfect. How did you manage this?"

"There are times when money comes in handy. I would have bought you some new clothes, but I had no idea what size. There is a boutique in the hotel we can finish shopping for you there."

"This is great. Thank you."

"You are most welcome. Go ahead and put them on. In the meantime, the pilot and I will transfer l your things to the car."

Sierra nodded, not trusting her voice. She didn't want to embarrass The Shark by bursting into tears, overwhelmed by his thoughtfulness.

It was the nicest thing anyone had ever done for her.

***

Skinbone rubbed his eyes. Falling asleep, even for a short time, had done him more harm than good. He was irritable, and groggy and would do anything for a cup of coffee, even hospital swill. Unfortunately, he'd have to do without. He was not about to leave Luke's side.

The bleep of the monitors told him Luke was hanging on. What he needed most was a reason to keep on living. There were three things Luke wanted: to find his son, to bring down Kepler International, and to see Skinbone settled with a good woman.

Only one of those was in his power. He wished he could give the old man all of them. He squeezed Luke's hand, hoping he knew someone was there with him. It hurt like a sonofabitch to see him lying there, fighting for his life.

"You gotta fight old man. Don't you dare give up on me. So happens I need your advice. You heard me right. Old Skinbone has gotten himself into a situation. There's this woman who's gotten under my skin. Problem is..."

The door to Luke's room opened. Skinbone's words trailed off as a bright eyed nurse quietly entered the room.

"How's he doing?" she whispered.

"No change."

"He's a fighter. He made it through the night and that's a good thing."

Skinbone hoped she was right. He wouldn't rest easy until Luke was sitting up in bed, cracking jokes, and giving him a hard time. He stood up and walked over to the window, giving the nurse space to go about her business. Sure enough, it was a new day. The sun was shining hot and bright. People were milling about, going on with their day, like nothing had changed. Maybe for them, nothing had. His world, on the other hand, had been tilted on it axis.

Shit. When the hell had things gotten so complicated? In what world was it fair that Luke was barely clinging to life?

Kepler was going to pay. If he knew what was good for him, Hollywood was riding their asses right now, making their lives a living hell. It was what they deserved. They'd blown up enough lives. They didn't give a damn who they sold Foxtrot to; even knowing it could decimate the free world.

What kind of sick sonofabitches were these people?

***

They checked into a Residential Inn. Shark had managed to procure new identities for them both. They were now Roger and Sarah Morton, on holiday from Poughkeepsie.

Sierra didn't ask how he'd pulled it off. She didn't want to know. "You know what I find strange? The newspaper article didn't mention FBI involvement; it only mentioned the Chicago Police. So why was Donovan St. James at our old hotel?"

Shark barely looked up from the computers. "Coincidence, perhaps?"

"Not likely, considering he has ties to Neil, Grace, and me."

"Personal, then?"

She shrugged. That didn't feel right either.

"Perhaps the FBI is involved and keeping a low profile. If I'm not mistaken, isn't it standard for them to be involved in all alleged kidnappings?"

"Maybe." She wasn't convinced. The Donovan she knew would leave no stone unturned in finding her or figuring out what happened to Grace and Neil. He wouldn't be content to take a backseat. At the very least, she'd expected to see a quote from him somewhere in the article, reaching out to her or beseeching people to aid in her safe return. *He couldn't possibly believe Neil was alive, could he?*

She plopped down on the sofa with a weary sigh, eyeing the stack of banker's boxes from Grace's house. Biting the inside of her cheek, she peeked out the window. What she wouldn't give to be able to go out exploring, and enjoy the day like a tourist.

Enough dwelling. No one was going to wave a magic wand and fix her problems. If she wanted to save herself, she was going to have to work for it. Sierra reached out and dragged the boxes towards her, groaning at the effort. She wanted to go through them one last time to make sure she wasn't missing anything.

Shark's phone rang, shattering the silence. They shared an uneasy look. "I don't recognize the number."

"Maybe you should answer."

He flipped the phone open, bringing it to his ear. "Yes, this is Walter Marx."

She couldn't tell much from his end of the conversation. For the most part, he was giving one word replies. Her muscles tensed, wondering if it was bad news. She didn't have to wait long. A smile broke out on his face and he gave her a thumbs up. Mystified, she waited anxiously for him to conclude the call.

"That was the realtor. Change of plans. We can move into the Shadow Lake property at any time."

His news did nothing to alleviate her fears. "Did she say why?"

"Seems the renovations were completed sooner than anticipated."

"Doesn't that strike you as odd? First we couldn't have it for weeks, now suddenly it's available?"

"Perhaps, although the end result works in our favor, doesn't it?"

She was getting wound up. "I'm not so sure. Think about it. The timing is all out of whack. I run into Skinbone Harris, manage to get away from him, and as far as we know, we weren't followed. Whoever is after me has no idea where I am. All of a sudden, the news is calling me a kidnapping victim and now you get a call from the realtor telling you the property is available? It smells like a set up to me."

"Damsel, I know it looks that way, but you are forgetting something important."

"What?"

"No one knows of our connection. No one could possibly tie you to me. This is indeed a fortuitous turn of events."

"Would you please not use that word?"

"Which word?"

"Fortuitous. It makes my skin crawl. I get this weird feeling whenever I hear it."

His smile drooped. "It was not my intention to upset you."

"No, Shark, it's okay. I'm edgy, that's all."

"Understood. Then perhaps we should get back to work so we can conclude this unfortunate chapter in your life."

Sierra forced a smile. "Good plan." *But is it,* she wondered, *or are we asking for trouble?* She removed the lid from the nearest box, and unwrapped the sea shell she'd salvaged from Grace's burned out home, wondering yet again why her friend had displayed it in such a prominent place in her room.

Chapter Twenty-Four

Angelica smoothed down the black sheath dress she was wearing, and rose to greet her guests. "Father has yet to come out of his room. We will have to start the cocktails without him."

Ethan Wilde arched a brow. "Are we drowning our sorrows?"

Angelica's lips curved in a knowing smile. "I see no reason for that, do you?"

Ethan's eyes shifted to Donovan St. James. "I would hazard a guess my shadow might think so?"

Donovan flashed his pearly white teeth. "You make my job sound tedious. I am here to protect our assets. We have paid you well for Foxtrot. My superiors want to be assured I am on hand when it is recovered."

"*If* it's recovered," Wilde corrected.

"If it *isn't*," Donovan quipped, "Kepler International stands to lose a fortune."

Angelica listened to the exchange with amusement, enjoying the way each of the men's hackle's rose with each word. "Gentleman, I believe we can all behave in a civilized manner. We all want the same thing, don't we?"

Neither of them met her gaze. *More's the pity*, she thought. She would have enjoyed watching a human cockfight. It was rather disappointing they chose the more civilized route of lapsing into silence. She moved between them in a fluid motion, brushing against them both. No doubt both their eyes were riveted on the form fitting dress which displayed her figure to advantage. What God didn't provide, elective surgery corrected. The power her surgically enhanced face and form gave her over men was worth a few weeks of pain every now and again.

She let her arm trail over the bar, and then prepared their cocktails. Ethan and Donovan eyed each other, to her amusement, reminding her of two bulls in adjoining pens. Dampening her lips, she unabashedly let her gaze devour Donovan first. He was impeccable, as always in a dark blue Pierre Cardin suit that accentuated his ice blue eyes and blonde hair. Then she shifted to Ethan, growing warm as she drank in his dark, dangerous appeal. His black hair was worn long, European style, and his impenetrable jet-black gaze aroused her. It delighted her to no end that she had made both men her lovers, sharing supposedly confidential information with each of them. She wondered if either one of them suspected. She would have loved to taunt them further, heightening their jealousy but this was neither the time nor the place. Business first, pleasure would have to wait. For now.

Angelica mixed the martinis, pouring them into three glasses. She raised the first one to her lips and took a small taste, her red lipstick leaving a stain, before handing the glass to Ethan. He caught her eye, took the glass from her, and raised it in acknowledgement. Smiling provocatively, she repeated the process before handing a second glass to Donovan. He gripped her wrist hard enough to make her gasp before taking the glass from her trembling hand.

It disappointed her that Ethan missed the exchange between her and Donovan; he was staring at the small table which she'd set up next to the bar. A black satin swatch of material covered an angular object resting beneath it. His fist clenched and unclenched at least five times while she watched. The poor boy seemed a bit tense.

Not to be outdone, Donovan reached out and fingered the fabric. "What have we here?"

Her eyes narrowed, bottom lip protruding in a pout. It irked her that the men were paying more attention to each other than to her. A situation she planned to rectify. She slapped Donovan's hand sharply; Ethan smirked. "You do not touch what is not yours," she admonished. "But if you must know, we received a special delivery last night."

"Foxtrot?" Ethan's voice was almost as sharp as her slap.

She sidestepped the question. "We should wait for Father to join us for the unveiling. Until then," she speared an olive, putting on a show of slowly sucking it between her red lips, "let's enjoy our cocktails. I enjoy a little suspense, don't you, boys?"

"Where is Jared?" Ethan asked.

"You haven't been paying attention. He's in his room, sulking. We must be patient. Father will join us when he's ready."

"Is he still bereft over the death of Grace McGinley?"

Angelica shuddered. "Please, that *woman* was nowhere in his league. I will never understand what possessed him to get involved with someone so distastefully common."

"Your claws are showing, Angelica," Donovan chided. "Not everyone can be as wealthy as the Kepler's. Grace McGinley undoubtedly garnered your father's attention because she had a brilliant mind."

"A brilliant mind does not make up for lack of breeding," she snipped.

"Well, the suspense is killing me. Perhaps you should go check on him," Ethan suggested.

"I agree," Donovan seconded.

"Fine." Outnumbered, she slammed her drink down on the bar, glowering at Ethan. Her dark eyes flashed with annoyance, treating both men to an icy stare. "I'll see what's keeping him."

Ethan downed the rest of his martini and turned towards Donovan. "What is your angle? What are you *really* doing here?"

"Excuse me?"

Before Ethan could rephrase his question, a shrill scream echoed through the penthouse. Both men went running, stumbling over each other to reach Angelica first.

She stood at the foot of her father's bed, shrieking loud enough to wake the dead.

Jared Kepler would not be joining them tonight, or any other night. Two bullets had been fired, one to the chest, and one to the head, leaving Jared Kepler lying on a mattress soaked with blood and gore. His accusing eyes, wide open.

***

Sierra was craving dinner. Ribs precisely, which disturbed her to no end. Barbecue reminded her of the little hole in the wall place in Memphis, where she'd first met Skinbone Harris. Pushing him from her mind, she shifted through the last of Grace's things.

She intended to keep everything for sentimental reasons. She tossed some photos on the coffee table, trying to summon up a taste for Tex-Mex, food she normally loved. Her mind zeroed in on a carafe of Sangria. She'd bet anything a few glasses would help her sleep through the night, which would be a welcome change. The cat naps she'd been taking were no substitute for the real thing.

All she had to do was pry Shark away from the computers. "How much longer?"

"Patience, Dear Damsel. With any luck, all will be revealed no later than then tomorrow morning."

"I won't last that long," she whined without thinking.

"Excuse me?"

"We need to take a break. It's a beautiful night, and we have to eat. If I don't feed my howling stomach soon, I'm going to turn into the wicked witch of the west. Trust me; I get cranky when I'm hungry. It's not a sight you want to see."

"It was foolish of us not to stop at a grocery store and load up on supplies. Now that you mention it, I'm a bit hungry myself. I should have warned you that I get absorbed by my work. Unless someone reminds me to eat or sleep, I forget to do either."

"It's settled then. I'll go change and put on my wig. In the meantime, why don't you work your magic on the computer and find us a halfway decent restaurant."

"Shall I find a diner, or would you prefer to sample local fare."

"Let's live it up. Local fare it is."

"Excellent choice."

***

Half an hour later, they were speeding down North Highway 89A, to sample authentic Mexican and Southwestern Arizona cooking. Shark insisted on driving and Sierra was too hungry to object. She couldn't take her eyes off the scenery, finding herself glued to the passenger window.

The view was breathtaking; under different circumstances, she could see herself kicking back and enjoying the town, so it was difficult to explain the chill slithering up her spine. Looking out at the red rocks, she found herself experiencing flashes of déjà vu.

It was a hot night, the temperature hung in the mid-nineties. The air conditioning in the car barely made a dent against the heat. Despite the warmth, Sierra rubbed her arms, fighting an inner chill. Her face twisted in confusion. "I've been here before."

Shark sat ramrod straight in the driver's seat; his hands gripped the wheel in the ten and two position. He shot her a quick glance. "I have the strangest sensation, that I too, have spent time here in the past. Although, until today, I would have sworn I'd never set foot here."

"Exactly what I was thinking." Her words hung between them like a misplaced clue. Neither one of them knew what to make of it. "I'm getting these flashes, like something is trying to jog my memory."

"Yes! Repressed memories. It's odd that we're both feeling the same things."

"More than odd. It's damn creepy."

"I agree."

Without warning, voices rang out in her head. Snatches of childish laughter. Playing hide and go seek amidst the red rocks. Sierra frowned, wrapping her arms around her body. She was dimly aware of Shark slowing the car.

Something painful had happened here. It wasn't a coincidence she'd picked Arizona out of all the places they could have gone. They'd come here for a reason, even if they hadn't been aware of it.

Shark searched the landscape, a look of puzzlement on his face. He was searching his memory, same as she was. Despite the glimpse into childhood games and the echo of laugher, Sierra was certain evil lurked here, hidden somewhere deep within.

The laughter grew louder in her mind. She closed her eyes. A vivid memory sprang to life. She was maybe five years old. Her hair was still platinum blonde and she was wearing a cool, white cotton dress with splashes of purple flowers. Her hands covered her eyes, and she was counting to ten. She saw her fingers open wide enough to peek through. Another little girl, dressed in a plaid jumper, ran to hide. The girl was giggling; she scurried behind a large rock formation and crouched down behind it. Her face darted out for an instant, as if she wanted to be sure she'd chosen a good hiding place.

Sierra gasped. *It was Grace. Grace was the little girl in the plaid jumper.* Her mind reeled. That was impossible. Grace moved to their neighborhood in the second grade. They'd become fast friends, sticking to each other like glue. This memory showed her meeting Grace at least two years earlier.

Was she going crazy?

Shark grasped her hand hard enough to jolt her back to the present. "Are you okay?"

"No." Truth be told she was shaken to her core. "Maybe my imagination is playing tricks on me, but I remembered playing a game with Grace. The problem is, I didn't meet her until two years *after* the memory."

For the first time since she'd met him, Shark looked rattled. "I too, am having vague impressions of having spent time here. They are dim, but they are also very real."

Sierra broke out in a clammy sweat. "And yet, neither of us remembered until right now, until we were back here."

"It's most unsettling."

She leaned out the window, feeling a pull to the land. "We were meant to be here, just like we were all meant to meet." Her voice was faint, fading out into the twilight.

The Shark shivered. "This is giving me the heebie jeebies."

Ordinarily she would have laughed at his choice of words. Not tonight when they seemed apropos. "The real question is what the hell does this have to do with Foxtrot?"

***

The penthouse swarmed with activity. Angelica sat on a sofa, flanked by Ethan Wilde and Donovan St. James. A homicide detective sat across from them, firing off questions.

Angelica leveled a glacier stare at the detective. "My father has just been murdered. Show a little respect please, Detective."

Donovan laid a hand on her shoulder. "He's only doing his job."

"He's right, ma'am. This is standard procedure. We need to rule you out as a suspect so we can concentrate on finding whoever did this to your father."

She pursed her lips. "Fine, let's get this over with then." Turning to Ethan, she brushed her hand across his thigh. "Would you be a dear and get me a drink?"

The detective raised an eyebrow at the implied intimacy. Jotting down a quick note, he raised his head and resumed his questioning. "Was anyone threatening your father?"

"Not that I am aware of."

"Has he received any ransom demands?"

"That's an odd question."

"Ma'am, a scientist who worked for him is dead, another is missing. We need to establish whether there is a connection," the detective snapped.

"That's ridiculous. Do you know how many people my father employs? It's far more likely the two scientists were screwing each other and a jealous girlfriend is responsible for their death and disappearance."

Ethan raised a brow and handed her a drink. The detective caught the exchange and scribbled in his spiral notebook.

"What about you, Mr. Wilde? Did Mr. Kepler have any enemies?" the detective continued.

"I am certain he had many. A man with his wealth and power is bound to have adversaries. But I am not aware of any who made specific threats or who wanted him dead."

"Fair enough."

The chief medical examiner emerged from Jared's bedroom, a solemn expression on his face. A gurney carrying the remains of Jared Kepler followed. Angelica covered her eyes at the sight of the black body bag, burying her head against Donovan's shoulder.

"I've been through enough for one day, Detective," she said in a shaky voice. "Are we done here?"

The detective nodded, flipping his notebook shut. "I have enough for now. Again, Ms. Kepler, I am very sorry for your loss. I'll be in touch."

She rose, swooning slightly. Ethan steadied her. "Thank you. Find whoever did this, Detective. Find the bastards who murdered my father."

"Yes, ma'am," his eyes traveled over the strange trio one last time. He had the sour look of someone who'd inadvertently waded into a waist high pile of shit. Angelica didn't notice. She sank back down on the sofa, seeking comfort from her companions.

***

Skinbone's voice was raspy. He did his best to keep up a steady stream of conversation so Luke would know he was there with him. He didn't want the man to feel like he was alone. Time lost all meaning for Skinbone.

His entire world narrowed down to Luke and the sterile hospital room. He might have been there for days, or hours. It felt like he'd been at Luke's bedside forever, but it didn't matter. Until the old man recovered, this room was where he planned on being.

There was a soft knock at the door. A pretty nurse entered, a gentle smile on her face. She came bearing gifts. "I know this is against the rules, so I'm trusting you not to tell on me," she whispered, handing Skinbone a large container of coffee and a sandwich. "You need to look after yourself too, you know. We can't have you collapsing on us."

Skinbone took the food and drink, his eyes welling up with gratitude. "Thank you. You're an angel."

Her cheeks turned a sweet shade of pink, "You look like you could use the food – and a friend."

He noted her shy smile and the hint of interest sparkling in her bright green eyes. They were a balm to his weary soul. It felt good to be looked after. *This* was the kind of woman he should be falling for. "I appreciate it. Maybe I can return the favor sometime."

Her smile widened. "I'd like that. Now enjoy your meal. I'll be back to check on you both later."

He grinned as he watched her leave the room, "See, old man, there might be hope for me yet. That pretty little nurse was making time with me. You may get your wish, after all."

Skinbone hoped his words would elicit a response from Luke. When none was forthcoming, he unwrapped the sandwich and wolfed it down. He reached for the coffee, scalding his mouth with the bitter hospital brew. He didn't give a damn. Nothing had ever tasted so good.

He savored his coffee to the last drop, wishing he could squeeze more out of it. Crumbling the cardboard cup in his hand, he stretched out his legs with a sigh. "Don't know why you live in this town. The memories here can't be good for you. When you're back on your feet, we're gonna need to talk about moving you out to Texas. Hell, any place would be better than Arizona."

Skinbone closed his eyes for a moment. Memories of the camp his parents had been tricked into sending him to came rushing back. He didn't know if he was one of the unlucky ones who remembered because memory suppression hadn't worked, or if his memories hadn't been successfully erased due to his family's connection to Luke and his son. While he was haunted by memories of his time at the camps, he would never fall victim to Kepler's treachery again, unlike thousands of others who weren't as lucky. All the more reason retrieving Foxtrot was so vital.

Thanks to Luke, he could live his life a free man, without fear of being manipulated into performing unspeakable acts against his will. Skinbone knew evil existed; he had firsthand knowledge of it. Though some might find it contradictory, that's how he'd become an assassin. Someone had to rid the world of the sonofabitches hell-bent on destroying it.

He reached up and fingered the small scar embedded in his scalp. It was a living reminder of what had been done to him and the havoc these bastards planned to wreak. There was no doubt he was one of the lucky ones. Because of Luke Preston, he'd escaped being an unwilling accomplice to the reign of terror Foxtrot was poised to unleash.

***

They ate in silence. Had this been a normal day, Sierra would have loved the rooftop cantina Shark had chosen. The scenery was breathtaking, the view nothing short of spectacular. The smells wafting from the kitchen should have made her mouth water. It was a shame she couldn't enjoy any of it. Beneath the beauty and the lively atmosphere lurked an ominous presence, setting her nerves on edge.

She reached for the carafe of Sangria, replenishing both of their glasses. "Do you think there's a connection?"

"I don't know what to think." He hunched forward across the table, speaking in a whisper. "On the surface, it's highly unlikely the two are related. Nothing hints at a possible connection. On the other hand, what are the odds that we would both have suppressed memories of having spent time here as children? The mind boggles because that brings into play a whole spectrum of events that are beyond my belief system."

She took a large bite of her fajita, staring out at the view. When she finishing chewing, she wiped her lips with the napkin and met Shark's eyes. "Predestination. I know how weird this is going to sound, but Skinbone Harris used those exact words the night the night I met him—that we were predestined to meet for a reason that was as yet unclear to both of us. I didn't know it at the time, but he had to be referring to Foxtrot. That's the only possible connection between us. Now, it's looking like you and I were also predestined to meet, but is it because of Foxtrot, or because of what happened to us here as children? And then there's Grace." She folded her arms on the table. "This is all so confusing. Did my meeting Grace here, all those years ago, set this whole thing in motion? Or is the whole situation nothing more than a cluster of bizarre coincidences?"

"I can't begin to comprehend the odd twists and turns that are playing out before our very eyes. I can only surmise that it is in our best interest to get back to work and find out what is on those computers."

Appetite gone, Sierra shoved her plate of food aside. "Let's get out of here. The sooner we get to it, the better."

Shark started to push his chair away from the table when his eyes fixated on a spot near the bar. The color drained from his face. Seconds later, his jaw dropped open and a look of sheer panic replaced his worried expression.

Sierra turned to see what he was looking at. A big screen TV was mounted behind the bar, a Breaking News banner displayed near the bottom of the screen. He grabbed her wrist in a death grip, pulling her out of her seat, dragging her towards the TV.

The volume was turned down but they were close enough to read the story as it scrolled beneath the footage.

Jared Kepler had been found shot to death in his Chicago penthouse.

Goosebumps rose on her arms. *If Kepler, with all his money, power, and security couldn't save himself, what chance did they have of staying alive?*

The contents of her stomach slammed into her throat, gagging her. Shark swayed on his feet, clutching onto the bar for support. Belatedly, she remembered Jared Kepler had almost been his father-in-law. She pried his fingers off her wrist and put her arm around him in an attempt to provide comfort. His body was rigid beneath her hand. Violent death had now touched both their lives, tightening the strange bond between them.

She rubbed his back, afraid he was going into shock. Signaling to the bartender, she ordered a shot of tequila. Most of the Sangria they'd ordered with dinner remained untouched. Not that it mattered. Shark needed something stronger.

While they waited for the drink to arrive, Sierra struggled for something appropriate to say. Somehow 'sorry for your loss' didn't cover the gamut of emotions either one of them was feeling. She hadn't known Jared Kepler, but all of their lives were inexplicably intertwined.

There was nothing she could say, or do, to ease the pain and the fear Shark was experiencing. She knew, because she was feeling it too. For the moment, they were of one mind. She knew each and every one of his thoughts as intimately as if they were her own. At least he didn't have to be alone, the way she had been after she watched Neil die.

Sierra opened her mouth to tell him everything was going to be okay, stopping herself in time. She had no right to make promises she couldn't keep. The truth was, she was terrified nothing would be okay ever again.

The news switched to another story. "Are you alright?"

Her words sounded hollow, ridiculous, even. Shark shook his head, sagging onto a bar stool. She bit her lip, wishing she knew how to get them out of trouble. "Maybe you should go home, back to Chicago."

That roused him out of his stupor. "And leave you to deal with this alone?"

"Yeah, if it will keep you safe."

The bartender set the shot of tequila in front of Shark. Her friend gripped it with an unsteady hand, raising it to his lips. Her eyes drifted back to the

TV. An image of Luke's face filled the screen. The caption was an update on an earlier report of his shooting. The news wasn't good. He was in critical condition and hadn't regained consciousness.

For a moment, she couldn't breathe, and then agony caught fire inside her. They switched to a shot of his bullet-ridden house. She choked out a sob. It was her turn to clasp Shark's hand in a death grip. Pointing to the screen, she felt the words tear out of her. "That's my Luke. He's been shot too."

Her legs buckled. She teetered backwards, clutching a stool for support. A shot of white hot fear burned through her veins. She turned to Shark, eyes swimming with tears. "Oh, my God, none of us are safe."

Chapter Twenty-Five

Sierra's jaw tensed. Shark scrunched down in the passenger seat, shell shocked. Up till now, he hadn't experienced any of what she'd gone through first hand. It was easy for her to want to blame herself for getting him involved; she had to keep reminding herself there was a good chance that everything happening was far beyond their control.

Except for Luke. If she hadn't left the damn netbook behind, he wouldn't be lying in a hospital bed fighting for his life. He'd probably never had a chance. She thought back to the train. Bullets shattered the windows minutes after she logged on. There was no way in hell anyone could track an IP address that fast; Neil's netbook had to be equipped with a more sophisticated device, allowing them to trace it instantaneously. She pounded the steering wheel with her fist. The bastards must have hit squads stationed everywhere in the damned country to be able to react with such speed. Whoever wanted Foxtrot had deep pockets and long arms. She swallowed hard. It was amazing they hadn't gotten to her yet, considering the resources at their disposal.

She was worried about Shark. He'd retreated into his own little world. He seemed to have gone numb. She had to find a way to snap him out of it. Spotting a liquor store, she made a sharp left turn, peeling rubber before sliding into a parking spot. She had no idea if tequila was a remedy for shock, but Shark definitely could use another shot.

They were back on the road minutes later, making it back to the hotel in record time. Shark roused himself out of his stupor the moment they arrived, beating her to the door. She followed him inside, flipping on the lights and setting down the bottle on the small kitchen counter. He was already at the computers. "Shark, what are you doing?"

"We have to get answers, now, tonight. I fear for your safety. If anything happens to you, I will never be able to live with myself."

"Shark, whatever happens to me isn't your fault. I never should have run in the first place. If I'd called the police like I should have, neither of us would be in this position."

He glanced up at her with eyes as wide as saucers. "I am forced to disagree. If you'd called the police, you'd be dead. If they can get to Jared Kepler and your friend from the train, they can get to anyone, anywhere, at any time. If anyone is to blame, it is I. I discouraged you from calling your

FBI friend while you had the chance."

She pulled off the wig and raked her fingers through her hair, "Look, neither one of us is to blame. We didn't start this."

He raised his index finger. "But we can finish it."

Sierra wished she shared his confidence. She tossed the red wig on the sofa, and rubbed her scalp where the bobby pins had dug in. Since seeing the newscast, the need to see Luke throbbed inside her. If she'd been alone, she wouldn't have bothered coming back to the hotel—she would have headed straight to the hospital—but there was no way she was going to abandon Shark, not in the shape he'd been in. Her first priority had been getting him back to the hotel and making sure he was okay. Her lips curved in a sad smile. His behavior on the ride home may have scared her, but he bounced back quickly. She guessed he needed time to process Jared Kepler's murder.

The night had taken a dangerous turn, leaving her more on edge than ever. A part of her had clung to the hope she was being overly paranoid, that she'd blown the danger she was in out of proportion, making it bigger than it was. Tonight proved without a shadow of a doubt her imagination wasn't working overtime.

Shark was immersed in his work, attacking it with renewed urgency. There wasn't anything she could do to help him and she'd already gone through Grace's things enough times to know she wouldn't discover anything new. She wasn't needed here.

"I'm going to run out for a while."

Shark swung around from his work, eyeing her with trepidation. "It's not safe for you to venture out alone, Damsel. Based on what's happened tonight, I'd go so far as to say I don't think either one of us should leave until we accomplish what we've set out to uncover."

"I have to go see Luke, see how he's doing. I have to apologize to him."

He blinked in confusion. "The news report stated he hasn't regained consciousness. While I applaud your concern, how can you justify putting your own life at risk to see a man who won't even know you're there?"

"It doesn't matter. *I'll* know I was there. I'm responsible for what's happened to him. For God's Sake, Shark, the man saved my life." There was a note of hysteria in her voice. She took a deep breath, knowing she had to calm down. "I can still say what needs to be said."

Shark shook his head. "It's not safe. As you succinctly put it, Luke went to great lengths to save your life. I don't mean to sound cruel, but he did you a great service. By placing yourself in jeopardy, you will be dishonoring the very thing he did for you. This may not be my place to say, but I don't think he would want that. His actions were heroic; don't take that away from him to soothe your conscious."

His words had the impact of a ton of bricks raining down on her. He was right. She'd been ready to run off halfcocked. She perched on the edge of the sofa, feeling her face turn a bright shade of scarlet.

Shark hurried over to her. "I am so sorry. I didn't mean to hurt your feelings."

Sierra bit her lip, trying to get a grip on her emotions, "No, Shark, you're right, but you hit a nerve. She slid off the couch and walked over to the window. A full moon glowed low in the sky. "I do want to see Luke, though."

"Even if you had gone running over to the hospital, odds are you wouldn't have been able to see him. If he's in intensive care, visiting hours are very strict, and, if I'm not mistaken, you need to be an immediate relative.

"I'll be his long lost daughter."

"I sense your impatience, but this needs to be thought through. What do you even know about him? You can't go barreling into his room claiming to be his daughter without knowing a thing about the man. For example, he may actually *be* surrounded by friends and family. How would you explain yourself? Or, what if he is a prominent member of the community? The hospital staff would expect you to know his history. And, of course, the most obvious concern of all—what if the people who tried to kill him are watching his room? You could be walking into a death trap."

The air deflated out of her. "Okay, you win. For now."

"Thank you. Why don't you use my laptop while I'm working and see what you can dig up on Luke. If you can't find what you need, I'll help you later."

She wasn't thrilled with waiting, but she couldn't ignore Shark's reasoning. "No matter what happens, I am going to see him tomorrow."

"Fair enough. I know how much this means to you, but you also have to think of your welfare."

"Agreed." She frowned. "Oh my God, Shark, I got so caught up in everything tonight, I didn't even realize. Neither did you."

"Realize, what?"

"What we were talking about earlier. Predestination. I met Luke on a train to New Orleans. What are the odds that you and I ended up in Arizona at the exact same time Luke got shot? Are we supposed to write that off as yet another coincidence?"

She could see the wheels turning in his head. He backed away from her, covering his mouth with his hand. A shudder raced through his body. She hurried over to the counter and twisted open the bottle of tequila, pouring a splash into a glass before pressing it into his trembling hands. "You okay?"

He shook his head. "The heebie jeebies again. Can't seem to shake them tonight."

Sierra hesitated for a minute before pouring a healthy dollop of tequila for herself. "We'll find a way to get through this. I don't know how, but we will."

He swallowed the drink in a single gulp. "Tomorrow, we'll figure out a way to get in to see your friend. For now, I need to get back to work. I need to focus on something I can understand."

Sierra took a sip of the tequila and grimaced. Straight shots weren't her thing. "And I'll see what I can find out about Luke. Would it bother you if I turned on the TV? I'll keep the volume low. I want to find the news channel."

"I won't be distracted by the TV."

She picked up the remote and settled on the couch near the window. She noticed a strong wind kicking up while she booted up Shark's computer. In the dim light, she typed in the words Luke, Sedona and Shooting. She'd only caught the tail end of the newscast, missing most of the details.

The wireless connection was slow. She yawned, waiting for the search engine to show its results. Coverage of Jared Kepler's death and Luke's shooting was taking a backseat to a volcanic eruption in Iceland. She yawned a second time, glancing back at the laptop. The cursor was still spinning. She closed her eyes, hoping to rest them for a few minutes while she waited. Deciding it wouldn't hurt to stretch out, she propped a throw pillow behind her head. *Two minutes,* she promised herself, *then she'd get to work.*

Seconds later, she was fast asleep.

***

The entire scenario sickened him. In his experience, the death of a powerful man had a tendency to turn into a farce. In these situations, grief took a backseat and a carnival-like atmosphere took over. The vultures began circling the carcass and there was a palpable sense of excitement permeating the air. He knew he shouldn't generalize. There were instances among the rich and powerful where those left behind were racked with grief, wandering empty rooms in a fog of true bereavement.

This wasn't one of them.

He extricated himself from the odd tableau on the sofa, viewing the situation with a sense of the macabre. The grieving daughter dressed in black, the chosen color of mourning. The other lover, hovering over her, speaking in a sickening, solicitous tone.

His lips curled in wry amusement. No doubt an engagement announcement would be forthcoming. He could, of course, stir the pot, and be the first to present himself to her on bended knee, murmuring sweet nothings to the tune of what a powerful couple they would make. Seduce her by playing the subservient male, pumping her up to enlarge her overinflated ego.

As if.

She thought she had him wrapped around her finger. He raised an eyebrow, cutting off the bitter laugh at the image of Angelica perched on her pedestal, weighing her options, deciding which lover to choose. The twit had no idea how little she mattered.

Did she really think her plastic body was enticement enough to discourage him from his original plan?

He was here for one reason and one reason only—it sure as hell wasn't to get into the daughters pants, although that had been a necessary and sometimes pleasurable evil.

He wanted Foxtrot, plain and simple. No amount of death or drama was going to discourage him.

Angelica's shoulders shook with delicate grief. The poor dear. She bowed her head, burying her gorgeous face behind slender fingers. The room went still, heightening the drama. Seconds passed. He cocked his head, anticipating an eruption. She didn't disappoint. Her gut wrenching sobs tore through the room on cue, splintering the silence.

He watched as Donovan St. James pulled Angelica close, smoothing his hand over her thick raven tresses. It was enough to make his stomach turn. Angelica sunk her claws into any man she met. She'd done the same to him, and now she was flaunting her newest lover in his face.

Ethan sauntered over to the bar and mixed himself another drink. His companions were too engrossed in each other to spare him a glance. Considering the circumstances, their negligent behavior bordered on insulting. Angelica had shared his bed often enough to know what he was capable of.

Perhaps they needed a reminder. After all, the night deserved a fitting climax to mark the passing of Jared Kepler. Besides, his curiosity could only be contained for so long; the beast inside him demanded to be fed. He'd been patient long enough. It was time to force the rat to scurry out into the open.

"It's been an eventful night," Ethan began, confidence oozing through his deep timbre. He continued in his theatrical cadence, "However, we have come together this evening at the behest of Jared Kepler. And so, we shall honor his wishes, albeit from beyond the grave."

Angelica's head whipped towards him, eyes crackling with an ice cold-hearted warning he pretended not to see.

"What's wrong with you, man?" St. James objected, his tone incredulous. "Can't you see she is beside herself with grief?"

Ethan ignored his rival and flicked a fuzz off his suit coat, fixing his icy gaze on the pair. It disgusted him to be a part of this group. A cruel smile marred his face. "And yet Foxtrot, and the mission lives, does it not?" He dared St. James to challenge him. After all, it was Foxtrot that had brought them all together. Crossing over to the small table, he ripped the black satin covering off the item that rested upon it, "Let us all see why we have gathered here tonight."

Angelica leapt to her feet, her face gnarled with hatred, "How dare you?"

"How dare I?" He raised his eyebrows and looked down his nose at the unveiled item, fury pounding in his veins, "How dare *you? This* is what we were called here to see? A shot up computer? What the bloody hell is this?"

She drew herself up to her full height, snarling at him. "*That* is Foxtrot, you fool. What else could it be?"

"Foxtrot? Riddled with bullet holes? This is a worthless piece of crap." He fought the temptation to grab her by her elegant throat, clenching and unclenching his fists instead. "If this is any indication of Foxtrots power, Kepler International is a joke. *This* is what your team brings back? They've destroyed it, for God's sake."

Angelica blanched at his words, moving forward to touch the broken computer. Her shock seemed genuine; it was possible Jared had initiated tonight's meeting after all. Her eyes narrowed into angry slits, "It wasn't *my* team," she snapped, catching herself before she revealed too much. "I expected more. I expected Foxtrot to be intact."

Donovan St. James spoke up, "This is only one piece of the puzzle. There are other computers out there. McGinley and Thornton both worked on Foxtrot."

Angelica didn't appear to be listening. Her eyes glazed over as she stared at the computer.

"Now it all makes sense," Ethan continued. "Your ex-fiancée, the computer geek. The one your father was so high on you marrying. What was his name again?" he demanded, his gaze flickering between Angelica and the man who had inserted himself into both their lives.

"Shark," she whispered with a shudder of disgust, "Wally, Walter Marx."

"The computer genius. No wonder Jared was so furious when you kicked him out of your bed. He's the only one who can help us."

Angelica shrank beneath the scalding eyes trained on her. It was clear Wally "The Shark" Marx didn't figure into her plans. "No," she said, stepping backward.

"Too damn bad, we need him," Ethan barked. "Get him here."

Her eyes flew between the two men. "My father was murdered tonight. No one will be making any demands on me. I suggest you both leave. Now. Before I call security."

Ethan smirked, loving every inch of her discomfort. St. James appeared hard pressed to control his anger at being dismissed.

All in all, he'd done a damn good job of shaking things up. It would be interesting to see how things played out. He hoped Jared Kepler was enjoying the tribute to his memory. This was only the prelude to the final showdown. The stakes were higher than anyone imagined. A fight to the death loomed on the horizon, and he planned to win.

God had forsaken him long ago, but the truth was he'd rather rot in hell for the rest of eternity than live in a world controlled by Foxtrot.

***

Daylight was waning. Sierra ran past the red clay rock, desperate to find Grace. Her little white dress was stained with sweat, her small body trembled with fear.

The children were allowed two hours of play each day. When the alarm sounded, they spilled out of the laboratory like frightened mice, out into the penned yard, scattering to its furthest corners. A few of them had discovered a small hole in the chain link fence, which they crawled through when no one was looking, pretending they could escape the camp. It was a game, really. There was no way to escape. The camp was located in the middle of nowhere. No one would come to their rescue. Ever.

Sierra was frightened. Her small shoulders shook with sobs. "Grace," she cried out, "Come out, come out, wherever you are. It's time to go in."

Grace didn't answer. Sierra glanced over her shoulder. The guards were herding the children back inside. There would be a headcount; any child not accounted for at the predetermined time would be severely punished. Sierra wiped the tears from her eyes, smudging dirt across her face. She had to go back. Maybe Grace was already inside. Falling to her hands and knees, she crawled back through the small opening in the fence, and ran towards the laboratory as fast as her small legs would carry her.

A hand swooped down on her out of nowhere, lifting her into the air. Her screams splintered through the yard, striking terror in the hearts of the other children. Sobs turned into hiccups of fear when the guard clamped his hand around the back of her neck, carrying her inside like a stray dog.

They passed through the assembly hall, where the children gathered for attendance before being fed dinner, and a fresh round of tests were performed on them. None of the other kids would meet her frightened eyes. She was taken to a small, dark chamber the size of a closet, and tossed inside, scraping her knees on the concrete floor. Before the door swung closed, she saw Grace being carried away by another guard. She was shrieking, her tiny hands and feet pummeling the air.

Sierra curled into a ball, unsure of what to expect. It was so dark she couldn't see her hands when she held them out in front of her. Her tummy rumbled; she'd worked up an appetite while playing. She was always hungry here. The meals were meager—if she missed dinner, breakfast was a long time away. No snacks were allowed.

All alone, she started to cry. She wanted to be home, with her mommy and daddy, away from this awful place with the mean men, scary doctors, and the needles they stuck into her arms. She received shots twice a day. Sierra rocked back and forth, petrified of the punishment she knew was coming. She hated it here. They forced all the children to do tricks all day and evening with their minds. The only time they were allowed to speak to one another was during play time. The rest of the time they were kept isolated, performing the same tasks over and over again until the grown-ups were satisfied. Some of the tricks were frightening. One little boy could set things on fire. Another could send large objects flying across the room. Her bottom lip trembled, thinking of some of the things they made her do.

They strapped Sierra into a chair, attaching all kinds of wires to her. Some of them were hooked up to machines; others were attached to a box that shocked her with jolts of electricity if she didn't do exactly what they told her to do. One of the other little girls was terrified of heights and of water. They tortured Sierra until she used her mind to force the frightened little girl to climb a tall ladder, onto a narrow gangplank, over a deep swimming pool. It wasn't a normal swimming pool either, or diving board, like Sierra had seen before on TV. The gangplank was only a foot and a half wide, fashioned out of unfinished wood, and was at least ten feet above the water. The pool was built into the ground, the waters churning and bubbling with waves.

A strong wind blew through the room, something Sierra never understood. Wind happened outside, not indoors. But there was wind and waves, both making loud roaring noises. The girl stood on the small strip of wood, crying and shaking like a leaf, covering her ears to block out the noise.

They jolted Sierra with electric shocks until she used her mind to make the little girl walk off the plank, plunging ten feet down into choppy waters.

And they used other children to force Sierra into doing things that made her wish she was dead.

The fire had been the worst of it so far. They'd taken her outside and tied her hands to a wooden pole. An earpiece was shoved into her ear, though no sound came from it. She was scared to death, wondering what they were going to do to her, what her instructions would be. No one talked to her. A group of men started to erect walls around her, made out of logs, sealing her off in a wooden room. Her mind raced in terror, anticipating the threat she would have to overcome. No amount of imagination prepared her for what happened next.

The logs burst into spontaneous flames surrounding her. She couldn't run, there was no door to escape through, and her hands were bound to the wooden pole. The acrid smell of smoke began to choke her. Tears gushed out of her horrified blue eyes. She was going to burn to death, burned at the stake like the martyrs she'd heard about in Church.

And then a voice boomed in her ear. "Use your mind to douse the flames."

She was so scared she could barely think. The flames were getting closer; the grass caught fire, sending sparks racing towards her. Fighting the urge to close her eyes, she stared down the flames, extinguishing them one by one, and carved a doorway for herself. She used her mind to untie the ropes fastening her to the pole and ran to freedom from the smoldering pile of rubble around her. Her eyes met those of a little boy. He was hooked up to wires, same as she'd been when she made the little girl leap into the curling dark waters. The boy smiled at her as she ran to safety. Despite the heat, a chill ran through her. He had the coldest, blackest eyes, she'd ever seen.

Sierra awoke with a start, her heart racing a mile a minute. It took her a moment to get her bearings and remember where she was. The dream came hurdling back to her. She gasped in horror, realizing it wasn't a garden variety nightmare. Being back in Arizona jogged her memory of the camp she'd been sent to. *Her nightmare had been real. The black eyes of the little boy—she'd seen those eyes again, as an adult, seconds after Neil burst into flames.*

Covering her mouth with her hand, she raced to the bathroom, oblivious of Shark's worried cries following her. She flung up the toilet lid, and sank to her knees, losing her supper.

This was no coincidence. She shook her head, trying to quell the violent trembling seizing her body. *Everything tied together in some impossible, inexplicable way.* The nightmare was crisp in her mind. Shark pounded on the bathroom door. She used her feet to scramble away from the toilet and leaned up against the tub for support. Covering her ears she tried to drown out the noise, as another memory came rushing back to her.

She was fastened to a metal table in the center of the laboratory/camp. This time she wasn't alone. Grace lay prone on a table to her right. To her left was the little boy with the cold black eyes. A doctor hovered over her, holding a drill in his hands.

"They won't remember a thing," someone said, "We will erase all their memories, and their abilities until technology catches up to us. The drugs and brainwashing will wipe their minds clean. All we need to do is implant the chips in their brains. And when the time is right, we will activate their powers. We will have the perfect army, controlling their minds and their psychic powers. Tracking them like robots, making them perform to our specifications. Twenty, thirty years from now, our people can take over the world. Until then, they will function like normal human beings, with normal lives, until we give the command. Now drill the damn holes in their heads—this isn't the first time we've done this. We've been planting the chips since the late sixties. We will cause a revolution the likes of which has never been seen. Do your job, Doctor, *or you will be one of the first causalities of the revolution we have planned. My only regret is that I most likely will not live to see it. But my son, Jared, he will be king of the world, and what a magnificent*

world it will be."

Sierra clutched her stomach, succumbing to dry heaves. Her hand reached out to trace the scar hidden beneath her hair. She remembered the doctors talking. It had been right after the car accident which had taken the lives of her parents. She'd escaped the worst of it by being in the backseat, but she'd experienced extensive head trauma. They had to operate on her brain to reduce swelling and remove the shards of glass embedded in her scalp. The doctors talked about a metal piece they'd removed from her brain; they hadn't understood how it had gotten there. The metal shard hadn't been a result of the accident.

It had been the chip those bastards had implanted in her brain.

She curled into a little ball, horrified by what she was remembering. The magnitude was enough to crush her.

Shark burst through the door, eyes wild. "Damsel, have you fallen ill?"

She raised her head in slow motion. No matter how bad she wanted to escape from the memories, she couldn't. Grace had one of those chips embedded in her brain. So had the killer. And now she'd sucked Shark and Luke into this atrocity. She gripped the edge of the bathtub and hauled herself up. "I'm okay."

Shark breathed a sigh of relief and ran over to her. "Are you certain? It looks as if something dastardly has befallen you."

Sierra nodded. She was in a daze, but she couldn't give into it. If there was ever a time in her life to be strong, it was now; she would not allow herself to wallow in the memories It was then she noticed Shark's eyes danced with morbid excitement. He was jumping out of his skin.

"What's happened?" she asked.

"I have broken the code. Come sit down. The files are being converted as we speak. Within a matter a seconds, we will have the answers to Foxtrot."

The air whooshed out of her body. She doubled over, feeling a hit to her solar plexus. The missing pieces were falling into place.

"Damsel?"

Her mind reeled. She grabbed Shark, overcome with sudden terror. "Shark, you were at the camp. You're one of *them*."

"One of *whom*?"

"We need to get you to the hospital right away."

"What are you talking about?"

An alarm sounded from the other room. A computer generated voice announced the file conversion was complete. He broke into a smile. "Success at long last."

She shook her head. "Shark, that's not important right now. You have a microchip implanted in your brain. We have to get to the hospital and get it removed."

"Damsel, you have me most concerned. I will do my best to head your warnings, although I think your distress is the result of a nightmare. You had a fitful sleep, tossing and turning and mumbling out loud. Forgive me for saying so, but you look like you are still absorbed in what I am certain were quite vivid dreams. While it is my express desire to help you, first, we need to see these files."

There was no talking to him. He'd see for himself that her nightmares were real. She allowed him to link his arm though hers and lead her towards the living room area. He pulled a chair up next to his, beside the computers. Her eyes drifted to the TV droning on in the background. Luke's picture filled the screen. The announcer looked somber, "Former FBI chief, Luke Preston remains unconscious…"

Her eyes widened. *Luke was with the FBI?*

Shark's hand coiled around her wrist, yanking her back to the present… and the computer. "Holy Mary, Mother of Moley. This is unspeakable. Horrific. Insidious. Dear God, Damsel, we must find a way to stop this. Are you seeing these files? I have reviewed them all, but the situation is most dire."

She dragged her eyes to the computer screen, already knowing what she would see. "We need to get you to the hospital, Shark," she repeated in a deadpan voice. "You are one of *them.*"

His eyes met hers. "If I didn't know you had my best interest at heart, I would be crushed by your words. Have I not proven my devotion? Become your most trusted ally? Surely, you cannot truly believe I am one of *them*."

Sierra could feel her desperation rising. "Shark, you don't understand. I remembered, in my dream. I *saw* what happened at those camps. I saw what they did to me, and to Grace, and to the other children. It was what they did to *you* too, years later. My God, Shark, *I* was one of them."

"What are you saying?" His voice held a note of fear.

She grabbed his hand, placing it on her head, moving his fingers over her scar. "Do you feel that?"

He ran his hands over the spot, eyes flickering in confusion.

"I had a microchip in my brain. It was removed years ago. At the time, the doctors thought it was a shard from a car accident, but it wasn't. It was a microchip." Tears welled up in her eyes, "They can't get to me, but they can get to you. We have to have it removed. Now. Tonight."

His Adams apple trembled above his collar. He remained silent while he digested her words. He nodded once, looking up at her with frightened eyes. "Be that as it may, you have no proof I have one of those chips inside me and we have only skimmed the surface of what these files contain. First we need to know exactly what we are dealing with. No danger will come to me right now. We have what they need."

"We don't know that. Don't forget, Luke had the netbook. If they took it from him—they have access to whatever Neil had, to whatever information is important enough to kill for."

Shark hadn't thought of that. His eyes darted from her to the computer screen to the TV. "Holy blazes, Mother of Moley." He pointed to the TV, face collapsing before her eyes. She turned to what he was pointing at.

Donovan St. James and another man supported a breathtakingly beautiful woman between them.

Donovan. If Luke wasn't conscious, he could help them. Foxtrot was too huge for them to deal with alone. They needed someone they could trust. Someone with the enough power to fight the enemy.

Shark cocked his head, tears spurting into his eyes. He raised a finger, pointing at the screen. "Angelica. And her lover." His voice broke with heartache. Her eyes flew back to the screen. The second man with them had cold, black eyes. Like the little boy at the camp. Like the person who had killed Neil.

Dear God, could they be one and the same?

A headache brewed. She rubbed her temples in an attempt to stave it off, but questions continued to pound away at her. *Why is Donovan St. James with them? How is Skinbone Harris involved?*

The net was tightening. Shark turned an unhealthy shade of white. There was no time to waste thinking about Donovan or Skinbone. Shark was her first priority. She needed him to understand the urgency. Her hands flew to his head, searching for a scar. She found one, halfway between his ear and his forehead.

"Feel that, Shark. Now tell me you aren't in any danger."

He wouldn't meet her eyes. "I know I have a scar, a result of what I always assumed was a childhood mishap. I never questioned it. Children fall."

"You know better."

He shook his head. "I know we need to go through these files tonight. Even if what you say is true, *especially* if what you say is true, our mission has taken on a greater urgency than ever. We have to know exactly what we are dealing with. So far, all we have uncovered is an accounting of things that have happened before…what they refer to in the documents as The First Wave. If I do indeed have a chip inside me, we will lose precious time while I recover from the procedure. What if you are recognized at the hospital or, God forbid, the evil-doers have someone watching Luke's room? Your life and freedom are at stake, as are mine. Surely delaying my visit to a doctor for the tiniest time isn't the end of the world. I implore you, let's finish our work here first. As a precaution, have everything packed and ready to go in case we need to leave in a hurry."

Damnit, she thought, *it was an impossible situation.* Shark pled his case well, making valid points. She couldn't fault his logic. She was also afraid for him. Unless his chip was removed, he was for all intents and purposes, a dead man. A drone, controlled by powers they had yet to fully understand.

"Damsel? Are we agreed? I promise you, as soon as we go through all the data, I will go to the hospital. I could not, in good conscious, abandon you until our work is done."

She nodded vaguely in agreement, terror crackling inside her at the fate that could befall him if they took too long. Sierra offered up a silent prayer that Luke would regain consciousness or that she would be able to reach Donovan.

"Thank you." Shark said, returning to the computers. His demeanor changed, exposing his analytical side. This was his field of expertise. She could see it in the way his body straightened with confidence. His boyish exterior was replaced by an air of command, revealing a true genius at work.

His morbid excitement at breaking the code drew her eyes back to the monitor. She read along with him, feeling her overworked heart drop at the insidious plan churning out before her very eyes.

They had to save the world.

But first, she was going to save her friend.

Chapter Twenty-Six

Skinbone Harris felt his cell phone vibrate for at least the twentieth time that night. He rested his head against the guardrails surrounding Luke's bed and squeezed the older man's hand.

"Hollywood is all fired up about something," he explained to Luke, "but I ain't gonna risk using a cell phone in this room. They have rules for a reason. I'm going to step out for a few minutes and find out what's got his knickers in a knot. Now, don't you dare do something stupid on me, like die, or I swear I will haunt you in Heaven or Hell or whatever damn place we both wind up. You got that, old man?"

Luke's fingers twitched. Skinbone's stomach leapt to his throat. He sucked in a wad of air and hunched over the railings. "Did you hear me? Are you coming out of this?"

Maybe he was half-daft, but he swore he saw Luke's eyes working beneath his eyelids. He stood up, willing life into the old man. "You damn well better not be coming back to me because I mentioned Hollywood, or I will kick your damn ass."

Hell's bells. Was he imagining things or had Luke's lips curved into a hint of a smile. Skinbone grabbed onto the guard rails to keep himself steady. His voice was gruff, "Come on back to me, Luke."

The fingers on Luke's right hand moved. This time he knew he wasn't imagining it.

"Hallelujah!" Skinbone broke into a wide smile, tightening his grip on Luke's hand, "Squeeze if you can hear me, okay?"

The old man's fingers curled around his.

Luke licked his dry lips, his voice weak and raspy, "Don't think you can start bossing me around."

Skinbone didn't bother hiding the tears of joy running down his face. He leaned over and kissed Luke square on the forehead. "I knew you were a tough old sonofabitch. Hot damn."

Luke tried to lift his head. "Need to tell you something…"

Skinbone could see the effort was taking a toll on Luke. "They'll be plenty of time for talking later. You need to rest."

"The girl." Luke's voice grew weaker, "You have to save the girl. She's one of you. She was one of the children."

Skinbone frowned. "What girl?"

"Flash drive… in my pocket. Foxtrot. Will tell you everything. Find her, son, before it's too late." The old man was getting worked up. His eyes took on a frantic gleam. "Save her."

Luke's monitors started to beep wildly; he needed to calm down.

"Who? Who do you want me to save?"

"Sierra..." The old man's head fell back on the pillow, his words fading out. Skinbone panicked until he heard a gentle snore. For a minute, he'd feared the worst.

The burst of activity on Luke's monitors alerted the staff to a change in his condition. The doctor came bursting through the door, skidding to a halt when he saw Skinbone's face.

"What happened?"

Skinbone was still reeling from Luke's words. It took a moment to register what the doctor was asking. "He woke up. He squeezed my hand, said a few words, and fell asleep. That's a good sign, right?"

"He actually spoke?"

"Sure did." *But had he known what he was saying?*

"He's not out of the woods yet, not by a long shot, but yes, it's a good sign. I'm not going to lie to you he has a long road ahead of him, and it's still touch and go."

It wasn't what Skinbone wanted to hear. He was hoping for something more encouraging. Hell, right about now, he just wanted to know what Luke meant. Five minutes ago, Sierra Montgomery had a bulls-eye between her eyes for landing Luke in the hospital and playing a intricate role in Foxtrot. He'd been wrestling with his conscience, trying to work his way through his dilemma. Killing the woman he'd fallen in love with. And now the old man used what could be his last breath, begging him to save her. He shoved his hands in his pockets. The whole situation was a train wreck.

"I need to examine him. If you could please step out of the room for a few minutes?"

Skinbone nodded. "Sure." He was itching to look through Luke's things. He needed to know if the flash drive existed or if Luke had been delirious. In the meantime, he'd get himself a cup of coffee and see what had Hollywood all fired up.

***

There was no remorse. Jared Kepler had to die. He was too weak to handle Foxtrot or its implications. It was clear he was in over his head with the project. Obvious he'd gone soft. He'd been more upset about Grace McGinley's death than the loss of the information and the prototypes.

From that point, it didn't take much to discover he'd been paying off Grace in secret, from one of his offshore accounts. It was amazing how foolish people were. They'd go to great lengths to initiate a cover-up, only to be careless with their personal correspondence. To be fair, Jared had no way of knowing Grace would end up dead or that the work would be stolen; no reason to think his secret would be exposed.

Jared Kepler wanted Foxtrot to fail. He had been sabotaging the project from the beginning, a measure that not only endangered the Kepler empire, but the careful plans which had been laid out for the future.

In retrospect, it was a shame someone had killed McGinley. She'd been a brilliant scientist and could have remained useful. There was a delicious irony in having her work on Foxtrot, oblivious to the fact that she had one of the microchips implanted in her brain. Her creation would have been used against her, robbing her of her will, turning her into their unwitting pawn.

How unfortunate she made the fatal mistake of getting tangled up with the wrong man.

Kepler's ineptitude created the hailstorm they were now in. Whether he'd done it for love or had developed a conscience late in the game, was of no consequence. Once Foxtrot was recovered, he would have been in the way. There'd been no choice, he had to be eliminated.

There was no point in looking back. With Kepler out of the picture, he now had free reign to use whatever means necessary to move forward. The list of adversaries was growing shorter by the day. Luke Preston and Jared Kepler were no longer an issue.

Two down, two to go.

***

The clock was ticking. She felt it in every fiber of her being. Raking her hands through her hair, she peered over The Shark's shoulder. "What is all that?"

"It's running lists of names. All the children who were subjected to the camps."

She'd been about to scream at him to hurry up until she saw his anguished expression and the deep shadows beneath his eyes. Biting her lip to keep quiet, she reminded herself this discovery was hard on both of them.

They were running out of time. She needed to find a way to get Shark to speed things up. Then it hit her.

"Wait a minute. Whose computer is that? Neil's or Grace's?"

"Miss McGinley's."

"Doesn't that strike you as odd? Even if Foxtrot is related to the camps, why would she have all those names?"

He frowned. "You have a point. I got so caught up in the enormity of the situation the thought didn't occur."

"Maybe she was sending a message. Can you pause that and do a search?"

"Certainly. What do you have in mind?"

"We need to find the connection. I say we throw in everyone who we know is involved in some way. Let's find out if anyone else was in the camps. Start with you, me, Grace..."

His fingers flew over the keyboards. "Gotcha, who else?"

"Neil Thornton, Skinbone Harris, Donovan St. James, Luke Preston, Jared Kepler, what was the name of the dark haired man with Angelica?"

"Ethan Wilde."

"Okay, add him."

"What about Angelica?"

"A long shot, but add her too."

"Anyone else?"

"No one I can think of. You?"

He shook his head. "I think that covers the main characters."

"Okay then, do the search." She held her breath, having no idea what results she hoped for. Or what they would even prove.

The Shark leaned back in his chair and whistled. "Okay, here they come."

She gripped his shoulder hard, watching the screen. "Good Lord."

"Indeed. With the exception of Luke Preston, Jared Kepler and Ethan Wilde, the rest of us, at one time or another, were all subjected to the same atrocities." His hand stroked the computer screen. "Even my beloved, two-timing Angelica. Why would *she* have been subjected to the same torturous treatment as the rest of us? How could Jared have allowed his daughter to endure such unspeakable horror?"

Sierra didn't give a damn about Angelica. Something else caught her eye, "Wait, what's that?"

Shark frowned, "Those are the nearest hits to our search."

"Ethan Hania Preston." She rubbed the knot in her brow. "Do you think that means something?"

Shark shrugged. "Ethan Preston? Doubtful. It's most likely a random result of the search criteria which included the names Ethan and Preston."

Sierra wasn't convinced, but she let it go for now, stumbling back a few steps when the full impact hit her. *Skinbone Harris* had suffered through the camps too. He was *one of them.* They were all tied together, her, Shark, Grace, Donovan, Neil, Angelica...and *Skinbone.*

Knowing that muddied the waters. It didn't make Skinbone any less dangerous; he could be under their control, brainwashed to eliminate any threat to Foxtrot or he could want the information for his own purposes. Either way, she had no doubt he would kill for it, which made him the enemy.

She fell back onto the sofa, running a hand over her forehead. "Okay, now, wait. Something else doesn't make sense. How does Luke fit into all this?"

The more they discovered, the more perplexing the situation became. "Luke worked for the FBI. Could he have been investigating Foxtrot? We need more, Shark. You have to go deeper. The list of names is important, but so far, we haven't learned anything we didn't know or already suspect." Hopping off the couch, she pulled another chair over to the table. "Let me help, we can go through the files faster together. You work on Grace's netbook; I'll work on the laptop I took from Neil's house," she banged the desk with her fist. "God! I wish I hadn't left Neil's netbook behind for Luke to pick up."

Sierra couldn't slow the racing of her heart. Until they had hard facts backing them up, she couldn't take the story to Donovan or anyone else in authority. No one would believe their wild accusations; they'd be sitting ducks for the murderous bastards behind all of this.

It had been pure genius to murder Jared Kepler, making him the fall guy. All roads would point to Jared being the mastermind behind the insidious plot, allowing the true villain to hide behind a veil of protection.

She might not have proof…yet…but there was no doubt in her mind. The sonofabitch had killed before; he wouldn't hesitate to do it again. Neil and Grace had been taken from her and he'd almost succeeded in killing Luke. This was personal. Too many people she cared about were involved.

She had no idea how many faces lurked behind the cover of evil, but she knew one damn thing for certain.

They'd messed with the wrong woman.

***

Skinbone slipped a dollar bill into the hospital vending machine and watched a paper cup tumble down, and fill with foul smelling coffee. Didn't much matter to him what it tasted like, he needed to stay awake.

He burned his hands on the paper cup, and carried it over to a beat up table. He sat down and took a swig of coffee before punched in St. James' number on his cell phone.

"Where the hell have you been?"

Skinbone's hand curled into a fist. "It may have escaped your attention, but Luke Preston's house was shot up with him inside it. The bastards left him there like a dog, dying in a pool of his own blood."

"It's too bad the old man is dead, but we have bigger fish to fry."

Skinbone was hard-pressed to contain his rage. No expression of sympathy. Self-absorbed prick. It suited Skinbone fine to keep St. James twisting in the wind. "I don't give a rats ass about your fish and I sure as hell don't appreciate your attitude."

"Yeah, you're right. Sorry. I know you and Luke were close, but things are heating up back here in Chicago."

"Meaning what?"

"Jared Kepler was murdered last night. Found shot to death in his own bed. We've recovered a netbook belonging to Neil Thornton. All shot up, but we have a bead on a man who might be able to retrieve the information. A computer whiz who used to work for Kepler. Wally Marx, goes by the name The Shark."

Either Hollywood was a moron, or the coldest damn asshole this side of the Mississippi. Skinbone flexed his fingers. Had St. James been within spitting distance, he would have rung his neck. *Where the hell did he think the shot up netbook came from? More than likely, it was stained with Luke's blood.*

"Did you hear what I said?" St. James prodded.

It took every ounce of strength to keep his tone neutral. "Yeah, got it. Sounds like you're handling things. What else?"

"What else? We have a job to do. How soon can you get back here?"

"Not yet. Things need to be done."

"Things more important than Foxtrot? I need you on the next plane."

"I don't work for you, *Hollywood.* Get that straight."

"Luke may be gone, but he'd want us to follow though."

Luke *would* want him to keep at it. He had to respect the old man's wishes. But first he had to find Sierra. Skinbone swallowed his anger. It went down like a ton of bricks in his gut. "Going to be few days before I can head back. Keep your eyes open. Odds are, whoever killed Kepler will be at the funeral. That's the way these S.O.B.'s work and, right now, you have a better in with these people than I do."

Dead silence greeted him. Skinbone was short on patience. "You there?" he barked.

"Yeah. That's the thing. I got a problem. You might call it a conflict of interest," St. James began.

"What the hell are you talking about?"

"I can see you haven't been keeping up with the news. We still have doubt as to whether Neil Thornton is dead. Forensics went through the house with a fine tooth comb, I think I mentioned that to you right before you left town. I thought they might have missed something, so I pulled rank and had them go through it three, four times. There's no evidence he was killed."

"Let me get this straight. You actually believe Thornton is our man? Didn't we address this once before?"

St. James ignored the question. "Thornton's girlfriend is also missing. Could be they were abducted, because of Foxtrot, or could be…"

"Spit it out."

"Or it could be the girlfriend is our man."

Skinbone felt a tightening in his chest. "You're talking in circles. Get to the damn point."

"Thornton's girlfriend used to be my fiancé."

Sonofabitch. That was the last thing Skinbone expected to hear. He had a bad feeling about what was going to come next. St. James didn't disappoint him.

"I don't want her harmed. We would have been married right now if Grace McGinley hadn't introduced her to Thornton."

Skinbone felt a sharp pain right between the eyebrows. The veins on his forehead popped out. "You should have excused yourself from this case. How can you be objective with your personal connections?"

"I didn't believe she was involved, but it's looking more and more likely that she's been running the whole operation.."

"I get the point." Skinbone crushed the coffee cup with his bare hand. The hot liquid scalded him. He disconnected the call, not even registering the blisters from where he'd been burned.

Chapter Twenty-Seven

This was bad. It was real bad. Sierra went to stare out the window. It was almost morning. They'd worked through the night.

"We have to get to the hospital. We need to see Luke and warn him, if possible, or at least make sure he's being guarded. And we have to get that damn chip out of your head."

"The chip can wait, Damsel. We need to stop this before it goes any further. Do you know how many people are at risk?"

She whirled around to face him. "Yes, of course I know, but my first concern is you."

"While I am most appreciative of your concern, my life pales in comparison to the damage that will be done if we don't stop this."

Sierra ground her teeth, trying to think. "Will you stop being so damn noble? Your life matters, alright? It matters to me. I'm not about to let you sacrifice yourself for the *cause.*"

"Okay," he sighed. "What do you propose?"

"If we take what we know to the authorities, we'll lose time while they investigate. I was wrong all along. Neil and Grace completed their work on Foxtrot before they died. These computers may contain all the research, but it's not the finished project. Grace must have hidden Foxtrot somewhere... and we have to find it. If the wrong people get their hands on it first..."

"We're all doomed."

"On some level, I understand. You hear rumors about things like this, all kinds of conspiracy theories, and you figure the people trying to 'expose the truth' are crackpots. That's what we would be classified as, Shark, crackpots. Enemies of the State. No one would take us seriously, except the people after Foxtrot, and they want us dead. We need hard evidence and even then we have to be careful. Jesus Christ, the *government* commissioned this project."

"Jared Kepler's father was an evil genius. He took things much farther than the government ever intended. They didn't know about the camps, or the chips, or what was done to the children. They just wanted to know if these things were possible as a way to protect us from future acts of terrorism." Shark was a patriot. Go figure.

"I know. That's why we need tangible proof. We don't have time to waste. Is the jet waiting?"

"Yes, but if I follow your advice and have the chip removed, who knows how long it will be until I can fly?"

"The new identities you created for us are flawless. No one is looking for Roger and Sarah Morton from Poughkeepsie. We'll be safe until you heal."

"Too much can go wrong."

"We'll take extra precautions." She took his hands in hers. "Look, to be on the safe side, we pack up everything and load it in the car in case we need to make a fast getaway. If only we knew…"

Her mind scrambled backwards at record speed. *Damn it, the clues had been staring her in the face all along, she just hadn't known what to look for.* She bolted away from Shark and began tearing through the boxes of Grace's things.

"She left me a key," Sierra yelled over her shoulder. "It was hidden in a place that only I would know about. No one else would ever think to look there."

He came up behind her. "You think this key has meaning?"

"I'm positive. Grace was clever. She insinuated in the documents you uncovered that she suspected someone was working against her and Jared—someone who wanted Foxtrot. She knew her life was in danger, so she took precautions. Whoever murdered Jared Kepler probably thought he knew more than he did. Grace was protecting him." She realized the implication with a heavy heart. Grace had loved Kepler; they'd been protecting each other. And now they were both dead, a fate her and Shark could easily share if they weren't careful.

The Shark rubbed his face. "I still don't understand. We don't know what the key unlocks."

"If she left one clue, she left another. It's here, somewhere. I know it is. It wouldn't be visible to the naked eye, she was too smart for that." She pounded her forehead with her fist, "I have to think like Grace. Like the key, she would have hidden another clue in plain sight. Somewhere that would be overlooked. Something that only had meaning to me."

The TV droned on in the background. They'd left it on all night in case there were further updates on the murder of Jared Kepler or a change in Luke's condition. Shark's face twisted with pain, startling her. He clutched his stomach; for a wild second she feared that he'd been shot. She grabbed him, immediately checking for injuries. He shook her off and hurried to find the remote, turning up the sound.

Their lives changed again in a split second. Her face filled the TV screen, staring back at her with an expression from happier times. Blood rushed through her head so loudly, it drowned out the newscaster's words. The words under the Breaking News headline told it all.

Sierra Montgomery wanted for questioning in connection of the murder of Jared Kepler.

***

Pain blasted in his head. The past came rushing back. He thought he'd eradicated the residual effects of the atrocities he had endured. He'd channeled that energy into rage, into a desire to destroy anyone connected to the development of Foxtrot and its predecessor, the First Wave.

Ethan Wilde had no illusions of grandeur. Not anymore. Those illusions died a painful death long ago when he realized he was not who or what he seemed. Hatred had taken hold, ruling his life like an iron fist.

What a fool he'd been To think he was "The Chosen One." The environment he'd grown up in stoked those feelings of grandeur. He'd been able to perform miracles for Christ sake; believed he was a hero, a vessel for good. But then his abilities were challenged, and the truth surfaced, forever shattering his illusions of being a good man.

He wasn't good. His childhood had been robbed from him. Those at the camp had seen his talents and infused him with evil incarnate. There was proof in the microchip he had ripped out of his head. They lost control over him but the power and the evil remained. There was no stopping his urge to destroy. He *was* evil. Hatred and his need for vengeance fed the evil, allowing it to take over his soul.

He thought back to when he learned the truth; the anger had nearly killed him. He went wild for a time with only his wits to prevent him from teetering over the deep edge. That's when he knew. He couldn't go up against *them* alone. Not if he was going to succeed. He needed to be sanctioned; to have a free pass to kill. Didn't mean he was going to follow the rules; if a few bodies turned up dead he was clever enough to cover his tracks. He'd killed the scientists. There hadn't been a choice. They'd had to die.

Thornton and McGinley had been hired to develop Foxtrot, an insidious project commissioned to resurrect the horrors inflicted during the First Wave. Granted it was only a job to them, funded by a government contract, but once again, Kepler International took things too far. He couldn't let them live. They would have gotten in the way, thwarting his intentions of eliminating Foxtrot and the back-up research, ensuring it could never be recreated.

He would destroy Kepler International from the inside out, blasting Foxtrot into oblivion, and removing all traces of it from Earth. But he hadn't killed Jared Kepler—someone beat him to it. Someone with an agenda of their own who wanted Foxtrot for a far more deadly purpose.

His hands balled into fists. *Focus on one problem at a time. Take care of them in order.*

Sierra Montgomery was still out there, a free woman. She needed to be stopped. He didn't know who she was working for, and didn't much care… until he saw the newscast.

He should have kept his mind on the mission. Instead he chosen to gratify his need to soak as much pleasure as possible out of Kepler's demise as possible. He may not have pulled the trigger to eliminate Jared, but the mighty house of Kepler International was starting to crumble. He poured himself a cup of coffee, and sat down to watch the news, relishing the fact his enemies were feeling a world of hurt, knowing he set it all in motion.

Switching on CNN, he settled in to enjoy himself.

That's when it happened. He saw a face he'd never expected to see, not in a million years. His coffee went flying. The pain in his head, and the memories roaring back brought him to his knees. His mouth contorted into a snarl, the rage inside him spewing forth, strong enough to make the floor quake.

The quest for vengeance burned inside him. *There was one more person who had to pay.*

***

Sierra tossed her clothes in a suitcase. "We'll go to Shadow Lake. With any luck, no one will look for us there."

"Finally." Shark breathed a sigh a relief. "It brings me great joy that Damsel is thinking about herself for once.

"Don't get too overjoyed. We're stopping at the hospital first to have that chip removed."

"That's insane. The risk is too great, especially in light of this most recent news cast."

"We have to see Luke and tell him what we know. We need to find out how to get in touch with him once we discover Foxtrot's location."

"Wouldn't it be far safer to call Donovan St. James? Granted, I have no wish to have any part of the man. In fact, I would shudder to be in close proximity to him, but that doesn't mean he can't help you."

"What are you talking about? You don't even know Donovan."

"I know enough." Shark's voice was grim.

She paused, hand on her hip. She was on the verge of asking what he had against Donovan when her cell phone rang. "It's Skinbone Harris. He must have seen the news. Are you sure these disposable phones can't be traced?"

"The phone itself, no, but as I've mentioned they might be able to pinpoint a location based on the satellite towers. The call could be a ploy, a way to narrow down where you are."

"We have to move. Now."

They hauled everything into the car. Sierra got behind the wheel. "Maybe you should stay behind, and get the chip taken care of. I can go on to Shadow Lake alone."

"I refuse to leave you. Not now, in your most desperate hour of need."

"Okay. Under the circumstances, I'm not going to argue, but once we get to Shadow Lake we are finding you a doctor."

It took every ounce of strength she had not to speed. She was worried. Seeing Luke was a risk, but she had to put her trust in someone, and he'd already saved her life once. She prayed he'd be willing to help her again.

Her stomach was in her throat by the time they reached the hospital. *What if there were guards outside Luke's door?* She turned to Shark, doing her best to hide her fear. "How do I look?"

"If I didn't know better, I'd think I was looking at Sarah Mortan from Poughkeepsie."

"God, I hope you're right." She pulled the visor down and examined herself in the mirror. The red wig and floppy straw hat didn't look out of place in Arizona; neither did the huge designer sunglasses. She'd made liberal use of the make-up Shark purchased, slathering on bright orange lipstick and long, coral fake nails. False eyelashes and sea green eye shadow topped off her new look. The brightly colored, loose fitting sundress disguised her figure.

Sierra sucked in her breath and forced a smile. "Let's do this."

The bright lights and bustle of the hospital jarred her. For some reason, she'd been expecting empty hallways and silence at this hour of the morning. Shark reached for her hand and squeezed. It was show time.

She let Shark do the talking. "We're here to see Luke Preston. He's in Intensive Care."

"Immediate family only."

Shark nodded. "My wife is…"

Sierra dabbed her eyes with a lace-edged handkerchief. "It's alright dear, you can say it."

He pulled Sierra close against his chest. "My wife is his daughter, by way of…"

The clerk cut him off, not interested in the details. "I only have one pass. Your brother has been by his side the entire time. Only one of you will be able to go in at a time."

"Thank you," Shark said, signing the register as Roger Mortan.

Sierra held her tongue while they navigated their way towards the elevator bank. Once inside, she swore. "*My brother?*" She hissed. "Now what do we do? We need a distraction."

"Too late." The elevator doors opened to Luke's floor.

She pressed the visitor's pass into Shark's hand. "You'll have to go in for me."

"Me? Why?"

"It will look better. You could say you worked with Luke at the FBI and talked your way past the nurses."

"I hardly look like anyone's idea of an agent."

"Fine." She snatched the pass. "I'll go."

Holding her head high, she marched down the hallway. She'd bluffed her way through other situations; she'd figure out a way do it again. Shark hurried alongside her, mumbling words of encouragement. None were needed. Luke's room was devoid of visitors.

Sierra couldn't stifle the sob escaping her lips. He looked small and frail in the bed. She remembered him as larger than life. A hero, invincible. She rushed to his bedside, tears running down her cheeks, "Oh Luke, I am so sorry."

His eyes blinked open; he looked confused.

"It's Sierra, from the train."

He raised a shaky hand. She grasped it, holding on gently. "I am so, so sorry to have gotten you involved in this mess. I have so much to tell you and I need your help. I know I have no right to ask, and you have no reason to help…"

"Shhh…" Luke licked his dry lips. "You need to listen. I know everything. Recovered the files from the netbook. Know how much danger you are in. You ran when your boyfriend, Neil Thornton, was killed. You have no idea what you stumbled into."

"You know about Foxtrot?"

"Foxtrot was my mission. My son…was in the camps…I didn't recognize you all grown up. You were there. You were one of the little girls with him."

She nodded, not bothering to wipe away her tears. "Yes, I was at a camp here in Arizona. I started to remember after I got to Sedona."

"You know…about the microchips?"

"Mine was removed years ago. It's a long story and we don't have time. I came here to beg your forgiveness and to get your help. I don't know who to trust. Neil and Grace completed Foxtrot before they were killed. The technology exists. If whoever is after me gets to it first, all they have to do is flip a switch and Foxtrot will be activated."

Luke's eyes bulged. "You need protection. I'll call my contacts at the FBI, get you into a safe house."

"No, it's too late for that. Grace left me some clues, but I haven't figured out where Foxtrot's hidden yet. I need to find it. And then I need to know what to do with it."

"Trust no one, for your own safety. This is too dangerous for a civilian. You can search for the clues while you're under protection. My boy can take care of the rest."

She glanced around to make sure no one was within hearing distance. "I need to do this. These bastards have messed with my life too. I've rented a house. Don't worry, it's under someone else's name. It's in Shadow Lake. I'm heading there as soon as I leave here."

"Wait…let him…keep you safe."

"Let who keep me safe? Your…boy?"

Luke's eyes fluttered closed. She froze, afraid he was gone. Steeling herself, she leaned over and checked his pulse. It was strong and steady beneath her fingertips. She sagged against the guardrail in relief. Their conversation must have worn him out. She'd wait around until he woke up. He'd tell her what to do and who he trusted to keep her out of harm's way.

Chapter Twenty-Eight

Skinbone pulled Luke's flash drive out of the computer. Sierra Montgomery might be innocent, but she sure as hell had bad taste in men. Donovan St. James aside, Neil Thornton was a real piece of work.

He tipped back his chair and stared at the ceiling, wondering what he would have done if he had been Thornton. He sure as hell wouldn't have been diddling around with his girlfriend—not when he knew full well his actions were putting her life on the line.

Letting the chair fall forward, he strummed his fingers on the table. This whole damn mess was more twisted up than a mangled old tire iron. Before he went back to sit with Luke, he needed to think. He found a worn out old sheet of paper in his back pocket and hunted down a pen. Face set in stone cold hard lines he decided to draw himself a tree and see what shook out.

The contents contained on the flash drive were encrypted, most of it was impossible to decipher. Skinbone assumed the files were a detailed accounting of Foxtrot—from inception to completion. At first, he didn't understand what Luke wanted him to see…until he came across a subfolder Luke had flagged. Within that file were Thornton's personal notes. They were benign enough at the beginning. Later, Thornton's entries became frenzied, the ravings of a paranoid man who was certain someone was out to get him. He alluded Grace was out to sabotage the project, felt that she was working for someone on the inside and that she wanted Foxtrot to fail. Then came the most damning evidence of all. Thornton was approached by someone…a person he referred to simply as X…and that person was trying to coerce Thornton to join forces with them. It was at that point Thornton began to fear for his life.

Except Thornton hadn't been paranoid. And he paid the ultimate price.

Who had Thornton feared?

At the top of the sheet, Skinbone wrote the name Jared Kepler. Drawing a long line beneath it, he went to work, adding four horizontal lines under Kepler's name. Beneath it, he wrote Thornton, McGinley, Angelica Kepler and Ethan Wilde. So far, he had squat. He added a series of lines to the left of Thornton's name and wrote in Sierra Montgomery. Next he penciled in a makeshift triangle, starting to the right of Jared Kepler and ending at Ethan Wilde. He added another series of broken lines to the right, printing Donovan St. James, Luke Preston, and his own name.

He studied the sheet of paper a good long time, hoping something would jump out at him. When nothing did, he decided to start eliminating. He put a slash through Jared Kepler. The man was dead; he wasn't behind this. He crossed out Luke, Sierra, and himself. Grace had been involved with Kepler, he could probably cross her out too.

That got him thinking about connections. He remembered those old word puzzles back when he was a kid. Finding hidden words and circling them. Words that were hidden in plain sight.

Someone had been threatening Thornton to turn over Foxtrot upon completion. Skinbone slapped his hand down on the table. The pieces starting falling into place. X wouldn't have killed Thornton. Not until *after* he'd gotten what he wanted. The scientist's death had thrown a huge monkey wrench into his plans.

If X wanted Foxtrot for his own purposes, Jared Kepler was another stumbling block. X had killed Kepler, knowing the murder would be tied to Thornton's and McGinley's. The cops would be looking for one killer, not two. He'd get off clean for Kepler's death, leaving him free to hunt down Luke and Sierra.

Even if that's how it went down, he still didn't have the answers he needed. He was missing something, but what? Throwing down the pen, he rubbed his hands over his face, feeling the stubble against the palms of his hands. He couldn't remember the last time he'd shaved. The answer was right in front of him, he knew it. He just had to find the connection.

He started circling like a madman, using distinctive strokes so that he could keep the groupings separate.

Who would benefit most by controlling Foxtrot? What were they after? Power? Or money?

Angelica Kepler had plenty of both now that her Father was dead.

When he finished, a single name jumped out at him.

Skinbone crumbled the paper in his hand. "Sonofabitch."

He leapt to his feet so fast, the chair crashed to the floor behind him. He didn't give a damn. He had to protect Luke.

***

Sierra slipped out of Luke's room, motioning for Shark to follow her to the waiting room.

He looked at her with his puppy dog brown eyes and a woebegone expression on his face, "Damsel, I hate to push you, but we really need to leave."

"I know, but we can't leave yet. We'll go soon, I promise. I want to wait a little while longer to see if he wakes up again. He looked awful. I don't know if he's going to make it."

"You have to think positive."

"Easier said than done. How can anyone think positive under these circumstances? You weren't in the room. In spite of everything Luke's been through, he was worried about me. About my safety. He offered protection."

"Not a bad idea."

"I got the sense he was referring to witness protection. Maybe it wouldn't be so bad for me, I have no one left. But you do. And if we let them take away our freedom, we'd be letting them win. I refuse to let that happen."

"But we'd be alive."

"That's no kind of life…" she stopped, and stared at Shark. " Unless… I'm sorry, this isn't a decision I should be making for you. Maybe witness protection is something you want to consider?"

He shook his head. "No, I was thinking of what might be best for you. So far, I've managed to remain off the radar. No one knows I am working with you. I have nothing to fear, no reason for witness protection. But I must urge you again, we have to leave. You aren't safe here."

"Okay. I want to peak in on Luke before we go. He was going to give me a name before he fell asleep—someone who can help keep us safe, and who he wants me to give Foxtrot to once we find it."

Shark looked uneasy. "Damsel," he began.

Sierra held up her hand to cut him off. "No, it's okay. I think I know who he was talking about. It has to be Donovan. It fits. They're both FBI and Donovan must be working the case. That's why he was in Chicago with Angelica and Ethan Wilde. He's working undercover."

"That's one way to put it," Shark mumbled under his breath.

"You really don't like him, do you? I appreciate your sticking up for me, but I broke up with him, remember?"

"A wise move on your part, I might add."

They were nearing Luke's room. "Shark, if I didn't know better, I'd think…"

Sierra stopped dead inches from the door. A man was inside, bending over Luke's bed. It looked like he was shaking him—or choking him. She didn't pause to think. Racing into the room, she picked up the first weapon she could find. A pair of safety scissors.

She plunged forward, burying the scissors into Luke's attacker's chest. His hand shot out, grabbing her wrist. He twisted her arm backward, deflecting the worst of the blow. She wrenched her arm free, recoiling in shock when he turned to face her.

Their eyes met for a split second.

"Sierra?" There was a stunned expression on his face.

She backed away, shaking her head in denial. "You?"

He glanced down at the tip of the scissors protruding from his left shoulder and yanked them out. They clattered to the floor. "What are you doing here?"

She watched them fall and skitter across the floor. "What the hell? Are you superman or something?" She gasped, remembering she'd teased him with those very words the first time they'd met.

"Or something." He smiled, taking a step towards her.

She grabbed a metal tray, swinging it at his head with all her might. It connected with a sickening thud. Skinbone swayed, gripping the bed rail for support. She swung a second time, hitting him again, harder this time. He sank to one knee, struggling to speak.

"Sierra, wait…"

He knew her real name. She'd be right about him all along. Skinbone Harris was the enemy.

"Sierra," he called again, reaching out to her. His voice sounded weaker.

She didn't want to hear what he had to say. *He'd been about to hurt Luke.* Throwing the tray to the floor, she grabbed Shark's hand, "Let's get the hell out of here. Now, before the staff starts racing in here."

Behind them, she heard the sickening thud of Skinbone's body hitting the floor.

The sound tore her up inside.

***

Angelica stood at the window in her Father's penthouse, staring out at the glittering lights of the city. The contrast to the black depths of Lake Michigan was stunning. She tilted her head, looking out into the night with fresh eyes. Tonight, the view possessed a haunting quality. It reminded her of a city teetering on the edge before dropping off into pool of darkness. A black abyss, where nothing and no one could survive.

She should have been out there taking all it had to offer, feeling the pulse of the city throb within her veins, enjoying the last gasps of a society for the people, by the people. She enjoyed decadence. More power, more pleasure, more money. She should have been free to indulge in the fun for at least another twenty years. Now it all fell on her.

If history taught one anything, it was that a nation which catered to its baser needs was destined to topple. The downfall of the United States had begun years before her birth, back when the nation suffered a giant hiccup and spit out the sixties generation. Her grandfather had been among the few wise enough to realize the time had come to prepare for a new world order.

The old man had been right. It hadn't taken long for the nation to crumble. Only fifty years.

The country was in a giant freefall. Unemployment too high, wages too low. Education falling way beyond the levels of other countries. The nation could no longer sustain itself. Yet the borders remained open, allowing in the poor and the desperate to drain what limited resources they had left. Poverty levels climbed as more and more citizens fell on hard times. Companies collapsed, banks went under, the Real Estate Market had already crumbled. Despite the turmoil brewing within the States instead of taking action, jobs continued to go overseas, raising desperation levels at home. Aid continued to pour out to other countries, while countless Americans lost their homes, and could no longer afford food.

It was a sorry state of affairs. A joke, really. One would have to be a fool not to see what was coming. For a country who touted equality, and a no class system, the lines between the rich and poor were distinctly drawn. It wouldn't be long before there was a revolution, or an emerging country hungry for power made a move on the U.S.

Her grandfather had seen the future and made provisions to save a sinking nation. The First Wave and Foxtrot had been created to protect the country's shores from invasion. A worthy endeavor. But what protected the nation from imploding? It might take another ten or twenty years before society was pushed over the edge, but why sit back and allow it to happen?

Why indeed when she could have anything she wanted? The groundwork was laid for her, it would only take one more step. Her eyes swept the skyline. Under her, the city, hell the whole damn country, could rise to glory. Democracy was a joke. Look at where it had gotten them? The States should be run like a business, with the best and the brightest rising to the top. The uneducated and the common beholden to a single ruler, performing the menial tasks they were suited for in exchange for housing, food, clothing. Their dependency would keep them in check. Those who refused to honor the new order would be jailed or executed, purging the country of undesirables.

A new world order, the one her grandfather had dreamed of. The fairytale world he had regaled her with stories of when she was a tot upon his knee. A fantasy world where she reigned as Queen, her lover by her side. *He* was the perfect mate. He would quickly gain the confidence of the people, precipitating a smooth transition. Assuring them all would be well. His position would lend credibility to her mission.

There would be bloodshed and chaos. Death, tears, and resistance. The nation in an uproar until the dust settled

She caught sight of her reflection in the glass. Her eyes softened, dazzled by her own beauty. A thrill raced through her. Raising an eyebrow, she stared into her eyes. She craved power and control and it was all at her fingertips. All she had to do was reach out and take it.

Her father had been too weak to appreciate the gift he'd been given. She wasn't about to repeat his mistake.

Ethan Wilde cleared his throat. Donovan St. James remained silent, sipping his drink.

Her eyes glittered as they met her partners. He gave her an imperceptible nod. For the plan to succeed, they would need allies, a trusted few who shared their vision for the future. It was time to test the waters, to discern if their companion was a worthy candidate.

According to plan, Angelica turned to the men with a smile. "Gentleman, I've carefully considered your suggestions. We must move forward with Foxtrot. To that end, I have decided we need to bring Wally Marx, The Shark, back into the fold."

"And if he doesn't respond to your summons?"

"We may need the technology of Foxtrot to utilize the microchips for their intended purpose, but I've found someone who can use the chips as a tracking device. If Shark won't come willingly, we will retrieve him."

"That means…"

"We will take back what has been stolen from us and put it to use. Now that I have free reign to run Kepler International as I see fit, the world gentlemen, as they say, is our oyster." She paused for effect. "A new day in history has begun."

Chapter Twenty-Nine

Hospital staff raced towards Luke's room. Sierra braced herself, expecting security to block their escape. Her legs pumped with energy she didn't know she had. When Shark lagged behind, she grabbed his wrist, pulling him along with her.

They managed to exit the hospital unscathed. Shark collapsed against the passenger seat, winded. Panting, she started the car. She'd foiled Skinbone Harris in his plot to kill Luke. With any luck, he was getting a pair of handcuffs slapped on him right now.

The bastard didn't deserve her. She forced herself to be consoled by the thought. The instant she saw him, she knew she loved him, and she hated what that made her. Not only had she fallen in love with a virtual stranger on the heels of her fiancée's death, he was a stone cold killer. An assassin, like he'd told her from the start. There had to be something wrong with her, something broken deep inside to make her keep falling for the wrong men. She wanted to lay the blame at Foxtrot's door, but she was a grown woman. It was up to her to own her mistakes.

She peeled rubber leaving the parking lot. They had to get to Shadow Lake. Gripping the steering wheel, she headed for the airport, hoping she'd saved Luke in time.

"What happened back there?" Shark asked when he regained his breath.

She tightened her hands on the steering wheel, answering through clenched teeth. "That was the infamous Skinbone Harris. He was trying to hurt Luke."

"Ah. That explains it."

"Explains what?" she snapped.

"The way he looked at you."

"What are you talking about?"

"You weren't imaging the connection between you and Skinbone Harris. He's got it bad for you."

Shark's words sliced her to the core. "Who cares? He's evil."

Shark grabbed the door handle when she made a sharp turn. "I hesitate to point this out, especially at such an inopportune time, but you've got it bad for him too."

"Are you insane?"

"I am not convinced Mr. Skinbone Harris meant Luke any harm."

"Oh my God, have you lost your mind? Skinbone was shaking Luke. For all I know, he was choking him."

"Or… perhaps he was simply trying to wake him?"

Sierra hit the gas hard, jerking Shark back in his seat. "What is wrong with you? Why are you defending him?"

"Because I know love when I see it, and if Skinbone loves you, he can't be all bad."

She glared at him. "Do you even hear yourself? And Skinbone is *not* a good man."

"The lady doth protest too much."

"Oh the hell with you. You lost your marbles somewhere in those hospital hallways."

"If that's what you choose to believe."

Shark's cell phone rang, starling them both. They shared an uneasy glance while he pulled the phone from his pocket. His face turned white. He stared at the phone for a good, long second, and then it slipped from his hand, falling to the floor.

"What is it? What's happened? You look like you've seen a ghost."

"Indeed, I have. A ghost from the past, that is. The call was from Angelica."

Her eyebrows shot up. "That's a surprise. You didn't have the most pleasant break-up."

"No we did not. Angelica is… a different breed of woman. She has this mindset where she can do whatever she wants and never suffer the consequences. At first I was attracted to that quality. I mistakenly believed it was strength."

Shark was quiet for a few minutes. "Angelica violated my trust. She hurt me and, given the opportunity, she would do it again. What I mistook as strength was petulance. It is easy to be taken in by her great beauty, and the air of refinement she portrays, but I fear what lies beneath her façade is a contorted version of the face she shows the world. There is ugliness behind her beauty, a selfish entitlement. If she doesn't get her way, she thinks nothing of stabbing one through the heart with her stiletto heels."

"Wow, Angelica doesn't stand a chance with you. I have to admit, I'm glad. She doesn't deserve you."

"I made my feelings clear when I ended things with her. The fact that she would call me shows how little she understands the human heart."

"Is it possible she was calling to tell you about her father's death?"

"I don't see why she would. She knows I would hear about it on the news. She would consider it beneath her to solicit symphony."

"Maybe she wants to invite you to the service? I'm sure it will be private."

"That's possible. My quarrel was never with Jared Kepler, although now, given Foxtrot, I see him in a new light."

"Do you think Angelica knows about Foxtrot? How involved is she in the business?"

"Angelica's main preoccupation is herself. She has an office and a title, but I've never known her to do any actual work—other than deposit hefty paychecks to her account."

"Is she the sole heir?"

He shifted in his seat to look at her. "In fact, she is. Kepler International must be in total disarray. She is in no way equipped to take over, and will need someone to help run the company until she is up to speed."

"She may need more than one person."

"Are you suggesting I offer my services?"

"I'm not suggesting anything. I'm thinking out loud. How sympathetic do you think Angelica would be towards our mission?"

"If Foxtrot can make Kepler International money, not sympathetic at all. She makes no secret of enjoying the finer things in life."

"Even considering the mass chaos Foxtrot would cause?"

"As long as Angelica remained unscathed, I doubt she would lose any sleep over it."

"So much for a simple solution to our problems."

"There would be a certain ironic appeal to infiltrating Kepler to bring down Foxtrot. I would be rather like a modern day James Bond. The down side, of course, would be I'd come face to face with the ne'er-do-well she enjoyed intimate relations with while engaged to me."

"Let's not get ahead of ourselves, Double-oh-Seven. With any luck, we'll find what we need at Shadow Lake. The airport is right up ahead, but hold on tight, I have to floor the engine. I'm not sure, but I think I see flashing lights behind us. Say a prayer we make it to the plane without getting stopped by the cops."

***

They scraped him off the floor. Skinbone felt the lump on his head, feeling a warped sense of pride. Sierra Montgomery didn't take shit from anybody, not even him. The flip side of the coin was she'd put herself in a hell of a lot of danger.

The nurse's cool hand soothed his aching brow, "You need to see a doctor, you may have a concussion."

"My head is too hard for a concussion."

"And you're bleeding," she tsked and examined his chest where the scissors had pierced his skin. "You need to let us take care of you." She glanced up at him from beneath her lashes. "I'll even make sure you have proper home care."

A few short weeks ago, he would have lapped up her attention, milking it for all it was worth. The fact that he was anxious to decline the pretty nurse's offer was a clear signal he had it bad for the lady who'd clocked him.

"Most appreciative, ma'am, but I don't imagine I'll be sticking around long enough to be cared for."

Luke let out a hoot from his bed, "I never thought I'd see the day. You got hit harder than you're owning up to boy. Never known you to turn down a pretty lady." The older man took a minute to get his bearings. His eyes narrowed as he took in the scene. "What the hell happened to your head? And where is Sierra?"

Skinbone's face burned red hot. "You might say we had a difference of opinion."

It took some effort, but Luke propped himself into a sitting position. He almost looked like his old self. The nurse excused herself, leaving Luke and Skinbone alone. "Mighty big difference of opinion," Luke remarked. "You want to tell me what's really going on?"

Skinbone knew he was giving Sierra way too much of a head start. She was in a shitload of danger. He also couldn't walk away from Luke. Doing his best to ignore the nagging sense of urgency, he recounted their first meeting at the Memphis diner and subsequent encounters.

Luke forgot his pain, studying Skinbone hard, "You've fallen for her, haven't you?"

Skinbone spent a few minutes studying his shoes. A crooked smile softened his chiseled features. "I may have developed certain feelings for her."

"Good Lord, son, you have to go after her. You shouldn't be wasting time with me."

"I can't. Not yet. There's something you need to know first. I figured out who's behind this. I know who killed Jared Kepler."

Luke heard him out, looking every inch the man who'd raised him. Looking at him now, it was hard to believe all he'd been though. When Skinbone finished talking, Luke nodded wisely. "Go find her son, and save her. Once this mess is sorted out, it's not too late to make me a granddad."

"Hold your horses there, old man. Sierra Montgomery isn't exactly fond of me right now. She sure as hell doesn't trust me, not one damn bit. And I'm not going anywhere until I take care of a few things. I don't like the idea of leaving you alone. I'm damn sure going to make sure you're safe first."

CHAPTER THIRTY

The plane took off without a hitch, though neither Sierra or Shark were in good shape. Too many ghosts haunted them.

"What are you thinking?" he asked after they reached cruising altitude.

"I'm wondering if there will ever be an end to all this. Are we crazy to try and take this on by ourselves? Luke isn't going to be any good to us right now. He needs time to heal, which means we'll have to hand this all over to Donovan. I'm not looking forward to that meeting. To have to turn to him for help after leaving him for Neil…"

"Perhaps Luke will be in better shape by the time we sort this out. We still have plenty of work to do."

"Yeah, maybe." She couldn't get the look of betrayal in Skinbone's eyes out of her mind. Why had he looked at her that way? Her life was one hell of a crazy mess. She missed her house and her life, but there was one thing she didn't miss, she realized with sickening clarity—her relationship with Neil. She was sorry he was dead; but she shouldn't have had to work so hard at the relationship. Not if they'd really loved each other.

Shark extracted a computer from his bag. "I know we should take advantage of this time to sleep, but I am too keyed up to rest."

"I am too. I can't seem to shut my mind off." She moved across the aisle to join him. "What have you got?"

"It mystifies me that so much focus has been on our enemies hunting for Neil's computers. The information contained on the laptop you took from his home is cut and dry, whereas Grace had a plethora of details far beyond the scope of her assigned work. I have to assume this is courtesy of her relationship with Jared Kepler. It appears he had notes from the initial project, The First Wave, transcribed so Grace might use them in order to sabotage Foxtrot."

"Wait a minute, you're saying Kepler wanted Foxtrot to fail?"

"Not only did he want it to fail, from what I gather, he was looking for a failsafe to disable the project from ever moving forward."

She scooted closer. "Seriously?"

"It's clear Jared Kepler was conflicted. He received a government contract to develop Foxtrot. According to this, it was earmarked as anti-terrorism weaponry in the event of an attack." Shark sat back, staring out into space. "When you look at Foxtrot from that angle, it truly is the most brilliant of weapons. It would make our country virtually untouchable."

"How do you figure?"

"Let me start from the beginning. The initial project. The First Wave came into existence in the nineteen sixties which was a time of revolution and evolution. Interest in psychics and psychic phenomena was at an all-time high. Think Jean Dixon or even the popularity of Edgar Cayce, though he was deceased. The frenzy for psychic exploration and dominance even extended to the U.S.S.R. The world was hungry for prophesies, predictions, and for proof these things were true."

"That's all well and good, but as it stands now, today, Foxtrot would be so random. Think about it, are you in anyway prepared to stave off an enemy attack?" Sierra asked.

"Not in my current capacity, no, but as outlined in the government plan, anyone possessing proven psychic abilities would be called to duty, briefed and deployed as a second army so to speak. The U.S. would have millions of soldiers capable of using Pyrokinesis to ignite enemy planes or suicide bombers before they reached their intended targets. Telekinesis could be used to manipulate weapons of mass destruction, sending them back to enemy shores. Precognition could be used to alert us of impending attacks, astral projection or bilocation would enable us to actually travel to enemy territory and see exactly what they are planning, while maintaining a presence here. It's brilliant—or it would have been if Kepler hadn't defiled the program by replacing it with their own agenda."

"I never looked at it from that angle."

"Because the original project was corrupt, courtesy of Jared Kepler's father."

"Out of greed and a hunger for power, the bastard."

"It's a wonder he escaped prison. Allegations of corruption and selling the technology were what shut the project down. And you will never guess who pointed the finger at them."

"Luke Preston."

"Bingo. But the elder Mr. Kepler remained unscathed and nothing was ever proven. In the end, some of the original scientists served prison time for selling information to China and Mexico. The Indigo Children. Within the last twenty five years, children with super psychic abilities have been emerging in these areas. They started surfacing a few years after The First Wave was implemented here. The original project was never intended to go as far as it did. Children were invited to the camps purely to be tested for psychic abilities, and those abilities were supposed to be nourished and nurtured over time. What actually happened was an abomination."

"We can attest to that."

"It get worse. Shortly after incarceration, the jailed scientists met untimely deaths in prison. It's not a stretch to assume someone shut them up."

"They were the fall guys."

Shark nodded. "There is a lot more here, but I'll cut to the chase. Jared Kepler realized the value of Foxtrot if it was done correctly. With the project starting up again, he became privy to the original files kept hidden by his father. Most likely, if the government hadn't given him the contract for Foxtrot, the original plans and files would have lain dormant and undiscovered for years, perhaps forever. At the onset, Kepler hired Neil and Grace to work on the project. When the atrocities came to light, he must have started to rethink the whole thing. Long story short, somewhere along the line, he and Grace fell in love. He shared his findings…and concerns… with her, and paid her off the books from his private accounts to delve deeper and find a way to undo all the damage his father did. It also explains why, even though they had a lab, he allowed them each to work from their own homes, giving Grace the ability to work independently from Neil."

"And no one aside from Jared Kepler knew what Grace was doing."

"Correct."

Sierra rubbed her forehead, digesting the information. "Wait a minute. If what you say is true, whoever killed Grace and Neil wanted to destroy Foxtrot. They had no way of knowing Grace was trying to sabotage her own work. The person who murdered them saw them as a threat."

"A safe assumption."

"Grace's house exploded. All of her work *should* have been destroyed. Neil was supposed to be alone the night he was killed. The killer should have been able to grab his computer and destroy it. But I got in the way, both times."

"And considering your connection to them, the killer believes you are also a threat."

"But Jared Kepler wasn't. Not after Foxtrot was stolen. His scientists were dead, all their data was missing. On the surface, he was a victim. Why kill him?"

Shark shrugged. "It doesn't fit."

"Unless someone knew Jared was trying to sabotage Foxtrot, someone who wanted Foxtrot to be developed, someone who planned on picking up where Jared's father had left off."

"I hate to add fuel to the fire, but Luke Preston wanted Foxtrot stopped."

"He wouldn't have murdered Grace and Neil. He'd use his FBI contacts to shut down their work."

Shark's complexion turned ashen. "You know what you're saying, don't you?"

"Yeah. We're being pursued by three groups of people, although I think we can safely assume Luke knows we're on the same side, so he'll have called his dogs off."

"It's comforting to know we won't be killed by the good guys."

***

Sierra and Shark reached Shadow Lake before dusk. A car dropped them off at the property where the realtor handed them the keys.

Sierra looked at Shark. "I don't know about you, but my mind is on overload. I'm going to be worthless unless I get some sleep. I need twelve hours alone in a nice, comfy bed."

"I know this is the part where I should say we need to save the world from Foxtrot, but I agree. This may be the one place we can feel safe for a time. My brain feels like mush."

Exhaustion had a way of blurring the senses. She didn't know what day it was, or how much time had passed since she'd run from Neil's house. Shark wasn't faring much better. His eyes were half closed and he was yawning. She would have thought everything they'd discovered on the plane would have invigorated them. Instead, they barely made it up the stairs.

They reached the second floor. Sierra sagged against a wall. "At least we have a better handle on things. We know Luke is on our side, Skinbone is a stone cold killer, and we'll turn Foxtrot over to Donovan if and when we find it."

"I'm not sure the picture is quite as clear as you think."

She raised her hand. "No more debates, not tonight. Tomorrow we start fresh."

"Then I'll bid you goodnight."

"Take the Master Suite. You're footing the bill, it's only right."

Shark peaked inside the room, "I'll be more comfortable down the hall."

"Okay," She said, too tired to argue. She flipped on the light, and stared. The bedroom was spectacular. No wonder Shark insisted she take the Master Suite, she smiled. It was probably too frilly and lilac for his taste.

Sierra dumped her things near the bed, marveling at the room. She almost wept with pleasure. The bed even had satin sheets—it was a far cry from dozing in cars or airplanes. She promised herself, if she survived their ordeal, she'd treat herself to the something special, no matter how expensive. She'd earned it.

Deciding to forego her shower until morning, she rummaged in her suitcase for a t-shirt, and slipped into bed. If they were going to stay at the rental property for a while, she needed to make time to shop. Her meager belongings had already taken a beating.

Her muscles unknotted the minute she stretched out on the bed. She ran her hands over the satin sheets, sighing out loud. She wiggled her toes in pleasure; she could definitely get used to this. Tucking the blankets around her, she curled up on her side and promptly fell asleep.

The sound of a door slamming woke her. She was out of bed in an instant, padding to the bedroom door in bare feet. She cracked it open and nearly screamed. Shark stood right outside, a worried look on his face.

"You scared me half to death."

Holding a finger to his lips, he pushed his way into her room. "Did you hear that?" he whispered.

"Yes. A door slamming. It woke me up."

"Someone's here. Do we have any idea who it can be?"

"Not a clue." She thought quick. "Have you unpacked?"

"I didn't even turn down the bed. I passed out on top of it. When I heard the door slam, I shoved my stuff underneath it and came to check on you."

"Okay, good. Help me push my things underneath while I make up the bed. Until we know what we're dealing with, it's best if nobody knows we're here. This way, we'll have the advantage."

"Good thinking."

Within minutes, the room appeared untouched. They'd left the bedroom door open a crack. Together, they tiptoed towards it, listening for signs of the intruder. They didn't have to wait long.

A shape lurked in the shadows, too dark to make out. Shark gripped her wrist, his fingers digging into her skin. Sierra resisted the urge to peel them off, the pain would help her focus.

"No one's here. He hasn't moved in," said a deep voice.

Sierra glanced at Shark. His eyes were glued on the figure below.

"Yes, I'm sure. I haven't checked the upstairs but nothing's been disturbed. There's no sign of life."

"Cell phone," Shark mouthed. She nodded.

"If anyone else shows up, we'll know. The area is secure."

Sierra sagged against the door frame, wrapping her arms around herself. *They weren't safe anywhere. Shadow Lake wasn't the haven they'd hoped for.*

Shark released his death grip on her wrist and rubbed her back in the awkward way people do when trying to comfort.

"I had checked the kid out, like you requested. He'll buy us the time we need."

Shark raised soft brown eyes to her, giving her a thumbs up. She wasn't as encouraged.

"No. Got bounced out of college for hacking and drifted a few years. He was never convicted of anything. If he broke the law, he was smart enough to avoid leaving a trail. The guy's a genius. Not too swift in the real world, though. Kepler offered the kid a sweet deal to stay on after the daughter screwed around on him. The kid didn't even bite. Turned his back on the both of them and left the company. I would have found a way to stick it to them, but not this guy. He's as clean as they come. Bottom line, the kid's coming here to lick his wounds. His rich daddy is footing the bill."

Sierra glanced at Shark. The man downstairs knew far too much.

"From what I can tell, he's a real loner. Outside of the fling with Kepler's daughter, he keeps pretty much to himself. No matter how it falls out, it works to your advantage."

A pause while he listened to the voice on the other end of the line. "I'll do a quick sweep upstairs to make sure the place is empty. I say let the kid move in. He'll keep away unwanted visitors."

Sierra grabbed Shark's arm and motioned to the heavy drapes. She hoisted herself up on the window ledge, gesturing for him to do the same on the opposite side. They were perfectly concealed. As long as the guy didn't look under the bed, they were home free.

He didn't. He checked the bedrooms, closets, and bathrooms, spending a cursory amount of time in each room. They were safe for the moment.

"What do you think that was about?" Shark whispered.

"I have no idea but it's obvious we can't stay. Whoever he was talking to knows way too much about you and has a vested interest in Foxtrot."

"They don't seem to consider me a threat."

"It's a bad idea."

"No one knows of my connection to you. Who knows what I might find out if I stay?"

"Too dangerous. I say we spend the night. I don't think he'll be back for now. Tomorrow we'll have to figure out a way to get out of here without being seen."

"If you insist."

"I do. Let's try and get some sleep. I have a feeling tomorrow is going to be a long day."

It was clear Shark wanted to challenge her decision. She wasn't about to let him. "I'll see you in the morning. Goodnight."

He hesitated. "But..."

"No. I'm tired, scared, and thoroughly disgusted. We needed this place. Time to figure out why Grace had the brochure and what she'd been doing here, and for you to finish going through the files. I'm sick of running like a damned criminal, but I sure as hell won't put us in danger. Now I'm going to bed."

"Goodnight." He walked away with his head hanging down. She kicked the door closed in frustration, feeling like a shit for hurting his feelings. It couldn't be helped. The intruder rattled her far more than she cared to admit.

The bed which had seemed so inviting earlier mocked her. She'd been a fool to think they could rest easy. The chill she'd felt earlier settled deep in her bones. Rubbing her arms, she walked over to the windows. In the distance she saw several sail boats docked for the night. Unlike most lake houses, they were isolated. *Odd, usually lake front property was at a premium.*

There had to be a reason they were so isolated. Why would such an inviting location be sealed off from the rest of the world?

Unless.

Unless there was activity which had to be protected from prying eyes or curious neighbors. Heart racing, she let the curtain drop. She sat down on the bed and forced herself to slow down. Too many things nagged at her. She was having a hard time processing them all.

"Damn you, Grace," she whispered. "You should have trusted me."

She glanced at the windows, thinking yet again what a strange location Grace had chosen. Why would a woman who hated water rent a house right on top of it? Sierra had a clear memory of coming back from Hawaii and hurrying over to Grace's house with the large seashell, anxious to give her best friend the souvenir.

Grace had backed away, a plastic smile plastered on her face, loath to even touch it. She'd politely asked Sierra to set it down. It remained in that exact spot for weeks until it finally disappeared altogether.

Why had it been prominently displayed on Grace's shelf, all these years later?

Sierra dropped to her knees, yanking boxes out from under the bed until she came across the one with the seashell. She pulled it out, trying to figure out what it meant. It certainly wasn't a clue to come to the Lake House. The flyer had taken care of that. There had to be another meaning.

The key and the seashell had been hidden in plain sight. Grace knew no one except Sierra would give them more than a cursory glance.

"What were you trying to tell me?" She lifted the seashell to her ear, listening for the sea. Nothing. Shaking the shell, she heard a slight rustle. Sierra set it on her lap, wedging her fingers inside. Something brushed against the tips of her fingernails. She forced her hand in deeper and felt the edge of a sheet of paper.

Desperate, she searched the room for something that would help her pull it out. When that didn't work she stood up and smashed the shell against the edge of the dresser, breaking it open.

Tucked inside were several neatly typed sheets. *Grace had left her a message.*

***

Skinbone Harris snapped his phone shut. He was in a foul mood. He'd no sooner finished releasing a statement about Luke's condition to the press when a storm opened up overhead, the worst to hit Sedona in over forty years. The airport shut down. No planes were leaving the ground, period. He had no choice but to wait it out.

He'd done all he could to protect Luke. Other matters demanded his attention.

He sat in the small airport, watching the rain pound against the windows. A fierce wind kicked up, fueling his bad mood. He thought of the words Luke whispered to him.

Shadow Lake. The safe place Sierra was going to hide.

A strange emotion gurgled inside him, courtesy of the call he'd just finished listening in on. He refused to put a name to it, no matter how bad it gnawed at him. Sierra Montgomery had done it to him again—she was shacking up with another man.

Damn fool woman. Wally "The Shark" Marx was a real operator, bouncing from Angelica Kepler's bed into Sierra Montgomery's. Skinbone wanted to throttle the punk with his bare hands.

The addition of Wally Marx into the mix put a whole new spin on things. He was the computer genius Donovan St. James had *a bead on.* The one capable of retrieving data from Luke's shot up computer.

How in the hell had Sierra managed to hook up with Marx? Unless she'd been in cahoots with him the whole time, playing all of them for fools.

It didn't bode well for the future.

He looked out at the storm, wondering if there'd even be a future—for any of them. He'd used an IMSI catcher to listen in on the call from Shadow Lake to his primary suspect in the plan to steal Foxtrot. There was no way this could turn out well. Either Marx was using Sierra to get the information, or he was being used. Either way, when he showed up at the lake house with Sierra in tow, they were screwed.

Skinbone raked his fingers through his hair. He felt like a ping pong ball, bouncing back and forth between emotions. *How the hell did your average girl off the street get so deeply embroiled in such a deadly situation? He could understand her being afraid after witnessing her fiancée's death, but why not call the cops instead of setting up false trails, and all the other harebrained things she'd done since then. Most people sure as hell wouldn't have headed back to Chicago for the sole purpose of digging up more information. You'd think getting shot at on the train with Luke would have been a major deterrent. Not to Sierra. No, instead she decided to jump headfirst into the deep end of the pool, not even bothering to think it might get her killed.*

He couldn't decide if he was proud of her bravery or if he wanted throttle her for her stupidity. Given her newfound connection to Wally Marx, he wasn't entirely sure she was innocent. No one in their right mind would take the risks she had. *If she actually had stumbled into this whole mess by accident, her luck was due to run out.* Especially if she thought she'd found a safe hiding place, like she'd told Luke.

Sierra Montgomery was a sitting duck. If the storm didn't let up soon, he'd fly the damn plane himself to Shadow Lake.

Chapter Thirty-One

Angelica was a nocturnal creature. She loved the night, the power it gave her, the control she had over men when she descended upon them under the cloak of darkness. How helpless they were to resist her, how eager to give her what she wanted.

In the future, she would need to be more discrete. At least until everything was in place, then she could do whatever she damned well pleased. He couldn't pull this off without her; he needed her every bit as much as she needed him. For the time being.

Afterwards, he would have no choice but to accept the fact that she had other lovers. No one man would ever be enough to satisfy her. He would soon learn *this* was what she needed, if he wanted her to be happy. And how could he deny her anything? She was handing him the keys to the kingdom he craved.

The doorman let her through without buzzing upstairs. *He* knew better than to question her or to look askance at the raincoat she wore on a hot summer night. He was the type of man she liked, one who knew his place.

She knocked as a courtesy. When he didn't answer, she let herself in, dropping the coat on the floor behind her. Her hips rocked from the sway of her stilettos. The black penior she wore left nothing to the imagination. The only purpose it served was the thrill she would feel when she commanded him to rip it off her body.

Angelica eased the bedroom door open, intending to pounce on him unaware while he slept. A fitting punishment for ignoring her knock. Her body was flush with heat. She entered the room with the stealth of a cat, eyes trained on the bed.

It was empty.

Her eyes narrowed. She flung the bathroom door open, hoping to startle him. He wasn't there. She'd already passed through the living areas. They'd been unoccupied.

The condo was empty. Too empty, she realized, tearing through the closet and dresser drawers. Nothing of any consequence had been left behind.

He was gone, without notice, without warning.

She ripped the sheet from the bed, shredding it with her bare hands. Her lips curled in anger. How dare he do this to her? This was no accident. He hadn't been called away. No one in their right mind would walk away from Kepler International. Or from her.

He was going to pay for his mistake. Grabbing her coat from the living room floor, she stormed out of the house. His disappearance could only be taken one way. An admission of guilt.

He was going to be very, very sorry.

No one crossed her and got away with it. And these were far from ordinary circumstances. He'd shared her bed, been privy to their secrets, held a position of power at the company.

Her limo driver dropped his cigarette, turning a deep shade of red at being caught outside the car. He hurried to open the door for her and returned to his place behind the wheel. She kept a keen eye on the driver, hoping he'd make a mistake. She wanted to unleash her fury on someone.

He'd been working against them the whole time, playing the role of solicitous lover and confidant. Venom spewed from her lips, twisted thoughts of revenge grew inside her. Death was far too good for him. She seethed. Her father had invited a traitor into their midst, leaving her to clean up the mess. He'd fooled them all, blindsiding her with betrayal at the worst possible time, when triumph was within their grasp.

"Bastard," she hissed when a new worry sprang to mind. The netbook. What if he had taken it?

Lucky for the driver, he kept his mouth shut. He did what he was told, not even daring to look at her when he opened the car door in front of the Hancock Building. All men should be so well trained.

She'd taken possession of her father's penthouse the day after his death. Now she ran through the lobby, cursing the elevator for taking too long to arrive. By the time she made it up to the penthouse, she was shaking with rage.

Tossing her bag on the nearest table, she hurried towards the great room. He stepped out of the shadows, catching her off guard. There wasn't time for her to stop; she ran smack into his chest. It only took a second to regain her composure.

"Get out of my way."

He grabbed her by the wrists, a move she didn't appreciate. She was in no mood to play. "What kind of greeting is that, Sweetheart? Especially in the light of the fact I come bearing good news."

"I don't give a damn about your good news. We're in the middle of a disaster. How the hell did you get in here anyway?"

"You aren't the only one who can talk themselves in somewhere, darling. I'm a very good persuader."

"You won't be much good for anything unless you let go of me right now. The computer with Foxtrot may be gone. We've been had, made fools of. The bastard's been right under our nose the entire time."

His eyes turned to angry slits. "What the hell are you talking about?"

"Let go of me so I can check on the netbook and I'll explain."

He released her. She glared at him, ramming him with her shoulder while she hurried past. He kept pace behind her, close enough for her to feel his hot breath on her ear.

She came to an abrupt halt, clutching her chest in relief. The computer remained in its original position, untouched. "Thank God. At least he didn't get away with all we have left of Foxtrot." Angelica turned to companion. "But why? If it's his intention to betray us, why wouldn't he take it?"

"Angelica, you're blathering on like an idiot without telling me a damn thing. What the hell are you talking about?"

She brushed the back of her hand against her forehead. "I need a drink. This is all so confusing."

He grabbed her by the shoulders before she could pour her wine. "Where were you tonight? And why are you dressed in this coat? It's ninety degrees outside."

For the first time, she remembered what she was wearing. She didn't need another scene, not tonight. She had to change before he saw what she had on underneath—and before she told him about the betrayal.

She needed time to concoct a plausible story. Gripping her stomach, she let her hand fly to her face, "I'm going to be sick." Brushing past him, she ran to her bedroom, slamming the door behind her. She yanked off the raincoat and the sheer penior, almost breaking an ankle in her haste to put on a simple sheath dress. He walked in before she could finish zipping it up.

For the first time since they'd met over a year ago, she was afraid of him. Their eyes met across the bed. She saw the murderous gleam in his eye.

"What are you not telling me, Angelica? What are you hiding?"

She let her arms fall to her sides. "What is wrong with you tonight? Would you please give me a minute to change into something more comfortable and then maybe we can continue this conversation in a civilized manner."

"Something more comfortable." He lifted her raincoat from the chair, exposing the sheer black penior hidden beneath it. "Like this?" He dangled it in front of her, advancing in her direction. "Do you take me for a fool? Whose bed were you in tonight, Angelica? Who the hell are you sleeping with? Is that who betrayed you? One of your lovers?" He ripped the nightie in half with his bare hands, coiling a length of wispy fabric between his fingers.

Angelica backed away from him. She needed to think fast, not liking the turn the night was taking. *This* was not the type of future she envisioned. He was her lover, not her inquesitioner. His behavior was ludicrous, bordering on insane. She had to turn the tables on him. "Don't be absurd. Just because I have lingerie in my room is hardly any reason for you to accuse me of sleeping with someone."

"Don't lie to me."

She arched a brow, hiding her fear behind a veil of anger. "You think I'm lying? Do you?" Keeping her eye on the fabric he was twisting, she forced herself to remain calm. She took a small step forward, then another, pushing the unzipped dress down her shoulders.

"What are doing, Angelica? Trying to seduce me? Don't be pathetic."

"I wouldn't let you touch me right now if you begged." The dress slid past her waist. A slight tug sent it dropping to the floor. She stepped over it, walking right up to him, staring him in the eye. "Go ahead. See for yourself. Do I feel like sex? Can you smell it on me? Can you? I didn't think so. Don't you *dare* ever question me again."

She turned her back on him, reaching for a robe. He caught her off guard, slamming her against the wall, wrapping the wisp of fabric around her throat tight enough to choke her. "Let's get something straight, darling. You may not have been with a man tonight, but you are no innocent. Don't think for one minute I'm going to put up with that sort of behavior after we are married. I'm not about to have a two bit tramp for a wife. I will not be cuckolded, and I will not be made into a laughingstock."

The fabric was strangling her, but she was not going to give him the satisfaction of seeing her claw at it. "I'd be careful about issuing orders if I were you," she hissed between clenched teeth. "You can't do this without me."

"And you can't have the power and position you crave without me, darling. You need me."

"Kepler International is mine. Foxtrot belongs to *me*."

He barked out a laugh, pulling the makeshift noose tighter around her slender neck. "And who do you think made that possible, darling? Your father was standing in the way of our plans."

Her eyes bugged out of her head, her vision started to blur, "You killed him? It was *you*?"

"He never would have allowed us to go through with it, darling. He lacked your vision of the future."

There was no more breath left in her. She slumped against the wall, on the verge of passing out. Without warning, he released his hold on her. She crumpled to the floor.

"Our country is going to need a strong leader, someone they believe in. Once we unleash Foxtrot, there will be utter chaos. They will throw their support to me. Hell, in those first few months, they'll look to me as their savior. I'm perfectly positioned. I will have their trust. I'm the one who can turn this country from a democracy into the empire it was meant to be. Something you could never pull off. You're nothing but a socialite. You may have the brains, sweetheart and the cunning, but what you don't have is respect. As my wife, we will rule together, as equals. But I will not have you acting like a two-bit whore. Those days are over. Now put some clothes on, something decent. I have a minister coming over. We are going to be married tonight."

She rubbed her throat. "You think I'm going to marry you after what you just did to me?"

"I'm certain of it. I found your ex-boyfriend, The Shark. After the ceremony, we are flying out to see him, with the computer. Like you so eloquently put it the other night our time has come. It's time for a new world order and we have to be ready."

Angelica pulled herself up from the floor, seeing her life flash before her eyes. She hadn't signed on for the future he was painting. There was no way in hell she was going to live her life under his thumb, giving in to his demands. She had sought him out. All of this had been her idea. She'd been the one with the vision, not him. "What about…?" Her other lover had always been part of her plans. She couldn't let on he was gone.

"What about him? We'll leave him here while we 'honeymoon.' Then we'll see where he fits."

She needed a diversion. Telling him about the betrayal would encourage another outburst. Until she thought of something, she'd have to play along, even if that meant going through with the marriage. No matter how distasteful, it would buy her time to come up with an alternative plan. She needed leverage, a way to turn the tables on him.

He should be groveling at her feet. Without her, he had nothing, and Foxtrot belonged to her. Let him have his small victory. He'd made a grave mistake by playing his hand tonight.

He'd just become expendable.

Chapter Thirty-Two

The smile died on her face. Something was wrong. Instead of sharing her excitement, Shark looked pained. *No, that was impossible. He'd gone to bed. Nothing could have gone wrong while he was sleeping.*

She thrust the papers she held towards him. "I haven't read it yet, but it has to mean something. This could be the clue we've been searching for. We can read it together."

Shark studied the floor for a moment and then pulled her into a hug. The paper fluttered from her fingertips, falling to the floor. *Oh, God,* she thought, *this is going to be bad.*

"Let's sit for a minute."

She went numb, not understanding what could have happened in the short time they were apart. Wanting to delay the inevitable, she tried to stall. "Maybe we should read Grace's message first."

"Please. Sit."

At a loss, she complied. Shark sat down beside her. "There's no easy way to say this. There was a news bulletin. It seems your friend Luke passed away this afternoon."

The tears came instantly, pouring out of her before she had any chance of stopping them, "No. No, that can't be. We saw him. He was getting better, he can't be dead. He just can't."

Shark gathered her into his arms. "I am so sorry. I know how grateful you were to him, and the connection you felt."

She shook her head. "There has to be a mistake. I can't believe it. I *don't* believe it. How could this have happened?"

He didn't have an answer. Her words hung between them, weighing heavily in the night air. She buried her head against Shark's shoulder, shaking with the force of her gut-wrenching sobs. His t-shirt was soaked with her tears before she pulled away.

"If something's happened to Luke, there's only one person who could be responsible. Skinbone Harris. I swear to God, if he had anything to do with this, I will kill him with my bare hands."

"You can't assume…"

"He was there, Shark, standing over Luke's bed. What else am I supposed to think?"

"Often, things are not quite how they appear. All I am saying is keep an open mind."

"How can you be so trusting after what Angelica put you through? How can you still manage to give people the benefit of the doubt?

"Because, despite how it seems right now, the world isn't all bad. Good does exist. Look at you, for example."

She reached out and squeezed his hand, "Thank you, but you're a far nicer person than I am. I'm lucky to have met you."

He waved away her compliment, but she could see how pleased he was by the slight blush on his cheeks. "Let's read Grace's letter."

She'd forgotten about it in the wake of Shark's news. She glanced at the bed, where she'd dropped it after hearing about Luke's passing. Her hand froze. "I told Luke about Shadow Lake. What if he told somebody where we are?"

"First off, we don't know that he was murdered. Second, he was a trained FBI agent; I don't think he would have revealed our location."

The seed of doubt was already planted in her mind. She was beginning to think coming to the Lake House was a huge mistake. Snatching up Grace's letter, she held it between them. Her eyes skimmed the page while Shark took his time, lips moving while he read.

"It's here," she screamed. "Foxtrot is here, at Shadow Lake."

"That's not all that's here," Shark answered in a cryptic tone. "This place also served as a camp. How could someone live in this house, amidst the most luxurious of surroundings, while deep below, in a sub-basement, children were being experimented on?"

"You don't think any children are here now, do you?"

He jumped up from the bed and started to pace, running his hands through his hair."I doubt it. It's clear Jared Kepler decided not to move forward with the project. If this was a government sanctioned camp, it's nothing like what we were subjected to as children."

"You're right. If any of these camps are operational, they would be voluntary. They would be tested for psychic abilities, not tortured or locked away."

"I agree with your assessment."

"It still complicates things." She turned over the paper. "Grace drew us a map of the vault Foxtrot is locked in. The key I found unlocks it but, from what I can tell, the vault is in a sub-basement. What if we this is a camp? We'd be on government property stealing government property. Why can't anything be simple?"

"It doesn't appear to be our lot in life to stumble across anything simple."

Sierra stood and crossed over to the window. Looking out at the lake, she was reminded of the crazy speedboat ride Luke had taken her on to save their lives. She had to do the right thing now, for him.

"The way I see it, we have two choices. Retrieve Foxtrot, hand it over to the government, and risk it falling into the wrong hands. Or we could destroy it."

Shark sat down. "We never discussed those options."

She turned to face him, "In light of everything that's happened, all the lives that have been lost, I think it's something we need to consider."

He raised his hand, fingering the small scar on his head. She knew he was thinking of the microchip implanted in his brain. When he spoke, his voice was barely more than a whisper. "I think we should destroy it."

She shivered, knowing the risk involved. "So do I."

***

His eyes snapped open. Skinbone tensed, ready to lash out, until he recognized the pilot staring at him.

"The storm has cleared. We're ready to go, Sir."

He must have fallen asleep. Small wonder, considering the emotional turmoil he'd been dealing with. Nodding, he grabbed his bag, and followed the pilot to the tarmac. The satchel containing his weapons was already on board. He'd never bothered to unload them, having no use for them while he kept vigil at Luke's bedside. Heading to Shadow Lake without back-up was a different story. He'd need all the tools at his disposal.

The stress was catching up to him. He could feel the strain in his body when he mounted the stairs. He couldn't afford to be off his game, not if he was going to honor his promise to keep Sierra safe. *What a joke,* he thought, fingering the lump on his head. It wasn't going to be easy to reason with her. He could imagine the fight she'd put up when he tried to take her home to Texas until the mission was complete. He was going to have his hands full. Sierra was a handful enough—he hadn't bargained on Wally "The Shark" Marx thrown into the mix. He'd given his word to Luke, but things were going to get mighty ugly if Marx was sharing her bed. Even uglier if Marx was involved in the plot to steal Foxtrot.

Jesus, he rubbed his eyes, entering the cabin. *I'm getting too old for all this drama.* He wanted a nice, simple life. It was time to retire for good. Maybe open up the agency he'd daydreamed about. Do something that wouldn't put him toe to toe with a woman who crawled under his skin like a bad itch he couldn't scratch. The quiet life suited him fine. He didn't need this heartache.

He dropped his bag and looked up, ready to take his seat. He froze, feeling a sucker punch to his midsection. Skinbone stared at the back of the plane in shock. The pilot was already speeding down the runway. Swearing up a blue streak, he gaped at the unexpected passenger, feeling his innards turn inside out.

"What the *hell* are *you* doing here?"

***

Sierra pushed the hair out her eyes. She'd involved Shark in too much already. She wasn't going to make him a party to treason.

It seemed a lifetime ago since this all first started. She twisted on the small Mag light she'd found at the bottom of her purse and shined it on the directions to the vault Grace's map provided. With any luck, she'd find Foxtrot and be able to destroy it. She prayed that would be enough.

The floorboards creaked overhead, giving her pause. Shark should have been in his room, fast asleep. What if the intruder had come back? This time there'd be no hiding from him.

Crouching beneath the stars, she held her breath, listening for another sound. She couldn't leave Shark alone and defenseless. Unless it fell into enemy hands, Foxtrot didn't pose an imminent danger. Shark, on the other hand, could be in peril.

Seconds stretched out into minutes. The upstairs remained silent. Buildings creaked; she'd let her imagination get the best of her. Glancing down at Grace's directions, she tried to get her bearings. From what she could decipher, she had to pass through the first basement in order to reach the entryway to the subbasement.

As she traveled through the hallway, a number of doors opened up into white rooms that had a quasi-medical feeling to them. She reminded herself the building had been used as a camp in the past. Grace must have hated it here.

Tears welled up in the corners of her eyes. Brushing them away with the back of her hand, she thought of how Grace had fallen in love, with Jared Kepler, and how they'd tried to do the right thing. They'd both died for their efforts, and now Sierra was following in their footsteps. The chill surrounding her had nothing to do with being below ground. It had everything to do with the danger she'd placed herself in.

It was too late to back out. Steeling herself, she moved forward. She had to see this through, no matter what the cost. Inching her way through the hallway, she tried to empty her mind. Destroying Foxtrot was all that mattered. Everything else could wait until she had time to sort out her feelings.

Then she heard it. A distinctive female voice. The sound of stiletto's overhead.

"Shark? Shark, Sweetheart, are you here?"

The voice could only belong to one person.

Angelica Kepler.

***

Angelica waited in the elegant foyer. Marble floors gleamed beneath her, giving the entryway an austere quality. She shivered, wishing she could turn back the clock, knowing it was already too late.

She glanced around the room, listening for Shark. So far, she hadn't heard so much as a creak in response. A part of her prayed he was wrong, and that Shark wasn't here. She'd have a little more time to think her way out of her current situation.

The last twelve hours played over in her mind. He hadn't given her a minute alone since he'd announced their impromptu wedding. No matter what anyone thought, she was a clever girl. She knew how to get by. And she knew how to work men, keeping them firmly under her thumb.

Not this time. She assumed he'd allow her time to dress for the wedding. She'd intended to use that time to call Shark, but he hadn't let her out of his sight, the bastard. He suspected she would double cross him.

She wanted him dead. The problem was she needed a man with position and power in order to bring her plan to fruition. It was too late in the game to change sides now.

"Call him again," he hissed in her ear.

Angelica dug her fingernails into the palms of her hands to keep from lashing out. He'd placed her in an impossible situation, one she couldn't think her way out of with his constant hovering. Struggling for composure, she tapped her foot on the marble floor hoping to irritate him. It worked. He dug his fingers into her arm, "I said, call him."

"I don't bellow."

"Too damn bad. We want him to know it's you. Otherwise he might get spooked and call the cops."

"Fine." She glared at him, and yelled out, "Shark, its Angelica."

The mansion remained deathly silent.

He swore under his breath. "I'm going round back. If your former lover doesn't appear in the next few minutes, I want you to go upstairs. If he's sleeping, wake him. We have work to do."

Angelica listened to the sound of his footsteps echoing through the hallway. Finally, a reprieve. If she was going to get the upper hand, she had to act soon. She had two choices: find Shark and beg him to help her or locate the kitchen and find a weapon. Closing her eyes, she imagined raising a knife and burying it deep inside her husband's wicked heart.

What if she didn't succeed in killing him on the first try? She could see him pulling out the knife, lurching towards her like something out of a horror film. She couldn't take the risk.

"Angelica? What are you doing here?"

She jumped, stifling a startled scream. Shark had caught her unaware. She smoothed trembling fingers over her dress in an effort to calm her nerves. Tossing back her hair back, she looked up at him. He stood at the top of the staircase, blinking down at her in surprise.

He looked exhausted. His hair fell across his forehead; there were dark shadows under his eyes. She wondered if he was still inconsolable over their break-up. With any luck, he'd be so grateful to see her he'd bend over backwards to help.

"What are you doing here, Angelica? How did you find me?"

Not the greeting she'd expected. His cool tone set her on edge. She glanced over her shoulder, making sure they were still alone, and hurried towards the staircase. "Shark, we need to talk. I've made a huge mistake and I need your help. There isn't much time."

He squared his shoulders, exhibiting a strength she hadn't believed he was capable of. "If I'm not mistaken, I don't recall inviting you upstairs. Stay where you are, I'll come to you."

Her hand faltered on the railing. This wasn't the man she had manipulated. He was cold. Defensive, even. Worry fluttered in her stomach. What if he wouldn't help? She slowed her breathing, hoping to quiet her racing heart. Survival instincts kicked in. Shark wasn't the only one acting odd. She was allowing her desperation to show through, giving him a ringside seat to her fear and confusion.

She was Angelica Kepler, damn it. This was her world, her rules. No one had the right to challenge her. Not Shark, not her husband, no one. All she had to do was turn on the charm to win Shark over and he'd be salivating to help. A delicious thought crept into her mind. Her lips curved into a smile, knowing she had all the power she needed. It was a simple matter of stirring up the jealousy lurking inside Shark and pitting the two men against each other; rile Shark enough to force him to defend his honor.

Shark would lose, of course, but that would hardly be her fault. She'd make her escape while the men locked horns. Her ex-fiancée's death could actually work in her favor—without him available to break the encryption, her husband wouldn't have access to Foxtrot.

And she would have the time she needed to formulate a new plan.

It was perfect.

She leaned forward, brushing her lips against his cheek, treating him to an ample view of her cleavage. Her fingers worked their way over the back of his neck. He shuddered in response.

"I've missed you," she whispered, confident of her power, knowing she had him right where she wanted him.

Chapter Thirty-Three

Sierra crouched in position, straining to hear what was happening upstairs. She heard Angelica call out a second time, and then…nothing. Beads of sweat formed on her brow. She was torn between rushing to Shark's defense or continuing onto the vault.

They were no longer alone. Destroying Foxtrot had to take priority. *Unless…could Angelica have been the enemy all along?*

It was a no win situation. She couldn't leave Shark twisting in the wind. It would be a hollow victory if she managed to destroy Foxtrot at the expense of her friend's life. But what if she raced upstairs only to discover Angelica had genuine feelings for him and had come to make amends?

She didn't think that was the case. There was nothing endearing about Angelica. The woman was a viper. If she'd come looking for Shark, there was one reason: she wanted something.

If only she could hear what was going on. Creeping forward, she kept her eyes trained on the ceiling. There had to be air ducts somewhere. She shoved the map into her pocket and pointed the flashlight overhead. *What was she going to do if Shark was in danger?* She had nothing to defend them with. She thought back to the rooms she'd passed. Was there anything she could use as a weapon?

The walls were starting to close in on her. She flashed back to her summer at the camps, when she and the other children were confined to small spaces. A jolt of anger snapped her out of her indecision. If Angelica was part of this, she would wring the heiress' neck, weapon or no weapon. Too many people had suffered at the hands of the almighty Keplers.

Enough was enough.

The arms came out of nowhere. They wrapped around her in an unbreakable vise, stealing the breath from her body. She grunted. Her arms were useless, but she used her legs and head as weapons against her attacker.

She heard a swift intake of breath when her head connected with his chin. She was thrown forward for a split second. There was no time to recover before she was turned and crushed against his body. His hand tangled in her hair, lips fastening on hers, silencing her screams. The death grip he held her in relaxed into an embrace. His mouth softened, deepening into a sensual kiss.

A whimper escaped her throat. Nothing had ever felt like this. A rainbow of lights exploded behind her closed eyes. She felt her entire life boiling down to this moment.

Her eyes flew open, remembering where she was. Sanity restored, she went rigid, clawing at him with her fingernails.

He swore under his breath, black eyes glinting in the darkness.

She stared back at him, scrambling away in disgust. "How *dare* you? Were you in on this with her all along?"

The hurt on his face was palpable. "After that kiss, can't you tell we're on the same side?"

"*Never*," she hissed. "We will *never* be on the same side."

"We already *are*."

Disgust started in her belly, racing up to her throat. "You killed Luke."

"Ah, hell. You heard about that."

Her face twisted into an expression of horror. "I *heard* about it? That's all you have to say? You cold-hearted sonofabitch!" She flew at him, knocking him against the wall. Her hands pummeled his body.

He grabbed her wrists and reversed their positions, pinning her to the wall. Chest heaving, she kicked out at him, spitting in his face. He brushed his face against his shoulder, towering over her. "Damn, you're a hellcat."

She brought her knee up to his groin. "You ain't seen nothing yet."

He grunted, doubling over in pain; he managed to keep a firm hold on her wrists.

Their eyes locked. Hatred seethed through her. She brought her mouth down to his wrist, biting hard.

"Goddamn it." He pulled his hand away, using his body to prevent her escape. "You think you're so smart? Deny this."

He pressed his mouth against hers again. She writhed against him, struggling to deny the explosion inside her. *It was wrong to feel anything for him. What in God's name was wrong with her?*

Squeezing her eyes shut, the tears started to flow, dousing the passion between them.

He released his hold on her. "Ah, hell, don't cry. Do you have any idea what a pain in the ass you are?"

"What kind of sick bastard are you? Is this what you call the kiss of death? Kiss me now, kill me later? I have news for you, buster, you won't get away with this. My friend is right upstairs."

He bristled, words tumbling out in a snarl. "You mean your lover, Wally Marx? Sure didn't take you long to take up with him after Thornton's death."

The blood drained from her face. "How do you know about Shark?"

"Shark? Are you kidding me? Is that what you call him when you whisper sweet nothings in his ear?"

She raised both her hands, shoving him hard. "You disgust me. You want to kill me, fine, go ahead. That's what you're here for isn't it? But leave him out of this."

He moved forward, a troubled look on his face. "So it's true. You *are* involved with him."

"Oh, for Christ sake, why do care? You've hunted me down like a dog. You've proven you're the big, bad assassin." Her face flamed an angry red. *It had all been for nothing. Running hadn't done any good. She was going to die.*

Sierra slid down the wall, crumpling to the floor. "Get it over with already."

Skinbone crouched down beside her and gathered her trembling body into his arms. "Do you love him?"

She swiped at the tears running down her cheeks. "Go to Hell."

"Answer the question."

She refused to meet his eyes, searching for an escape route. Realizing she was trapped, she decided to answer, hoping to spare Shark's life. "I'm not in love with him. He's a friend. A friend I pulled into this mess. All for nothing."

"Shhh." He stroked her hair. "It wasn't for nothing. I came here to save you. You don't want to believe it, but I'm on your side."

"That's not true. Luke was on my side and you killed him."

"You really do care about Luke, don't you? You're awful invested in a man you only met once."

A chill washed over her. Though it was hard to tell in the semi- darkness of the basement, she thought she saw a shadow of a smile flicker across his face. "He saved my life. A pretty good reason for me to care, don't you think?"

"If memory serves, at the time, he thought the bullets were meant for him."

"And he saved me anyway, knowing I probably couldn't keep up with him. He could have left me there, but he didn't." She thought back to her initial impressions. "I thought he was a crazy man at first. Once I got to know him, he turned out to be a good guy."

Sierra couldn't stop shaking. Raising her tear-stained face, she glared at Skinbone. "How could you hurt a man like him? What kind of cold- blooded monster are you?"

Skinbone sighed, shifting his body closer to hers. "You have to stop thinking you know everything and start listening, okay?"

She stared down at her engagement ring, twisting it off her finger. It was hard to imagine the bright shiny diamond she'd worn with such pride and expectation had led to a trail of death and destruction.

"Hey." He reached out and tilted her chin up, studying her face. "It's going to be okay. You just need to trust me."

Her face twisted in disgust, her tone flat. "I repeat, go to Hell."

"You've got your facts all wrong. I would never hurt Luke, not in a million years. You are right about one thing—he's a good man, good as they come. What you don't know is he's been a father to me since I was a teenager. When my parents died, he took me in, straightened me out."

"But, I saw…"

"You saw me trying to wake him up. I had something important to tell him."

Her head started to swim. "I don't believe you. He was FBI. You're an assassin. What you're saying doesn't make sense."

"Good Lord, woman, have you always been this distrustful? You could try the patience of a saint."

Her mouth dropped open in indignation. "*I* could try the patience of a saint? Are you kidding me? The last time I trusted someone unconditionally, I ended up here, crouched in the basement of a lake house, in some godforsaken town, running for my life and chatting with a hit man. Forget the fact this place was used as a camp to torture innocent children. Maybe I should also forget there are a whole slew of people who want me dead. Or that Foxtrot is a ticking time bomb if it falls into the wrong hands. And why? Because I trusted someone, and that trust landed me in the wrong place at the wrong time."

It was his turn to be surprised, "Wait, back up a minute. If you're so innocent, how do you know all this?"

"Like I would tell you. You want to talk so bad, let's talk. You know what I think? You've been after me this whole time and now you want to play nice to make your job easier. Is that what you did with Luke? Chatted him up for information before plunging a knife into his back?"

Skinbone threw back his head and started to laugh. She inched away from him. The man was crazy. There was no malice in his laughter. If she didn't know better, she might have believed he was honestly amused. He was a madman, pure and simple. Her skin crawled at the thought of how she'd been attracted to him.

The gap between their bodies widened. She calculated her odds. If she could put enough distance between them, she might be able to make a run for it.

Her spine tingled. This was her one shot to get away. Her muscles tensed, ready to spring into a run. Taking a deep breath, she scooted a little further away. It was now or never. She hoisted herself up. Keeping her head lowered, she vaulted forward.

Skinbone's arm shot out, clamping around her ankle. She tumbled forward, watching the concrete floor rush up to greet her, and braced herself for impact. His arms folded around her body seconds before her head slammed into the floor. She struggled against him, knowing he'd prevented her from injury. It was small comfort. Better to die in an instant than endure this prolonged agony.

She went limp in his arms, praying Shark had heard their scuffle and had escaped. Skinbone dragged her backwards, depositing her on her fanny. Towering over her, he shook his head, "You sure as hell don't understand the meaning of talk, do you?"

Sierra pressed her lips together, chin trembling, refusing to look at him.

He paced back and forth in front of her, looking like he was at his wits end. "All right." He twisted his hair back into its customary ponytail and sat down beside her. "I propose a truce and an honest exchange of information. At the end, if we decide not to work together, we both walk out of here alive."

Her eyes sparkled with anger. "I don't trust you."

His face turned a mottled shade of red. "Don't you think if I wanted to kill you, you'd be dead by now? Do I really need this aggravation?"

Sierra snuck a glance at him. She conceded with a begrudging nod. "You go first."

He blew a long stream of air up at the ceiling, "Where the hell do I start?"

"You claim you had a connection to Luke. Start there."

"Okay, yeah. Good choice." He fell silent. She didn't know if he was lost in thought, or gathering his words. "I was a wild kid heading for trouble when my parents died." He looked her straight in the eye. "Lost them both to accidents, a couple years apart. I hit a real rough patch."

She searched his face for any traces of a lie. Not finding any, she nodded. "I lost my parents the same way. I know the rough patch you're talking about."

"I'm sorry," he said simply. When she made no move to elaborate, he continued. "Growing up, our families were close. My mother and Luke's wife were both Hopi. Native American. They'd grown up together, two little girls with big dreams, both falling in love with white men."

He shook his head. "All that is ancient history. Me and Luke both ended up alone. I think, for a time, he needed me same way I needed him. It was hard for him, what with his wife taking off with their son. He set me back on the right path, helped me get my head screwed back on straight, and groomed me for the FBI. It wasn't long after I finished my training in Quantico when I was recruited as a government assassin. It takes a special breed of man to do that kind of work. I knew how to set aside my emotions. I'd seen too much pain as a kid, you know. I learned how to shut off my feelings to protect myself from getting hurt."

Sierra tried to imagine a young Skinbone Harris. Her heart ached, hearing his story, wondering how a young boy could grow into a man capable of killing without remorse. He stretched out his long legs, pausing to look at her.

"You shouldn't judge. Not unless you've seen the kinds of things I have. Evil doesn't only exist in horror stories. It's here on Earth, all around us, every day. Sometimes there's no alternative. There's nothing pretty or romantic about what I do. It's not always easy to stomach. But I'll tell you this, it's a job that needs doing, and you only get one chance to do it right."

She opened her mouth to say something. Skinbone pressed his fingers against her lips, "Shhh, let me finish please."

Sierra drew her legs up, hugging them against her chest. Nodding, she kept silent, allowing him to continue.

"That kind of life takes a toll on a man. Some years ago, I retired, went independent. I still contracted for the government from time to time, but it was on my terms. I only took a job when I knew the lives and well-being of many were at stake. When the threat was so evil, the mark had to be eliminated, otherwise hundreds, maybe thousands were at risk, and there was no other way to stop it."

He reached out and took her hand. "It's a lonely life, not to mention a dangerous one. Moving from town to town, using aliases, staying underground. Doesn't leave much room for relationships—not the sort worth having, anyway. After a while, I pulled out. I set my sites on retiring. For good this time, and I meant to keep things that way."

She felt herself softening towards him. Maybe it was because she wanted to believe him. "So what happened?"

"Luke happened. He put together a special task force to bring down Foxtrot. He lost his son because of Kepler International. I couldn't turn him down. Not when he needed me."

"I know that part of the story. Turns out I was at the same camp with his son."

Skinbone's eyes filled with worry. He gripped her head with both hands, searching for a scar. "Then you're in greater danger than you realize."

She covered his hands with hers, easing them back down. "My chip was removed years ago. Massive head trauma, courtesy of the accident that killed both my parents."

"I don't understand. I thought you were a victim in all of this. That you managed to get yourself tangled up in this whole mess when you ran off with your boyfriend's computer. Now you're telling me you've known all along?"

"Don't look at me that way. If I hadn't been at Neil's house that night, if I hadn't seen the killer's eyes, I wouldn't know a damn thing about Foxtrot. I would have lived out the rest of my days in ignorant bliss. I had no idea what Neil and Grace were working on. The first time I ever heard of Foxtrot was when I found a photo in Neil's car and the word was scribbled on the back."

"Wait. You're glossing over some important details here. After all the grief you've put me through, the least you can do is fill in a few blanks."

"Grief?" The word came out in a shriek. "What grief did I put you through? I was the one with a bull's-eye on my head, scared to death you were trying to kill me."

"Don't change the topic. I've had a firsthand taste of how well you evade things."

She jabbed a fingernail into his chest. "How dare you say that about me? I've jumped headlong into this whole mess, trying to save myself and everyone else I've involved. The only thing I evaded was *you,* and that was out of self-preservation."

His fist curled around her finger. "I already have one stab wound thanks to you. I'll take a pass on a second."

Her cheeks grew warm, remembering the scissors. "What do you need to know?"

"For starters, if you knew nothing about Foxtrot, how did you wind up at Grace McGinley's house and clear out all traces of her work?"

"Do we really have time for this? It's a long story."

"Short version."

Grace's death hurt the worst, making it difficult to talk about. "Grace was my best friend. I was in shock over Neil's murder, on the run, terrified of the killer coming after me. The photo I mentioned, the one I found in his car? It was of Neil and Grace. I jumped to the wrong conclusion. I thought they were having an affair. I can't even begin to explain how that made me feel. I needed to know if it was true, so I decided to confront her. I figured I'd set up a pretty good false trail and the killer would never expect me to backtrack to Chicago."

Her voice trailed off. She shook her head. Reliving the moment she pulled up in front of Grace's house was too hard.

Skinbone understood. "And instead, you found a burned out building and learned your friend was dead."

"I knew something was off. I had to go inside, to look for clues, and to save any memento's I could. That's when I found the money and the encrypted files. I also found the flyer for this place hidden beneath her computer. At that point, I had no idea what was going on, or that they were working together, but it wasn't hard to figure out they were deep into something and it was serious enough to get them killed."

"Jesus. The two people you were closest to were murdered. No wonder you were running scared."

"By then it was too late to go to the police. I figured I'd look like the prime suspect. With the way the media is these days any exposure from being arrested would have led the killer right to me." She stared up at the low ceiling. "There were times I thought I was losing my mind, when I was trying to fit the pieces together. That maybe between stress, exhaustion, and grief, I was conjuring up theories that didn't exist."

"Back up a second. You mentioned finding money at Grace's house. What's that about?"

"I don't know if you know this, but Grace and Jared Kepler were involved. Romantically. He was paying her off the books to sabotage Foxtrot. He didn't want the project to move forward."

Skinbone let out a long whistle. "So it's true then. I'd heard something to the effect they were involved, but I wasn't certain how trustworthy my source was."

"They were in love. Another secret Grace kept from me. I didn't know a thing about it at the time."

"You had no idea what was going on?"

"No. Not at first, anyway. I didn't start figuring things out until later." She pushed a stray strand of hair behind her ear. "It was a stroke of luck I met Shark. Without him, I never could have accessed the computers."

Skinbone's feature's sharpened, "Wait a damn minute. You just met this Shark character?"

"It's hard to believe. We've been through so much, I feel like I've known him forever," she marveled. "The truth is, I met him the day after I found out Grace was dead. What a pair of sad sacks we were. I was terrified and grieving and he was nursing a broken heart over his break-up with Angelica."

"Wait a minute." He repeated, pressing the heels of his palms against his eyes. "Slow down. That didn't strike you as odd?"

"At the time, no. I had no idea Kepler International was involved in any of this."

"But afterwards, when you found out? Good Lord, woman, didn't it occur to you that he could be in on this whole thing?"

"Shark? Don't be ridiculous. He was devastated. Jared Kepler made him an offer to stay on, but Shark wanted nothing to do with any of them."

"It doesn't feel right. There's no such thing as coincidences as I've told you before." He rubbed the knot between his brows, shaking his head. "In a big city like Chicago, you just *happen* to bump into Angelica's ex-boyfriend. He, in turn, is only too happy to offer his services to you. Never mind that he's putting his life at risk by running around the country with a woman he barely knows. A woman whose fiancée and best friend were just murdered and who's terrified a killer is after her. And this guy Shark, out of the blue, out of the kindness of his heart, decides to tag along for the ride? Do you know how insane that sounds?"

She thought of Angelica's unexpected appearance. *It was a tad too convenient. They discovered Foxtrot's location and hours later Angelica bursts onto the scene...* Sierra pushed down the flicker of doubt. "It didn't happen like that," she snapped, unwilling to concede that it sounded a bit fishy. "You don't know Shark. You're concocting this devious plot after the fact. I do have a brain in my head, though you don't seem to think so. I know who I can and can't trust."

"Do you?"

"Yes, I do." She folded her arms across her chest, refusing to look at him.

"Just like you were so certain I was out to harm you."

"Weren't you?" she challenged.

"You did do a hell of a job throwing me off my game. For a while there, you were the wildcard. I had you pegged as a new player who had entered the game, wanting Foxtrot for malicious purposes. You drove me to distraction because I couldn't bear knowing you were up to no good. I didn't know what in the hell to do about you."

"And you were wrong about me, weren't you?" She wasn't willing to let it go until she made her point about Shark.

"All right, yes, I was wrong about you. Turns out we were on the same side." He tugged at her elbow, "I get what you're trying to say, but I'm still going to keep my eye on this Shark character. I'll even take the blame for you turning to him instead of me. We could have made real progress if we'd worked together, instead of tying each other up in knots."

A hint of a smile played across her lips. She'd won round one. It was time to move on to more interesting topics. "What did you mean when you said I threw you off your game?"

He smiled, white teeth gleaming in the darkness. "Ah, hell, you gonna make me spell it out for you?"

She sniffed loudly, wiping away the last of her tears. "Yes."

"You couldn't tell by that kiss?"

"No."

"Damn it, woman, you got under my skin. I started having feelings for you."

"Feelings?"

He ran his hand through his hair, looking uncomfortable. "Love, okay? I was starting to fall in love with you. Are you satisfied?"

"Well that's a hell of a lot better than having you want to kill me."

He groaned. "Keep it up, and I may wring that pretty little neck of yours yet."

She grinned. "This conversation has taken a major turn."

"We've gone from trying to kill each other to talking love in record time. It's gotta be some kind of record, don't you think?"

She arched a brow. "Did I mention anything about love?"

The look on his face was priceless. "Have I just made a total ass of myself?"

A weight lifted off her shoulders. All those feelings that had been churning inside her could finally be set free. There was no more second guessing herself. Smiling, she snuggled into his arms. "Not exactly."

"Maybe this will tip the scales in my favor." He pulled her close, crushing her mouth against his. For an instant, nothing else mattered. She shivered from the thousand tiny electrical currents running down her spine.

He drew away. "Did I win any points?"

Her breath came in short, little gasps. "Maybe a few."

His jet black eyes bore down into hers, "Is this crazy? We barely know each other."

"My world has been crazy since the moment I laid eyes on you."

His gaze darkened, his arms tightened protectively around her. "Ah, no, you can't blame me for that. It had already turned crazy by the time I met you."

She hated him for pulling her back to the real world. There was no guarantee of a happy ending. Nothing had been resolved, except their feelings for each other. A new thought flitted through her mind. She sobered in an instant. "It doesn't feel right to be happy. Luke…"

"Luke isn't…"

A sound erupted overhead. Sierra gripped his arm, panicked.

"What the hell was that?" she gasped.

"Does your friend Shark own a gun?"

"No."

"Then we've got trouble. That was a gunshot."

Chapter Thirty-Four

Shark scrambled to get his thoughts straight. Angelica, here, coming on to him was the last thing he'd expected. *She wanted something.* It was in his best interest to play along. Tilting his head to one side, he studied her. There was no doubt she was gorgeous, but how was it he never noticed her blatant sexuality before?

Her body hummed with arousal. She took a step closer to him, throwing off heat. He remembered to smile, to wet his lips. The most stunning thing of all was that he felt nothing despite her thinly veiled attempts to throw herself at him. He'd become immune to her charms.

He cleared his throat. "I've missed you too," he lied. "How did you find me?"

She linked her fingers through his, "Let's go upstairs and I'll tell you."

Going upstairs would be a mistake. She'd see the computers; discover he knew about Foxtrot. He had to keep her downstairs and talking if he was going to maintain the advantage.

He pulled his hand away, striking an indignant pose. "You broke my heart. I believe you owe me an explanation first."

His words didn't sit well with her. Her eyes turned anxious. Pressing forward, she whispered, "Let's go upstairs, please."

"I have no desire to play the bed sheet game unless I know you have changed your ways."

She glanced over her shoulder, looking nervously at the doorway. "I have but I'm in trouble and I need your help. I've been coerced into marriage and I'm afraid he's going to kill me unless I give him what he wants."

Shark wavered. Her honesty was raw, brutal. Admitting she had a husband, begging for help. Perhaps she was not the evildoer he'd painted her out to be. "What sort of help do you need?"

Her eyes glittered. For the first time, he noticed the harshness of her features, the callousness of her heart. She reached inside the large bag she wore slung over her shoulder, withdrawing a netbook damaged beyond repair. "He wants you to access the data on the hard drive. I want you to tell him it's impossible. He needs to believe all the information has been destroyed."

Shark took the netbook from her shaking fingers, knowing exactly what it was. Neil's missing computer, the same one Luke was killed over. He turned it over in his hands, making a show of it. "There's a good chance I could retrieve the data."

She breathed a sigh of relief, "Excellent. You just can't let *him* know that."

He favored her with a lopsided grin, thinking back to the conversation he'd had with Sierra. If he could secure a spot on the inside, he might be able to gain information they needed. Deciding he'd put up enough of a protest, he glanced up from the computer, "Who is this man who is threatening you?"

She bit her lower lip. "He'll be here any minute. I need you to convince him the hard drive is worthless, that the entire computer is fried. But you can't give it back to him. I *need* the data that's on there. It's encrypted; I also need you to break the code."

"I would be happy to assist you, but in all good conscious, if you are afraid for your life, perhaps you should give the man what he wants."

Her eyes narrowed. "Never. He's trying to steal my legacy, my dreams for the future. The information on this computer belongs to *me,* and me alone. If he thinks he can double cross me, he's sadly mistaken."

Shark saw the fanatical gleam in her eyes, the way her chest heaved at the imagined injustice she'd encountered. "The way you double-crossed me, Angelica?"

She dampened her lips. "That was a mistake. A huge, huge mistake."

"We'd planned a future together. A very nice future, I might add."

"Yes, yes we did." She eagerly grabbed onto the lifeline he offered her., "And we can still have one. But only if you help me."

"No more secrets between us?"

"None," she lied.

He saw right through her. He knew she would betray him in a heartbeat, the minute she'd gotten what she wanted. She was in for a rude awakening. This time, he was going to get what he wanted from her. "Very well, then, you can count on my help."

"Thank you, Shark."

He clutched the computer to his side. Her gratitude at least was genuine. Too bad it wouldn't last. The few words they'd exchanged spoke volumes. He knew without any doubt, what, and who, he was up against.

"I will get to work posthaste." He turned on his heel and headed in the direction of the great room. He mumbled a silent prayer, wondering where Sierra was. She would ruin everything if she chose this inopportune moment to appear. The sound of Angelica's stiletto's clicked behind him. He hoped he was playing this right; one mistake on his part, and his plan would go terribly awry.

He set down the computer, quietly taking in the room. The understated elegance served as a perfect backdrop for the magnitude of the scene about to unfold. Angelica hovered beside him. He could feel the nervous energy bouncing off her in waves.

A mild sweat formed under his collar. He powered up the computer, wondering if it would chug to life. If it didn't, he was screwed. There was, of course, another way to retrieve the information, but that wasn't a road he was willing to go down.

Angelica wrapped her arms around his neck, peering down at the computer from behind. He wanted to pry her hands off him, but she was clinging to him like a deadly vine.

"I see you've returned to your whorish ways."

The voice startled both of them. Shark looked up to see his nemesis standing in the doorway. Clearing his throat, he feigned an impervious tone. "Your *wife* is rightly concerned about the integrity of the computer. Her actions suggest her desperation, not any designs on my body."

Donovan's laugh was brutal and swift. "You make a good point. Why would she settle for you when she can have any man she wants? Our sweet Angelica has already made her choice in that department. You aren't man enough to handle her."

"And yet I come to her aid. Perhaps you are sadly mistaken in the qualities Angelica values most in a man. While you may possess certain *attributes* she finds appealing, what she craves most is a man who will do her bidding. A point you fail to understand. I freely admit I am in awe of her and will perform any task, simply to see the look of pleasure which crosses her face. You, on the other hand, strive to control her, which goes against her grain. In the end, who do you think she will choose?"

Donovan sneered. "Her choice is made. She is my *wife*. A fact any amount of wishing on your part won't change that."

Shark shrugged. "If that's what you need to believe."

Angelica laughed nervously, moving to stand beside her husband. "I thought I made myself clear, Shark. I offered you a job, a way back into Kepler International. My husband is correct. I've made my choice."

Her tone dripped with hidden meaning. Shark remained focused on the computer. He swallowed hard. The fates were stacked against him. It wasn't booting up.

"Then I wish you both much happiness." Shark's eyes remained on the computer.

"So what's going on there?" Donovan waved a gun in his direction.

Shark hit a few keys in order to stall. "It's too soon to tell. The computer is damaged. I need time to work with it."

"That's a crock of shit. You know damn well it won't boot. There are other ways to retrieve the information."

"Sometimes, with patience and a little coaxing…"

Donovan shoved Angelica aside, leveling his gun at Shark's head. "Don't feed me any bullshit. You never go anywhere without your laptop and all your gizmo's. Go upstairs and get them. I don't have time to deal with your lame excuses."

Shark couldn't risk Donovan following him upstairs. "That's where you are wrong. I am here on retreat, to heal from my broken heart. I may have my laptop with me, that much is true. But I don't have a way to connect the computers."

"I don't believe you."

"Believe what you like. Might I suggest, instead of hurling threats, you take a trip to the nearest store to purchase the supplies I will need? It's the only way I will be able to…"

"You have five seconds. If you don't make a move to go upstairs, I will blow your head off."

Shark stood, holding his arms out in supplication. "Do what you want, but without the proper equipment, my hands are tied."

Donovan clicked off the safety, garnering Shark within his sites. "Three, two…"

"There is nothing I can do." Shark felt a chill of terror snake down his spine. He'd done his best to call the man's bluff.

Donovan's eyes were cold, the gun steady in his hand. "One."

Shark tore off his glasses, sending them flying across the floor. Donovan's gaze wavered for just a moment. It was all the time Shark needed. He drew himself to his full height and let out a cry, lunging at the FBI agent. The momentum sent them both tumbling to the floor. Shark managed to straddle the larger man and made a grab for the gun, in an effort to knock it out of Donovan's hands. A struggle ensued, Shark wrestling with St. James to try to force the gun downwards towards the floor.

A gunshot exploded. Shark staggered backwards, a look of shock on his face. Angelica fell to her knees with a scream.

Chapter Thirty-Five

"Stay here."

Sierra pressed her hand against her mouth, watching Skinbone race down the narrow hallway. If Shark was in trouble, she couldn't stand helplessly by.

The gunshot could only mean one thing: someone had found them, someone who wanted them dead.

Skinbone would stop her if he knew what she planned to do. Inching down the hallway, she listened for the sound of Skinbone's footsteps beating a path upstairs. Once she knew it was safe, she continued her quiet journey. Too many people had died because of Foxtrot. She wanted to face the bastard who'd make her life a living hell head on.

Her toe caught the edge of something. She stumbled forward, breaking her fall with her hands. A metal case gleamed in the darkness. Certain it hadn't been there before, she bent over to examine it. Skinbone must have carried it down into the basement and left it behind. Feeling ill, she moved her shaking hands over the case, searching for the clasp. It took three attempts before she managed to pop it open. Her breath caught in her throat. It was filled with guns.

She hesitated. She'd never fired a weapon before, but being armed would certainly level the odds. Reaching out, she lifted one from the case, testing its weight in her hands. Her mind scrambled to remember anything she knew about guns. She looked for the safety, slipping it back. Her insides turned to ice at the sound of the click.

It was now or never. Driven by instinct, she made her way up the stairs, careful not to make a sound. Skinbone had a good head start. She searched her memory for the long ago prayers she'd said at her bedside each night, praying she wasn't about to walk into a scene of carnage.

Her prayers didn't help the cold sweat drenching her body. Without warning, she flashed back to those last few moments in Neil's kitchen, right before the *click boom* that changed her life forever. Now she was fighting for the lives of two more people she cared about. She wasn't about to lose them too.

She flattened herself against the wall, the same way she had when she'd first escaped the killer. An eerie sense of déjà vu dizzied her. The gun almost slipped from her fingertips. Taking a deep breath, she wiped the palms of her hands on her pants and eased forward to peer around the corner.

The foyer was empty. Sierra craned her neck, hoping to catch a glimpse of Shark. Still nothing. *Now what?* She didn't think the shot had come from upstairs. It sounded too near. If she stepped out into the foyer, she'd be exposed.

She had to chance it. There wasn't any other choice.

Moving the hand with the gun behind her back, she slipped out into the open, maintaining her position against the wall, and froze.

Sounds of a scuffle echoed from the living area. A woman screaming. The sound of a chair toppling over. And a familiar voice.

Help had arrived, and not a minute too soon.

Breathing a sigh of relief, she hurried forward, stopping dead when she came face-to-face with Donovan St. James dragging a bleeding Shark alongside him. She didn't take the time to assess the situation. "Donovan, thank God! How bad is Shark hurt? Who did this to him?"

The look on her former lover's face was chilling. "Sierra. My, my, isn't this a nice surprise. Now I can kill two birds with one stone."

Sierra stiffened in shock. *No, this couldn't be happening.* Donovan couldn't be *the one.* He was FBI, her ex-boyfriend. For God Sake, he'd been friends with Neil, *and* Grace. He couldn't possibly be behind the plot to steal Foxtrot.

She tightened her grip on the gun behind her back, forcing herself to act normal. "I'm so glad to see you. Let me take a look at Shark's wounds and then we'll need to talk."

His smile was cold, turning his handsome features to ice. "We do need to talk, Sierra. You are in serious trouble. Wanted for Neil's murder, for stealing government property. Tell me, how long have you been conspiring with Shark? Months? Years?"

"Donovan, what are you talking about?" she shook her head, twisting her lips into a smile, She inched a few steps closer. "Let's go somewhere and talk."

She glanced at Shark, wincing at the blood streaming from his abdomen. His face was pale, contorted in pain. He raised an eyebrow, tilting his head in Donovan's direction. She knew what he was telling her. He was warning her not to trust the FBI agent, signaling he was the one.

There had to be a mistake.

She scanned the room, searching for Skinbone. *Why wasn't he here? He had a head start.* She forced her eyes to go soft, and gazed up at Donovan with a sweet smile. "We can sort this all out. I can help you."

His laughter frightened her. "Yes, you *can* help me. You can be a good girl and give me what I want."

She braced herself, knowing what she had to do. Minutes ago, she'd asked herself if she could actually use a gun on someone. She'd imagined shooting from a distance, not close up, and not someone she used to love.

Sierra batted her eyelashes, gripping the cold steel in her hand, mentally preparing herself to use it. "I'll give you anything you want. Just please, let me take care of him."

Donovan glanced at Shark. Sierra looked over Donovan's shoulder at the figure coming up behind him. Her breath caught at her first glimpse of Angelica. The woman was stunningly beautiful. She held a thick vase in her hand, creeping silently towards her husband. Their eyes met for a fraction of a second and Sierra almost lost it—Angelica's were ice black, as cold and deadly as Neil's killer's. They also begged her not to let on that she was advancing.

Sierra didn't give a damn about Angelica or her quiet plea. Seizing the opportunity, she brought the gun forward and aimed it straight at Donovan's head.

At that precise moment, the door banged open, distracting all of them. Sierra exhaled, certain it was Skinbone. Her knees went weak with relief. The growing tension in the room was the only thing that kept her from collapsing.

Bold footsteps headed towards them, accompanied by a spray of bullets. Acting on instinct, Sierra dove to the floor, taking Shark down with her. She rolled onto her side to shield him, clutching her gun in two hands.

Angelica shrieked and dropped the vase she was holding, sending shards of glass flying everywhere. A jagged edge of the vase grazed Sierra's forehead, blood trickled into her eyes, momentarily blinding her. She wiped the blood with her sleeve in time to see Angelica cowering behind Donovan.

Sierra's mind raced as she wondered who was behind the attack. A bullet slammed into the floor, inches from her head. She pressed her face against the cold tile floor, tucking her knees to her chest, trying to make herself as small a target as possible. When she glanced up, she saw that Donovan had raised his gun and was firing back. She watched in disbelief as the bullets from Donovan's gun spun uselessly in the air, raining down to the floor before reaching their mark. A red mist clouded her vision from the wound on her head. She swiped at the blood in anger. If they had any chance of escaping, she needed to be able to see.

Donovan snarled. He swung his arm, grabbing Angelica by her hair and pushing her in front of him, making his wife a human target.

There was a brief lull in the gunfire. Sierra raised her head, risking a look at their attacker. She gasped in horror, feeling herself go numb. She would never forget those eyes. The face she'd glimpsed the night of Neil's murder came into sharp focus. Dead black eyes, jet black hair. *This* was the man who'd torn her world apart. *He* was the one she'd been running from. Seeing him again, the similarities between him and Skinbone were obvious. The complexion, the features, they could have been brothers.

Brothers.

Angelica cried out, breaking her concentration. "Ethan, please, don't let him hurt me. He's kidnapped me. You don't know what he's capable of."

"You'll have to shoot through her to get to me." Donovan taunted.

"You think I give a damn about her?"

Donovan wrapped his arm around Angelica's throat. "You should. She's shared your bed often enough."

"She was a means to an end, my man, a means to an end. She's nothing but a well-dressed whore. Do you know how many times she jumped from your bed to mine? And I mean that quite literally. Too bad the joke is on you, Angelica. You had your pleasure, thinking you were dominating each of us, when all the while; we were both using you."

"Ethan, no, you can't mean that," she whimpered. "Please, help me."

Sierra listened to their exchange. For the moment, no one was paying attention to her or Shark. Something tugged at her, a memory she couldn't quite place. She lay on the floor unmoving, watching the drama unfold in slow motion before her.

"Help the likes of you?" Ethan smirked and turned his head, concentrating on a spot beside them. A fire ignited, swiftly turning into a fireball, burning swift and hot. "I'd see you in Hell first."

Angelica screamed. The sound was blood curdling. Sierra screamed along with her, reliving the agony of Neil's death, the flaming ball, which had eaten away at him, melting him into the floor.

And then she knew. Good Lord, she knew.

The little boy, back at the camp, surrounding her with fire.

Luke's words played back in her head. "I didn't recognize you at first. You were at the camp with my son."

She replayed the memory of standing over Shark's shoulder while he scrolled through the names of the children at the camps. One didn't quite fit. Shark identified Ethan Wilde as one of Angelica's companions. The name wasn't on the list. The name Ethan Preston had come up instead.

Her mind was spinning. Luke had been married to a Native American woman. She'd run off with their son. Luke had never been able to find him. Skinbone's mother was Native America. The jet black hair, dark eyes, and coloring explained the resemblance between Skinbone and Neil's killer.

Sierra dragged her focus back to the scene playing out in front of her.

"There's a simple choice to be made here," Ethan continued, reaching inside his pocket. He pulled out a badge. "No doubt I'll be bounced off the force, but I don't care a whit about that. The job was a simply a means to infiltrate Kepler International, to bring a bit of authenticity to my mission. My sole purpose was bringing you bloody bastards to justice. The badge provides me authority to kill without fear of repercussion...assuming there are no witnesses to challenge my story. "

Donovan leaned forward and squinted, reading the badge. "Interpol? What a joke. You don't honestly expect me to buy that, do you? What a damn fool you are—I'm not a flunky sent by a foreign government to babysit the purchase of Foxtrot. You have no idea what you are dealing with."

"Oh, I know very well who you are. You climbed up the ranks of the FBI, intent on a political future. The Presidency, no less—the one office your father couldn't attain because he married the wrong woman. Your mother didn't have the social standing to be the wife of a President, nor was she willing to make an effort. You weren't going to make the same mistake. You needed a woman who would be an asset to your political ambitions. And then you met the lovely and devious Angelica. She was a dream come true, wasn't she? Two peas in a pod, the both of you. Delusions of grandeur. Nothing but blackness in your souls. The two of you were in on this from the beginning. In fact, you engineered the whole thing. What, you couldn't trust your political ambitions to fate? Knew you weren't good enough without her money and clout? I have proof of all of it, you know." Ethan leaned forward and winked at them conspiratorially, "I've had your rooms bugged from the get go. Trust me, my superiors won't question your deaths. Neither will the American government."

"You sonofabitch," Donovan spat, hands curling into fists.

"Perhaps. My mother *was* a bitch. She believed I had the devil inside me, made my life miserable, chipping away at me until I had no choice but to think I was evil incarnate. I'll be damned if I let Kepler International ruin another life."

"What the hell are you talking about?"

"Play innocent if you choose, or play the fool. I was in those camps. Ripped from a normal life and turned into a monster. The deprogramming didn't work on me. Some of my memories were erased, but my abilities grew stronger. I know exactly what you and Angelica have done, and why. Jared buckled. He wanted no part of the madness, so he had to die. Tell me, did you kill Kepler?" He swung the rifle at Donovan, then pointed it at Angelica. "Or are you a sadistic enough bitch to have murdered your own father?"

Angelica struggled in Donovan's arms, ripping and clawing at her capture. "Ethan, you bastard," she hissed. "How can you be so hateful? After all we shared?"

"I seem to have struck a nerve," Ethan smirked. "We shared *nothing*, Angelica. Tell me, whose grand plan was this? Using Foxtrot to cause anarchy in the States? Mobilizing hundreds of thousands of unwitting citizens with chips implanted in their brains to cause chaos and ruin. What an enlightened idea, setting civilization back hundreds of years. Destroy the free world.

Really now, did you honestly believe you would get away with it?"

Donovan raised his pistol and aimed it between Ethan's eyes. Without hesitation, the FBI agent fired his sidearm. The bullets were no match for Ethan's psychic powers. They dropped to the floor inches away from Ethan. He'd managed to create an invisible shield around him, blocking any threat to his person.

Ethan laughed. "Ironic, isn't it? The fact that I'm indestructible is thanks to Grandpa Kepler. Of course, we need to give him credit for my madness too."

Shark moaned beside her. Sierra cringed, hoping her friend wasn't in too much pain. She pressed her hand against his midsection, trying to staunch the bleeding. So far, they'd managed to stay on the outskirts of the battle. She had no doubt that at some point the attention would turn to them. On impulse, she pulled the gun closer to her body, hiding it under her belly. She was going to have to do whatever was necessary in order to protect them. It would be a useless effort unless she came up with a way to penetrate the protective barrier surrounding Ethan Wilde.

The smoke grew thicker. Sierra stifled a cough and pulled Shark's shirt over his face. There had to be *something* she could do to level the odds in their favor.

"I can take the two of you in," Ethan continued, "or hurtle you both into the flames."

"Your choice," Donovan smirked. "Neither option will get you what you want."

"I think either choice will do. It doesn't matter what happens with Foxtrot if the two of you are dead or behind bars."

"You're mistaken. I'm not the one you're after. You can have her." Donovan shoved Angelica towards Ethan. She fell, landing at Ethan's feet, sobbing hysterically. In two quick strides, Donovan towered above Sierra and Shark.

Keeping her eyes trained on Donovan, Sierra moved the gun she held out of sight. Her body tensed, waiting for the opportunity to strike.

"These two," Donovan motioned with his pistol, "these are the two you want."

Ethan's eyes narrowed. The spotlight was shining on Sierra now. Donovan's hateful glare rained down on her. She sucked in a breath; she wasn't going down without a fight.

Donovan nudged her body with the toe of his boot. "You want Foxtrot? The power and the glory that accompany it? We're on the same side, man. I came here to bring these two in. I already shot one of them when he resisted. Did you think you were the only one playing Angelica's game? You and me? We want the same things."

"Like your partner, Skinbone Harris? Don't imagine him showing up to help you. He's already been dealt with," Ethan replied with a cruel smile. "Neither of you played this game very well."

Sierra stifled a sob. Skinbone was dead. Luke was dead. Donovan was a sick twisted bastard. Shark was bleeding out beside her.

She was on her own.

"You won't walk away clean from this, not without my help," Donovan said, his voice calm and easy. "You're hands are too dirty. You killed Thornton and McGinley and you messed up. You didn't get what you wanted. And you left a witness."

Ethan barked out a laugh. "You can't prove it. Hell, you won't be alive to prove it, so it doesn't much matter, does it? Once you and Angelica are dead, the threat dies with you. I did kill McGinley and Thornton. I thought if I could eliminate them, I'd put an end to Foxtrot. But I won't cry any tears over their deaths, chum. My problems are nothing a new identity won't cure. And then I can take my sweet time looking for Foxtrot."

"You're delusional, man. Kill me and you'll have the United States government to contend with. You won't have a chance in hell getting your hands on Foxtrot if you kill a federal agent. There is a simpler alternative, of course. Angelica and I can make a spot for you, if you chose to work with us."

At the mention of her name, Angelica pushed herself to her knees and wrapped her arms around Ethan's legs. "Ethan, please, don't listen to him. I'll give you anything you want. *Anything.* We were good together, no matter what you say now. Foxtrot belongs to me and I'm the only one who can give it to you."

Ethan glared at Angelica. "Shut up. The two of you deserve each other. At the risk of repeating myself, you both must be daft, truly. Such an auspicious plan. Activate the chips inside the minds of all those hapless souls, altering their stream of consciousness into a united power strong enough to cause floods, earthquakes, tornadoes, fires, poverty—weakening the States to the point of collapse. Kill the President, and decimate the chain of command. Then the handsome, white knight Donovan St. James rides to the country's rescue, the gorgeous Kepler heir on his arm. It's Camelot all over again, isn't it? The country rallies for a new leader, sealing its own fate. You use and reuse your army of psychic soldiers, embattering your citizens until you establish a monarchy. And from there, then what? Conquer Russia? China? The United Arab Emirates? That was your plan, wasn't it, to enslave the world through your treachery?"

Sierra sucked in a gasp. Good Lord, this was far worse than she'd ever imagined.

Donovan's hand swooped down, pulling Sierra up by the hair. She twisted in his grasp, keeping her head lowered. Her ex-lover slapped her hard across the face, knocking her off balance. Her ears rang, blood gushed into her mouth. Anger pounded inside her. There was no time to second-guess herself. She couldn't bear to look at Ethan. He'd murdered Neil and Grace without a hint of remorse, but he was working *against* Foxtrot. No matter how despicable he was, they were on the same side, a fact that was impossible to stomach. She couldn't steel herself to look him in the eye.

"You need proof that you and I are on the same side?" Donovan grabbed her by the chin, turning her face towards Ethan. Sierra understood. She was his trump card. After everything she'd been through, she'd played right into the hands of the madman.

She would get one shot before all hell broke loose.

Ethan's gaze fixed on her face. "Ah, the lovely Sierra Montgomery. Well now, isn't this an interesting surprise. I really must commend you, my dear. You are a worthy adversary. I never thought you'd elude me for so long. "

She spit out a mouthful of blood, drawing on the drama to distract them. She needed to stay alive long enough to make her shot count.

Donovan pulled her upright, holding his gun to her temple. "She's the weak link, the one person who can bring you down. I will blow her away right now, as long as you and I reach an agreement."

"A devil's bargain." Sierra was surprised her voice was so clear. "I have Foxtrot. It's well hidden and impossible to get to without me. Kill me and all of your plans go up in smoke."

Angelica's head whipped towards her. "*You?* You have Foxtrot?" She scrambled to her feet, a maniacal look on her face.

Sierra ignored Angelica, remaining focused on Ethan, "You know what Donovan is capable of. Don't buy into his act. He's lying to save his sorry ass. That man bleeding on the floor over there? He's been working with me. We came here to destroy Foxtrot, to put an end to it. Donovan came here to stop us. And that's not all. I have information for you, information you can't get anywhere else."

Ethan cocked his head. *Good*, Sierra thought. *Now I've got your attention.* "What kind of information?"

"I know everything, Ethan," she baited him. "I know about what happened to you after the camps. I also know the damage done to you can be reversed. I spoke to your father right before he died. He spent his life searching for you, working to find a way to make up for what happened to you."

"You're lying. My father sent me to the camp. He's responsible for all of it."

"No, no he wasn't. He's been looking for you ever since your mother took you away."

Ethan grabbed his head, wild eyed. "That's not true. It's not possible! I don't even know my father. You're making this up."

Sierra took a huge gamble, "I think you do know who your father is, Ethan. I think that's what led you here."

It happened in an instant.

Sierra caught a movement out of the corner of her eye. Angelica flew towards her, hands poised like claws, ready to attack. Ethan grabbed at Angelica. The tramp twisted away, slipping out of Ethan's grasp, losing her balance. Her feet slipped out from beneath her. With a startled cry, Angelica fell forward, head slamming into the marble floor with a resounding crack. A pool of blood immediately surrounded her.

"Bitch, look what you've done!" Donovan's anguished cry rang in Sierra's ears. He smashed his fist into her face, snapping her head back. For a terrifying moment, Sierra feared she was going to pass out, and then her vision cleared.

Heart hammering in her chest, she watched Donovan raise his arm, finger on the trigger of his gun. Adrenaline kicked in. Her arm flew backwards, reaching behind her. Sierra whipped out her pistol and fired.

The report sent her stumbling backwards. Donovan's blood splayed everywhere, soaking her. Screaming in horror, she dropped the gun and raised her arms to protect herself.

"Looks like it's you and me, now."

For a moment, she'd forgotten Ethan. The horror of taking a life had wiped everything else from her mind. Wrapping her arms around herself to control her shaking, she turned to the madman in a daze.

The black eyes that had terrified her on the night of Neil's death focused on her. There was an ugly smirk on his face. "You've made my job easier. Unfortunately, it doesn't change anything. There's no reason to keep you alive, though I do commend you for making a valiant effort for survival with that nonsense about my father. There was a brief second where I almost believed you."

"It's true," Sierra whispered, freezing in her tracks. Her heart skipped at least three beats. Skinbone Harris stood behind Ethan, leveling a gun at the man's head. Blood dripped from a gaping wound on Skinbone's forehead. Ethan must have knocked him out earlier, and thinking he'd struck a fatal blow, dragged Skinbone's body outside.

Her lips turned up in a slow smile, dizzy with the fact that Skinbone Harris, the man she loved, was alive.

Ethan followed her gaze. Skinbone ducked in time to avoid the blow Ethan leveled at his head. Skinbone got off a single shot before Ethan pumped a bullet into his belly.

Ethan howled in anger. The room burst into spontaneous flames, licking at the windows and doorways. "You can all burn in Hell, and Foxtrot along with you."

Eyes wide with shock, Skinbone clutched his belly, dropping to one knee. The smoke thickened, making it hard to see. Sierra felt around on the floor for her gun, knowing she had to get Skinbone and Shark out of the building before it was too late. The acrid smell brought it all back; Neil shrieking in agony, while his body was consumed by flames, the stench of Grace's death lingering in the burnt out shell of a house.

New balls of fire erupted throughout the room, making it impossible to know which way to crawl. Her hand closed around Shark's ankle. She pulled him along with her, still searching for her gun.

Ethan's menacing laughter filled the room. Her sobs were swallowed by the crackling fire. She could feel the heat. The edge of her jeans caught a spark, flames ignited around her ankle. The pain was excruciating.

Through the flames and smoke a familiar figure emerged. She rubbed her eyes, certain she was hallucinating. The figure rushed Ethan, tackling him, knocking him to the floor, and straddling him.

Sierra crawled forward in time to see Luke place the barrel of a gun between Ethan's eyes. She couldn't let him do it.

"Luke, no," she screamed, "you can't kill him! Ethan is your son."

Luke hesitated, disbelief clouding his face. "My son?"

"Luke Preston," Ethan interrupted in a raspy voice. "Can't be you. You're dead."

"Surprise. You didn't succeed in killing me, you bastard."

"Wasn't me. That was all St. James. I did go to the hospital after I saw your face on the news. I planned on killing you after you explained why my mother saved a locket with your picture in it. She left me a letter, warning me about you."

"What?"

"She told me…you ruined my life…because of you, I turned into a monster."

Luke eased his hold on the younger man. "What the hell is going on?"

"It's true," Sierra gasped. "He's your son."

Luke picked Ethan up by his collar, staring hard into his face, "After all these years? No, it can't be…"

It was the last thing she heard. Fire danced up her leg. Rolling on the floor, she tried to douse the flames. Her lungs filled with choking smoke, robbing her of breath.

It's going to end this way, she thought. There wasn't time to save herself. Mercifully, she somehow managed to find Skinbone's hand, collapsing from the effort of reaching him.

"I love you," she said, feeling him squeeze her hand in return.

She tried to lift her head to see Skinbone's face one last time.

"I love you too," he said.

The world faded to black.

EPILOGUE

Three Months Later...

The day was gorgeous. Sierra smiled, feeling the sun beat down on her upturned face. She wanted to pinch herself, thinking it was impossible to be this happy. For the first time in her life, she *belonged.* She had purpose. A reason to get out of bed every morning, knowing she had something to look forward to.

The agency would officially open tomorrow. She pushed open the door, feeling a sense of satisfaction at the little ding of the bell.

Skinbone rushed to her side, planting a kiss on her cheek. "Sweetheart, you should be home resting. What are you doing here?"

"And leave you men to your own devices? Besides, my burns have healed." Her eyes twinkled. "I like to think of them as my badge of honor. We all have scars to prove what we went through."

"I have two," Shark piped up, touching the spot on his scalp where his chip was removed.

Sierra smiled up at Skinbone. "Looks like you didn't waste any time putting Shark to work."

"You were right, the guy is amazing. He's going to be a hell of an asset to our little agency here."

Sierra glanced toward Shark. "I was so afraid for him. I didn't think he was going to make it."

Skinbone pulled her into an embrace, "Hell, I didn't think *any* of us were going to make it. You're a scrappy little thing, you know that? One of the many reasons I love you."

She punched him in the arm. "I still haven't forgiven you for letting me think Luke was dead."

Skinbone winked at Luke. "You should know the old man is too crazy to die. Once I figured out Donovan was working against us, it was the best way to protect Luke from any further attacks. Of course, I didn't count on him being a stowaway on my plane."

"Hey, that's my plane and don't you forget it," Luke objected.

"Yeah, giving me one more thing to worry about."

Luke rolled his eyes. "That's the thanks I get for saving every last damn one of you. On my deathbed, no less. You think it was easy escaping from the hospital?"

"Pay no attention to Skinbone. He's still pissed off that he didn't get to play the hero. How's Ethan doing?" Sierra asked Luke.

"Good. The treatments are going well. He's starting to get antsy and he's also been asking about you. He's grateful to you for saving his life, after everything he put you through."

"I couldn't let you kill your son," she said softly.

"You saved both my sons."

Sierra couldn't hide her happiness. "I think me and Skinbone saved each other."

Skinbone cleared his throat. "Before we all start laying it on too thick here, take a walk with me."

"A walk? I just got here."

"We're not going far. Only to the park across the street."

Luke and Shark grinned at her like two idiots. "What's going on here?"

"Will you stop with the questions and come with me?" Skinbone said, offering an outstretched hand.

Feeling outnumbered, she accepted his hand, glancing over her shoulder at Shark and Luke. She felt nervous suddenly. Putting her life back together had been no easy task. She liked knowing exactly what to expect out of each and every day. Starting this agency in Texas with the three men in her life had been a huge step for her. She'd had to twist all their arms to agree to opening a second agency in Chicago once this one got off the ground. Her life was full, she didn't need any more surprises.

Skinbone led her to a bench in front of the fountain, motioning for her to sit down. "You said something really important back there. That we saved each other."

"We did," she said softly.

"You changed my life, Sierra Montgomery. Something I didn't think any woman could ever do."

"You changed mine too."

"It's like I said the first time we met, we were predestined to find each other."

"It was fortuitous."

He grinned. "It was at that. What I'm trying to say is, you mean more to me than anyone I've ever known. No matter how long I live, I'll never have enough time with you. You mean the world to me. You are my world. Which is why," he dropped down to one knee, "I have something to ask you."

Sierra stared down at him, feeling a flutter in her stomach. She couldn't take her eyes off him. He pulled a small box out of his pocket, looking up at her with love. "Sierra Montgomery, will you do me the honor of being my wife?"

She smiled, overcome with emotion. She reached out, cupping his face with her hands, "Only if you'll do me the honor of being my husband."

His hands closed around her wrists, sealing the deal with a kiss.

Behind them, Luke popped the cork on a bottle of champagne. Shark held out the glasses. "Don't you just love happy endings?"

"I do at that." Shark's eyes twinkled.

Luke winked and threw his arm around Shark. "We got us a nice little family here, son."

Sierra laughed looking at them all with love, amazed at what had risen out of darkness. "We do indeed."

Skinbone's eyes clouded with emotion. Sierra accepted the flutes of champagne Luke handed her, passing one to Skinbone. She smiled, raising her glass in a toast, "To the future."

"To the future," they echoed.

Author's Biography

Lori Gordon resides in Chicago with Livvie Rose, a four-year-old black and white kitty. Her short stories have been published in Pill Hill's "Quest for Atlantis" and "Fem Fang Anthologies", Static Movement's "Caught by Darkness" and "Madness of the Mind" Anthologies and Abandoned Towers Magazine. She is currently at work on a Crime Thriller, "Red Herring."

STATE OF PANIC

CPSIA information can be obtained at www.ICGtesting.com
Printed in the USA
239455LV00001B/69/P

9 781617 060786